Into the
Night

Into the Night

Janelle Denison

St. Martin's Paperbacks

This is a work of fiction. All of the characters, organizations, and events portrayed in this novel are either products of the author's imagination or are used fictitiously.

INTO THE NIGHT

Copyright © 2011 by Janelle Denison.
Excerpt from *Night After Night* copyright © 2011 by Janelle Denison.

For information address St. Martin's Press, 175 Fifth Avenue, New York, NY 10010.

ISBN: 978-0-312-37227-9

Printed in the United States of America

St. Martin's Paperbacks edition / April 2011

St. Martin's Paperbacks are published by St. Martin's Press, 175 Fifth Avenue, New York, NY 10010.

10 9 8 7 6 5 4 3 2 1

To the three best writing pals a girl could ever ask for: Carly Phillips, Julie Leto, and Leslie Kelly. Thank you for your unending support, your advice and critiques, and for helping smooth out all the kinks in my plot. I couldn't have written this book without your help!

And to my husband, Don. My own personal hero. I love you.

Chapter One

Being called to the boss's office didn't happen often for Nathan Fox. But when it did, there was usually a damn good reason for the summons.

Sometimes, meeting with Caleb Roux was all about discussing a security or surveillance problem they were having at The Onyx Hotel and Casino. Today, judging by Caleb's serious demeanor and the familiar red folder sitting on the surface of his desk stamped CONFIDENTIAL, this one-on-one was all about The Reliance Group and a case Nathan was about to get briefed on.

A familiar rush of anticipation surged through Nathan. As a surveillance supervisor at The Onyx, he enjoyed his security job and outsmarting the criminal element who thought they could beat the system. But as a former undercover vice cop with the Las Vegas Metropolitan Police Department, being a part of TRG was a nice little side job that fulfilled the part of him that still loved the thrill of the chase and the adrenaline rush of a challenge.

"What do you have for me?" Nathan asked, getting right to the point.

His boss splayed his fingers on top of the folder but didn't open it, as if he was protecting secrets he wasn't quite ready to reveal. At the age of thirty-six, Caleb exuded a quiet confidence and intelligence, along with sharp instincts Nathan had come to respect. Most knew Caleb as the operations manager of The Onyx, but a select group of employees at the casino knew him as something else as well—the astute leader of The Reliance Group, the very discreet and covert team Caleb had organized a few years ago.

TRG consisted of an interesting mix of "specialists" who possessed unorthodox skills and took on assignments other agencies refused to touch. Depending on the job or the situation, they were hired out privately and confidentially, using whatever means were available to complete the mission.

Nathan was certain today's case would be no different.

"As you might have guessed, I have a new assignment for you, and this one is going to require you to go undercover, which we both know is your specialty."

After acknowledging Caleb's statement with a nod, Nathan waited patiently for him to continue.

Leaning back in his chair, Caleb gave away nothing with his relaxed posture as he revealed the facts of the case. "I was contacted by a man named Tom Ramsey, a lieutenant colonel in the marines who recently retired. According to my initial interview, he's had a hard time integrating back into his marriage and family after being on active duty for so many years."

Nathan himself had spent four years in the marines, and he could relate to Ramsey's difficulties. After spending years in war-torn countries, making the mental and emotional transition back into a normal civilian life wasn't always easy.

"This assignment involves Ramsey's sixteen-year-old daughter, Angela, who recently ran away from home," Caleb went on. "Over the past two years that Tom has been home, his daughter has grown increasingly hostile and resents the fact that he hasn't been a real part of her life since she was a baby. Now he's taking an active role in disciplining her, and she's rebelled big-time. She's been caught drinking alcohol, smoking pot, and shoplifting. While she's left home before, this time it's been much longer than a few days."

A runaway. Nathan felt a solid kick to his gut over that bit of information as a past he desperately wanted to forget flashed through his mind. He inhaled deeply and did his best to keep his focus on the facts pertaining to this particular case. "How long has she been missing?"

"Over three weeks," Caleb told him as he rubbed his hand along his clean-shaven jaw. "Ramsey hired a private investigator to find her and discovered she'd made her way from their home in Arizona to Vegas. Problem is, Tom can't get to his daughter."

Nathan frowned. "What's the issue? She's a minor. A call to Metro and they'd pick her up, haul her ass back to Arizona, and hand her over to her parents where she belongs."

"There's a catch." Caleb's jaw clenched ever so slightly, but his gaze remained as direct as his personality. "According to the PI, Angela hooked up with Preston Sloane here in Las Vegas. The PI's final report has Angela living at Sloane's estate home in Summerlin."

Nathan's mind reeled, and a chill raced through his blood.

Preston Sloane. The prominent fifty-four-year-old man was rumored to have a penchant for young girls, a fact Nathan was well aware of since Sloane had been on his radar when he'd been a vice cop. During the time Nathan had worked undercover in a prostitution ring, he'd seen and heard enough about the arrogant, mega-rich financier and his sleazy appetites to verify that there was a lot of truth to the gossip surrounding the billionaire's sybaritic lifestyle.

Sloane was a man who lured young girls into his life with irresistible promises of excitement, luxury, and expensive gifts. Once he enticed them into his debauched world of sex and narcotics, getting them hooked on drugs ensured they stayed until he grew tired of them. Or until someone younger and prettier grabbed his attention. That's when he abandoned them to the unforgiving streets of Vegas to fend for themselves, where they were eventually snatched up by pimps looking to add to their stable of working girls.

Just as Sloane had done with Katie, the girl Nathan had sworn to protect all those years ago.

Sloane had destroyed first her innocence, then her life when he'd cast her aside to survive the only way she knew how. By the age of seventeen, she'd been picked up by a pimp and was working as a prostitute to support her drug addiction. Sloane might not have been the one to put the bullet in Katie's head that had ultimately killed her, but Nathan held the man responsible for taking advantage of her youth and vulnerability and changing the course of what should have been a long and promising life for Katie.

Sickened by what he'd been unable to prevent, Nathan felt his stomach twist into a huge knot. The guilt sliced deep, just as it always did whenever he thought of Katie and how he'd failed to save her.

"Tom already went the police route," Caleb continued, seemingly unaware of Nathan's inner turmoil, but Nathan knew better. His boss was well aware of the demons that still haunted him. "They paid a visit to Sloane's estate in Summerlin and were greeted by Preston himself, along with an invitation to search anywhere they pleased on the premises, which they did."

"All twenty-five thousand square feet of the place?" Nathan asked, doing his best to focus on this case, and not his past.

"Supposedly, yes." The shrewd look in Caleb's eyes told Nathan the other man was skeptical, too.

Nathan knew Sloane's estate sprawled over ten acres. A virtual fortress on the outside, and a palace inside, the massive domain had been built to house over a dozen guests. The entire place was surrounded by twelve-foot walls, state-of-the-art surveillance, and armed guards; it was as impenetrable as Fort Knox. To get anywhere beyond the gilded gates, an invitation from Preston Sloane himself was required.

Caleb absently tapped his finger on the red file folder. "Needless to say, they didn't find Angela, or any evidence she'd been there. I suspect someone warned Sloane before the cops arrived with a search warrant."

Nathan couldn't disagree. While working for Metro, he'd quickly learned that the man was untouchable, and well insulated by people who were paid to protect him.

"So, either the girl is hiding and doesn't want to be found, or she's being held against her will," Nathan speculated out loud.

"That's what it narrows down to," Caleb said with a

succinct nod, then leaned forward and finally pushed the red folder across his desk toward Nathan. "It's your job to infiltrate Sloane's circle, get into the estate, and find Angela so we can bring her back safely to her father."

Normally, Nathan would have reached for the file and given the contents a look just in case he had any other questions for Caleb. Hesitation rose within him now, though, along with deeper, darker emotions from the past he'd worked so hard to suppress.

"Getting close to Sloane is going to take time," he said, his tone gruffer than he'd intended.

"Take a week and get everything set up," Caleb said, not backing down. "After tonight, your shift at the casino will be covered so you can start on the case. All the information we currently have on Sloane and the case is in that folder, along with a current photo of the girl. Let me know if there's anything else you need and I'll get it for you."

"Okay," Nathan replied, unable to quell the churning in his gut, that sense of walking into trouble before it even began.

"Lucas is processing your new identity, and the documents you'll need to support your new persona for the case will be here in a few days."

Nathan nodded, familiar with the routine of undercover work.

Caleb stood and rounded the desk. Stopping next to Nathan's chair, he gripped his shoulder. "I know you can handle it, Nathan, or I wouldn't have put you on this assignment. You have the experience to tackle this case. You can save a girl and give her a happy ending. Her father is counting on that, and on *you*."

Shit. Tom Ramsey's unconditional trust in his ability to get his daughter home safely was the last thing Nathan wanted on his conscience.

Caleb left the office and closed the door behind him, leaving Nathan alone with that damn red file and his own turbulent thoughts. Leaning forward in his chair, he braced his arms on his knees, released a harsh breath that seemed to burn his lungs, and cursed the other man's tough-love approach.

Caleb knew Nathan's past, and the reason he'd quit the force. The bastard knew exactly what he was doing when he'd handed him this case. There were just too damn many similarities to his last undercover assignment as a vice cop.

He didn't even know Tom Ramsey or his daughter Angela, but the case was fast becoming personal, which had been Caleb's intent. The other man was forcing Nathan to face his greatest fears and failure, and was giving him the chance to right a wrong and maybe lay his guilt to rest.

If that was even possible.

Life had shown Nathan there were no guarantees, and promises didn't mean shit because there was no controlling fate and her plans for a person. She certainly hadn't forgiven him for letting a young girl die.

Swallowing hard, he reached out and picked up the red file folder. He opened it and finally put a face to Angela. The attached high school picture showed a pretty girl with blond hair and bright blue eyes shining with the kind of youth and guilelessness a man like Preston Sloane wouldn't hesitate to take advantage of. She smiled at the camera, capturing a moment of happiness that somewhere along the way had turned into teenage angst and defiance, and had driven her to run away from home into a world that would destroy her innocence and leave her a mere shell of her former self.

He'd witnessed that kind of transformation with other young girls who believed that working the streets and giving their bodies to strangers would give them the love and attention they craved. And they usually paid with their souls. Some, with their lives.

As much as Nathan wished this assignment didn't exist, he knew he couldn't turn his back on Angela. He refused to let another young girl die because he didn't do his job.

He'd take the case, just as Caleb knew he would, his main goal to locate Angela and extract her from Sloane's estate by whatever means were necessary. While he'd like to believe it would be a quick in-and-out mission, Nathan had to consider what he was likely to find once he managed to gain entrance into Sloane's world.

If he was lucky, and fate truly was on his side this time, he'd find evidence that would finally put Preston Sloane behind bars for a very long time.

Finished with his surveillance shift later that night, Nathan made his way down to the main bar in the casino in an attempt to relax and unwind before he headed home for the evening. There were only a few guests at the bar, and Nathan grabbed a seat at the far end, away from the other customers. He waited for Sean, the bartender, to finish making a martini for an older woman, who eyed Sean appreciatively as he mixed the drink and flirted shamelessly with her.

Nathan grinned, his mood lightening as he watched Sean O'Brien, player extraordinaire, in action. The man possessed an abundance of charm and had a way with females most guys envied.

Once the martini was served, Sean strolled down to his end of the bar. "Hey, Fox." The other man greeted him by his last name, as he always did. "What can I get for you this fine evening?"

"The regular, on the rocks."

Sean shook his head, his Irish blue eyes dancing with unabashed amusement. "A root beer," he emphasized in that drawl of his. "You are such a teetotaler."

Nathan didn't take offense, since the other man always enjoyed ribbing him about his drink of choice. "It's what I like, so there's no point in pretending otherwise."

"Real men drink beer." Sean continued to give him a hard time. "The kind that's *not* sweetened."

A smile quirked the corner of Nathan's lips. "Luckily, I'm a secure guy and don't need to prove myself by tipping a bottle of Heineken."

"Yep, you da man." Sean saluted him and moved to the soda station.

Admittedly, on rare occasions Nathan indulged in a shot of Johnnie Walker Black, but there'd been a time when his sole reason to drink was to forget. Still, after spending a good six months abusing hard liquor and existing in a continuous drunken state to keep his personal nightmares at bay, he'd finally pulled his head out of his ass and sobered up in time to salvage what was left of his life.

Unfortunately, he'd been too late to save his relationship with his fiancée, Jill. Unable to handle his mood swings and the guilt he hadn't been able to resolve, she'd walked out on him and hadn't looked back.

Not that he could blame her. He'd been a miserable

son of a bitch after that last undercover mission, and his self-defeating behavior had put a huge strain on their relationship. Liquor had numbed his senses at a time when he'd badly needed it, and as much as he sometimes still wished he could drown that ever-present dull ache in his soul with a bottle of whiskey, dealing with reality, and everything he'd lost, had become his personal penance.

And soon, he was going to step right back into that dark life he'd once been a part of. Caleb Roux had made certain of that.

"Two's your limit. I don't want you driving under the influence," Sean joked as he placed a tall chilled glass of root beer in front of Nathan, then glanced at his watch. "What are you still doing here, anyway? Can't get enough of this place, or what?"

Nathan shrugged as he ran the tips of his fingers along the condensation gathering on his glass. "I'm not ready to head home yet."

"Maybe if you had someone to take home, you'd feel differently." Sean grinned wolfishly as he cleared a few dirty glasses from the counter. "I know for a fact the redhead over there is single and looking for a good time." He gave a subtle nod toward the young, perky-looking woman sitting across the bar who was nursing a frothy drink while casting seductive looks toward Sean whenever he happened to glance her way.

Nathan shook his head. "I think she's pining for *you*, my friend."

"So many women, so little time." Sean sighed but didn't seem put out. He habitually juggled more than one woman at a time. "Seriously, if you're looking for a good night's sleep, getting laid will do the trick."

"I don't think it would help. Not tonight, anyway." Nathan took a long drink of his root beer before sharing the real reason why he was sitting at the bar at two in the morning. "Caleb put me on a case and the gears are shifting and grinding, if you know what I mean."

Sean, also a Reliance team member, nodded in understanding. "I totally get it. Let me know if you need a refill."

Sean moved on to a new customer who'd taken a seat at the bar, an older gentleman who appeared down on his luck. Nathan took a sip of his soda and watched Sean give the man a friendly pep talk as he poured his drink, making his customer laugh at something he said. The gift of gab was one of Sean's many skills, a knack he'd mastered as a former con artist and used to his advantage when bartending, as well as on cases with TRG.

Despite Sean's shady past and the time he'd spent behind bars for his scams, thanks to Caleb he'd cleaned up his act and was now a valued operative of The Reliance Group. Many of TRG's team members either had secrets in their pasts or carried physical and emotional scars that could have destroyed their lives. Yet Caleb had seen beyond their flaws and had given them a reason to turn past mistakes into something positive. He'd given them a chance to redeem themselves and reclaim their self-respect.

Just like Nathan and the Ramsey case.

Before he could get mired in the darker thoughts he'd been resisting for most of the night, Valerie Downing slid onto the vacant bar stool beside Nathan, surprising him with her sudden appearance. Valerie was a casino host at The Onyx, where she catered to patrons' and players' whims to keep their business, and their gambling, confined to The Onyx. Her psychic abilities, however, made her an integral part of The Reliance Group.

Friendly as well as beautiful, Valerie flashed him a smile that lit up her soft brown eyes with threads of gold. "You're just the man I've been looking for."

Immediately thinking she was having a security issue with one of her clients, Nathan became alert. "Is there a problem on the floor?"

She shook her head, her silky brown hair sweeping across her shoulders with the movement. "No worries. This isn't about work. It's more about . . . pleasure."

Out of nowhere, Sean appeared on the other side of the counter. "You've got *my* attention."

Valerie laughed, the husky sound filled with a wealth of amusement. "You are so easy, O'Brien."

He grinned like the rogue he was. "Only when it comes to pleasure."

She rolled her eyes. "I need a favor, and I'm hoping one of you will come through for me. Keep in mind what I'm about to ask you to do is for a very good cause."

Nathan was immediately suspicious. A quick glance at Sean told him the bartender wasn't nearly as eager to step up to the plate now that *pleasure* was no longer the sole focus of their conversation.

"Good causes don't come without some kind of personal sacrifice, Val," Nathan said, and finished off the last of his root beer.

"A monetary donation is definitely involved, and I'll need your time, too. About three hours of it." She glanced from Nathan to Sean, her expression oh-so-hopeful. "Is either of you free tomorrow after six?"

The question caught Nathan off guard, and he tried to think fast . . . except he already knew he had nothing planned.

"You know, I just remembered I have a date tomorrow night," Sean interjected smoothly, appearing apologetic, but Nathan knew better. "I'm really sorry."

"Bummer." Valerie sounded truly disappointed, then she switched her optimistic gaze to Nathan. "How about you, Nath? Are you free? And before you answer that question, remember that you owe me a favor."

He lifted a brow. "I do?"

She nodded, looking much too confident for Nathan's comfort. "Remember last week with Trey Blackmore?"

Nathan groaned, recalling the incident too well. Blackmore was one of The Onyx's high rollers, a whale who dropped hundreds of thousands of dollars in the casino during his visits without flinching. Yes, the man was filthy rich and an asset to The Onyx's coffers, but he was also an arrogant bastard who was always trying to bend gambling rules and regulations because he believed he was entitled.

Just last week Nathan had gotten into a heated argument with Blackmore when he'd once again overstepped his boundaries with one of the pit bosses, and it had taken Valerie interceding to smooth things over. Her job was to keep their whales content and satisfied so they didn't take their gambling elsewhere, and she'd managed to placate Blackmore's ego while making sure he conformed to Nevada state gaming law.

Yeah, Nathan owed her for that one.

Fine. Whatever she needed, he could handle. How bad could her request be, anyway? It sounded like a fundraiser-type event, and at worst he'd have to attend some kind of shindig and schmooze for a few hours. He really wasn't in the mood, but for Valerie, he'd help out.

"Okay." He would suck this one up for good karma in the future. "Whatever you want, whatever you need, I'll do it for you."

"You are the best, Nathan." The smile she gave him spilled over with gratitude. "And who knows, you might even enjoy yourself."

The sudden mischievous gleam in her eyes sent a ripple of unease through him. "What, exactly, are you recruiting me for?"

"Actually, it's for a good friend of mine, who is an event planner. She's hosting an event where all the proceeds are donated to the battered women's shelter. There's just a few itty-bitty details you need to know ahead of time so you understand exactly what's required of you."

There were requirements. Great. "I'd be really happy if a suit and tie weren't involved."

"No, it's a casual affair. Nice slacks and a collared shirt will be fine," she said, making him extremely happy with the low-key dress code. "The event is being held at Simply Fondue, from six to nine tomorrow night."

He'd heard of the five-star restaurant, located on the Vegas Strip, but had never been there. He didn't see himself as a fondue type of guy, but he'd endure it for the sake of charity.

"This is a speed-dating charity event," she said, her words fast and rushed, leaving no room for interruption. "There's a cocktail hour, which will segue into the speed-dating game for another hour or so, and a bit of socializing afterward. It's really easy and simple and fun. And it's a great way to meet women. *Nice* women."

Sean, who'd been standing nearby drying wine-glasses, choked back laughter. "Oh, man, you are so screwed."

What the hell? Nathan's head spun, and not necessarily in a good way. "What in the world is *speed dating*?"

"Just the newest way to meet the opposite sex," Valerie said, then went on to explain how it all worked. "It's a fun process that eliminates the awkwardness of meeting new people, or spending hours with a person you may not connect with."

He gave his head an adamant shake. "I don't have a problem meeting, or mingling with, the opposite sex."

She delivered a quick, placating squeeze to his arm. "Nobody said you did. And just because you participate in the game doesn't mean you're going to marry one of the women you meet." The sigh that escaped her sounded way too wistful and romantic. "Then again, how amazing would it be to find the woman of your dreams there? What a great story that would be, huh?"

Nathan cringed. Things were quickly going from bad to worse. His mind filled with images of women frantic to find a husband and ready to sink their claws into the next victim.

He shuddered at the thought and suddenly felt desperate to find a way out of the commitment he'd just made. "Why do you need me to do this for you? Doesn't your friend already have people signed up for this speed-dating thing?"

"She did, but three of the male applicants pulled out earlier tonight."

"Smart guys," Sean said, chuckling.

Valerie sent Sean a chastising glance before returning her attention to Nathan. "Cindy was only able to replace two of the guys, so she needed one more man to balance out the ratio of men to women and I promised her I'd help out." Obviously sensing Nathan's indecision, she rushed on to hook him for good. "It's only one night, and just a few hours of your time. All you have to do is talk to women and be nice to them. If you aren't attracted to any of them, no big deal. And if you did this for Cindy, *for charity,* I know she would be so grateful."

Awww, hell. Those expectant eyes gazing at him with such hope did him in. He was a sucker for a pretty face and sweet smile. He blamed his three older sisters for using the same tactics on him and taking advantage of that intrinsic male part of him that wanted to please the females in his life.

Like attending a charity event that involved dating strange women.

He couldn't bring himself to disappoint Valerie. It was only a few hours of his time, and wouldn't interfere with his TRG case since this weekend was all about compiling information on Preston Sloane and figuring out a strategy before going undercover. Nathan figured the event would be a good distraction from everything else weighing so heavily on his mind.

He sighed. "Fine, I'll do it."

He'd go to Simply Fondue tomorrow night. He'd meet and mingle with single women and gently deflect any interest, because he certainly wasn't looking for a relationship. He'd flirt, enjoy the cocktails and food, and chalk it all up to an interesting experience.

Then, with his good deed out of the way, he'd concentrate all his time and attention on the Ramsey case. His sole focus in the upcoming weeks would be finding sixteen-year-old Angela and bringing her safely back home to her parents, where she belonged.

Chapter Two

"I swear, the things I do in the name of journalism," Nicole Hutton grumbled in disgust, not for the first time since she'd been handed her current assignment. After two years at *The Las Vegas Commentary,* she didn't deserve such a rookie story. "Speed dating, of all things. It's truly mind-boggling what the good people of Vegas find fascinating, isn't it?" And she was frustrated because *she* had to report on such a frivolous event when she was eager to report on a story with depth and substance.

Fresh from a shower and wrapped in a silky thigh-length robe, Nicole strolled out of her bathroom and into the adjoining bedroom where her friend, Michelle, was stretched out comfortably on an upholstered second-hand lounge chair in the far corner. Michelle, a co-worker as well as her roommate, was newly engaged to a great guy, and that meant Nicole would be searching for a new roomie in the near future. Which sucked big-time, because after two years together, Nicole really enjoyed Michelle's company, advice, and friendship.

"Well, speed dating does seem to be one of the hottest

trends right now, so I guess that counts for something," Michelle said, trying to make sweetened lemonade from the sour lemons Nicole had been handed. "Inquiring minds want to know what it's all about."

Nicole rolled her eyes as she sat down on the small chair in front of her mirrored vanity. Keeping her annoyance at the whole situation in check, she picked up a tube of body cream and started rubbing the scented lotion along her bare shoulders and arms. "Fine. I'll tell our readers what they want to know, and hopefully move on to something more intelligent with my next assignment."

Michelle bit her bottom lip, a reluctant look passing over her delicate features before she spoke. "I heard Sharon say if they get a good response to this article in next week's issue, she's going to make *Dating in the 21st Century* a monthly segment."

Nicole groaned out loud. She wanted to ask if Michelle was kidding, but knew it was no joke. Sharon, the editor in chief at *The Las Vegas Commentary,* would undoubtedly put Nicole in charge of the column, and the thought of spending the next six months reporting on current dating trends was enough to make her break out in hives. Which would be a really bad thing right before her speed-dating assignment this evening.

"Sharon is killing me with all these fluff pieces she keeps tossing my way." A legitimate complaint considering what she'd been promised when she took the job at the *Commentary*. "God, will she ever give me something I can investigate and make a name for myself?"

Michelle sighed, silently understanding Nicole's irritation and disappointment. "You know how strict Sharon is about having to work your way up the editorial ladder."

"I've been climbing for almost two years." Swiveling her chair toward the vanity mirror, she began plucking the hot rollers from her hair. "I think I've more than proved myself as a reporter. She knows I'm capable."

"You can always sleep with the boss," Michelle suggested, tongue in cheek. "It worked for Justin."

Loose blond curls fell to Nicole's shoulders as the heated rollers were removed, one by one. She met Michelle's gaze in the mirror and grinned wryly. "It's been a long dry spell for me in the sex department, but I'm not desperate enough to go girl-on-girl, and I know that's not Sharon's scene, either. So, the whole sleeping-with-the-boss thing just isn't going to work for me."

Michelle rolled her light brown eyes. Then, turning on her side, she propped her head in her hand, her expression suddenly somber. "You're feeling restless at work, aren't you?"

"I just feel . . . undervalued, and uninspired as a journalist. I'm bored and I want exciting stories that give me a rush of adrenaline and actually make a difference." She swiped on eye shadow and rimmed her upper and lower lashes with a soft kohl liner before adding mascara.

Because as things stood, she was sorely in need of a career boost of some kind. She hadn't spent all those years at Columbia University on a full scholarship to be a minion at a mediocre, socially driven newsmagazine. She'd rather take risks with difficult, uncompromising reporting that kept people up to date on important current issues.

News was Nicole's true passion, and she dreamed of

being a tough journalist on top of breaking events. A reporter who relished the challenge of discovering deep, dark truths and documenting stories that were shocking, yet so riveting you couldn't help but read all the sensational, and sometimes scandalous, details.

When she'd hired on at the *Commentary,* the new and upcoming magazine's vision had been different—definitely more in line with Nicole's personal goals. Somewhere along the way, the editorial input had turned soft, indulgent, and much too complacent for Nicole's liking. And as tonight's speed-dating assignment proved, the weekly publication wasn't taking her career in the direction she'd pictured. And most likely it never would.

And that meant it was time to reevaluate her current place of employment. But until she found an alternative, she needed a steady paycheck and had a story due on Monday. So, instead of going into tonight's assignment with a negative attitude, she'd decided to focus on the more positive aspects of the evening. And maybe, while she gathered the information she needed to write her article, she'd have a good time, too.

After running her fingers through her hair, she headed to her closet and changed into the outfit she'd bought earlier that day. She returned moments later and twirled around in the middle of the bedroom for Michelle's approval.

"So, what do you think?" Nicole asked, perching her hands on her slender hips, now encased in a slim-fitting, hot-pink, summer-style dress.

Michelle's wide-eyed gaze echoed her surprise. "Wow, you look amazing. And hot. Sizzling hot," she added with a grin as she sat up on the lounge chair to get a better look at what Nicole was wearing. "I've never seen that dress on you before. Or those shoes, for that matter. I'm used to you wearing more tailored outfits for work, not something so blatantly sexy."

Tonight was certainly about work, and a bit of fun, too. Hence, the sexy playfulness to her wardrobe. "I found both the dress and shoes on sale at Nordstrom and couldn't resist getting the outfit for the summer." It wasn't something she'd ever wear to work, but she'd find a few reasons to wear the dress again after tonight, because she really did love it. "I didn't want to go tonight wearing a pair of slacks and a button-down blouse. Talk about boring."

Michelle laughed. "Oh, you look anything but boring, especially in those three-inch heels and baring more skin than I've ever seen on you in public." She tipped her head to the side, her gaze turning much too speculative. "In fact, I'm beginning to wonder if tonight is more than just an assignment for you, that maybe you're finally open to finding Mr. Right during this speed-dating event."

Nicole shot her friend an are-you-out-of-your-ever-lovin'-mind? look. "Hell, *no,* I'm not looking for Mr. Right, or anything serious for that matter." Her voice was emphatic as she pushed a pair of silver hoops into her earlobes, then followed those up with three matching bangle bracelets.

Getting tied into a committed, long-term relationship wasn't on her radar for a good long time. She'd been there, done that. The experience had been more than she'd ever bargained for emotionally, and had nearly destroyed her self-worth, along with her self-confidence. It had taken a long time to recover from the aftermath of giving her whole heart and soul to a man who'd used her as his plaything—and dismissed her from his life as soon as someone younger and just as guileless caught his eye.

She'd been so naive, so trusting back then, but she wasn't that romantic, starry-eyed teenager any longer. She was jaded, she supposed, and toughened by the experience. At twenty-five, she just wasn't ready, or willing, to risk her heart and emotions on anything beyond building her career as a journalist.

These days, the only thing she relied on a man for was sex. And even at that, it had been nearly six months since she'd indulged in one of those seductive, tempting, feel-good kind of romps between the sheets. Nicole had made do just fine on her own since then, but the truth was, a vibrator didn't compare to the real thing. She missed being touched and caressed by strong, capable hands, and kissed by a soft, warm male mouth. She loved the feel of a man's hard body moving against hers, enjoyed the friction and slow climb to a powerful orgasm that drove him equally wild.

Though she enjoyed the intimacy of being with a man, she insisted on a friends-with-benefits arrangement, one specific go-to guy for hot but uncomplicated sex. No strings attached, and especially no messy emotions involved. Just mutual, physical pleasure, and no obligations to mess with her head or her heart.

How was *that* for dating in the twenty-first century?

Nicole shook her head on those thoughts and looked on the bright side of things. "I figure if I'm stuck with this assignment, I might as well enjoy myself," she told Michelle as she double-checked her purse for everything she needed, then pulled out a tube of her favorite lip gloss that tasted like crème brûlée and shimmered with pink undertones.

Michelle lifted a delicate brow. "So, you're going to mix business with pleasure, hmmm?"

"Why not?" After swiping the gloss across her lips, she dropped the tube back into her purse and snapped it closed, then grinned at her friend.

"God, you are so bad sometimes," Michelle said with a shake of her head, though her tone was light and infused with amusement. "Well, have a good time, but don't do anything I wouldn't do."

"Now, what fun would that be?" Nicole wrinkled her nose at her friend, who'd become much too conservative since getting engaged.

She sashayed out of the bedroom, a smile on her lips. Tonight Nicole planned to make the most of her humdrum assignment and her sexy new outfit. She might not be looking for a serious relationship like the rest of the applicants at the event, but that didn't mean she couldn't have a good time and enjoy any male attention that came her way—even knowing she'd be coming home alone to a cold, empty bed and her own personal vibrating Casanova stashed in her nightstand drawer.

Nathan noticed her as soon as she walked in, as did all the other guests mingling in the private banquet room situated in the back of Simply Fondue. Despite his initial reluctance to be here, for Nathan it was lust at first sight.

She'd snagged the men's attention because she looked so vibrant and gorgeous in her formfitting hot-pink dress—a direct, in-your-face contrast with the more conservative, button-up outfits most of the other ladies had chosen to wear to this evening's event. She looked so incredibly sexy with all those tousled blond curls falling to her shoulders, so alluring with that sweet, sensual smile curving her full, shiny lips. Then there were those high heels accentuating her slender legs and prompting a man's thoughts to travel down an erotic path that included some very steamy fantasies with her in the starring role.

What man wouldn't be drawn to all that sensuality, tied up in such a neat and totally hot package waiting to be unwrapped like a decadent present? A guy would have to be a eunuch not to notice, and appreciate, her sultry beauty.

And he was *not* a eunuch.

If anything, the woman in pink's appearance was going to make for an interesting evening. Nathan couldn't help but wonder if she was on the prowl for a husband, or just looking to have fun.

Before arriving at the restaurant, he'd cleared his head of the Ramsey case for the night in order to get through this dating event and fulfill his obligation to Valerie. The TRG assignment would still be waiting for him tomorrow, but for now, he forced himself to relax and go with the flow for the next few hours.

He kept to the perimeter of the room until the actual event started, politely talking to the women who approached him but not going out of his way to mingle like many of the other guys were doing. This was all about him filling a vacant seat for Valerie's friend, and he was already counting the minutes until his good deed was done.

Swirling the ice in his glass of root beer, Nathan

glanced back in Pink's direction. She was at the sign-in table, getting her name tag and filling out the required paperwork before the event began.

Grabbing a pen, she bent at the waist to write down her personal information, and Nathan nearly groaned out loud. God, she had a nice, shapely ass—smooth, firm curves that would undoubtedly fit quite well in the palms of his hands. Or against his thighs if he molded himself to that tempting behind . . .

Another woman appeared in his line of vision, effectively interrupting his little fantasy. She was dressed in a navy-striped power suit and wore a pair of black-rimmed designer glasses. Her hair was twisted up into a severe knot on her head, and she held a glass of white wine in her hand.

"Hi. My name's Heather," she said formally, and held out her hand for him to shake.

Not so surprisingly, her grip was as strong as a man's, backing up that power suit she was wearing. "Nathan," he replied with a smile. "Nice to meet you."

Her own smile was slight, as if she didn't want to give up too much all at once to the wrong guy. "I'm a paralegal for a law firm here in Vegas. What do you do?"

Okay, that was direct and to the point. "I work in security."

She wrinkled her nose at him, not at all impressed with his profession. "Oh, like a rent-a-cop?"

Because he didn't care for her overall attitude, he didn't bother to correct her assumption. "Yeah, something like that."

That's all it took to make Heather bolt. Obviously, she was looking for a guy with a more stable, and prominent, career. And that was fine with Nathan.

He went for a refill on his drink and caught sight of Pink again, who'd moved on to the buffet table set up across the room. He experienced a jolt to find her subtly watching him with an inviting smile on her lips as she selected some strawberries from a fruit tray. Just when Nathan decided to head toward her, another guy moved in.

Which gave another woman the opportunity to corner him at the same moment.

Well, hell. The petite redhead standing in front of him introduced herself as Cleo, and while she dominated the conversation with information about herself and what she was looking for in a husband, Nathan only half listened to what she was saying, nodding when he thought it appropriate. He was too damn distracted by Pink's husky laughter drifting from the other side of the room and how she'd every so often give him a private I'm-totally-attracted-to-you glance before resuming her discussion with the men around her.

She was teasing him from a distance. Flirting with her body language. Slowly driving him mad with the need to meet her up close and personal and see if the heated awareness between them was real, or just his imagination.

Before he had a chance to implement his plan, Cindy stepped into the middle of the room and rang a bell, the signal that the speed-dating event was about to begin. All the lively chatter settled down, and everyone's gaze turned to the woman hosting the evening's event.

Cindy's warm smile was designed to put everyone at ease, and seemed to do the trick. "First off, I want to thank everyone for coming tonight, and I hope you all have a good time getting to know one another."

She went on to explain the rules, which were simple and straightforward. They'd all received a scorecard, which they could use to write down notes during their quick, seven-minute dates. Ultimately, they had to check the YES or NO box next to the name of each person they met, depending on whether or not they'd made a connection and were interested in a future date with that individual. At the end of the session they'd turn in their scorecards, and those who'd mutually chosen each other by checking YES would be e-mailed by Cindy tomorrow morning with further information on behalf of the interested parties. Regrettably, only exact matches would be given contact information.

No regrets about it. Nathan was relieved he wouldn't have to worry about a potential stalker.

Chairs and small tables had been set up in a large circle in the private room, and Cindy asked the women to take a seat at the table with the number that matched the one on their scorecard. The men were encouraged to do the same. Pink ended up at table number three, while Nathan had to sit at number seven.

Because the men were the ones to move from table to table, he had to get through eleven women just to get his seven-minute date with Pink, who'd given him one last slow, sensual smile before returning her gaze to the guy sitting in front of her.

Satisfied the event was ready to begin, Cindy set the timer for the first seven minutes. "Relax, have fun, and good luck, everyone."

And so it began . . . the personal questions from the string of women he met, the hopeful, one-sided interest, and the casual interrogations for the sole purpose of sizing him up as that one guy who lived up to their high standards. He deliberately kept the verbal exchanges light and pleasant, and was careful not to lead any of the women on.

As each round ended and Nathan came closer to reaching Pink's table, the excitement of finally meeting her, the anticipation of talking to her, grew. He was curious to know more about her, to see if those vibes lasted beyond their initial introduction.

Then again, she could be all fluff, a pretty face and a killer body with no substance. What a crying shame that would be.

Two more rounds passed, and then it finally happened. He was sitting across from Pink, who smelled good enough to eat. He inhaled the scent of something sweet, like a rich buttercream-frosted vanilla cupcake, and knew it was her. The thought of her tasting as good as the luscious scent emanating from her aroused him on a multitude of levels, and had him shifting in his seat.

The smile lifting her glossy lips was filled with feminine awareness, and up close, he couldn't help but notice she had the most fascinating eyes—a stunning, deep, dark, velvet blue that seemed to seduce and mesmerize.

Admittedly, he was both. And that just didn't happen to him when it came to women. She intrigued him, and if he played his cards right and they clicked beyond this basic physical chemistry, maybe they could get together later this evening—before he immersed himself in his new identity and the Ramsey case.

The bell rang, and the session began.

"Well, we finally meet," she drawled, her warm, friendly voice making him feel instantly at ease. "I'm Nicole."

"Nathan." He reached across the table and shook her hand, not at all surprised to find her grip firm, but her skin womanly soft, as it should be. He wondered if she was equally soft and supple everywhere, and instinctively knew she would be.

She tipped her head ever so slightly, causing her soft, wavy hair to caress her shoulders, which also drew his gaze to the gentle swells of flesh pushing against the low-cut bodice of her dress. Her breasts were small, but definitely more than enough for him to enjoy.

"So, how are you holding up after all these quickie dates?" she asked, the tinkling sound of the silver bracelets on her wrist snapping him out of his lust-induced thoughts.

Realizing he was spending an inordinate amount of time eyeing her chest, he dragged his gaze back up to hers, not sure what to expect. He was a healthy, red-blooded man, therefore a visual creature by nature. Certainly she couldn't blame him for admiring her sweet curves and perfect-looking breasts. And judging by the amused glimmer in her eyes, she didn't seem to mind at all.

Okay, if he remembered correctly, she'd asked him how he was holding up after more than an hour of pure dating torture. "Well, the good news is, the end is in sight." He grinned.

She laughed in agreement and picked up the pen resting on top of a small notebook next to her on the table. The top page had been filled with what looked like comments and notes, and she flipped to a clean piece of paper. "You're not having a good time?"

Considering how every other woman had started right in with the soul-searching, dirt-digging, relationship-seeking questions and tried cramming as much information as she could into her seven minutes, this woman's ordinary conversation surprised him, in a good way. He relaxed and decided to be honest with her.

"You want the truth?" he asked.

Still smiling, she blinked those long, dark lashes at him. "Of course. The truth, and nothing but the truth. I can handle it."

He was beginning to think this woman could handle anything. "This isn't exactly my idea of a good time," he confessed, completely entranced by her shimmering lips, and the luscious mouth made for all kinds of sin. "How about you?"

"It's been . . . interesting," she replied thoughtfully, her secret smile charming him even more. "So, if this isn't your idea of a good time, what prompted you to sign up for a speed-dating event?"

Definitely a legitimate question, though again, not a typical one in this venue. "I was pretty much roped into it. Cindy, the event coordinator, needed an extra guy to fill in for someone who couldn't make it, and my arm was twisted until I said yes."

She arched a blond brow, her blue eyes twinkling playfully. "This keeps getting better and better." She wrote something on her pad of paper he couldn't read from where he sat, then met his gaze again. "So, you don't really want to be here?"

"No, I don't *need* to be here," he clarified.

She laughed, the sound stroking across his libido in ways he never would have anticipated. "Ahhh, so you're not looking for love or a woman you can spend the rest of your life with?"

He shook his head, wondering if he was about to kill

all his chances with the alluring Nicole, but he wasn't going to give her any false hopes. "I'm sorry to disappoint you, but no, I'm not anxious to settle down anytime soon."

She propped her chin in her hand, her entire demeanor changing and softening in a sensual, inviting way. "I'm not disappointed at all. Actually, I find it incredibly refreshing compared with all the other guys here."

Now it was his turn to ask, "Why are *you* here?"

"Truth?" She bit her lush bottom lip. "I'm not interested in a relationship, either. I'm here to do research for an article I'm writing about dating trends."

He chuckled. No wonder she had a pad full of notes. "Well, well, well. Aren't we a pair?" They were probably the only two people there who weren't angling for a love match of some sort. A lust match, however, was entirely feasible, and he tested the possibility. "So, is this all business and no pleasure for you?"

She gave him a slow once-over that sent a surge of heat straight to his groin. "Now, that all depends on what kind of pleasure you're referring to."

The images filling his head went from sexy to X-rated. Definitely the kind of erotic stuff that had no business playing through his mind, especially in a room full of strangers.

With her bold words, her brazen responses, she fired his blood like no woman had in a very long time. She was a challenge he couldn't resist. Bracing his forearms on the table, he leaned in closer and held her gaze. "Whatever you want, however you want it, it's yours."

Her eyes widened, not in shock, but excitement—a combination of desire and need she didn't even try to hide. "Wow," she breathed. "You're good."

He grinned. "You started it." But he was more than willing to finish it, if that's where she wanted to take things.

She didn't deny the charge. Instead, she picked up her pen again and tapped it against the open notebook. "You know, you're totally skewing my research since you're not here for honest reasons." Her voice was light and teasing, belying the sultry look in her eyes.

She was one to talk! "And because your sole purpose for being here tonight is for research, and *not* a relationship, you're tempting every man in this room with something he can't have," he countered, enjoying their lively banter.

Her tongue darted out and moistened her bottom lip, making him wish he were the one tasting that mouth of hers. "Do I tempt *you*?" she asked huskily.

Oh, yeah. *Hell,* yeah. His body echoed the sentiment. Arousal hummed through his veins and settled directly in his lap.

The bell rang, shattering the flirtatious moment between them. The sound jolted him back to their present situation, and was a stark reminder that they weren't the only two people in the room.

"Your current session is over," Cindy announced. "Men, please move on to your next date."

Nathan didn't want to go, didn't want to leave Nicole. But her next date was there in a flash, not giving him the chance to say anything more or to see where this compelling conversation might have led. To see if the spark between them had any chance of becoming a live flame.

He'd have to find out when the event was over, because he wasn't done with Nicole.

Not by a long shot.

Chapter Three

Nearly two hours later, the speed-dating event finally came to an end, and not soon enough for Nicole. She stood and stretched her legs, then shoved her notepad into her purse and turned in her scorecard, along with the rest of the crowd.

Unbelievably, she'd dated fifteen men in one evening, and while she'd been able to gather enough interesting information to write her article, this particular game wasn't something she wanted to repeat anytime soon. If ever. It wasn't her thing, though it did add up to an entertaining experience.

The guys she'd met and talked to had been nice enough, but it was clear they were searching for something long-term with a woman. A few were even hoping for marriage out of the deal if they were fortunate enough. Well, almost every guy but Nathan. He'd been the exception in so many ways.

During each round, she'd been careful not to lead anyone on, or give the wrong impression about wanting a serious relationship. She tried, for the most part, to lead the direction of the conversation with her research questions. Luckily, she'd discovered that most of the guys enjoyed talking about themselves and didn't mind sharing their reasons for attending the speed-dating event.

Including Nathan, who'd nearly bowled her over with the surprising truth of why he was here—not for his own personal gain, but as a favor. That in itself had surprised her, not to mention being ambushed by his striking good looks, sexy smile, and those dark, seductive caramel-colored eyes that made her feel all warm and mushy inside—and good God, she so wasn't the type of female to melt into a pool of infatuation because of a man. But even from a distance, their attraction had been strong and immediate, and the moment they'd sat across from each other the awareness between them had spiraled to dizzying heights—all in seven short minutes.

Their playful banter had invigorated her, aroused her, and damn if she didn't want to know how he would have answered her last question before their session had ended.

Do I tempt you?

But much to her regret, the sexy, heated moment had gone without a reply from him. And even now, she couldn't help but wonder where it all could have led.

The men and women at the event started to mix and mingle again, and despite telling herself Nathan had been most likely toying with her with no intentions of following through on the undeniable chemistry between them, she found herself glancing around the room for him, anyway.

He wasn't anywhere she could see. No doubt he'd bolted once his obligation to Cindy, and the speed-dating event, had ended. Smart man, she thought, and decided to do the same before she was cornered by some guy she had no desire to talk to.

Just as she started for the door, a deep, male voice called out her name from somewhere behind her, bringing her to a hopeful stop.

"Nicole!"

Automatically, she turned around, her breath hitching in her throat when she caught sight of Nathan cutting through a group of people while he politely dodged other women's advances, his gaze locked on hers as he strode toward her with a single-minded determination that made her weak in the knees. Silly, yes, but there was something about a hot, take-charge kind of guy that totally turned her on, and Nathan did it for her in a major way.

She absently licked her bottom lip as she watched him approach. And what a mighty fine view it was. He was dressed casually in tan Dockers pants and a knit polo shirt, but there was no mistaking the powerful, rock-hard body beneath his clothes. His shoulders were broad, and his biceps were built with firm, toned muscles that hinted at the strength in those arms. A lean torso gave way to a flat belly, narrow hips, and lower, a pair of solid thighs.

Then there was his face—big girlie sigh here—gorgeous and masculine, with intense eyes and dark, silky brown hair that was a bit longer, and certainly more unruly and tousled, than most of the short, executive cuts in the room. It made him look rebellious and untamed, as if rules didn't apply to him.

And oh, how those bad-boy qualities appealed to her, and called to her on a feminine level.

Swallowing to ease the sudden dryness in her throat, she managed a nonchalant smile when he came to a stop in front of her. "Hey."

He pushed his hands into the front pockets of his pants, his hypnotic eyes searching her features. "You're leaving?"

She shrugged. "There's really no reason for me to stay."

"Not even for me?" An irresistible, toe-curling smile edged up the corners of his sensual mouth, and a surge of heat settled low in her belly.

The man didn't play fair. He was tempting her with his grin, his words, that totally hot body—and Lord help her, she was helpless to withstand all that enticing charm. Going so many months without sex was making her weak, weak, weak.

She figured the best defense was to flirt right back. "Is that your roundabout way of *asking* me to stay?"

"Yes, it is." Uncaring that they were standing in a room full of people, he reached out and stroked the pad of his thumb along her jaw, his touch electric against her sensitive skin. "To answer your earlier question, you tempt me. More than you can imagine."

She could imagine, all right. The corresponding fantasies filtering through her mind were definitely carnal.

"Except I don't want to stay here with all these people around," he went on, his voice low and intimate. "Let's go have something to eat in the restaurant, just the two of us."

Just that easily, he swayed her. Besides, it was still early, and it wasn't like she had anything or anyone waiting for her at home. "Okay."

With his big, warm hand riding low at the base of

her spine, he guided her out of the back room and into Simply Fondue, where a hostess seated them at a cozy booth with tall partitions for privacy. She slid along the leather seat, and Nathan moved in close beside her. Then he went ahead and ordered a cheese fondue, a chocolate caramel fondue for dessert, and a recommended bottle of Sauvignon Blanc.

Once the wine was delivered and a glass poured for each of them, Nicole turned to Nathan and clinked her goblet to his. "To a very interesting evening."

"And just think, it isn't even over yet." He winked at her and took a drink of his wine.

Grinning, she shook her head at him. "I'm thinking you and I have broken some serious rules about speed dating."

He looked completely unconcerned. "How so?"

"Well, we both came here tonight under false pretenses and not really wanting to meet anyone, yet here we are, hooking up on the sly."

He rested his arm along the back of the booth behind Nicole, and his fingers threaded through her hair until she felt them sliding along the nape of her neck. The sensual contact sent delicious shivers down her spine and made her breasts tighten and tingle in reaction.

"Is that what we're doing?" he asked huskily as his fingers continued to stroke her skin and wreak havoc with her sorely neglected libido. "Hooking up?"

"Maybe." His caress was so inviting, seducing her senses and all those female body parts that had gone much too long without a man's touch. "If you're lucky."

"I'm sitting here with you now, aren't I?"

She laughed. "That part has nothing to do with luck."

He cocked a dark brow, his eyes alight with humor. "What would you call it then?"

"Pure, unadulterated desire," she said, and took a slow sip of her wine, letting those words sink in before she continued. She was feeling bold and daring, and she embraced the sensation. "The way I see things, I want you and you clearly want me, and we're testing things out, maybe seeing if we like each other enough to take that desire one step farther."

He leaned closer to her, so close she could inhale the intoxicating scent of his clean, crisp cologne. So close, he could have kissed her if he wanted—and she would have let him, just to see if he tasted as good as she imagined.

"Just to set the record straight," he murmured, the flare of heat in his tawny eyes sending sparks to all those secret, warm places deep inside her. "I like you, Nicole. A *lot*."

"I like you, too," she admitted.

He gave her a reckless grin. "A lot?" he cajoled, a teasing note to his voice.

The man was too confident, though all that self-assurance worked really well for him. However, she wasn't about to give him everything up front. "I'll let you know. In time. You have to earn it first."

"I'll do my very best." There was just enough arrogance in his gaze to let her know he had the ability to wrap her around his finger, and other more masculine body parts. In time.

Their waitress arrived, interrupting the sensual mood as she delivered the pot of Swiss cheese fondue, along with grilled chunks of steak, vegetables, and pieces of bread for dipping. She refilled Nicole's nearly empty wineglass, then moved on to the next table to take another couple's order.

Nicole picked up one of the long fondue forks, pierced a slice of medium-rare filet mignon, and dipped it into the creamy cheese sauce. "So, what do you do for work?" she asked, wanting to know more beyond the fact he was totally hot and sexy as sin.

"I work in security."

She finished eating her steak and went for an artichoke heart. "So, are we talking security alarms?" she guessed.

He shook his head, washed down the bite of meat he'd eaten with his Sauvignon Blanc, then answered. "I'm a surveillance supervisor at The Onyx Casino. I work in the control room and deal with security issues that occur in the gaming areas."

She was impressed. "Now, that's far more exciting than a rent-a-cop or a man who spends his time installing alarms," she teased. "Have you always worked in a casino?"

"No." He paused for a moment before continuing, as if thinking his reply through before answering. "I joined the marines out of high school, then worked for Las Vegas Metro for a while before taking on the job at The Onyx."

Reaching for her glass of wine, she focused on what they had in common. "My younger brother, Eric, is currently serving in the military."

"Really? What branch?" he asked curiously.

"Army." He dunked a piece of sourdough bread into the creamy Swiss cheese, and she watched in fascination as he brought it to his mouth, his tongue catching a drop of sauce before it could fall to his chin. "He's been in Iraq for nearly two years now."

He met her gaze, the look in his eyes somber and very knowing. "I've been there. It's a tough assignment."

She'd read the news and researched enough about the war to know he spoke the truth about the horrific and deadly conditions the troops dealt with on a daily basis. "Eric loves what he does, and because of that I respect the career path he's chosen. It's my parents, my mother especially, who has a difficult time with him being there."

Nathan winced. "Yeah, my mom, too. She had a hard time watching her only son go to war."

Finished with the cheese fondue, she set her fork on her plate. "You're an only child?"

"No, I have three older sisters." He set his fork aside, too. "And let me tell you, it was hell growing up in an all-female environment. Though I did learn at a young age to cater to their whims to get what I wanted."

Despite his complaint, his voice was infused with a wealth of affection for his siblings. "So that's how you became such a charmer, hmmm?"

"What can I say?" His tone was playfully unapologetic, as was his grin. "It was great training when it comes to dealing with women. I learned all kinds of secrets from my sisters." He winked at her.

She laughed, and liked him even more than when they'd originally sat down at the table. He was open and honest and genuine, and those were qualities the men she'd dated in the past had lacked. It was true everyone who signed up for the speed-dating event had to undergo a criminal check and background screening for safety, but there was something about Nathan that made her feel safe and comfortable—whether it was his military and previous law enforcement credentials, or the fact that he clearly adored his mother and sisters.

Their dinner dishes were cleared away, their glasses of wine refilled, and a few minutes later dessert arrived in the form of a small pot of milk-chocolate-and-caramel fondue, with an array of fruit, tiny cakes, and other sweet treats for dipping.

Five minutes ago she would have sworn she was stuffed and couldn't eat another bite, but resisting anything drenched in chocolate was impossible. She didn't hesitate to skewer a bright red strawberry and dive into the decadent dessert.

"So, enough about me," Nathan said, as if he'd just realized how she'd deliberately kept most of the questions about *him*, rather than focus on her. "Are you native to Vegas?"

Okay, that she could handle. Nothing too deep or intimate. "No. I'm a small-town girl, born and bred. Prattville, Iowa, population three hundred sixty-seven." She grinned.

He swirled a chunk of pineapple into the rich, sweet sauce, his gaze curious as he glanced at her. "What brought you to the city?"

Again, nothing too revealing there, either. "I'm a journalist, a graduate of Columbia University. I didn't care for living in New York City, and there's not a whole lot to report on in Prattville, so I chose Las Vegas because it seemed like an exciting place to live." She speared a fluffy white marshmallow and drenched it in the caramel chocolate.

"Do you like your job?" he asked.

"At the moment I'm a little frustrated," she admitted, playing it cool and casual. "I mean, come on, it doesn't take a genius to write an article on speed dating."

He chuckled, and before he could keep up his line of inquiry, she spun the spotlight back on him. "Speaking of which, what were some of the more amusing questions you were asked tonight?"

"Let me think." He turned thoughtful as he considered his night of dating more than a dozen women. "One woman asked me, 'If aliens landed on earth and selected you to visit their home planet, would you go with them?' "

She burst out laughing. "Oh, that's just plain scary," she said, then shared one of her own. "After a few minutes in one of my sessions, I had a guy ask if he was cute enough for me, or did I need more to drink? Talk about a cheesy pickup line."

Nathan groaned. "It's guys like him that give us all a bad reputation when it comes to dating women."

"Just so you know, you passed our speed-dating round with flying colors."

After submerging a small cheesecake square into the melted sauce, she popped the tidbit into her mouth and moaned at the rich, sweet flavors sliding across her taste buds. The delicious combination melted on her tongue, and she closed her eyes and groaned again, certain she'd died and gone to dessert heaven. This creation was by far her favorite.

"That good, huh?" Nathan asked, interrupting her near-orgasmic experience.

Her lashes fluttered open as she swallowed the last of the treat, immediately noticing that his eyes had grown dark from watching her. "Oh, yeah," she murmured in a low purr of sheer satisfaction. She speared another cube of cheesecake and drenched it in the fondue. "Here, try it for yourself."

Just as she lifted the cheesecake toward him, dripping with the scrumptious sauce, it slid off the end of the fork and fell to her plate. Without really thinking her actions through, she picked up the morsel and hand-fed it to him.

And that's when everything changed, from light and fun, to a mood that unleashed the underlying desire simmering between them from the beginning. Undoubtedly, it was a sensual experience just slipping the soft, gooey cheesecake past his lips, and it was more than enough to give her pulse a nice little jolt of awareness. But then he did the unexpected, and when she would have pulled her hand back, he grasped her wrist and held it captive.

"Hold on a sec," he said in a deep and sexy tone. "I'm feeling cheated. All the good stuff is still on your fingers."

The challenge in his heated gaze was undeniable. The wicked grin on his lips was just as daring. Would she or wouldn't she let him lick all that caramel chocolate off her?

She wasn't in a position to say no. And didn't want to. He brought her hand back to his lips and flicked his tongue across the tips of her fingers, wringing a groan from deep inside her. He licked and sucked and nibbled the chocolate sauce off her skin, and took his sweet time doing so, setting off a whole different kind of hunger between them and sending a wave of lustful heat rushing through her veins. It was all she could do to keep from straddling his lap and kissing him senseless.

"Mmmm, good," he said huskily, and gave her index finger one last slow lick she felt all the way down between her thighs.

Completely aroused, she squirmed on the leather seat beside him, and knew she was breathing harder and faster than normal.

Done turning her inside out with wanting him, he dipped a clean linen napkin into his water glass and used the damp cloth to clean the rest of the stickiness from her hand and fingers. All the while she couldn't stop thinking about pressing her lips to his and tasting all that male heat—deeply, thoroughly.

All alone in their private booth, the aching need grew, until it could no longer be ignored and the bold and brazen words were tumbling from her lips before she could stop them. "Nathan . . . I want to kiss you. Can I?"

A slow smile spread across his gorgeous face. "Yeah, I'd like that."

He rested his arm along the back of the seat and remained where he was, waiting for her to make the first move and doing nothing to meet her halfway. Yes, she'd been the one to ask for the kiss, and he was definitely going to make her work for it. A delightful, exciting surprise, considering most guys would have been all over her by now.

The truth was, she liked being the one setting the pace and calling the shots when it came to anything sexual. It was a control thing for her, a way of keeping physical pleasure separated from any emotional involvement—an arrangement that worked well for her.

Placing her hand on his chest, she leaned in closer, tipped her head to the side, and settled her lips against his with a sensual sigh. His mouth was soft and warm and

oh-so-inviting, and—unable to resist the temptation—
she slipped her tongue past the seam of his lips and was
greeted with the heady taste of chocolate, caramel, and
the kind of pure male heat that could threaten to consume her if she let it.

While he had allowed her to initiate the kiss, once she
delved deeper, turning the chaste caress of lips to more
provocative play, Nathan didn't hesitate to join in, ex-
ploring with equal leisure. His tongue stroked inside her
mouth, so seductive, so coaxing, and her entire body
hummed with intense pleasure.

Her hand slid around his neck, her fingers tangling
in the rich, dark strands of hair curling over the collar
of his shirt. It was clear Nathan was a man who appreciated the fine art of foreplay, enjoyed every nuance,
and loved the chase as much as the capture. The slow
sweep of his tongue was as luxurious as it was arousing, and his mouth promised to pleasure her in every
way imaginable.

She nearly whimpered at the thought, but somehow
managed to pull back and end the kiss. They were both
breathing rapidly, and his gaze glittered with a passion
and a fire that matched her own. A passion that had the
potential of filling the aching emptiness within her, if
she dared.

Oh, God, she wanted that. Wanted *him*. It had been
so long since she'd felt so alive, so wildly attracted to a
man. She'd already told him she wasn't looking for
anything complicated or long-term, and he'd admitted
the same. There was nothing wrong with them enjoying the rest of the evening together and what had the
potential to be some incredibly hot sex. It was what her
body needed. It was what she craved.

One night only, no strings attached.

"This is going to sound very forward, but I know if I don't ask I'll regret it later." She inhaled deeply and let it out real slow, grasping the fortitude to finish her question despite the warmth suddenly suffusing her face. "How do you feel about going somewhere quiet and private so we can be alone, just the two of us?"

There was no mistaking what she meant. "Are you sure about that?" he asked as he gently pushed a tousled curl from her cheek.

It was that tender touch that sealed the deal for her. "Absolutely, one hundred percent positive."

A devastatingly sexy grin curved his mouth. "Your place or mine?"

The anticipation making its way through her system was very, very sweet. "Yours."

Chapter Four

Even though Nathan was anxious to be alone with Nicole, he drove just under the speed limit and kept the sight of her car in his rearview mirror at all times as she followed him to his house. He'd recently moved from a small apartment in the city to a neighborhood on the outskirts of Vegas, and Nicole was the first woman he'd ever brought to his new home. But somehow it felt right, and he didn't regret offering his place as an option.

When he'd agreed to be part of the speed-dating event, he never would have anticipated that this was how the evening would end. It was a pleasant surprise, and while the Ramsey assignment was definitely in the back of his mind, there wasn't anything he could do about the case tonight.

He intended to enjoy a few hours with Nicole—a mutual satisfying night of hot sex—and in the morning, they'd go their separate ways. They'd already established she wasn't interested in anything serious, and neither was he. It was the perfect arrangement. They were two adults attracted to each other, and they were taking advantage of the chemistry between them. It was a straightforward, cut-and-dried situation, and exactly what he needed before he immersed himself in Preston Sloane's sordid world.

Arriving at his house at the end of a cul-de-sac, he pulled his silver Audi Coupe into the garage and she parked in the driveway behind him. He got out of his car, noticed she was in her vehicle and on her cell phone, and waited for her to finish the call. Most likely, she was letting someone know where she was, just in case. Smart girl.

Less than a minute later she was walking toward him with a sultry smile on her lips—just for him. He held his hand out to her, and she placed her fingers against his palm and let him lead her inside the house, through the kitchen, and into the adjoining living room. He flipped a switch, and a lamp next to the leather sofa illuminated the area in a soft glow.

She looked around, taking in his basic furnishings, making him see the interior of the house through her eyes. "Sorry the place is so empty and sparse. I used to live in a small studio apartment and I've only had this house a few months. I haven't had time to buy more furniture." And he honestly didn't need much.

Smiling, she set her purse on the long table situated in the entryway where he'd left his keys, then started back toward him, a playful glint in her eyes, along with a whole lot of heat. "All that matters is that there's a bed somewhere."

He liked the way she thought. "There is. I have a really nice four-poster king-sized bed with a pillow-top mattress." A completely new mahogany bedroom set had been his only indulgence when he'd moved in, and now he was glad he'd splurged.

"I can't wait to see it," she said, but it was obvious by the single-minded way she tugged his shirt from his pants and pushed it up and over his head, right then and there, that she wasn't in any big hurry to rush off to the bedroom.

Neither was he. They'd get there, in time.

He tossed the shirt aside and sucked in a sharp breath when she splayed her cool hands low on his abdomen, then slowly skimmed her palms upward, using her fingers to familiarize herself with the hard planes of his chest. Her soft hands felt amazing on his skin, and when her thumbs grazed his taut nipples, he couldn't contain the groan that ripped from his throat.

His response seemed to set her off, too. She went in for a kiss, nipping at his bottom lip as her hands slid back down to the waistband of his trousers and started unbuckling his belt, her movements quick and impatient, as if she couldn't wait to get to the main event. She was back to being the aggressive one, and at the rate she was going he knew that once she had his aching shaft in her hands this encounter was going to spiral into a hot, fast, no-frills coupling that would be over in minutes.

Normally, he wouldn't complain, but there was so much about this woman he wanted to savor—with his hands, his mouth, and eventually, his entire body. For him, there was no rush. They had all night, and he planned to make the most of those hours together—and that meant taking charge of the situation before he was too far gone to think straight.

Grasping her wrists, he pulled her hands away from his belt and drew his head back, breaking the contact of her lips on his. She looked up at him in confusion, and he took advantage of her momentary bewilderment to guide her back a few steps, until he had her pressed up against the nearest wall and his thighs bracketed hers.

Her eyes widened in surprise, and he smiled at her as he straightened her arms back to her sides, then flattened her palms against the cool surface behind her. "Keep your hands against the wall, and no touching."

She arched a brow, though her blue eyes had gone all dark and smoky at his command. "That hardly seems fair," she murmured, but didn't appear too upset at the role reversal.

He shrugged unapologetically. "My house, my rules," he said as he trailed his fingers along the gentle swell of her hips and the indentation of her waist, tracing the lean lines of her figure through her dress. He couldn't wait until she was naked and he could touch her bare skin and explore her sensual curves.

She blinked her lashes lazily, though the rise and fall of her breasts told him just how aroused she was. "And if I break them?"

Leaning into her, he brushed his lips against the shell of her ear. "There are consequences, of course."

She shivered in excitement. "Ummm, that just might be worth being bad."

He chuckled, amused by her feisty attitude. Lifting his hands, he threaded his fingers through the soft curls at the side of her face and met her velvet blue gaze. "Back at the restaurant, I let you have the first kiss. This one's mine. And remember, *no touching.*"

He dipped his head and took her mouth in a soft, chaste kiss. She groaned in frustration, clearly wanting more, and he made her suffer a bit longer, because it was so much fun to do so. He licked her bottom lip, teasing her, and gently nibbled the soft bit of flesh with his teeth.

She whimpered, her lips automatically parting, tempting him to take what she was offering, and it was more than he could resist. With his hands entwined in the silky strands of her hair, he angled her head to the side, aligning their mouths for maximum pleasure, and deepened the contact. His tongue sank into the sweet, hot depths of her mouth, and he finally kissed her like he'd been dying to. In an instant, lust and need collided in a combustible combination of liquid heat and uncontrollable passion.

God, she was like an addictive drug he couldn't get enough of.

Untangling his fingers from her hair, he dropped his hands to the zipper at the back of her dress, and she arched away from the wall so he could pull the tab all the way down to the base of her spine. When he was done, he ended their kiss and nuzzled the side of her neck, his mouth open and hot and damp on her skin as he dragged the sides of the dress down her arms, all the way to her waist, trapping her hands at her sides in the knot of fabric.

She gasped, the soft, shocked sound darting straight to his groin like a physical caress.

He inhaled a deep breath against her throat. She smelled warm and sweet and fragrant, and the scent only added fuel to his hunger for her. He wanted to taste her, everywhere, and he planned to start with the breasts he'd bared.

She hadn't been wearing a bra—a pleasant surprise he'd discovered as he stripped away the top portion of her dress and felt those mounds graze his bare chest.

He moved back just enough to look his fill of her. She was perfectly proportioned to her slender waist, her breasts small but firm, and as he watched her nipples puckered tight.

He didn't hesitate to take one into his mouth, his lips pulling and sucking on the engorged tip while his tongue stroked and swirled and eventually soothed her taut flesh. She moaned and moved restlessly against him, and he felt her fingers gliding across his belly as she reached for his zipper once again. She tugged on the top snap, and his cock leapt to attention when her palm cupped the thick bulge straining the limits of his trousers.

Somehow, she'd managed to free her hands and was disobeying his order. For that, he bit down on the curve of her breast, just enough to create an erotic sting to remind her of his no-touching policy. She drew a sharp, startled breath and returned her hands to her sides, her palms pressed against the wall.

"You're cruel and merciless." Despite the pout on her lips, her eyes gleamed with arousal and a deeper, darker desire that told him just how much she liked him calling the shots.

Lucky for her, he was about to get more ruthless.

He shoved her dress over her hips, and when it slid down her legs and pooled at her feet she stepped out of the circle of fabric and kicked it aside. Unable to help himself, he eased back just far enough to take in the provocative view of her wearing nothing more than white lace bikini panties and a pair of strappy high heels that made her gorgeous legs look endlessly long.

With all those frothy blond curls tumbling around her shoulders and that lithe body wearing only sheer white panties, she looked like a wanton angel. And she was all his. Every inch of her. Reaching out, he slid his hands beneath her pretty breasts, cupping and gently squeezing the weight of them. He rubbed his thumbs across her nipples, and her head fell back against the wall, her lips parted, and the oh-so-sexy moan she sighed added to the slow burn in the pit of his belly.

He dropped his mouth over hers and kissed her again. Slowly, languidly, as he smoothed one of his hands down her flat stomach and into the waistband of those flimsy panties. This time he released a low, deep rumble of pleasure when he encountered the softest, hottest heat between her legs. She was so wet, so ready, and he didn't hesitate to push one finger, then two, deep inside her.

She went wild, and he had to admit he did, too, his cock surging with sensory overload. She shuddered, hard, and then her hips were moving restlessly against his hand and the fingers invading her tight body as they stroked and thrust in the same seductive rhythm as his tongue sweeping through the dark recesses of her mouth.

He felt her naughty, rebellious hands again, this time splaying low on his back, her fingers digging into skin and muscle as she ground her hips urgently against his, seeking relief. The tantalizing gyrations pushed his fingers harder, faster, into the tight clasp of her sex, and he thought his head was going to explode.

With monumental effort, he broke the kiss and stilled his hand, waiting for her to understand the repercussions of her touching him. After a moment, she released a soft sob of frustration and let her arms fall back to her sides.

"Nathan," she said, her voice a low rasp of sound. "I want you inside me. *Please*."

He buried his face against her neck and trailed delicate, moist kisses up to the shell of her ear. "I *am* inside you," he whispered, and to make sure there was no doubt in her mind, he stroked her slick inner walls with his fingers. "I can feel how snug and warm you are, how soft and aroused."

She groaned and shook her head. "You're driving me crazy."

He chuckled, then pulled back so he could look into her bright blue eyes. "Yeah, maybe a little. But there's no sense rushing a good thing." He eased his fingers back out, then drove them deep again, watching as her breath quickened and her lashes fell half-mast. "I want to watch you come. I want to know what it's going to feel like when you tighten around my cock when I'm pushed all the way to the hilt inside you."

The image he must have created in her head had a rippling effect on her body. She shivered, the tips of her breasts piercing his chest, branding him, while lower, she clenched around his plundering fingers.

"Please," she begged shamelessly.

Smiling like the devil, he continued to decimate her senses with a heated caress here and a leisurely stroke there. "You're in way too much of a rush," he murmured. "You're going straight for satisfaction and bypassing all the good stuff in between. Don't you know foreplay is the best part of sex?"

She laughed huskily, even as her hips continued to strain toward his enticing touch. "Yeah, *I* know that, but most guys aren't so patient and generous."

"Maybe you've been with the wrong kind of guys,"

he suggested, and brought his thumb into play, sliding the pad through the weeping folds of her sex until he found what he sought. Her clit. And that's where he next focused his attention.

She bit her bottom lip and moaned as he glided his thumb over the hard nub of flesh, using her own slick moisture to enhance the pleasure. "I think you're right," she said breathlessly.

"Of course I am," he teased, then began in earnest to prove how *right* he was.

His mouth went back to work seducing hers, deeply and thoroughly and with infinite patience, while his fingers adopted the same slow, deliberate rhythm down below. He ignored the desperate, needy sounds she made, ignored her attempts to speed things up. Instead, he made her burn, inside and out. He gradually brought her to the breaking point, to that pinnacle where lust and desire meshed into the ultimate pleasure, then pushed her even higher, until she was unraveling, trembling. The strength of her orgasm completely consumed her, leaving her weak and spent and gasping for breath.

He gave her a few moments to recover, brushing his lips across her cheek and removing his hand from the incredible heat of her still-pulsing body. He was achingly hard, and it was all he could do to keep from taking her right there, up against the wall.

Her eyes opened languidly, and a content smile curved her kiss-swollen lips. "Oh. My. God. That was amazing."

Her compliment stroked his male ego and made him want her even more. "And just think, we're not done yet. Condoms are in the bedroom," he said, leaving the next decision up to her.

She didn't hesitate. "Lead the way."

Taking her hand, he guided her down the hallway to his bedroom, where Nicole was quick to turn the tables and take control. This time, he let her, because he was done with the teasing and beyond eager to be inside her. She obviously wanted the same thing.

He pulled off his shoes and socks while she went to work getting him out of his pants, her mouth kissing him with a reckless hunger and passion that fired his blood like never before. As soon as his trousers and briefs were off, her hands were seemingly everywhere at once—caressing his chest, skimming down his abdomen, and then her fingers were circling his thick erection. She stroked the length of him in a firm grip, her thumb grazing over the sensitive head that was already seeping with moisture.

His hips automatically thrust against her palm, now slick from his own arousal. He groaned like a dying man, knowing he was going to lose it right there in her hand if she didn't stop touching and fondling him.

He forced himself to step away long enough to grab a condom from the nightstand and quickly rolled it on while she kicked aside her heels and shimmied out of her panties. Without any further preliminaries, she pushed him down onto the mattress so he reclined along the pillows shoved up against the headboard, and then she straddled his lap. The dewy soft flesh between her thighs enticed the tip of his cock with the promise of ecstasy.

Holding his gaze, she lowered herself onto him, much too slow for his liking. Needing more, he curled his fingers around her waist, pulling her down with a firm tug as he pressed his way into her hot, silky depths. He shoved past the tight squeeze of her inner muscles until he could go no farther, until her head fell back, her spine arching. A small gasp of surprise escaped her parted lips as he filled her fully.

It didn't take her long to adjust to his size, to take charge once again. Splaying her hands on his belly, she rolled her hips and rocked against him, a woman intent on stealing whatever satisfaction she could while making him insane with lust in the process. Even as she smiled down at him with such sweet, sensual longing, he recognized the on-top position as aggressive and dominant, keeping her the one in complete control. He wasn't about to complain, not when this particular pose appealed to every one of his masculine senses. That, and he knew he wasn't without power. Not only could he clearly watch every move she made and her changing expressions as she took her pleasure, but he could touch and caress her, *everywhere*.

And he did. He swept his hands over her breasts, palming the soft mounds, feeling the swell of her flesh and the rise of her nipples as he feathered his fingers across the rigid tips. With a soft, needy moan, she arched into his heated touch with an uninhibited thrust of her hips against his, the curve of her body drawing him in impossibly deeper, until using only his hands was no longer enough.

He craved more. Because of the pillows stuffed behind his back, he was sitting up rather than lying down, and the position enabled him to lean forward and put his mouth on her breast. His lips latched on to a stiff nipple, and he sucked, hard. She cried out, not from pain, but excitement. Her fingers threaded through his hair, tugging restlessly on the strands, her breath catching in her throat as he used his teeth on her, nipping her gently, then soothing the sweet ache with his tongue.

Panting now, she tightened her grip on his hair, yanked his head back, and took his mouth in a hot, wet, tongue-tangling kiss that made his cock pulse with the raw, primitive need to possess her completely. She moved on him like a bold and brazen siren, impulsive and unrestrained, seducing his body with the most erotic lap dance he'd ever had the pleasure of receiving. His hips rose to meet hers, each vigorous lunge burying his thick length deeper inside her, taking them both closer to release.

She groaned into his mouth, her writhing body clenching around his shaft, stroking him like a velvet fist as the first white-hot surges of her orgasm rippled through her. The muscles in his stomach and thighs tensed in response and he pumped into her harder, faster, driving her climax on until she was coming in deep, shuddering waves that triggered his own mindless surrender.

She collapsed on top of him, all warm and soft and pliant, and nestled her face against his neck, her breath hot and moist on his skin. He welcomed her slight weight, the crush of her breasts against his chest, the fragrant scent of her hair, and the touch of her damp lips on his throat. He massaged his hands up and down her naked back, and after a while she rolled off him with a contented sigh he felt solely responsible for.

She looked at him, all soft and sated, and he couldn't help the arrogant male grin curving his lips. What he found more surprising was the need to keep her in his bed, rather than his usual compulsion to usher her out of it, as he normally did with the women he slept with.

It was a novel sensation, and one he refused to examine too closely.

Instead, he shook those thoughts from his mind. He decided that for tonight, they still had a few more hours to enjoy each other until they parted ways in the morning, and he planned to do just that.

Chapter Five

After a quick trip to the bathroom, Nathan returned to the bedroom to find Nicole no longer waiting for him on the bed, where he'd expected to find her. Instead, she was stepping into her panties and pulling them back on, a clear sign she getting ready to leave.

"What are you doing?" he asked.

She bent over and picked up her shoes from the floor, giving him a provocative view of her ass. "I'm picking up my things and getting dressed," she said, stating the obvious.

He was stark naked and close enough to take full advantage of her bent-over position, and his cock responded to the randy thoughts chasing through his mind, stirring his lower body back to life with a surge of lust. "Why?" he asked, and this time his voice sounded strangled, with desire and the surprising need to stall her departure.

Straightening, she turned back around to face him, thankfully not noticing what a horny bastard he was. Her gaze met his, and a slight smile tugged at her lips. "Because I don't want to drive home naked."

Under normal circumstances, he would have laughed at her attempt to crack a joke, but right now he was too intent on enticing her to stay before he lost the chance. "You don't have to go."

"Yeah, I do," she replied softly, though she didn't look completely convinced by her own words. "It was fun, fantastic actually, but no need to complicate things by me hanging around."

He witnessed the array of conflicting emotions in her blue eyes, a wealth of uncertainties clashing with a deeper longing she was trying very hard to deny. He didn't understand the doubts, so he focused on the more sensual aspect still lingering between them. Being with her felt good, a warm and inviting contrast with the darkness of the case looming before him. A few hours of pleasure wasn't a lot to ask for, and it wasn't as though he'd be getting any work done tonight.

He gave her an easygoing smile. "Look, I know we both said we weren't looking for anything long-term, but what's the harm in you and I enjoying the rest of the night together?"

She sighed, and he could see her resistance crumbling, just a bit. "I really shouldn't."

Knowing she was riding that fine line between fleeing and staying, he decided to bring in a heavier arsenal of persuasion. "Yeah, you really should," he murmured huskily as he stepped toward her. "And let me show you all the reasons why."

Before she could move away, he wrapped an arm around her waist and pulled her body flush to his. There was no mistaking the stiff erection prodding her belly, and she gasped at the physical proof of how much he wanted her all over again. His free hand cupped the back of her neck to hold her in place, and then he meshed their lips together in an all-out relentless assault to convince her to stay.

His mouth moved over hers with shameless purpose, his tongue stroking hot and deep, over and over, until the tension in her body eased and he felt her melt against him. Letting her shoes drop back to the floor, she entwined her arms around his neck and kissed him back with equal heat and passion.

Triumph was very sweet, indeed.

Grinning, he lifted his mouth inches from hers, just enough to taunt and tease, and she whimpered in protest. He chuckled huskily, knowing he almost had her exactly where he wanted her. "Are you sure you still want to go?" he whispered against her parted lips.

Her answer was to hook one of her slender legs around his hip, so his shaft rubbed against the damp silk lining her panties. "You so don't play fair."

He'd take that as a yes. "No, I don't play fair," he agreed as he guided her a few steps backward, toward the bed. "Not when it comes to getting what I want, and in this case that would be *you*. Again. And this time, I want to be on top and in charge."

She laughed, the sound so sexy it made him ache to get back inside her. "You can certainly try," she said, all sass and brazen challenge.

With a playful growl, he tumbled her back onto the mattress. Before she could scramble away or switch their positions, he moved over her, holding her down with the weight of his body as he proceeded to show her who, exactly, held all the sexual power this time around. After a while she gave in and let him have his way with her, multiple times—at his leisure and in his own good time, which drove her wild in the process.

He liked that. A whole lot.

Being with a woman had never been so hot, so fun, and so satisfying. He couldn't seem to get enough of Nicole, though he did his best to sate his hunger for her throughout the night, until he'd wrung every last bit of pleasure from their bodies and they finally collapsed into sexual exhaustion.

Nicole couldn't stay. Oh, she was certainly tempted to indulge in a sleepover with Nathan. To wake up all warm and snuggled next to him and enjoy lazy morning sex with a man who knew his way around a woman's body and had awakened all those erogenous zones that had been dormant for way too long. A part of her definitely wanted to have breakfast with him, possibly even spend the day together getting to know him better, and therein lay the problem for her.

Tonight was supposed to be all about a dark, gorgeous stranger, a few hot orgasms—a one-night stand meant to slake those carnal needs that had built over the past six months of celibacy. Nathan had done the job admirably and generously. Except between the shared laughter, the playful teasing, the intimate conversations and lustful groans, he'd become more than a sexual object for the sole purpose of giving her pleasure. He'd become *real* to her—a man with an honorable past as a marine, the younger brother to three older sisters, and a man who embraced his job as a surveillance supervisor.

There was nothing awkward about being with him, nothing to make walking away from him simple or easy.

Because somewhere along the way he'd gone from being her temporary fantasy guy to the kind of man she knew she could fall for, given the chance.

And that knowledge scared the hell out of her.

Instinctively she knew spending more than this one night with him would be detrimental to her emotions, and quite possibly her heart. That warm fluttering in her belly when she glanced at him, combined with a deeper yearning for something more, was a complication and distraction she didn't want or need in her life. For her, it was all about self-preservation, because Nathan had the ability to mess with her head and her goals as a journalist, and she wasn't about to get sucked back into a situation that consumed her to the detriment of everything else that was important to her.

That's why she was getting out while the getting was still good, while she could think straight and make the decision without her mind being fogged with the afterglow of phenomenal sex. And right now was the perfect opportunity to make her getaway, since she still had the advantage of being cloaked in anonymity. She hadn't given Nathan any personal information for a reason. She hadn't checked his name on the dating scorecard as a match, and that, at least, would help her make a clean break with him.

Wanting to avoid any morning-after awkwardness, she knew she had to slip out in the dark of night while he was sleeping. Quietly and carefully, she edged off the bed. She stepped into her underwear, picked up her shoes from the floor, and gave him one last look to tuck away for future dreams and fantasies.

He was snoring softly, the endearing sound making her smile. The sheet was tangled around his waist, and she memorized what she could see of his hard, muscular body, the stubble on his jaw, and the roguishly long hair that had felt like silk between her fingers. Undoubtedly, he was a gorgeous, masculine work of art she was going to miss more than she cared to admit.

Swallowing the regrets rising within her before they threatened to overwhelm her, she tiptoed out of the bedroom and made her way down the hall to the living room. She was grateful the lamp next to the couch was still on, which kept her fumbling-around to a minimum. Finding her dress in a heap on the floor, she quickly put it on, then made her way to the table in the foyer where she'd left her purse.

She absolutely hated leaving like a thief in the night, without a good-bye or an explanation, and that thought had her reaching into her handbag for a pen and the small notepad she kept with her. Tearing off a clean sheet of paper, she wrote, *Nathan, thank you for an amazing night. I had a great time. Nicole.* Then she placed the note beneath his car keys, where he was certain to see it at some point tomorrow.

She grabbed the strap of her purse, but just as she turned away, the bottom of the bag brushed across a file folder on the edge of the table and knocked it to the floor. The contents spilled out, and she whispered a curse beneath her breath at her clumsiness as she knelt down to retrieve the papers and photographs now strewn across the ground.

She picked up a picture of a pretty, young blond girl and what appeared to be an investigative report. At first, she gave the summary an indifferent glance, but a familiar name caught her attention and made her pause and take a second, more careful look.

Preston Sloane.

She knew she ought to stuff the items back into the folder without another glance, but as a journalist she had a curiosity streak a mile wide. What she'd discovered made her question Nathan's connection to a man surrounded by controversy when it came to his private life.

Unable to ignore what she'd inadvertently found, her reporter instincts kicked in, overriding the twinge of guilt pricking her conscience. She didn't have time to sit there and read through all the notes and reports at her leisure without the risk of him catching her, so she did the next best thing. Pushing aside the little voice in her head telling her she was straddling a fine ethical line, she pulled her BlackBerry from her purse and took close-up pictures of the contents of the file to peruse later. Within minutes she had everything back in its place and was quietly slipping out the front door.

On the drive home, she mulled over what she'd discovered, her mind spinning with her own thoughts on Preston Sloane. Once she arrived at her apartment, she headed straight for her bedroom, closed the door, and began uploading the pictures she'd taken to her laptop. She changed into her favorite pair of short PJs, crawled into bed, and began reading the information she'd copied from Nathan's file.

In her opinion, and from what she knew and had heard as a reporter, Preston Sloane was as sleazy as they came. He reminded her way too much of her own experience in college, when her English professor, nearly twenty years her senior, had taken advantage of her youth.

She was barely eighteen, a freshman, and Mark

Reeves's flirtation and attention had made her feel special and attractive. All the girls in his class had a crush on him, and Nicole was no different—except she was the one he wanted out of all those other girls, and in a matter of weeks she was dating him, then sleeping with him.

But what began as an exciting relationship with an older, experienced man gradually turned into something much uglier—including the use of drugs (to relax her, he'd told her), then on to kinkier sexual demands. She'd been so convinced that he loved her, so caught up in pleasing him, that she hadn't realized just how degrading and dysfunctional the relationship actually was.

Mark had been a master at seducing her body and manipulating her emotions, only to shatter her heart and self-esteem when someone younger, prettier, and more innocent came along to replace her in his affections. With Nicole well used, he'd cut her out of his life completely and without remorse, leaving her ashamed and humiliated.

At the time, she'd hadn't been able to see the silver lining in his cruel and abrupt breakup. Devastated and unable to focus on what was most important to her— her degree in journalism—she'd nearly lost everything that mattered to her.

She'd learned her lesson well and had thankfully recovered from the ordeal, but the emotional scars and inability to trust a man completely ran much deeper.

Now, as she scanned through the investigative report and the Internet articles on Preston Sloane and the supposed darker side to his personality, her stomach roiled in response. Then came the detailed information on a teenage girl named Angela Ramsey, a runaway who'd last been seen at Sloane's estate and had been missing for the past three weeks.

Nicole had no idea what Nathan's involvement was with Sloane and the teenage girl, or why he had a portfolio filled with so much personal data on each. He'd told her he worked in surveillance for The Onyx, so why was he interested in something that had nothing to do with casino security?

By the time she finished reading everything, she'd connected to Angela Ramsey's story on a personal level and felt compelled to do something to alter the course the young girl was currently on. Her journalistic side saw a breakout story. And the eighteen-year-old she'd once been wanted desperately to save other girls from enduring the humiliation and degradation of getting involved with a man like Preston Sloane.

She tried to get some sleep, but instead spent the rest of the night and early-morning hours tossing and turning fitfully. Her mind churned with her own foolish past, the choices she'd made, and how those choices had nearly destroyed her. Nicole wondered how many young girls like Angela had seen Preston Sloane as their own Prince Charming. A man reputed to use girls for his pleasure, at the cost of their own self-worth and sanity.

Oh, yeah, she'd been there, done that, and she couldn't deny the information struck a personal chord. By morning, she was determined to do what she hadn't done all those years ago with her professor: find a way to expose Preston Sloane for the creep he was.

Here was the substantial story she'd been looking for, just begging for her to research and write. Unable to resist such a challenge, or the chance to expose an unscrupulous man like Sloane, she saw this as an opportunity to make amends for past mistakes and hopefully save other girls from falling victim to the kind of emotional manipulation that could scar them for life.

Nicole knew her editor at *The Las Vegas Commentary* would never approve of her taking on Preston Sloane. Investigating the man's life, and proving he was guilty of statutory rape, would require meticulous research. Logic dictated she find a way to get close to the man so she could discover what really went on behind the high walls of his estate. Even if that meant going undercover to get his attention.

As for Nathan, she could only hope she didn't run into him again. But if their paths did cross during her investigation of Sloane, she'd just deal with the situation when, and if, it happened.

If waking up to find Nicole had snuck out on him sometime in the early-morning hours wasn't enough to bruise Nathan's male ego, then finding her brief message thanking him for a great time only added insult to injury.

After rocking his world last night, more than once, she was gone—and had left him the equivalent of a Dear John note. There was no explanation for her hasty departure, and while he knew every inch of her body intimately, he realized he had no information on how to contact her. No phone number, no e-mail, no home address, *nothing*.

Hell, he didn't even know her last name.

The only thing he did know about Nicole was she was a writer of some sort, and she'd attended the speed-dating event to research an article about dating trends.

But that information was too general to find out who she was, or to track her down. Not without a last name to help his search.

Last night, in the heat of passion, pertinent information about her hadn't been a concern, mainly because he'd thought this morning they'd have plenty of getting-to-know-you time to exchange those personal details about each other.

Unfortunately, she hadn't given them the opportunity.

After getting over the initial blow of finding Nicole gone, Nathan took a shower and tried to focus on work and preparing a plan to get close to Preston Sloane. He was determined to write off the entire situation with Nicole as a one-night stand, which had become his regular mode of operation over the years, ever since his downhill spiral after Katie's death and the loss of his fiancée, Jill, due to his alcohol abuse.

Emotionally, he just wasn't ready to give any woman what she needed out of a relationship, and he wasn't sure he ever would be. He'd already failed too many people in his life. He found it much easier to be alone and responsible only for taking care of himself; he didn't have the worry of disappointing someone he cared about.

Nowadays, hooking up with a female was all about physical pleasure and little else. He didn't do long-term relationships or emotional involvement, and he was always the one to walk away when things turned too demanding.

He realized Nicole had used his own tactics on him, and he didn't like being on the other end one bit. He couldn't remember a woman ever getting under his skin in just one night the way she had. So much about Nicole intrigued Nathan, and he would have bet money she'd felt the same about him—even if she had ditched him before the light of day.

Despite his frustration, he turned his concentration to the Internet and digging up as much information on Sloane as he could find. When he checked his e-mail later that afternoon and discovered a note from Cindy in regards to the speed-dating event, he felt a glimmer of hope that Nicole had checked his name on the score-card, as he'd done for her.

I'm very sorry. No matches were made.

She was the only woman he'd said yes to, but as he read the generic message blinking on his computer screen, he was forced to accept the fact that she truly didn't want to be found.

The final rejection stung, more than he cared to admit. But he'd never chased after a woman before, and he wasn't about to start now. In fact, she'd probably done him a huge favor by ending things so abruptly. With the Ramsey case demanding his undivided attention, and going undercover in the next week or so, the last thing he needed was a hot, sexy female distracting him.

Chapter Six

Nathan spent the next two weeks attending the same social events as Preston Sloane in an attempt to gradually work his way into the other man's social circle. Because of how personal this case was to Nathan, he was anxious to put an end to the assignment as quickly as possible and return to his job at The Onyx.

Thanks to Lucas Barnes's unsurpassed skill in creating forgeries of official documents, Nathan now had a new identity as Alex Keller, along with an ironclad background as a wealthy entrepreneur who had just moved to the Vegas area.

To keep in sync with his new affluent persona, Nathan had also endured an image overhaul. Faded jeans and T-shirts were replaced with slacks and designer-label collared shirts. He was now the proud owner of a high-dollar, tailored suit with a collection of designer shirts and ties. His too-long, shaggy hair had been shorn into a short executive cut, and he'd sat through his first-ever manicure to give his hands a polished, rich man's look.

The best perk of immersing himself into Sloane's

prominent world was the black Ferrari he now drove—a temporary rental car, but a very cool upgrade nonetheless. As Alex Keller, he'd taken on a short-term lease at Turnberry Towers and was currently living in a fully furnished suite. The luxurious condominium building wasn't the type of place he'd ever choose to live, but all the trappings were necessary to authenticate his new identity and image.

Networking in the same places Sloane frequented had paid off for Nathan. After discovering that Sloane preferred to meet with a personal trainer at a private athletic club for his morning exercise regimen, Nathan had arranged his own workouts to coincide with the other man's and afterward, in the sauna, had struck up a few casual conversations with him. During those times Nathan had managed to feed the other man information about his lifestyle, as well as drop subtle comments about his interest in the younger teenage girls who frequented the gym, rather than the mature women.

Nathan had also finagled an invitation to an elite, private casino-night party and had played a few games of high-stakes poker with Sloane sitting at the same table. A few times Nathan had deliberately arrived at the same restaurant where Sloan had reservations for lunch or dinner, and made sure he went up to the other man to say hello. Every move Nathan made in regard to Sloane was a calculated attempt to build their acquaintance into a more personal relationship—one that would eventually gain him access to a party at Sloane's estate so he could locate Angela Ramsey.

Over the past two weeks, Nathan had gotten plenty of face time with Preston Sloane, but it wasn't enough. He needed to figure out a course of action to gain the

man's trust in a way that would get Nathan what he ultimately wanted. He hoped tonight's appearance at an
art gallery exhibit that Sloane was also attending would
finally present him with the opportunity.

He turned into the parking structure for the Ethan
Layne Gallery, located downtown in the Las Vegas
Arts District, and brought his Ferrari to a stop at the
valet. An attendant hurried over to the driver's side,
the eager gleam in the other man's eyes telling Nathan
he was looking forward to getting behind the wheel of
such a rare, turbocharged sports car. Nathan tossed the
young guy the keys, retrieved his claim ticket, and
headed inside the building, where he took the elevator
to the fourth floor. The double doors opened directly to
the spacious gallery, where tonight's reception and exhibit was in full swing.

A waiter walked by with a tray of champagne, and
Nathan took one of the crystal flutes to sip on while
he mingled with the crowd, pretended interest in the
framed, black-and-white photography artwork on the
walls, and kept an eye out for Preston Sloane. Husky
feminine laughter caught his attention, and he turned
his head to see a young woman with long, wavy brunette hair, exotic dark brown eyes, and a willowy body
draped in a black silk dress.

He immediately recognized her as Stephanie Diaz,
the pretty, up-and-coming nineteen-year-old artist whose
photography was on display tonight. After a bit of digging, Nathan had discovered that Stephanie was linked
to Preston Sloane, who'd arranged tonight's exhibit for
her with his very good friend Ethan Layne.

Apparently, the girl had been one of Sloane's "favorites" for the past few years, and tonight's reception,

teeming with the who's who of Vegas, was his way of giving Stephanie a jump-start on her career now that she was getting too old for him. From what Nathan knew, the girls Sloane preferred ranged in age from fourteen to eighteen; he either discarded anyone older or—if she was deemed special—made sure her future was secured.

Katie, the girl Nathan had sworn to protect during his time as a vice cop with Las Vegas Metro, hadn't been as fortunate and had met with a tragic ending to her young life. Chances were that Angela Ramsey and the many other girls who passed through Sloane's estate home in Summerlin wouldn't be rewarded with the kind of generosity he had bestowed on Stephanie.

Pushing those dark thoughts out of his mind, Nathan shook off the tension gathering across his shoulders and continued perusing the gallery, the guests, and the artwork on the wall. He had to admit that Stephanie had talent. The black-and-white pictures she'd taken encompassed a wide range of subjects, from landscapes, to nature shots, to portraitures, and with Sloane's help she'd no doubt achieve success.

As he turned a corner that led to another section of the crowded gallery, he finally caught sight of Preston Sloane standing with two other couples, engaged in a conversation that was occasionally dotted with jovial laughter. For a man in his mid-fifties, Sloane had managed to keep the aging process at bay, most likely with the help of expensive cosmetic procedures. His hair was still thick and dark brown, without a hint of gray or signs of balding. The skin on his face and neck was tanned and taut, and his body was lean and toned, giving the appearance of a man in his thirties.

With so many people around, it was difficult to find an opening with Sloane, and Nathan mulled over the various ways he could steer him away from the other guests for a little one-on-one conversation. Reining in his impatience, he took a small drink of his champagne and pretended interest in the photograph of the Nevada desert on the wall in front of him before moving on to the next picture.

That's when he saw the girl across the room, slightly turned away from him as she took in the artwork on display. In a sea of women decked out in sophisticated, designer outfits, she stood out like a breath of fresh air in her simple white summer dress. The hem, ending modestly just below the knee, was trimmed with floral cutouts, a pale pink ribbon cinched her small waist, and a sparkly pink headband in her blond hair completed the outfit.

He could only see the soft lines of her profile, but he pegged her age at around sixteen. She was the first young girl he'd seen tonight and he wondered who she was with. She moved on to another picture, and Nathan noticed that Sloane's gaze was now following the girl, watching her with the kind of avid, predatory interest that told Nathan this girl had just become new prey for the older man.

Nathan tensed as old, protective instincts surged to the surface, flooding his veins with a rush of adrenaline. Refusing to let the girl become one of Sloane's casualties under his watch, Nathan circled closer just as Sloane excused himself from his group of friends and started toward the girl, leaving Nathan a good ten paces behind the man. Sloane reached her before Nathan could and said something to her that made the girl turn her head and smile at him.

Instantly recognizing those soft, velvet blue eyes and that pretty feminine face, Nathan jerked to an abrupt stop about five feet away from the couple.

It was Nicole—though a much younger-looking version of the woman who'd blown his mind with a phenomenal night of uninhibited sex.

Shock and disbelief warred within him. He gave his head a hard shake, but the vision of Nicole remained. Gone was the artfully applied makeup she'd worn when he'd first met her, along with her sexy, tousled hairstyle and head-turning pink dress. In her place was the look of a sweet, fresh-faced, guileless teenager.

No way. No fucking way.

He heard her giggle as Sloane did his best to charm her, much different from the husky, sensual laughter she'd shared with him during their night together. She'd never divulged her age to him, but as an ex-vice cop, he *knew* she wasn't as young as she looked today. She'd been too sophisticated and experienced with him, and no one under the age of twenty-one had been allowed to participate in the speed-dating event.

So what the hell was she doing here? And why was she pretending to be so young? He quickly flipped through his memory, recalling what she'd told him about being a journalist conducting research for an article on dating trends.

So, she was a reporter of some sort. Was she there to interview Stephanie Diaz on her debut at the gallery? If that was the case, Nicole's youthful appearance and the way she was subtly flirting with Sloane didn't jive with what he'd expect of a journalist.

Suddenly feeling on edge, he set his half-empty glass of champagne on a passing tray. This whole scenario didn't sit well with Nathan, and he needed a better handle on the situation and Nicole's reasons for being here before confronting her. And he *would* confront her, just as soon as he could get her alone.

He casually moved behind the duo so that he wasn't in their line of vision, but remained close enough to hear their conversation while he stared at another piece of artwork. Sloane was currently complimenting Nicole on how lovely she looked and she ducked her head demurely at his indulgent praise and murmured a bashful "thank you." Yet another reaction that belied the confident woman he'd met two weeks ago.

"I'm Preston Sloane," the other man said, introducing himself as he extended his hand for her to shake—undoubtedly a calculated move to touch her.

She slid her smaller palm against his, and Nathan watched as Sloane slowly stroked his thumb along the back of her hand—a very inappropriate caress between a man in his fifties and what appeared to be a teen.

Sloane was attracted to Nicole in her teenage facade, and that knowledge made Nathan's stomach turn with disgust and solidified the urgency of forging a friendship with Sloane so he could rescue Angela.

"I'm Nikki," she replied softly, then withdrew her hand with just the right amount of shyness.

Nikki. A girl's nickname. Oh, yeah, she was definitely up to something, and playing Sloane in the process.

"Are you enjoying yourself this evening, Nikki?" Sloane asked, his voice warm and inviting.

Nicole nodded and met Sloane's gaze, somehow managing to appear flattered by his attention. "Very much. I love photographic art and can spend hours in an art gallery. After graduating from high school next year, I'm hoping to attend the art institute here in Vegas."

High school? Nathan would have laughed at the tale she was weaving if the situation weren't so damn serious.

"That's an outstanding goal." Sloane smiled, and this time the slight curve to his lips held a hint of seduction, as if he was testing how she'd respond to the unspoken overture. "You know, I have quite a large collection of rare artwork that I'd love to show you sometime, if you're interested."

"Oh, wow, I would love that!" she said, her voice expressing her enthusiasm.

"Excellent." Sloane looked pleased with her easy acquiescence, obviously believing he'd just cajoled a pretty young thing one step closer to his lair. He retrieved a business card from his wallet and handed it to Nicole. "Here's my private phone number. Give me a call when you're free for a few hours, and I'll send a limo to pick you up and bring you to my estate. I have an entire room devoted to some of the most amazing artwork you'll ever see."

Nicole tucked the card into the small purse hanging over her shoulder, while still managing to project a wide-eyed innocence. "Thank you. I really appreciate the offer. I'll see what I can do about giving you a call this weekend."

"That would be great." He winked at Nicole, and she *blushed,* of all things.

And just like that, Nicole was *in.*

Nathan's jaw clenched in irritation. He was more than a little pissed at Nicole's appearance and whatever game she was playing with Sloane. The last thing he wanted was her obstructing his case, or inadvertently blowing his cover if she saw him. She had the ability to screw up the groundwork he'd already established with Sloane, and he refused to allow that to happen. Which meant he had to find a way to take control of the situation—pronto.

Sloane shifted closer to Nicole and inclined his head, his expression much too intimate considering their age difference. "Are you here by yourself, or are you with someone?"

Knowing this was the only opening he was likely to get, Nathan stepped up to Nicole before she could reply to Sloane's question. He slid an arm around her waist and felt her stiffen in surprise as he pulled her close to his side.

"Sweetheart! There you are," he said, his affectionate tone establishing that she was with him. He smiled down at her, noticing the stunned disbelief reflected in her big blue eyes at seeing him again. "I was wondering where you'd disappeared to," he chastised gently.

To his relief, she didn't struggle against him and went along with the pretense, confirming his hunch that she was trying to deceive Sloane somehow and didn't want to expose her own cover. "I, uh . . . I was just wandering around admiring the artwork."

"Alex," Sloane said, his gaze moving from Nicole to Nathan in a pleasant greeting. "You know this lovely girl?"

"I do." His hold on her tightened, and the possessive

move didn't go unnoticed by Sloane. "She's here with me tonight."

Even though Nathan had clearly staked a claim, the awareness in Sloane's gaze didn't abate one bit. Instead, the fascination seemed to intensify. "You have excellent taste in women, my friend," he complimented, his voice deepening with approval.

With those simple words, Nathan sensed a shift in his association with Sloane—from casual acquaintances to the stronger alliance he'd spent the past two weeks trying to forge.

And it was *Nikki's* presence that changed everything.

Before the situation escalated in a direction Nathan wasn't prepared for, he needed answers from Nicole. Hopefully, her explanation would help him figure out what was going on, and what he was going to do about her meddling in his case.

"There's something I need to discuss with Nikki," Nathan said to Sloane. "Will you excuse us for a few minutes?"

Sloane nodded, though his gaze hinted at his reluctance to let Nicole out of his sight. "Of course."

Taking Nicole's elbow, Nathan led her away, his firm grip not giving her any choice but to follow. Feeling Sloane's gaze on them, and wanting as much privacy as he could find, he guided her into a secluded area of the gallery that wasn't a part of tonight's exhibit. As soon as they were alone, he turned her around to face him and backed her into the nearest wall. Standing in front of her, he flattened one hand by her shoulder so that she couldn't easily escape. It also gave the impression that they were having an intimate conversation should anyone walk into the room.

Unfortunately, their close position also made him incredibly aware of her as a *woman*. One who'd spent hours in his bed, naked and willing and sexy as hell as she moved over him, and beneath him, in carnal abandon. He'd written her off as a one-night stand, an erotic memory to fantasize about when relieving his own needs in the dark of the night. Yet here she was, in the flesh, staring up at him with those seductive, velvet blue eyes and smelling like a frosted cupcake he wanted to eat.

Of its own accord, his body responded, wanting her despite the extreme and unexpected situation that had brought them together again. Heated desire surged through his veins and increased the pressure straining against the fly of his slacks. She licked her bottom lip, drawing his gaze to her lush mouth, making him remember how hot and heavenly she tasted. Making him ache with the need to kiss her again.

Stealing himself against her allure, along with his own reaction to her, he bent his head closer and narrowed his gaze in an attempt to intimidate. "What the hell is going on, *Nikki*?" he bit out.

The corner of her mouth quirked with dry humor. "It's nice to see you again, Nathan," she drawled sweetly.

He winced at the use of his real name when Sloane knew him as someone else—and Nathan needed to keep it that way. "Call me Alex and answer my question," he ordered, the sharp tone to his voice demanding her cooperation.

A smooth, bare shoulder lifted in a casual shrug. "I'm just enjoying the exhibit."

"Bullshit," he growled impatiently. "You look totally

different. You've transformed yourself into a teenage girl and it's clear you're leading Sloane on! What kind of game are you playing?"

Nicole arched a brow, subtly taunting him with her lack of fear when it came to his gruff interrogation. "I could ask you the same thing, *Alex*." Boldly, she slipped her hand just inside his sport coat, splaying her fingers against the material covering his chest. "You don't strike me as the artsy type, though I do have to say that you clean up real nice."

She shouldn't have touched him. Nicole meant to distract Nathan with her sensual caress, and judging by the lust flaring to life in the depths of his eyes she'd managed the feat. But she hadn't anticipated her own body's traitorous reaction to the warmth radiating from his hard, muscular chest. Her nipples hardened and her pulse thrummed in acute awareness. The sizzling chemistry that had burned between them during their one night together hadn't diminished at all. Instead, the sexual tension swirling around them now seemed hotter. Brighter. More intense.

With his hair cut short and his face freshly shaven, his masculine features appeared sharper, more refined than the flirtatious bad boy he'd been. His dark brown eyes glittered with a combination of reluctant attraction and a brooding edge of anger that was directly solely at her.

If she hadn't already witnessed the more charming and amicable side to his personality, she might have felt threatened by his menacing temperament. Clearly, he'd been watching her with Sloane, and he wasn't thrilled to see her again under the current circumstances. Yet despite the information she'd taken from Nathan's files, there had been nothing to indicate he'd be at tonight's exhibit, and she honestly thought she'd be able to execute her plan with Sloane without any interference.

And she nearly had.

But even though she'd been caught in the act, so to speak, Nicole wasn't willing to give up her story, or bend to Nathan's demands—no matter his intimidation tactics.

A muscle in Nathan's jaw ticked. "What is your association with Sloane?"

"I just met the guy," she said, her tone deliberately vague.

Her reply annoyed him even more, and beneath the palm still pressed to his chest, his body tensed. "Yeah, by pretending to be a girl in high school when I know damn well that you're a grown woman. What's up with the act?"

Realizing that touching him was too much of a distraction, she dropped her hand back to her side. "It's none of your business."

His brown eyes blazed with golden heat, singeing her in more ways than one. "I'm *making* it my business."

Feeling provoked, and irritated by the fact that he believed he had any right to *her* personal business, she straightened her spine and jutted her chin out defiantly. "Look, just because we slept together doesn't give you permission to interfere in my life or demand any kind of answers from me. I don't know you well enough." Besides, she had no idea what Nathan's affiliation with Sloane was, either.

Needing to put some distance between herself and Nathan, she attempted to step around him, but he was quicker. His free hand clamped onto her hip and pressed her back against the wall—gently, but firmly. He shifted closer, using his hard, muscular thighs to help keep her pinned in place and surrounding her with the heady scent of his woodsy cologne and something far more seductive.

He dipped his head closer, his gaze latching on to hers, direct and arrogantly male. "Whatever you're doing here with Sloane, you don't have the first clue what you're getting into," he warned in a low voice. "I suggest you turn your ass around and leave before you do something stupid that will get you into a whole lot of trouble."

She barely resisted the urge to knee him in the groin for inferring she was incompetent. Instead, she gave him a saccharine smile that did nothing to conceal her resentment. "I've done my research and I know exactly who and what I'm dealing with. I'm a journalist, remember?"

He arched a skeptical brow. "A journalist who writes fluff pieces on *speed dating*. Or was that a lie and you were angling for a bigger story?"

She might have omitted certain information about herself the night they'd met, but she hadn't lied about her assignment. "When I met you, that was the truth."

Unfortunately, her article had been so successful that *Dating in the 21st Century* had indeed become a monthly feature for the magazine, with Nicole in charge of researching and writing expositions on various dating trends. Currently, she was working on a piece about online dating, which gave her plenty of free time to pursue other interests. Such as Preston Sloane.

He studied her intently before responding. "Right now, I don't know what to believe when it comes to you."

Okay, that stung, and she hated that his opinion of her mattered at all. "Believe what you want, but I'd appreciate it if you'd let me go." Being this close to him was wreaking havoc with her mind and body.

"Not on your life," he said with a shake of his head, then cast a quick glance around the gallery to make sure they were still alone before returning his attention to her. "I have no idea what you're up to, but whatever you're doing with Sloane, I can guarantee that you're getting in way over your head."

"Why are you so concerned about Sloane?" she shot back in a heated whisper. "Are you trying to protect him from something?"

He jerked as if she'd slapped him. "I'm trying to protect *you*," he hissed indignantly.

"Thanks, but I'm perfectly capable of taking care of myself," she said before turning the tables on him. "You told me that you work at The Onyx in security, so what is *your* involvement with Sloane?"

Nathan wasn't about to spill his secrets, either, which put the two of them at a standoff. Frustrated, he swore beneath his breath. The woman was infuriating and stubborn, and he struggled between wanting to throttle her and pressing his body flush to hers and kissing her senseless.

Before he did either and brought unwanted attention to the two of them, he decided it was time to finish their exchange where they couldn't be overheard. "You and I obviously have a lot to talk about, and this isn't a conversation we should have in a public place. Did you drive here?"

She shook her head, and the overhead lights glinted off the sparkly pink headband holding her hair away from her face. "No, I took a cab."

"Perfect." This way, if anyone watched them leave together, it would be in his vehicle as a couple, instead of separate cars. "Let's get out of here."

Grasping her hand tight in his, he led her back through the gallery and toward the elevator. Before they could slip out undetected, Preston Sloane caught up to them.

"Alex," he called out, loud enough that Nathan couldn't ignore the other man.

Nathan brought them to a stop, and as he watched Preston head their way, he slipped his arm around Nicole's waist and leaned close to whisper in her ear. "Follow my lead," he ordered before facing Sloane again, hoping she'd preserve his cover.

"Are the two of you leaving already?" Sloane sounded disappointed.

"Yes." Nathan grinned at the older man. "Nikki and I have reservations at The Palm for dinner."

"A very nice way to impress a girl, Keller," Sloane said in approval, though his gaze lingered on Nicole with unmistakable interest before returning to Nathan. "Look, I'm having a private party at my nightclub, Bliss, this weekend and I'd like the two of you to come, if you don't already have plans." He withdrew a small card from the inside of his blazer and extended it toward Nathan. "Here's a card with the club info, and it doubles as your invitation. You can't get in without it."

Nathan accepted the information, but refused to

commit to anything since Nicole had just turned his case upside down. "I'll see what we can do."

"I'd love to see you two there." Even as Sloane said the words, his eyes were all over Nicole, a darker desire glimmering in his gaze as he took her hand in his. "Good night, Nikki, and I hope to see you again sometime soon."

Nicole gently tugged her hand from Sloane's and averted her gaze, keeping up the pretense of a shy sixteen-year-old girl. "Good night, Mr. Sloane."

The other man waved his hand in the air between them. "Call me Preston, please. Mr. Sloane sounds much too formal. And don't forget about my invitation to show you my art collection."

A small smile curved the corner of Nicole's mouth. "I promise I won't."

Nathan deliberately gave Nicole a possessive squeeze around her waist. "We'll talk about it, sweetheart." Nicole didn't know it yet, but no way was he going to let her spend any time alone with the other man.

Forcing an amicable expression, Nathan shook Sloane's hand. "I'll see you around."

He guided Nicole into the elevator, his mind spinning in a dozen different directions as the doors closed in front of them and the lift descended to the parking garage.

Sloane's invitation to his private nightclub was the *in* he'd been waiting weeks for, and Nathan knew the overture came with the expectation of him bringing Nicole. He should have been ecstatic to have finally gained a small measure of Sloane's trust, but Nicole's unexpected meddling changed everything. He now had to rethink his strategy.

Still, no matter Nicole's reasons for tempting the much older man, he was going to make it very clear that she had no business getting involved with someone as dangerous as Preston Sloane.

Chapter Seven

Nicole found herself tucked into the supple, tan leather passenger seat of a gorgeous black Ferrari that Nathan, aka Alex Keller, was currently navigating down the Las Vegas Strip with the expertise of a seasoned race car driver. Other than a terse "get in the car" when the parking attendant had delivered the vehicle, Nathan had been giving her the silent treatment ever since.

More amused than irritated, she cast a sidelong glance at her driver as he shifted gears to pass a car going much too slow for his liking. The Ferrari swerved around the Honda Accord with smooth precision, and outside the tinted windows the colorful lights along Las Vegas Boulevard blurred by as the sports car picked up speed.

The tension inside the Ferrari and between the two of them was palpable. Nathan was pissed, and there was no doubt in Nicole's mind that she was the cause. Yet despite the negative energy radiating from his side of the vehicle, she wasn't scared to be alone with him. This dark mood of his was definitely a different side to the man she'd slept with, but his actions thus far had came off as more protective than threatening, which she found very intriguing.

Honestly, *everything* about Nathan captivated her. From his warm brown eyes and the chiseled line of his jaw, to the large, strong hands gripping the steering wheel. Even the reasons behind his own involvement with Sloane piqued her curiosity.

They came to a stop at a red light, and Nathan glanced at her for a brief moment. The heat of anger had faded from his expression, but there was still a hint of uncompromising determination as he gave her a slow, appraising look that felt like a seductive caress over her bare skin. She shivered in response, as if he'd physically touched her.

He returned his attention to the road, and as soon as the light turned green the Ferrari roared to life again. No matter how annoyed he was with her at the moment, there was no denying that he was still attracted to her. And vice versa. Since their one night together she hadn't been able to get him out of her head. Not just the fantastic sex and multiple orgasms he'd given her so generously, but also how much she'd enjoyed their conversations before things had escalated to a night of pure, unadulterated pleasure.

Tired of being ignored, she decided to try to lighten the atmosphere. "Nice car," she said, more than a little impressed with his extravagant transportation tonight. "I had no idea security paid so well." Her voice held a teasing note.

"It's temporary," he said, keeping his reply short and succinct.

She rolled her eyes, even though the gesture was lost on him. So much for a lively conversation starter. She glanced out her window, watching as they drove past casinos and hotels, and realized she had no idea where he intended to take her.

"Where are we going?" She was more curious than worried.

"Back to my place."

She'd been to his house, which was in the opposite direction. "Umm, aren't you going the wrong way?"

"I'm living at Turnberry Towers."

Her jaw fell open as she stared at his profile, waiting for him to crack a smile or tell her that he was just joking. He looked completely serious. Between the Ferrari and now his claim of living in one of Las Vegas's most luxurious condominium buildings, she didn't know what to think.

"Wow," she said, the one word expressing her surprise. "Did you win the Mega Millions recently?" It was the only explanation that made sense.

He downshifted and made a left-hand turn onto Paradise Road, the street that led to the ritzy high-rise he now called home. "I don't play the slots. Like I said, it's temporary."

And that was that. Trying to extract information from this man was like budging an elephant. Impossible. And frustrating as hell.

"So, what's your real name?" she asked, figuring it was an easy enough question for him to answer truthfully. "Nathan or Alex?"

"It's Nathan Fox." He met her gaze for a moment, his mysterious eyes unreadable in the shadowed interior of the car. "But Preston Sloane knows me as Alex Keller."

Interesting. "Why the alias?"

He gave his head a quick shake. "You don't need to know specifics."

She swallowed an exasperated groan. "It would help to know a *few* details."

"Yes, it would." He pinned her with a silent look that told her he expected those details to come from *her*. "We'll have this discussion when we get to my place."

She didn't pressure him for more answers, but rather kept quiet as he let the valet at Turnberry Towers park his car, then ushered her into the elevator and up to the twenty-sixth floor of the high-rise. As soon as she stepped into the fully furnished suite, she gasped, awed by the luxurious contemporary decor and the magnificent view of the Las Vegas Strip right outside the floor-to-ceiling windows framing the impressive living room.

Nicole turned back around to face Nathan as he stripped off his jacket and loosened his tie. "Holy moly," she breathed, the two words summing up just how blown away she was by his new digs. "Temporary or not, this place is absolutely amazing."

The corner of his mouth quirked with the barest hint of a smile, giving her a brief glimpse of the fun, charming guy she'd spend the night with a few weeks ago. "I have to agree. The view of the Strip, especially at night, never gets old." He headed into the gourmet kitchen, separated by a granite-topped breakfast bar and cherry-wood stools. "Would you like something to drink?"

She shook her head. "I'm good for now, thanks." She was far more interested in getting back to their earlier discussion, and didn't hesitate to do so now. "I thought you worked security at The Onyx. Was that a lie, or are you also working privately for Sloane, or someone else?"

He strolled back into the living room to where she was standing, his fingers wrapped around the neck of what looked like a bottle of root beer. "Nosy little thing, aren't you?"

"Persistent, too," she added with a sassy grin, making sure he knew she could be just as determined as him when it came to extracting information. As a reporter, it was an ingrained skill. "I'm just trying to figure out your connection to Preston Sloane."

"I'd rather we talk about *your* involvement with Sloane," he countered easily, then took a long drink of his soda before continuing. "Are you trying to write some kind of exposé on him?"

She crossed her arms over her chest, refusing to respond to his question. Not unless she got her own answers in return. "Ever heard of the term *quid pro quo*?"

His dark brows lifted incredulously. "Are you suggesting we strike a deal that you'll answer my questions if I agree to answer yours?"

"Maybe I am," she said with a shrug. "We're obviously at a stalemate, so it seems like the best option. We're each involved with Sloane for our own personal reasons, so I'll share if you do."

Nathan's first instinct was to flat-out refuse. He didn't bend to anyone's demands, especially not a woman's. But it was quickly becoming apparent to him that he wasn't dealing with an ordinary female here. Nicole was obstinate, independent, and smart enough to keep him guessing—and he couldn't deny that those strong personality traits, and the woman herself, stimulated him mentally and presented a challenge he was more than willing to accept.

Considering they'd come to a standoff and he needed

her cooperation, he relented. "Quid pro quo," he agreed, and saluted her with his bottle of root beer in a promise to keep his end of the bargain. "I'm working under-cover."

"So am I," she said, giving him nothing more than he'd given her.

The laughter glimmering in her eyes told him she was good at playing his kind of game, enjoyed it, even. He decided to change tactics and ask questions that re-quired a more informative answer. "You're a journalist. Are you looking for a story?"

She hesitated a moment, as if contemplating how much to reveal. "I know there's one to be found with Sloane."

He tipped his head curiously. "And you know this how?"

"The man's a pedophile. He just hasn't gotten caught yet," she said, her tone laced with unmistakable dis-dain. "He's obviously really good at covering his ass, and it doesn't take a genius to figure out that a man like him has important people tucked deeply into his pocket to squash speculations before they turn incriminating."

She'd done her homework on Sloane and had pegged his MO incredibly well. Gathering any solid evidence to nail the man had proved impossible while Nathan had worked for Metro. Word on the street indicated that he had friends in very high places—from the up-per echelon of law enforcement, to powerful political figures, to a well-paid stable of lawyers who did a damn good job of protecting their client from prosecution. Sloane used his wealth to pay off, bribe, and intimidate witnesses and victims, and no one would testify against him.

Money, it seemed, could acquit the guiltiest of men, protected their lewd secrets, and shielded their depraved desires for young, innocent girls.

Nathan washed down the bitterness burning the back of his throat with a drink of his root beer before addressing Nicole again. "And you think you can nail Sloane where others have failed?" he drawled, a hint of sarcasm threading his tone.

Her chin lifted defiantly. "I'd like to try."

Aggravated by her response and the uncompromising set to her shoulders, he set his empty bottle of root beer on the coffee table and started toward Nicole. She really had no idea what she was up against, and he planned to enlighten her.

He stopped a foot away and stared down at her, still shocked at just how young she looked with her hair pulled back, her fresh-faced complexion and youthful features belying her true age. He wanted to scare her, make her run far and fast from a situation that could get her killed—and heap more unwanted guilt on his conscience.

"You're stepping into very dangerous territory," he said in a low, harsh tone. "Sloane eats little girls like you for breakfast. He's a ruthless man, and if he so much as *suspects* you're playing him, you're good as dead. And that's not going to boost your career, now, is it?"

She tossed her head back, fearless purpose firing in her gaze. "What makes you think I'll get caught?"

Jaw clenched, he leaned closer, intimidating her with his height and the anger now etching his features. "What makes you think you have the experience to deal with someone of Sloane's caliber?"

She didn't so much as flinch or back down from his

direct, in-her-face tirade. "I'm *very* familiar with Sloane's type," she said, just as fiercely.

He jerked back, startled by her unexpected response and everything it implied. "Is this thing with Sloane personal or professional for you?"

"Maybe a bit of both." As if realizing she'd revealed more than she'd intended, she sighed and turned away, putting distance between them. When she faced him a few moments later, she was composed once again, her expression all business. "What's the story with you? I thought you worked for The Onyx, but you just said you were working undercover. Are you a cop?"

"*Ex*-vice cop," he told her, and shoved his hands into the front pockets of his trousers. "I *do* work at The Onyx, but I'm currently undercover on a private case that's linked to Sloane." He didn't miss the questions in her eyes, but declined to explain anything about his involvement with The Reliance Group, because it was something she just didn't need to know. "It's . . . complicated."

Standing by the windows overlooking the bright lights of the Vegas Strip, she studied him for a long, silent moment, in a way that suddenly made him feel uneasy.

Finally, she asked, "Is this case about Angela Ramsey?"

Shock rippled through him like a live electrical jolt. How in the hell was she privy to something so confidential that only a few people knew about it? "Who told you about Angela?" His voice was as sharp as steel.

Immediately her gaze filled with uncertainty, and she pressed her fingers to her lips, as if regretting the

words she'd spoken now that she'd witnessed his vola-
tile reaction.

"Nicole, *answer me*," he said through gritted teeth,
and took a step toward her, willing to shake the explanation from her if need be.

She held up a hand to ward him off, looking more
nervous than he'd ever seen her. "Give me a minute."

Even though his patience was hanging by a thin
thread, he stopped and gave her the space she seemed
to need, while his mind spun with all kinds of scenarios. Was she a plant on this case? Was he being set up?
And the worst possibility of all—had his cover with
Sloane already been blown somehow?

His gaze narrowed and his gut churning with acid,
he watched as she made her way to the plush armchair
in the living room and sat down. Taking off her sparkly
pink headband, she ran her fingers through her hair,
disheveling the silky strands as they fell softly around
her face. That little change was enough to age her appearance a few years. Or maybe it was the worry lines
creasing her brows that made her look her true age. She
licked her bottom lip and rubbed her palms along the
skirt of her dress—sure signs of anxiety.

After inhaling a deep, fortifying breath, she brought
her eyes to his with dread glimmering in the depths.
"What I'm about to tell you is *really* going to piss you
off," she said in warning. "But I want to be completely
up-front with you about what I know, so try not to flip
out on me, okay?"

This didn't sound good at all, and he remained as
calm as possible under the circumstances. "I appreciate your honesty." That said, he refused to make any

promises about his reaction to what she confessed, because he had a bad feeling he wasn't going to like it.

She gave him a quick nod to acknowledge how important the truth was to him. "The night we slept together, when I was on my way out, I accidentally knocked over a folder that was sitting on the table in the entryway, and it was difficult to ignore the contents that spilled out."

That quickly, it all clicked together in his mind and everything about her involvement finally made sense. Anger welled inside him, and he let loose a ripe curse that made her wince. "How much did you read?"

"Enough to know that you're somehow involved with Preston Sloane and it has to do with a runaway teen named Angela Ramsey."

Nicole was right. He was royally pissed off and trying like hell not to flip out, as she'd put it. "And you decided all that juicy information would make a sensational story for you as a journalist? Beats the hell out of your assignment on dating trends, doesn't it?" His tone dripped with contempt.

She bristled with indignation, and the fire igniting in her eyes flared with her own brand of rebellion. "Look, *I* wasn't the one who left the file out in the open to be found, so I'm not entirely to blame."

Her accurate comment hit a nerve, but his temper got the best of him and he jabbed a finger at her in accusation. "You confiscated confidential information."

"I saw an opportunity and I took it," she admitted unapologetically. "I won't deny that. You would have done the same thing."

In her shoes, yeah, he probably would have, he silently conceded. The truth was, he was more furious with himself than with her—for leaving the file in a place anyone could have discovered it. Never mind that he hadn't been expecting company that night. Bottom line, it *was* his fault and he should have done a better job of protecting the file.

Even knowing he was responsible, a part of him felt scammed, though that hadn't been Nicole's intent when she'd accompanied him to his place. Yeah, she'd slept with him and had inadvertently stumbled across the information on Sloane, but what bothered him the most was that she'd never made any attempt to contact him again when she had two solid reasons to—her interest in Sloane and the connection they'd established. Admittedly, his male ego was involved, which accounted for a part of the resentment he was harboring.

Despite his own complex feelings over Nicole, he pushed them aside to focus on the issue at hand. "I want you to back off this story."

She shook her head. "I'm sorry, but I can't."

Stubborn, frustrating woman. Knowing he was in for a battle, he sat down on the sofa across from her and cocked his head to the side. "Can't, or *won't*?"

The wry twist to her lips almost made him smile, because he knew exactly what she was going to say.

"I won't. I need to expose Sloane for the slime that he is," she said adamantly. "And it's not just about the story for me. The man needs to be stopped."

He couldn't agree more. Undoubtedly, there was a deeper, personal element to this case for her, just as there was for him. "Doesn't matter. I'm not letting you near him again. I've got a job to do and I don't need you making things more complicated."

"Complicated?" She laughed incredulously. "In case

you've forgotten, I'm already *in*," she said, reminding him of Sloane's interest in her. "If anything, *you* need *me* to get close to Sloane."

His gut cramped at the thought of Nicole immersing herself in Sloane's world. The last time he'd used someone to help—when he'd hoped to nail the pimp responsible for running an international prostitution ring in Vegas—the results had been disastrous. Katie had *died* because he hadn't been able to protect her, and he'd sworn after that awful experience that he'd never, *ever* risk another person for a case again. And that included using the eager, intrepid reporter sitting in front of him to get into Sloane's estate.

Now he worked solo, and he meant to keep it that way. "I was doing just fine on my own."

She casually crossed one leg over the other and arched a blond brow. "Really? The way I see things, I have a personal, private invitation to Sloane's estate to see his art collection, and *we* have a joint invitation to a party he's having at his nightclub this weekend. Not to sound full of myself, but I think he's more interested in *me* than *you,* and I can easily do this on my own if you're not keen on forming a partnership."

Shit. They were at an impasse once again. Feeling stonewalled, he scrubbed a hand along his jaw and tried to keep his temper in check. He knew she wasn't going to back down or give up her golden ticket into Sloane's lair, and that knowledge forced him to reassess the situation, and her involvement in his case—despite his strong reluctance to do so.

He couldn't argue the point that she was the bait he needed to slip easily and seamlessly into Sloane's world. She could do things he couldn't, such as bond with the girls at the parties and at the estate, and gain their trust in a way that would lead straight to Angela Ramsey.

Engaging in a partnership with Nicole, even against his better judgment, would definitely speed up the process. And since time was of the essence, Nathan knew he wasn't in a position to turn down her offer—even though it pained him to give in to her demands. He absolutely *hated* the idea of taking her undercover with him, but at least this way he'd have some semblance of control over the situation and know where she was at all times. Rather than constantly running interference or worrying about her welfare.

He leaned forward on the sofa cushion and braced his elbows on his thighs, meeting her gaze head-on. "Because I know you're going to get involved with Sloane regardless of what I say or do, I would prefer you do it under my protection. I might need you to entice Sloane and get us into his estate much quicker than I could do it on my own—but you need me to make sure you're kept safe."

"Okay."

Her easy acquiescence was a surprise. Obviously, she was a smart girl and knew she was stepping into a dangerous situation. "I call the shots when it comes to making any decisions on how we're going to do things," he went on, taking advantage of her momentary compliance. "There's no negotiating on that fact. I don't need a power struggle between the two of us while we're working undercover. Got that?"

"Fine."

He stood up and paced in front of the windows, though his attention remained fastened on Nicole and making sure she understood his rules. "What I say goes. In order for this to work, we have to be in sync and you have to trust the decisions I make, without hesitation or questioning my orders."

"Fair enough."

He came to an abrupt stop and stared at her, wondering if there were any ulterior motives behind her amenable disposition—because there was one thing he'd learned about Nicole. She wasn't the docile type, and her current complacent behavior made him a little wary.

"Why are you being so agreeable?" he asked.

She laughed and stood up, too. "I want to work *with* you on this case, Nathan, not *against* you." She strolled toward him, a soft smile on her lips. "I might be ambitious in my goals as a journalist, but I'm not an idiot. You obviously know what you're doing and I trust you."

He was relieved that this wasn't going to be a power struggle between them. He hoped he didn't betray the trust she was extending to him. "Thank you."

"You're welcome." She came to a stop in front of where he stood, and now that they'd formed an alliance and their differences were resolved for the moment, the mood shifted, and that undeniable sexual awareness seemed to swirl in the air around them. "I really do appreciate you making this work between us."

With her so close and her eyes such a dark, sensual shade of blue, a warm surge of desire thrummed through him, teasing him with erotic memories of just how good the sex had been between the two of them. "Did I have a choice?" he asked wryly.

"No, not really, but I'd rather do this with your help than without." Lifting her hand, she slid her soft palm along his cheek and grazed her thumb along his lower lip. "You're a good man, Nathan, and I know you'll keep me safe."

"You think so?" His voice was deep and rough, her words unwittingly scratching the layers of old self-doubts that had crept up on him without warning.

"I *know* so," she whispered, then stood on her tip-toes and brushed her lips across his in a soft, warm kiss that ignited a deeper, hotter need for her. "I have a pretty good instinct about people, and you, Nathan Fox, are the real deal."

The pure belief in her voice impacted him like a swift kick to the gut, reminding him of another time, another promise he hadn't been able to keep—and the tragedy that had ensued. He squashed those ugly memories before they clawed their way to the surface. He refused to allow his greatest failure to undermine his ability to protect Nicole and resolve this case.

He clenched his hands into fists at his sides. Needing physical as well as emotional distance, he stepped back, severing the contact between them. "I'm going to take you back to your apartment tonight so you can pack up your things," he said, curt and business-like. "Until this case is over, you'll be staying here with me." Where he could keep an eye on her at all times.

"Okay." She watched him curiously, as if trying to figure out why he'd pulled away from her so abruptly. "But I still have other assignments for *The Las Vegas Commentary* that I need to work on. Though most of it can be done over the Internet and I don't need to be in the office to work on the piece."

"Another article on dating trends?" he asked.

"Unfortunately, yes," she said, and sighed in resignation. "What can I say? It pays the bills until something better comes along."

And Nathan knew exactly what Nicole was hoping for—a breakout exposé on Preston Sloane and his pre- dilection for underage girls. But even though Nathan had agreed to work undercover with Nicole, there were no guarantees that his case would lead to a big story— most likely, it wouldn't. Many had tried to bring down Sloane, and so far all had failed. Nathan didn't think Nicole would have any better luck. In fact, once they made their way into Sloane's estate and located An- gela, they were out of there. He wasn't about to let Ni- cole stick around for the fallout that would undoubtedly occur when Sloane realized he'd been duped just so she could get her story.

"Our first outing with Sloane will be Saturday night at his club, so we'll spend tomorrow discussing our strategy, and I'll give you the details of what you need to know about Angela Ramsey. Unless you already know everything?" he said, referring to the information she'd pilfered from his case file.

A pink flush of chagrin swept across her cheeks. "I think it would be smart to let you brief me so I know as much as possible about the case and the girl we're looking for."

He nodded in agreement. "Come on, let's head over to your place so you can get your stuff." He started for the front door of the suite, hoping like hell he wasn't making a huge mistake by allowing Nicole to go under- cover with him.

Chapter Eight

By the time they returned to Nathan's suite, it was nearing midnight. For Nicole, it had been an interesting night, filled with all sorts of revelations, along with a compromise struck between two people who needed each other to get what they ultimately wanted.

She still didn't know a whole lot about Nathan and his personal case involving Angela Ramsey—just the brief information she'd read from his case file. But before they went undercover at Sloane's private club this weekend, she intended to discover those details so she understood who, exactly, they were searching for, and why.

At her apartment she'd packed a suitcase with clothes and toiletries, and gathered her laptop and her own files of information on Preston Sloane to take with her. During that time, Nathan had waited for her out in the living room and talked to her roommate, Michelle. Her friend definitely wasn't happy about Nicole's decision to go undercover for such a risky story, especially without their editor's knowledge and approval, but Michelle understood Nicole's reasons for doing so.

Now, back at Nathan's place, she finished putting her clothes and personal things away in the guest bedroom and adjoining bathroom, then changed into the pajama shorts and tank top she slept in. She headed back out into the main rooms and found Nathan in the kitchen, leaning against the granite counter and eating a late-night snack of what looked like a bowl of Frosted Flakes cereal.

He frowned at her when he saw what she was wearing, even as his gaze seared a path from her chest to her bare thighs. Her breasts swelled in response to that visual caress, and her nipples hardened against the soft cotton tee. A muscle in his jaw ticced, as if he was annoyed with himself for being so drawn to her, and he lifted his heated gaze back to hers.

"Can you put on a robe, or something?" he asked, his gruff tone belying the sudden carnal heat reflected in his eyes.

His request surprised her, considering he'd already seen her completely naked. Then again, he'd been oddly tense around her since they'd struck their deal earlier, making it more than clear that he wasn't thrilled with their arrangement. That for him, forging an alliance to integrate them into Sloane's world was the lesser of two evils.

She headed to the refrigerator and pulled out a cold bottle of water before turning to face him again, noticing that he was still dressed in the shirt and jeans he'd changed into earlier to accompany her to her apartment.

"Why?" she asked, blinking oh-so-innocently. "Can you see through my clothes?"

His eyes dropped to her unbound breasts again.

"Having you run around in your skimpy pajamas is distracting as hell."

His admission pleased Nicole. That feminine part of her was thrilled he still wanted her, even if he was fighting the attraction. Since seeing her again at the art gallery, he'd been attempting to keep a physical distance between them and trying to maintain a business relationship, and she liked it that she could shake him up a bit.

"I'm wearing a tank top and shorts, not a sexy negligee," she said with a quirk of her lips, then took a long drink of her chilled water. "Besides, I don't own a robe. I've never had the need for one and I don't like feeling all bundled up and confined."

"Great," he muttered irritably, and finished off his cereal in two big spoonfuls. He rinsed his bowl, set it in the sink, then stalked off into the other room.

More amused than offended by his brusque attitude, she followed behind him, enjoying the decadent way her bare toes sank into the plush cream carpeting. "I have to ask, are you going to be this uptight every time we're together or when we're around Sloane?"

He spun around and shot her a look of annoyance that she'd dare insinuate he was the least bit on edge because of her. "When I'm working on a case, I'm *focused,* not uptight."

She almost laughed, but sensed that her finding humor in the situation would only agitate him more. "Well, it comes across the same way, and that scowl creasing your brows isn't very attractive. You're going to have to relax and loosen up when we're together, and try to act like you want me and that there's plenty of hot chemistry between us. Sloane is expecting to see that."

He stiffened as if she'd prodded him with a hot brand, and the depths of his eyes sparked with a hunger that was too restrained for her liking. "I don't need to pretend."

"Really? You could have fooled me considering you've been dodging me like a bullet with your name on it," she said in a teasing drawl, deliberately tempting him. Setting her bottle of water on the coffee table, she circled Nathan until she was standing behind him and had to resist the urge to press her body flush against his gorgeous, muscular backside. Instead, she stood up on her toes and whispered seductively in his ear, "If you want me, prove it."

Nicole's inviting words shot through Nathan like a red-hot dare, an irresistible challenge that quickened his pulse and spurred him into immediate action. He turned around, and quick as a flash he had an arm wrapped around her back and her soft, lush body crushed to his. He splayed his other hand at the back of her head to take control, and she gasped in surprise at his quick, aggressive tactics. The last thing he saw was her sultry smile of satisfaction as he slanted his mouth across hers and gave her exactly what she'd been angling for—irrefutable proof that he still wanted her.

Probably more than was wise.

At the moment, he didn't give a damn.

Coaxing her mouth open for him didn't take much effort, and as soon as her lips parted he didn't hesitate to deepen the kiss. Their tongues touched, tangled—the sweet taste of her going straight to his head and hardening him in an instant. Hot and eager, she matched his unrestrained rhythm with her own reckless abandon, the alluring scent of her rising around him, seducing his senses and igniting a pulsing demand for more.

God, he'd been fighting his attraction to Nicole since the moment he'd laid eyes on her earlier that evening, and he was loath to admit that a part of him was still smarting from her hasty departure the night they'd slept together. Now it all coalesced into this one blistering kiss that made him want to brand her, and make her realize exactly what she'd walked away from.

The hand around her waist skimmed lower until he was cupping her bottom in his palm. His fingers kneaded the soft curve of her ass through the thin material of her shorts, wishing he was stroking bare flesh instead. A low, primitive growl rose in his throat, and he instinctively flexed his hips and pushed his erection against her mound, so there was no mistaking just how much she affected him. How much he desired her. Hell, he was burning up with the need to strip her naked and take her right there, on the carpet in front of the windows overlooking the Las Vegas Strip at night. With his cock buried to the hilt inside her slick heat and her screaming his name as she came.

The possessive urge rising within Nathan shocked him, and he struggled to rein himself back before he completely lost control—something this woman made him do way too often, and in so many ways. He ended the kiss with a gentle nip of his teeth on her soft lower lip before pulling back completely.

She moaned in protest.

Wrapping his fingers in the long, silky strands of the hair at the nape of her neck, he gently pulled her head back, exposing the smooth, tender flesh of her throat. Her lashes fluttered open, and she stared up at him, her face flushed and her parted lips damp from his ravenous kiss.

Pure, unadulterated lust slammed through him. All he wanted to do was dive back into another passionate kiss and immerse himself in the mind-numbing pleasure of being inside her again. The same need pounding at him also reflected in her eyes, and he knew without a doubt she'd let him have his way with her, a willing participant every step of the way.

Yet he hesitated, needing an answer to the one question he hadn't been able to stop thinking about since they'd slept together. "Why did you leave in the middle of the night without telling me?"

She placed her hands on his chest and didn't pretend not to understand the question. "I wanted to avoid an awkward morning-after scene."

Her reply should have satisfied him; with any other woman he would have appreciated her being so considerate. Not so with Nicole, and he wasn't ready to analyze why this particular woman had such a profound effect on him. "What makes you think it would have been awkward?"

Her shoulders lifted in a casual shrug, though he swore he saw a flash of regret in her gaze. "We both agreed that neither one of us was looking for a relationship, and I just thought it would be easier if I left before morning."

"Yeah, well, maybe you thought wrong."

She looked stunned by his reply, but before she could call him on the wealth of insinuation lingering in his comment, he released her from his embrace and moved away.

Dragging his fingers through his hair, he exhaled a deep, tired sigh. "It's been a long night and it's late," he said, shifting to a more impersonal demeanor—which was exactly where his head should be considering they'd struck a business deal with the Ramsey case, and sex certainly wasn't a part of their agreement. "We've got a lot to cover tomorrow, so get a good night's sleep and I'll see you in the morning."

With that, he turned and headed for his bedroom, certain *a good night's sleep* would elude him.

Maybe you thought wrong.

Nicole lay in her bed, unable to sleep after that hot, hungry kiss she'd shared with Nathan and his very revealing comment hinting at the fact that he'd possibly wanted more than just their one night together—given the chance.

His admission had surprised her, and she couldn't deny there had been many times that she'd wished she hadn't snuck out on him the night they'd met. That she'd stayed until morning and seen where things had gone from there. Yet it was the deeper emotional possibilities with Nathan that had prompted her to slip out on him under the cover of darkness, and she couldn't deny that their kiss tonight had rekindled a fire and need deep in her belly.

She shifted restlessly on the cool sheets, her body revved up and the ache between her thighs a result of all the sexual tension that had blazed between her and Nathan. The flames of need had all but consumed her, and she would have been thrilled if things had escalated into a round of steamy, demanding sex. While most guys would have taken full advantage of the situation and her willingness to go the distance, he'd instead put an end to their hot and heavy embrace.

Judging by the hard, thick length of the erection that

had been pressing insistently against her mound, there was no mistaking just how much he desired her. The thought made her smile. Clearly, they both still wanted each other, so why not enjoy the benefit of being together for as long as it lasted? She still wasn't in the market for anything serious, but she was a modern woman who had no qualms about embracing her sexual nature and all the pleasure that came from being with a hot, sexy man like Nathan.

Now she just had to sway Nathan to her way of thinking.

Satisfied with her decision, she finally fell asleep and woke up after nine in the morning feeling rested and ready to start on whatever the day would bring.

She took a shower, dried her hair straight, and applied a minimal amount of makeup to her face. Dressed in a pink top and white capris, she followed the rich smell of coffee beckoning to her and padded out into the living room. She found Nathan standing by the windows carrying on what appeared to be a deep, serious conversation with someone on his cell phone. Giving him a semblance of privacy, she continued quietly to the kitchen to make herself a much-needed cup of caffeine.

As she stirred cream into the dark, steaming liquid, her ears perked up when she heard him mention her name, and she couldn't help but eavesdrop. Unfortunately, with only curt *yes*es and *no*s coming from his end of the exchange, she wasn't able to decipher why she was part of the discussion.

A few minutes later he disconnected the call, clipped his cell phone to the waistband of his jeans, and strolled into the kitchen.

"Good morning," she said, greeting him with a smile while trying to gauge his mood.

"Morning." Seemingly less on edge than when they'd parted ways the previous evening, he headed straight for the pot of coffee and poured himself a cup, keeping it straight-up black. "Would you like some breakfast?"

"Sure." Her dinner last night had consisted of a few hors d'oeuvres at the art gallery, and she was definitely hungry this morning. "What's on the menu?"

"How about an omelet?" he suggested.

"Only if you're making it." Honestly, she hated to cook and would rather have a bowl of cereal than labor over a stove.

When he glanced her way, she caught a glimpse of humor in his eyes. "Ham and cheese okay?"

"That sounds great." Glad to see that the strain between them had eased, she leaned a hip against the counter opposite him as he crossed the kitchen toward the stainless-steel refrigerator.

Wrapping her hands around her warm mug, she sipped her coffee and watched as he diced up some ham and began frying it in a pan on the stove. He cracked the eggs with one hand, dumped the contents into a bowl, and whipped the yolks into a creamy, frothy consistency. He looked so relaxed and self-assured, and she had to admit that there was something incredibly sexy about a man who knew his way around a kitchen.

"Sit down," he said, as he finished making her omelet and topped it off with shredded cheese.

She slid onto one of the bar stools at the granite counter overlooking the kitchen, and he placed a fragrant breakfast in front of her. Taking a bite of the savory egg, ham, and cheese, she gave a small groan of appreciation; it was delicious.

He grinned and turned back to the stove to make his own meal.

"I'm impressed," she said, meaning it. The omelet was better than any she'd ever had at a restaurant.

"Why?" He cast a quick, amused glance over his shoulder as he poured another round of the beaten eggs into a hot pan. "Because I can cook?"

"Yes, and do it well." She scooped up another forkful of the omelet. "Most bachelors I know are fast-food junkies."

He added chunks of fried ham and bits of cheese to the mixture and shrugged. "Actually, I really like to cook."

Smiling, she took a drink of her coffee. "Does that have anything to do with you growing up with three older sisters?"

His chuckle was deep and warm. "Yeah, I guess it does. My oldest sister especially, who always managed to rope me into helping her in the kitchen while she tried new recipes for the family. She'd put me to work cutting up vegetables or stirring sauces, and taught me what spices and seasonings to use in what dishes. Cooking with her was fun and I enjoyed it." After flipping the omelet, he glanced over his shoulder at her. "That sister is now a sous chef at a five-star restaurant in San Francisco."

"Did she make you wear an apron when you cooked?" she teased.

He slid his breakfast onto a plate, grabbed a fork from a nearby drawer, and gave her a mock reproving look. "She might have suggested it, but real men don't wear aprons."

She laughed, having fun with their light, playful banter, which reminded her of their flirtatious exchanges the night they'd met—before everything between them had turned so serious. "Of course they don't." And she knew for a fact that Nathan was 100 percent male, every lean, hard inch of him.

Finished with her breakfast, she set her utensils on her dish and took another drink of her coffee before turning the conversation to their business arrangement. "I heard my name being dropped while you were on the phone earlier. Who were you talking to?" Considering the bargain they'd struck to work together as a team, she had a right to know.

He didn't hesitate with his answer, proving to Nicole that he wasn't trying to hide anything from her. "That was my boss, Caleb Roux."

"Define *boss*. Is this your casino boss or your undercover boss?" She still found those two connections very confusing.

"Both." He remained on the other side of the counter separating them as he finished his omelet, his gaze suddenly too guarded for her liking. "There's a lot you don't know."

She refused to allow him to shut her out when it was imperative she knew everything she was up against. "Then enlighten me, because I need to understand who I'm going undercover with."

Releasing a deep breath, he set his empty plate in the sink, then grabbed hers and did the same. He pinned her with a direct, uncompromising look. "This is off the record."

His meaning was clear. Whatever he was about to tell her wasn't fodder for an article or story. "You have my promise." As a journalist, she prided herself on being honest and ethical, and her oath to him was no different.

Nathan braced his hands on the edge of the counter across from where Nicole sat at the bar area, knowing he had to trust her with a lot of private information in order for this partnership of theirs to work. He'd received Caleb's permission earlier to divulge his own involvement with TRG, just as long as Nicole didn't exploit it.

Ultimately, he chose to believe she wouldn't betray him, a first step in forging a strong alliance between them. "Caleb is the operations manager at The Onyx, but he's also the head of a private organization called The Reliance Group, and that's where the undercover work comes in."

She tipped her head to the side, her expression intrigued by what he'd just disclosed. "What, exactly, does The Reliance Group do?"

"TRG is a private organization that takes on complicated cases other agencies won't get involved with for various reasons," he explained. "Such as the situation with Angela Ramsey and Preston Sloane."

"I thought Angela was a runaway," she said, her tone confused. "Or did Sloane kidnap the girl?"

He shook his head. "No, she's classified as a runaway. Honestly, this case would have been much more cut-and-dried if Sloane *had* kidnapped her. At least then the police would have reason to arrest him."

"Right, but Sloane wouldn't put himself in that position."

"No, he wouldn't," he said, his voice filled with

disgust as he refilled his mug with hot coffee. "And unfortunately, the guy doesn't need to. He has a way of finding young, vulnerable girls and luring them into his world in a way that keeps him completely beyond the law. Which is why no one has been able to nail him yet."

She was quiet for a moment, seemingly processing everything he'd just told her before speaking again. "Isn't Angela from Arizona?"

He finished taking a drink of his coffee. "Yes."

"Your investigation report has her listed as a sixteen-year-old minor," she replied thoughtfully as she crossed her arms on the counter in front of where she sat. "So why not just place a call to Vegas Metro and let them handle the problem?"

A logical question from a very intelligent woman, he mused. "Angela's parents tried doing exactly that after their PI tracked her here to Vegas and Sloane's estate in Summerlin. The police paid a visit to Sloane's place, but didn't find Angela.

"Then there's the added complication that according to Nevada state law, since Angela is sixteen years old, she's legally the age of consent as far as any sexual activity is concerned," he continued, both frustrated and outraged by that particular law, especially in a city where sexual corruption ran rampant. "So even if she is having sex with Sloane, it's not a crime."

"But harboring a runaway is, no matter the age of consent," she countered, obviously familiar with the statutes.

"There's absolutely no proof that he's holding Angela against her will, which is why Nevada authorities aren't doing anything more about the case," he said. "The

police didn't find any evidence that Angela was at, or
had been at, Sloane's estate, and it's the perfect excuse
for them to quietly sweep the whole incident under the
carpet. Which is why Tom Ramsey contacted TRG to
track his daughter down and get her safely back home."

She nodded in understanding. "Well, we have the
private party with Sloane tomorrow night, which will
hopefully give us the chance to see if Angela is at the
nightclub. If not, I can give Sloane a call and set up a
time to go and see his artwork collection, and use that
as a way of getting into his estate and finding Angela."

"You're not going near Sloane without me. *Period.*"
The thought of anything happening to Nicole on his
watch made his stomach churn. "We're doing this *my*
way, remember?"

She sighed, but didn't bristle under his demand.
"Yes, I remember."

"Good. We really need to be careful how we handle
this mission. Right now, we have no idea if this is going
to be a hostile rescue or if Angela is going to cooperate
with us." Not to mention Angela's mental well-being
if she'd been influenced to stay through brainwashing
techniques or strong-arm tactics, or even drugs. There
were so many unknowns, which made this situation an
unpredictable one.

Leaving the kitchen, he headed into the living room
and grabbed the case file before returning to where Nicole was sitting. He sat down on the bar stool next to
hers, and set the folder—now fatter than when she'd found
it a few weeks ago—on the counter in front of her.

"I know you're familiar with the details of this case,"
he said, referring to the confidential material she'd pilfered the night they'd met. "But here's the file now that

it's been updated with recent information on Sloane. You also need to take a good look at Angela's photo so we can single her out at the nightclub tomorrow if she's there."

Nodding, Nicole opened the folder and studied the attached high school picture of Angela, then moved on to the other information Caleb had accumulated on the case, while Nathan tried not to think about the huge mistakes the young girl had made. First, running away from the security of home and parents who loved her. And second, trusting someone like Preston Sloane, even for a second.

At sixteen, Angela was still a baby, a spoiled kid who had so much growing up to do. A teenage girl who believed there was something better and more exciting to life than the rules she was expected to abide by at home. And predatory men like Sloane knew exactly how to take advantage of that innocence.

Nathan scrubbed a hand along his jaw, knowing that the girl had been gone long enough for Sloane to have completely immersed her in his world, and that included drugs, alcohol, and other forms of physical and mental control. Most likely, she'd been sexually exploited, emotionally manipulated, and they had to find her before Sloane passed her off to someone else—or worse, decided he was done with her and dropped her off on the streets to fend for herself.

Nathan knew exactly what would happen after that. He only had to think of Katie, and the way Sloane had used her, discarded her, and left her with only the option of turning to the cruel, unforgiving life of street prostitution.

Ultimately, she'd ended up dead.

He couldn't go through a scenario like that again, and the thought was enough to make Nathan feel nauseous. And now he wasn't responsible for just one civilian life, but two. Not only was he expected to rescue Angela, but he had to make sure that he protected Nicole, as well.

There was so much riding on this mission, and this time he prayed he wouldn't let anyone down. Himself included.

Chapter Nine

After a busy day spent prepping for tomorrow night's appearance at Sloane's club and discussing all the possible scenarios that could come up once they arrived, Nicole was ready to help Nathan find Angela and save at least one girl from making the biggest mistake of her life. And if she was able to get a story out of the recovery mission, all the better, to her way of thinking.

That afternoon, at her request, Nathan had driven her to Forever 21, a trendy store that catered to the fashion sense of teenage girls. She'd bought a fitted black lace tank top and a cute purple ruffled miniskirt that the salesgirl had promised her was all the rage. She'd found a pair of black strappy platform wedge shoes to complete the outfit and also purchased a sparkly black-and-silver butterfly necklace and matching earrings. The ensemble was casual, but fresh and flirty enough to give her the impression of being a teen—and attract Sloane's attention in the process.

While they were out, the two of them stopped at an Italian restaurant for a light dinner, and once they returned to Nathan's place, he'd announced he was heading downstairs to the fitness center to work out. She changed into her PJs, then settled on the couch in front of the windows overlooking the Strip and fired up her laptop to get some work done while he was gone.

She checked and answered her e-mail, visited her favorite blogs on the Internet, and eventually logged in to her online dating account at CupidsArrow.com to see if she had any hits. There were eleven messages awaiting her response, notes from men who were interested in contacting her based on the information she'd typed into her profile and a compatibility test she'd taken when she joined. She began checking out their profiles in turn, knowing the next step in researching her article was to set up a chat with a guy she found suitable to her tastes and personality to get to know him better.

Unfortunately, the only man she was remotely interested in was Nathan, who returned from the gym nearly two hours later. Despite being completely drenched in sweat, he looked incredibly hot and sexy in a fitted T-shirt and cotton shorts, his body all buffed from lifting weights. He disappeared into his room, closed the door, and she heard the shower turn on a few minutes later, which prompted all kinds of wicked, naughty fantasies of him completely naked and water sluicing down all those taut, sleek muscles of his.

The sharp pang of arousal arrowed through her, revving up her libido and making her ache for the kind of pleasure and satisfaction she knew Nathan was capable of giving her. Shifting restlessly on the couch, she attempted to force her mind back to her online dating quest, but she just couldn't drum up the enthusiasm to reply to any of the messages she'd received.

Her mind was on Nathan. The hungry way he'd

kissed her last night, and how he'd valiantly tried to avoid their attraction all day long. Including now, considering he'd remained secluded in his bedroom for the past hour and didn't show any signs of joining her for the evening.

She wanted him, and she was done waiting for Nathan to make the first move. Being the kind of woman who went after what she desired with a no-holds-barred kind of attitude, she decided to take the same approach with Nathan and make him an offer he'd be hard-pressed to refuse.

Powering off her laptop, she crossed the living room to his closed bedroom door, debating only a few seconds whether to knock or just walk in without warning. Opting for the element of surprise, she opened the door, sauntered into his male domain, and found him propped up in his king-sized bed reading a best-selling hardback novel. The only thing he wore was a pair of navy boxer shorts, leaving his chest and abs gloriously bare. His hair was still damp from his recent shower and tousled around his head, making her fingers itch to run through those silky strands.

Startled by her abrupt entrance, he frowned at her and set his book on the night table before concern gradually etched his features. "Is everything okay?"

"I'm fine." There was no sense beating around the bush about why she was there in his bedroom, and she wasn't taking no for an answer. "I think you and I should have sex."

Much to her amazement, the corner of his mouth hitched up in a charming smile. "I'm not sure I understand what you're saying," he drawled wryly.

She laughed. Yeah, okay, that was blunt, and she was about to get much bolder. "The way I see things, we're attracted to each other and we already know how good we are together," she said, slowly strolling toward the foot of his bed, watching his eyes darken with need as she moved closer. "I like sex. A lot. Especially with you. We're two grown adults who are capable of enjoying a fling, so why not take advantage of our time together, for as long as it lasts?" It was the perfect arrangement to her way of thinking.

"Because sex with you is too much of a distraction." A muscle in his jaw twitched, and she knew his restraint was crumbling despite his argument.

"You've got it all wrong. It's more distracting if we *don't* have sex." She climbed up onto the mattress and started a slow, provocative crawl up the length of his hot, hard body, her gaze locked on his. "You're fighting your attraction to me, and it shows in how tense you are when I'm near you. The last thing we want to do is go to the nightclub tomorrow night with you so uptight from all this sexual tension."

Before he could reply, she lowered her head and placed a warm, damp kiss just below his navel and right above where his fierce erection tented the front of his thin shorts. He sucked in a sharp breath as her lips branded his skin, then groaned deep in his throat when she gently bit down on the firm flesh of his abdomen.

She soothed the sting with a slow, leisurely lap of her tongue, and the ragged hiss that escaped him brought a gratified smile to her lips. It also tightened the knot of need coiling low in her belly, urging her to continue her upward advance, until her knees were straddling his waist and she was sitting on his lap—a familiar position with him. The thick length of his shaft pressed against her bottom, and she splayed her hands on his flat, muscular stomach and gyrated her hips, tempting him with the erotic promise of sliding deep inside her body.

He shuddered, but he'd yet to touch her. She'd already found irrefutable proof that he wanted her, and his ability to hold back only served to present her with the kind of challenge she couldn't resist. In fact, she looked forward to making him unravel and lose control.

There were too many clothes separating them, and she upped the stakes by removing her tank top and tossing it aside, leaving her completely naked from the waist up. The lust heating his gaze urged her on, and made her feel reckless and wild.

"Just in case you can't tell, I'm really hot and bothered." She rocked against the erection nestled so perfectly in the crux of her thighs and cupped her breasts in her hands, using her fingers to pluck at the stiff peaks. "So right now, there are two options for me. Taking care of things myself, which isn't nearly as fun as the real thing, or having sex with you, which is definitely *my* preference."

Smiling with seductive intent, she trailed one hand down her belly and into the waistband of her shorts, and a soft gasp fell from her lips as her fingers glided along her wet folds and found her aching clit. Shamelessly, she stroked herself, letting the pleasure build and tormenting Nathan in the process. With a low, breathy moan, she closed her eyes and let her head fall back as she arched against him, adding pressure and friction exactly where she needed it the most.

She heard him mutter a gruff curse, and knew he was close to breaking—thank God. Lashes half-mast, she looked down at him, taking in the clench of his jaw and the heavy rise and fall of his chest, and knew she almost had him.

"So, what's it going to be, Nathan?" she asked huskily. "You'd better hurry up and decide before I take matters into my own hands and you miss out on all the fun."

Quicker than she could anticipate, his hand shot out and he wrapped his fingers around the back of her neck, then pulled her mouth down to his. Lips touched and parted, the kiss instantly turning primal and possessive. Deep, demanding, and greedy. She reveled in the hot, arousing taste of him, the way her bare breasts crushed against his chest and how his large, warm hands skimmed down the slope of her back, then grasped her thighs and pulled her closer for a tighter fit against his groin.

Tangling his fingers in her hair, he tugged her head back, breaking their kiss so he could bury his face in the curve of her neck. "God, you're such a tease," he muttered, his breath hot and moist against her skin.

"Yeah, I know." She exhaled a quivering sigh when he grazed his teeth along a patch of sensitive skin, followed by a long, maddening lick of his tongue all the way up to the shell of her ear.

"Is it really such a bad thing?" she asked. From her perspective, teasing him had gotten her exactly what she wanted. Well, almost, anyway. All she needed now was his cock stroking deep inside her body and giving her the orgasm she craved.

"You make me crazy," he growled into her ear, sounding frustrated by the fact. "You make me so fucking hard I can't think straight."

His graphic words made her shiver, and she opened her eyes and smiled at him. "See, we need to do this, because I don't want to be responsible for you not being able to think straight while we're on this case."

He laughed, a ragged sound filled with amusement, and she knew then she had him hooked.

"You win," he said, and dipped his head again, this time trailing soft, damp kisses along her collarbone and down to her chest, where he nuzzled his face between her breasts.

"I usually do," she managed breathlessly, then arched her back so she could brush her nipples against his parted lips. "Besides, you and me, and having sex while we're together, is the perfect friends-with-benefits arrangement."

"Mmmm." He brought his hands up to palm both mounds of flesh, then dragged the flat of his tongue lazily along the curve of one breast, then the other, avoiding what she wanted the most.

"Is that what you're proposing?" he murmured as he flicked his tongue across her engorged nipples—a fleeting caress that only heightened her desire.

"Absolutely," she whispered, and squirmed shamelessly on his lap, every inch of her on fire from his slow-as-molasses seduction. Finally, just when she thought she couldn't bear any more torment, he took her nipple into his hot, wet mouth and sucked.

Her entire body shuddered, and her breasts swelled even more as he drew on the distended tips. *Oh, yes . . .* "Just hot sex and pure pleasure between two friends, without any messy emotions to complicate things." Pushing her fingers through his still-damp hair, she held him to her breast, fearing he'd pull away before she was ready to let him go. "It's a dream arrangement for most guys. Are you up for it, Fox?"

"Depends." His lips, teeth, and lascivious tongue continued to kiss, nibble, and lave her flesh as he talked. "Are you always going to want to be on top?"

The humor in his question made her grin. "It works for me."

He dropped his hands to her thighs and smoothed them upward, until his thumbs slipped beneath her flimsy shorts and sought more intimate places. He stroked across the damp silk panel covering her mons, before adding a subtle pressure that had her hips jerking against his with the need to feel a deeper, more illicit kind of touch.

"Yeah, but there are things I want to do to you that I can't with you sitting on my lap," he murmured.

A wealth of erotic images tumbled through her mind, adding to the arousal he was building inside her with his mouth against her breasts, and his fingers sliding along the weeping folds of her sex. "Good stuff, I hope."

"Yeah, *really* good stuff," he promised.

Unable to resist, she pulled his head back and stared into his dark eyes. "Show me," she dared.

A slow, wicked grin curved his lips right before he gently tumbled her onto her back. Instead of moving over her as she expected, he removed her shorts and panties, then pressed her knees wide open and settled between. She closed her eyes, feeling the brush of his hair against her skin, the rasp of stubble on his jaw, the warmth of his breath as he leisurely licked first one thigh, then the other, making her quiver with anticipation. Gradually, he kissed his way closer to where she was dying for him to touch her, where she was already slick and hot and wanting.

And then the shocking heat of his mouth was on her, so stunningly adept, so amazingly good. Her back arched as his tongue slid over the achingly sensitive point of her clitoris—stroking, suckling, each seductive caress sending a pulse of arousal spiking through her veins. He eased one long finger deep inside her, added a second, and she moaned helplessly as the tension in her belly, and lower, wound tighter and tighter toward release.

He pushed her higher, and she curled her fingers into the comforter to ground herself just as a tidal wave of an orgasm tore a strangled grasp from her throat and shook her to the core. The onslaught of pure ecstasy overwhelmed her senses, leaving her stunned and spent, yet craving so much more.

As her climax ebbed, he buried his face against her stomach, then suddenly swore in frustration, pulling her down from the hazy cloud of bliss where she'd been floating.

She couldn't begin to imagine what was wrong, especially since she wasn't close to being done with him. "Is everything okay?"

He lifted his head from her still-quivering belly, his eyes smoldering with raw hunger. *All for her.* "As badly as I want to be inside you, I don't have any condoms with me."

Relieved that she'd be able to ease his worry, she trailed her fingers along the taut line of his jaw and smiled. "You don't need any. I have an IUD, so I'm protected. And healthy," she added, just in case that was a concern.

"Me, too," he said, then slid off the mattress to stand at the foot of the high bed.

Her first thought was that he was leaving her even though she'd just issued him a very open invitation, and a surge of confusion washed over her. "What are you doing?"

He shucked his boxer shorts, and despite having seen him naked before, her mouth went dry at the sight of just how hard and thick that virile part of his anatomy was.

She was wrong, thank God. He wasn't going anywhere, and that incorrigible male grin, combined with the eager way he reached up to grab her hips, then dragged her down to join him, confirmed the fact. With her bottom positioned on the edge of the mattress, he hooked her knees over his arms, holding her thighs apart and giving him complete control of the situation.

Not to mention an unobstructed view of her sex, which he seemed to thoroughly appreciate and enjoy.

"You're not the only one with a favorite position," he said, before taking his cock in hand and rubbing the broad head along the slippery cleft between her legs.

Each brush of the smooth crest against her tender flesh stirred her desire all over again, bringing nerve endings back to life and making her impatient to feel him thrusting deep inside her. Yet he took his sweet ol' time getting there, using nothing more than the light pressure of his shaft to tease and dip and slide—until her hips were straining toward him and she was begging him to fill her.

Looking immensely pleased with her reaction, along

with the fact that she had no choice but to let him set the pace, he tightened his hold on her legs, pulled her closer, and fitted his erection snug against her slick opening. But instead of the fierce, hard thrust her body ultimately craved, he pushed into her oh-so-slowly, his hot gaze watching as her body took him inch by excruciating inch. When he was buried to the root, he closed his eyes, dropped his head back, and groaned, seemingly savoring the sensation of being clasped in her tight, silky heat.

How could he not move when she was aching for him to take her hard and fast? Needing more, she grabbed handfuls of the comforter and squirmed restlessly against him, wishing she could wrap her legs around his hips and force him to plunge deeper. "Nathan, *please*."

He opened his eyes and smiled down at her, a sinful gleam in his gaze. "I'm getting there, sweetheart," he drawled. "You're in way too much of a rush."

When he started to move, it was with slow, precise strokes designed to make her wild with desire—and his tactics worked like a charm. His hands slid down her thighs, still holding them apart for his viewing pleasure as he pumped leisurely inside her, the muscles across his stomach flexing with each disciplined thrust. His thumbs brushed lightly across the lips of her sex, tracing the damp folds with a teasing caress that rekindled the throb of a distant orgasm, but did nothing to assuage the growing, desperate ache within her.

Wanting to get even with him for his sensual torment, she decided to use the only ammunition she had in her arsenal—her hands, and her body. She wanted to show him just how resourceful she was, her ultimate goal to unravel that precious control of his and reap the benefits of a man who succumbed to the red haze of lust.

It became a sexy game between them. An irresistible challenge of who could arouse whom the most. And she was determined to win.

She touched her breasts, grazed her thumbs over her nipples, and moaned, feeling the tension rise within Nathan as he watched, his gaze burning with carnal hunger, his jaw clenched in denial. Biting her lower lip, she skimmed one palm downward, and when her fingers slid between their bodies to the hot, wet place where they were joined and glided over the hard nub of her clitoris, she gasped and tightened her inner muscles around him—and swore she felt him swell harder, thicker inside her.

He shuddered, but his features remained etched with determination. "Jesus, Nicole," he groaned raggedly, and pumped into her a little bit faster, but it wasn't nearly enough to satisfy the relentless arousal demanding release.

"Give me more," she taunted in a soft, heated whisper, and continued to push him closer and closer to the edge of his own sanity.

Done teasing them both, she closed her eyes and circled her clit with her fingers, knowing exactly what it would take to grasp the orgasm lingering just beyond her reach. Knowing, too, that her climax would trigger his own. With each deliberate touch and caress the thrill increased, the sensation amplified, the yearning grew . . . and with a defeated groan Nathan finally let go and began giving her *more* of everything she needed. Harder strokes. Deeper penetration. Faster thrusts.

He drove into her, impaling her on his cock, over

and over again, so solid, so rough, so powerful he sent her higher than she'd ever gone before. The pressure inside her became almost unbearable, then seemed to snap apart, battering her with a pleasure so intense she couldn't hold back the shocked cry tumbling from her lips, or the rippling aftershocks that gripped him tight.

She heard Nathan curse, felt him buck uncontrollably against her—once, twice, three more violent thrusts, then the hot, scalding rush as he came.

He collapsed on top of her with a rough groan, his breathing erratic, his body slack from his own vigorous orgasm. Feeling completely content for the moment, she laughed, enjoying every moment of his defeat.

Nathan woke just before dawn to find his face pressed against a fragrant spill of hair and his arms full of silky, curvy woman—a great way to start the day, in his opinion. Nicole was spooned against his chest, her tempting bottom tucked against his groin, her body all soft and warm and satiated from a night of incredible sex.

Unable to help himself, he smiled and gently trailed his fingers along the indentation of her waist and felt her stir sleepily against him. This time, she hadn't snuck out on him in the middle of the night, not even to return to her own room, and he had to admit he liked having her in his bed.

She'd proved last night just how weak he was when it came to her, that resisting her allure was next to impossible. Somehow, she'd wrapped him around her finger, coercing him into letting her be a part of his assignment and seducing him into having sex with her. Not that he was complaining about the latter, not when he already wanted her again this morning.

Would it really be such a bad thing to indulge in the friends-with-benefits proposition she'd suggested—a temporary agreement to enjoy sex with a woman he couldn't seem to get enough of anyway? Truly, it was a win–win situation—lots of physical pleasure without the emotional involvement. Just the kind of arrangement he preferred, especially considering that their reason for being together was temporary.

Bottom line, Nicole made him feel alive, more so than he had in years. She aroused him, frustrated him, even, but there was so much about her that intrigued him and kept him coming back for more. After last night, he was done fighting what he wanted so badly. *Her.*

He pressed his damp lips to her bare shoulder, then slowly kissed his way up to the warm curve of her neck. Nuzzling the side of her throat, he cupped a soft breast in his hand, and her nipple instantly beaded against his palm. His cock stiffened, and despite the numerous times they'd had sex during the course of the night, he was already aching to get inside her again.

She sighed, gradually coming awake, and tried to turn around to face him, but he had something else in mind. Gently, he eased her onto her stomach, nudged her thighs apart with his knee, then settled his hips between her legs. He covered her from behind, careful about distributing his weight as he aligned their bodies and the tip of his shaft glided along her slick, feminine cleft. Finding her hands, he laced their fingers together at the side of her head.

"Mmmm," she murmured as she instinctively lifted her bottom, seeking a deeper, more intimate contact. "Good morning."

"Yeah, it is." He slid into her with a sleek, heavy thrust that made them both groan in pleasure. "And it's about to get a whole lot better," he said, and proceeded to make good on his promise.

Chapter Ten

It amazed Nathan how Nicole could go from being such a sultry vixen with him in bed, to looking like a fresh-faced teenager *trying* to appear mature and experienced. From her cute and trendy outfit and accessories, to the soft curls framing her face and her practiced, youthful expressions, she pulled off the pretense quite well.

On a Saturday night, the Strip was congested with partygoers seeking the kind of excitement and entertainment that only a city like Vegas could provide. When they pulled into the circular drive for the well-known nightclub Bliss, there was a long line of people waiting for a chance to get inside. It didn't help matters that it was a long summer weekend that concluded with the Fourth of July, which attracted more tourists than normal.

Once the valet took his Ferrari to park, Nathan grabbed Nicole's hand tight in his and gave it an encouraging squeeze. "Ready or not, here we go."

"Don't worry about me," she said with a reassuring smile as they made their way though the press of people gathering on the sidewalk. "I'm more than ready to get in there and find Angela."

He believed her. At least a dozen times they'd gone over what they needed to accomplish once they got inside, and even though she wasn't technically trained for this sort of undercover work, he trusted her implicitly. She might be looking to nail a story on Sloane, but he'd seen enough concern in Nicole's gaze when they'd discussed Angela's predicament to know that she truly cared about extracting the young girl from a dangerous situation.

Nathan still believed there was some kind of personal slant to her interest in Sloane's lifestyle and his preference for underage teens. But whatever her motive for pursuing in-depth information on the man, it remained a mystery to him and she didn't seem inclined to talk about her reasons. Just like he wasn't willing to discuss his own private issues with Sloane and the case with her.

For now, their sole focus was to first locate Angela, then form a plan of action to get her out of the mess she'd tangled herself up in.

Nathan veered away from the main doors to the nightclub and headed toward the clearly marked VIP entrance. A hefty, bald-headed man dressed in black guarded the closed steel door, turning away party revelers trying to talk their way into the exclusive section of the club.

The man took his job seriously and wasn't letting anyone past him, which was why Nathan handed him the card that Sloane had given to him as an invitation. "I'm here for Preston Sloane's private party."

The other man glanced from the card to Nicole, then

back to Nathan again, his rugged face expressionless. "I need to see some identification."

Since Nicole looked barely old enough to drive, the guard was obviously more concerned with clearing Nathan's name before letting them through. Withdrawing his wallet, he flipped it open and showed the guard his Alex Keller driver's license. The man scanned the information carefully before making a call on his cell phone to verify his identity and to get approval to let him beyond the black metal door.

Sloane seemed to run a tight operation, and Nathan supposed the other man had to be careful about who he allowed into the private parties. His meticulous screening of the people he accepted into his inner circle was one of the reasons he had managed to elude prosecution.

After receiving confirmation, probably from Sloane himself, the guard disconnected the call, then unlocked and opened the door to let them through. Nathan led the way down a nondescript hallway that came to an end at another closed door and a younger man dressed in a dark suit. He, too, asked to see Nathan's ID before finally granting them access into the private club.

Once inside, Nathan discovered the atmosphere was much mellower than he'd anticipated—more like that of an intimate party than the frenetic mood that accompanied most nightclubs. The lighting was dim, and the music was kept at a reasonable level so conversations could be heard as guests mingled in the spacious lounge.

The decor was very provocative, with erotic art hanging on the walls, live girls dancing in gold gilded cages suspended from the ceiling, and strategically placed beds for couples to lounge on. Each one was draped with sheer red curtains and covered with a luxurious silk comforter and piles of pillows. Some were already in use, and while the veil of material had been drawn around the mattress, Nathan could clearly see what each couple was doing, which added to the erotic, sexual vibe in the room.

"I think this is what's called a den of iniquity," Nicole said from beside him, her voice tinged with awe. "I've never seen anything like this before."

"Yeah, it's quite impressive," he agreed, having seen his share of exotic places during his years as a vice cop. The underbelly of Vegas held some very licentious lifestyles, but Sloane's secret society was by far the most luxurious he'd ever encountered.

Hand in hand, they strolled deeper into the club, and Nathan took a moment to size up the guests. The men ranged in age from thirty-something professionals to older, wealthy gentlemen, and he even recognized a few athletes and lower-level politicians. Women in their early twenties, all dressed very provocatively, mingled with a younger group of girls who appeared to be in their teens.

All in all, it was a diverse group of females, providing plenty of choices for every male taste.

Nathan caught sight of Sloane, heading toward them with a young, pretty brunette by his side. The girl, who was wearing a red strapless dress with high-heeled shoes and had painted her lips a shocking shade of crimson, clung to his arm as they approached. While Nicole had gone the understated route with her choice of outfit and opted for a more natural look for her face, this girl appeared as though she was playing dress-up with her mother's clothes and makeup. And to Nathan, her appearance and demeanor screamed desperation.

With Sloane's blatant interest in Nicole, who managed to maintain an air of innocence in the way she presented herself, Nathan wondered if most of the girls whom Sloane was initially attracted to started out looking their age, then gradually felt the need to change their appearance to something sexier in an attempt to compete for his affection and hold his attention, only to be cast aside when fresh blood entered the picture.

Like now. Sloane was staring at Nicole, and while he'd minimized his desire for her at the art gallery, in this environment, teeming with sexual undertones, he did nothing to hide the lust in his gaze. The girl next to Sloane must have sensed the change in him, because she tightened her hold on his arm and moved closer.

Annoyed by the girl's possessive behavior, Sloane peeled her fingers from his shirt, severing the contact between them. Anxiety and dismay etched the girl's features, but Sloane didn't seem to notice, or he just didn't care.

"Alex and Nikki." Sloane welcomed them in a cheerful greeting, his gaze lingering on Nicole much longer than necessary. "I'm so pleased that the two of you came."

Nathan shook the other man's hand. "Thanks again for the invitation."

"It was my pleasure." Sloane's words held a dual meaning as he turned back to Nicole, picked up her right hand, and pressed an openly intimate kiss on the inside of her wrist. "You look absolutely beautiful tonight, Nikki."

"Thank you." Smiling shyly, Nicole tugged her hand back, giving the impression of being demure when

Nathan knew she was more likely repulsed by Sloane's display of affection.

He understood her disgust. It was all Nathan could do to keep calm when he wanted to beat the shit out of Sloane for even touching her.

The young girl had witnessed the exchange, too, and seemed to grow more distressed with each passing moment. Nathan guessed that she was Sloane's current "it" girl, and was feeling threatened by Nicole's appearance, and Preston's obvious interest in her.

"Nice place you have here," Nathan said, sounding suitably impressed.

"I'm glad you like it. There's plenty to enjoy, from the open bar, to the dance floor, and even private massage rooms." He inclined his head at Nathan. "Care to join me for a drink while Holly introduces Nikki to some of the other girls?"

"That would be great." Nathan couldn't have asked for a more ideal arrangement, which would allow him some one-on-one time with Sloane while Nicole tried to find out if Angela was somewhere in the nightclub.

They both had a job to do tonight, and the sooner they gathered the information they needed and located Angela, the sooner they could get the hell out of there.

Nicole followed Holly into an adjoining lounge area, feeling the resentment coming off the young girl in waves. Clearly, she didn't appreciate having to babysit Nicole—the new girl on the block who appeared to have captured Sloane's attention.

The first thing Holly did was beeline to the bar and order a mixed cocktail and a glass of water, not bothering to ask if Nicole wanted anything to drink. While the bartender set the water on the bar, then began pouring alcohol into a shaker to create her martini, Holly retrieved a pill box from her purse and shook out three tablets. She popped them into her mouth and washed them down with a huge gulp of water.

Nicole had no idea what Holly had just taken, but she was absolutely certain it wasn't aspirin. "Are you okay?" she asked, genuinely concerned for the girl.

"I just need something to calm my nerves," she said brusquely. "I'll be fine in a few minutes."

The guy behind the bar finished her cocktail, pushed it toward Holly, and she downed half of it in one long drink.

Nicole cringed, resisting the urge to take the martini from the girl and dump it out somewhere. Knowing her actions would draw unwanted attention, she opted for words instead. "Should you be drinking alcohol with those pills?"

Holly glared at her. "What are you, my mother?" she snapped.

"No. But I'm smart enough to know that taking pills with alcohol isn't a good mix." She sounded like an adult instead of a sixteen-year-old, but she didn't care— and Holly was too worked up to notice. With her own past experience under her belt, Nicole knew all about taking drugs to get through an increasingly unpleasant situation.

Which was why watching this too-young girl attempt to mask her emotions with narcotics made Nicole's protective instincts rise to the surface.

"Well, it works just fine for me." Holly finished off the cocktail, placed the empty glass on the bar, then walked away.

Grateful that she'd stopped at one drink, Nicole followed Holly, who continued to ignore her despite Sloane's instructions to introduce her to the other girls. It killed Nicole to see this young girl falling apart over Sloane, who didn't give a crap about her beyond his own depraved needs.

While Nicole wanted to shake some sense into Holly, she knew she had to take a different approach. She couldn't just come in and immediately change the girl's way of thinking and dealing with things. First, she had to gain her trust and put her at ease. Then maybe, just maybe, she could eventually reason with the girl.

It was a long shot, but she had to try, because in Holly, she saw her past. Mark Reeves, just like Sloane, had lured her in with sweet talk and promises, then used her sexually. Kinky desires had evolved into more deviant demands, and with him whispering in her ear how much he loved her, and her system pumped with just enough ketamine to keep her relaxed and compliant, he'd done things to her that with a clear conscience she would have flat refused.

Those memories were what spurred her with Holly now.

Gently, she grabbed Holly's arm to stop her, and the girl came to a halt—mainly because Nicole didn't give her a choice. She pierced Nicole with a spiteful look, but Nicole wasn't about to be deterred. Holly put on a tough act, but Nicole could sense the vulnerability beneath the girl's belligerent facade.

"I'm not interested in Preston," Nicole said, getting right to the crux of the problem between them, and hoping that her reassurance would help to soften Holly toward her. "I already have a boyfriend."

The tension stiffening Holly's spine eased a fraction, and the look in her eyes gradually filled with resignation. "It doesn't matter," she said, her voice choked with distress. "He's interested in you. I can see it in the way he looks at you. He used to look at me the same way."

Unexpectedly, Holly grabbed Nicole's hands, the sudden desperation etching her young features almost frightening in its intensity. "If you'll stay away from Preston, I can change his mind about me. I *know* I can."

Tears filled Holly's eyes, and Nicole could see the girl breaking down right in front of her. Her belly burned with fury at witnessing how Sloane's influence had affected this girl's psyche. Sloane had toyed with Holly's emotions and twisted her perceptions of their relationship to keep her amenable and dependent on him.

Bastard.

The girl was an absolute mess—from Sloane's manipulations, the drugs he'd obviously supplied, and the alcohol that Holly used to dull her pain. The instinct to protect the girl was strong, but Nicole knew from experience that convincing Holly she needed to escape this awful, mentally abusive situation wouldn't be that easy. Not when Holly had obviously been brainwashed and couldn't see past her need to be with Sloane.

Right now, Nicole could at least be a friend to the girl, someone she could talk to and maybe even come to trust. And in forging a friendship with Holly, she could hopefully gain the information she needed about Angela.

Wanting privacy for the two of them, Nicole led Holly to a secluded corner where they sat next to each other on a red velvet couch. By then tears were streaming down Holly's face, and Nicole retrieved a tissue from her purse and handed it to the other girl, who used it to dab at her eyes and wipe away the moisture on her face. In the process, she accidentally removed some of her makeup, and her true age began to emerge.

While Nicole waited for the girl to calm down, she casually glanced around the lounge, looking for a certain blond-haired girl. She saw a few mingling and flirting with the male guests, but none that resembled the photograph of Angela Ramsey.

"I'm sorry," Holly said after a few moments had passed and she was composed once again. She exhaled a shaky breath as her fingers played with the small, diamond heart pendant around her neck. "I don't mean to be such a bitch, but sometimes I just can't help it. You're so pretty and I'm so afraid that Preston is going to replace me with someone new."

Which would happen sooner or later, Nicole knew. It was inevitable, considering Sloane's track record. Holly hadn't learned that lesson yet, but Nicole was certain she would soon.

Holly's eyes had become glassy, and her body had gone lax as she slouched against the corner of the sofa. The alcohol and whatever pills she'd swallowed were taking effect, making her much more relaxed and mellow. Nothing more than an illusion until the narcotics wore off and the anxiety and fears returned.

Nicole eyed the sparkling diamond heart that Holly kept clutching in her hand, as if by embracing the pendant she could somehow hold on to the person who'd given it to her.

"Did Preston give you that necklace?" Nicole asked.

"Yes." A faraway look entered Holly's eyes, and she

smiled dreamily. "He gives me lots of nice, pretty things."

Nicole bet Sloane did. Whatever it took to give the girls a false sense of affection while they were with him. "What other kinds of things?"

"Fancy clothes and purses, and other jewelry," Holly said, speaking openly and freely about her life with Preston, more than Nicole had expected her to reveal. "He even gave me my own special room at his house and he let me decorate it just the way I wanted. It's beautiful. I've never had a room so pretty before. Or one I didn't have to share with someone."

There was definitely a backstory to Holly's tale, one that had led her to this point in her life where she'd become involved and dependent on a man who only cared for her as long as it was convenient for him and his needs. Nicole wanted to grab Holly and get the hell out of this place and make her realize that this wasn't the kind of life she wanted to live. That there was something better waiting for her outside the beautiful gilded bedroom that Sloane kept her in at his estate.

But Nicole couldn't act on the impulse, because there was no way for her to get Holly out of the nightclub safely, not when every exit was locked and guarded. She also couldn't jeopardize Nathan's case—not to mention that her actions would put her own life at risk. No doubt a well-connected man like Sloane would hunt her down and make her pay for her interference.

She might not be able to do anything about Holly tonight, but Nicole swore that she'd eventually find a way to rescue the girl, and help get her life back on track. Nicole knew all too well how difficult it could be to get out of a situation you were completely immersed in, and she wished she'd had someone who would have helped her to see how destructive her relationship with her English professor had been.

Nicole wanted to be that person for Holly.

With effort, she turned her attention to extracting as much information from Holly as she could about Sloane and this operation of his, eventually leading up to asking about Angela so as not to raise any suspicions. Any details she could glean from Holly would help her and Nathan understand what they were up against, and what to expect if they found themselves at Sloane's estate.

"Does Preston give you money?" she asked, keeping her tone light, curious, and innocent. Like a young girl who might be interested in making some extra cash on the side herself.

Holly shrugged. "Depends on what I need. If I want extra money, all I have to do is give his friends massages and pretend that I like them. Sometimes, they pay me even more to do other things with them. All the girls do it," she said, her tone slightly defensive, as if she felt she had to justify what she did. "I can make a lot of money that way, but the only one I want is Preston."

A surge of nausea rose up into Nicole's throat, and she had to tamp it back down. What Sloane did with these girls was no better than prostitution, and it sickened Nicole to the core that he got away with it.

"How old are you, Holly?" she asked, almost afraid to find out.

Holly visibly tensed, some part of her mind breaking through the drugs and alcohol's haze to register the importance of the question. "I'm eighteen."

Nicole didn't believe her, and called her on the lie.

"You seem younger. I'm sixteen," she said, giving Holly an opening to be truthful about her age.

Panic filled Holly's gaze. "You might want to keep that to yourself," she said in a low whisper.

Nicole found Holly's reaction, and her comment, interesting. "Why?"

Holly seemed more alert now. "Because it could get you, and Sloane, in a lot of trouble if the wrong people find out that he's seeing underage girls. The first thing we're told when we agree to stay at The Sanctuary is that we always say we're eighteen, no matter what our real age."

So that's how Sloane managed to keep his hands clean. The girls lied about their age, and he pretended to not know any different. While her mind came to that conclusion, her curiosity was piqued by something else Holly had said.

"The Sanctuary?" she asked, wondering what the other girl meant. "What is that?"

"That's Sloane's place in Summerlin," Holly said, and smiled. "It's absolutely beautiful there. So safe and peaceful."

Sloane had obviously chosen the word *sanctuary* for a reason, and it played right into the perception of him offering girls like Holly a haven from a previously troubled life, a refuge where they felt taken care of and protected. An illusion, Nicole knew, but to a young girl craving a place where she felt secure, the warm and welcoming atmosphere Sloane had created could seem very real.

There was so much more she wanted to know about Holly, like how she'd gotten involved with Sloane and if her family knew where she was. Certain that she was much younger than her claim of eighteen years, Nicole guessed that Holly was possibly even a runaway who'd seen Sloane as her salvation.

There were so many questions, and so little time to ask them. And before her time with Holly ran out, Nicole needed to find out if Angela was here tonight, and if not, where they could find her.

Nicole smiled at Holly, who'd relaxed once again now that she'd let the subject of their ages go without further questioning. "I have a friend I think you might know. Last time I talked to her she mentioned Preston to me, so she might even be here tonight."

Holly tipped her head curiously. "What's her name?"

"Angela Ramsey. She has blond hair and blue eyes."

A sullen look passed over Holly's features, making it clear that she wasn't thrilled to hear the name. "Oh, you mean *Angel*."

The innocent connotations of the nickname Angela had been given weren't lost on Nicole. "Angel?"

"That's what Preston calls her," Holly said, a bit of resentment creeping back into her tone.

"So you know her?"

Holly nodded, though she didn't look happy about the conversation revolving around another girl she considered a rival for Sloane's attention. "She's another one of Preston's favorites."

At least now Nicole had verification that Angela was still involved with Sloane. It was a start. "Is she here tonight?"

"No." Holly's lips pursed morosely. "Preston doesn't like to share Angel, but he will. Eventually."

The pain in Holly's voice tore at Nicole's resolve. She tried to keep her emotions out of the equation, but it was difficult not to empathize with Holly's situation when Nicole had been in a similar one herself.

"Do you know where Angela is?" Nicole asked, needing that last bit of information so she and Nathan could figure out their next plan of action.

"She's at The Sanctuary in Summerlin."

Before Nicole could ask Holly any more questions, out of the corner of her eye she saw someone approaching them. They'd been left alone up until this point, but whoever was heading toward them had Holly sitting up straighter and looking as though she was bracing herself for something very unpleasant.

Surprised by Holly's odd behavior, and curious to know who had evoked such a strong reaction, Nicole glanced at the woman who'd come to a stop where they were sitting on the couch. She was wearing a black low-cut dress and had a centerfold-type body that most men would appreciate, coupled with gorgeous blond hair that fell halfway down her back in soft waves.

This was no young girl, but a fully grown woman who looked to be in her mid-thirties—and was most likely the oldest female in the nightclub. There was a hardness about her despite her outer beauty, a shrewd-ness in her gaze that came from years of experience—and not necessarily good ones. Whoever she was, her appearance prompted Holly's expression to fill with dread.

The woman turned that discerning look toward Nicole, studying her through narrowed eyes. "Are you a new girl?"

Her inquiry was direct and to the point, and Nicole shook her head before any wrong assumptions were made. "No. I'm here with someone."

"And who would that be?" the woman asked, an unmistakable air of authority in her tone.

"Alex Keller."

"Fine," she said, as if she recognized the name, then she turned that cool green gaze back on Holly. "Derek is asking for you, and Preston said for you to do whatever it takes to make him happy. He's waiting for you in the sapphire room, so don't be long."

Reluctantly, Holly nodded her assent.

With that, the woman moved on. Her message was cut-and-dried, with no warm fuzzies to buffer the reality of what she was telling Holly to do. Nicole's chest felt heavy with heartache and grief for Holly—and a deeper rage against Sloane.

"Who was that?" Nicole asked, certain the woman was someone important to Sloane—and if that was the case, she and Nathan needed to know all the players the other man kept in his employ.

"That's Gwen. She's Sloane's assistant." Holly stood up, her gaze despondent, yet resigned to her fate. "I've got to go before I get in trouble."

Nicole watched Holly walk away, moving like a wooden, emotionless doll. She stopped at the bar, ordered another drink, then downed it in one gulp before disappearing down a hallway that Nicole assumed led to private rooms.

Knowing what awaited Holly in the sapphire room, it took every bit of control that Nicole possessed not to go after the young girl and rescue her from this degrading situation. She felt so damn helpless, and she knew why, but she had no time to dwell on her own past. Right now, she just hated being powerless to save Holly.

Pushing her own emotional turmoil aside, she exhaled a deep breath and focused on what needed to be done next. She now knew where Angela Ramsey was being sequestered, and she needed to let Nathan know so they could decide on their next plan of action.

Retrieving her cell phone from her purse, she texted Nathan the flirtatious phrase they agreed she'd use once she had information to share.

I'm ready for you, baby.

Nathan's conversation with Sloane went fairly well, with the two of them enjoying a drink while covering a wide variety of topics—from the Vegas casinos they preferred to play at, to Sloane's recent vacation at his villa in Italy, to the new business venture Nathan was considering investing in—a fictional deal set up by Lucas Barnes to add to Nathan's portfolio as an entrepreneur. Eventually, their discussion came around to Nicole and the young girls at the nightclub.

And there were many from what Nathan could see. Some had hooked up with the men in the lounge, while others were mingling and openly coming on to the older gentlemen; most of the beds were occupied with couples getting busy. A few girls who looked high on something, either alcohol or drugs, were dancing provocatively together, their youthful bodies writhing against one another and providing a classic girl-on-girl fantasy for most of the guys in the club.

For Nathan, the atmosphere was nothing short of sleazy and a repulsive display of depravity, at the very least. Sloane's lifestyle, and the careless way the other man exploited children, went against every ethical bone in Nathan's body and was a stark reminder of how imperative it was that this undercover case concluded much differently from his last mission as a vice cop.

And that meant treading carefully with a powerful man like Sloane. One wrong move or slipup, and innocent lives would be in jeopardy. And that was something Nathan refused to allow this time around.

"See anything you like, Alex?"

Sloane's curious question cut into Nathan's thoughts, and he glanced at the other man reclining in the red leather chair next to his. "You have quite a stable of girls to choose from."

Sloane casually swirled the dark liquor in his snifter glass and smiled. "Variety is a good thing, don't you think?"

"For some." Sensing the conversation held the undertones of a test, Nathan chose his words carefully. "Call me old-fashioned, but I prefer being with one girl, not many."

Sloane lifted a brow, a daring light in his eyes. "Are you sure about that, Keller?"

Before Nathan could reply, Sloane signaled to a girl standing nearby, who immediately moved toward them, eager to do his bidding. Like every other female in the club, she looked too damn young, yet too experienced in other ways. She was wearing a miniskirt, a too-tight top, and high heels, and her shoulder-length black hair framed delicate facial features and a sweet smile.

She came to a stop in front of them, a little unsteady on her feet as she waited for her next cue from Sloane.

"Alex, this is Jasmine," Sloane said, introducing the girl to him. "She's one of the favorites here at the club.

Whatever you want, she'll be more than happy to provide, isn't that right, sweetheart?"

Jasmine nodded, and before Nathan realized her intent, she sat down on his lap and wriggled her bottom suggestively against his groin, which did nothing to arouse him. If anything, it took supreme effort not to shove her right off his lap in disgust. He reined in the impulse and instead managed to pretend her brazen behavior didn't bother him in the least.

"I haven't seen you around before," Jasmine said, her voice soft and languid as she draped an arm around his shoulders and cuddled closer. "You're cute."

He couldn't smell any alcohol on her breath, but judging by her dilated pupils and her slurred speech, there was no question in Nathan's mind that she was on some kind of narcotic. Or maybe she sedated herself in order to deal with the nightmare that her life had become.

Aware of Sloane assessing his response and reactions, he reached up and gently brushed back the strands of hair that had fallen across her cheek, the caress more caring than sexual. "And you're very pretty," he said, returning the compliment and hoping that's as far as things went between them.

"Thank you," she whispered, and laid her head on his shoulder while pressing her free hand to his chest. "Would you like to dance? Or maybe I could give you a massage?"

The words sounded rehearsed, as though she'd said them dozens of times before, to at least that many men. It was a disturbing thought, and one Nathan couldn't dwell on at the moment. What he could do, however, was put an end to her advances.

"Maybe next time," he said, turning her down as gently as possible. The last thing he wanted was her getting in trouble for not persuading him to take advantage of her offer. "I promised my girlfriend that I'd be good tonight."

She pouted, but before she could do anything else to try to sway him, Sloane snapped his fingers and ordered the girl to leave them alone. Obeying, she slid off his lap, and moved on to a guy sitting across the lounge who immediately welcomed her overtures.

Unable to stomach what the girl was about to do, Nathan looked away and found Sloane watching him, his gaze a little too perceptive for his liking.

"You just passed up a sure thing, Keller," Sloane drawled, and downed the rest of his drink. "You could have had Jasmine and Nikki never would have known."

Sloane was questioning his motives, and possibly even his loyalty, and Nathan had to think fast on his feet. "What can I say? It's fresh and new and exceptionally hot with Nikki. Right now, she gives me everything I could want or need sexually."

"For now, yes," Sloane said, the look in his eyes changing, darkening with determination. "But every man has a weakness, and mine, at the moment, happens to be Nikki." His smile stopped just short of being perverse. "Now, we just have to find yours, and hopefully the two of us can come to some sort of gentleman's agreement."

Christ. Sloane was openly proposing a trade-off. Nicole for any one of his girls that Nathan wanted in exchange.

Having made it very clear what he desired, Sloane

stood and inclined his head at Nathan. "Now, if you'll excuse me, I have some business to take care of. You and I can catch up later."

The other man walked away, leaving Nathan feeling as though he'd just been sucker-punched in the gut. He sat there, trying to regroup, and less than a minute later the cell phone in his front pants pocket vibrated, startling him. He was so goddamn tense that the buzzing sensation nearly had him jumping out of his skin. He pulled the phone out and read the text message Nicole had sent to him.

I'm ready for you, baby.

He was relieved to see she wasn't in any sort of trouble, and hoped she'd been able to discover something about Angela's whereabouts. Tucking away his cell phone, he found Nicole and dragged her out to the dance floor, where they could be close and talk without being overheard.

Keeping plenty of distance between them and the other couples, he slid his arm around Nicole's waist and brought her body flush to his, from chest to thighs. To anyone watching, it was an intimate, sexual position, but Nathan's only concern was keeping their conversation private.

He took one look at her face, saw that she was shaken about something, and wondered what had happened to upset her so badly.

Caressing a possessive hand down her back, he brought his lips near her ear. "Are you okay?"

"I'll be fine," she whispered back, and slid her fingers into the hair at the nape of his neck, keeping her cheek close to his. "She's not here."

Disappointment coursed through him. "Damn."

"She's at his estate in Summerlin. The girls call it The Sanctuary."

Definitely a good-news, bad-news scenario. Good news because they'd nailed down her location. Bad news because now they had to find a way into Sloane's estate to get Angela out. After what Sloane had just proposed, Nathan loathed the idea of letting Nicole anywhere near the other man again, but she was ultimately the key to getting them both one step closer to Angela. Now he just had to devise a strategy to infiltrate Sloane's house in Summerlin, but without endangering Nicole in any way.

Over Nicole's shoulder, Nathan caught sight of Sloane heading toward another man who looked vaguely familiar. It took Nathan a moment to fully recognize the older gentleman as a superior court judge. A very powerful man to have on your side, especially when you dabbled in the kind of immoral misdeeds that Sloane did.

The two men talked for a few minutes, then exited the nightclub together. Nathan had hoped that he and Sloane would be able to talk again, but after casually asking around, he discovered that Sloane had left for the evening and wouldn't be back.

Which left him and Nicole back at square one.

Chapter Eleven

The first thing Nicole did when they arrived back at Nathan's apartment was head into her bathroom and take a long, hot shower. She washed her hair and scrubbed her skin with body wash, as if by doing so she could cleanse herself of all the perversion she'd witnessed at Sloane's private nightclub.

When the water turned cool, she got out and dressed in a pair of soft, loose sweatpants and a T-shirt, then ran a comb through her hair to let it air-dry. Still feeling restless, she headed into the living room. Across the way, she noticed that Nathan had left his bedroom door open in a silent invitation, but after everything she'd endured tonight she needed time alone to unwind and sort out her thoughts.

Preferring the cloak of darkness, she switched off the table lamps and sat down on the floor behind one of the couches in the living room facing the windows overlooking the Las Vegas Strip. In every direction, bright neon lit up the city like a never-ending light parade, and while she was normally awed by the amazing sight, tonight she found it difficult to enjoy the spectacular view.

She felt raw inside, and she couldn't get Holly out of her head. The despondent look in her eyes and how she was assuaging her inner pain and feelings with drugs and alcohol and barely functioning on her own. Then there was Holly's adoration and devotion to a man who had no qualms about using her—emotionally and physically.

It was such a horrible, grievous situation, and Nicole couldn't begin to imagine what had happened in Holly's life to make the young girl travel down this particular path—one that would undoubtedly end in heartbreak. Sloane had already stolen her youth and destroyed her innocence, and by the time he was done with Holly there was little doubt in Nicole's mind that there would be nothing left to salvage of the guileless girl she'd once been.

A mixture of anger and sorrow tightened her chest. But as upset as Holly's situation made Nicole, she understood all too well how easy it was to be swayed by a charismatic smile, to fall for a man who knew exactly the right words to make a girl believe she was the center of his universe.

Nicole, too, had been lured in by pretty lies and compliments that had gone straight to her head and made her think she was in love, to the point that she'd compromised her principles to keep her man happy.

The situation with Holly was worse than Nicole had endured. Nicole had been young and naive, definitely, but she'd been an adult at eighteen, not an innocent girl who had no one to turn to, and nowhere to go.

But it was the other similarities that ate at Nicole. The need to please a man so overwhelming that she'd succumbed to his perverse desires. The increasing dependence on some kind of relaxant to do the demoralizing, humiliating things Mark had asked of her. And how he'd shredded a little piece of her soul every time she'd allowed him to use her for his own twisted pleasures.

Mark had taken a once-outgoing, confident girl and destroyed her self-esteem. With his practiced manipulation, he'd made Nicole weak and insecure. He'd taken advantage of her vulnerability and emotions, until he'd grown tired of her and moved on to another young protégée, leaving her devastated and unable to focus on her college classes, exams, and the grades she needed.

It had been a dark time for her, a cruel life lesson that could have sent her spiraling down a much different path, and nearly had. Only with the help of a counselor had she managed to get her head back on straight and finish college with her degree in journalism, along with the drive to succeed.

But the whole sordid experience had left her determined to never allow a man that kind of control over her again. And to never let a man come before anything else in her life that mattered.

So far, so good.

Unfortunately, once Sloane was done with Holly she'd just remain broken, unless someone stepped in to save her. Even then, Nicole was certain a part of the girl would never be the same.

"Hey, what are you doing sitting out here in the dark all by yourself?" Nathan asked, startling her out of her deep reflection on the evening's events, and her own past. "Are you okay?"

She'd been so wrapped up in her thoughts she hadn't even heard him approach. He stood next to where she was sitting on the floor, his feet bare, and she just didn't have the energy to glance all the way up to his face. "I can't stop thinking about Holly." She'd told him about the girl on the drive home, and he'd been sympathetic and understanding.

"I know," he said softly, and sat down beside her. "It's not easy to witness what we did tonight and walk away unaffected. That's a large part of the reason why I quit the force. It's even more difficult to watch those girls sell their souls to the devil himself."

"And for what?" Nicole met his gaze in the shadowed darkness, feeling tortured from the inside out. "Jewelry? Crumbs of affection? A pretty room that Holly doesn't have to share with anyone else?" She shook her head in disgust, wishing she could make sense of it all. "What makes those girls living with Sloane believe that trading sex for expensive material things is a great life?"

Leaning against the back of the couch behind them, Nathan stretched his legs out and splayed his hands on his thighs, settling in to talk to her. "In my experience, I learned a lot of the girls are runaways. Either they come from a bad home to begin with, or they believe there's something better waiting for them outside their parents' rules."

"And sleazy guys like Sloane offer them just enough privileges and extravagant gifts to hook them in," she said, unable to keep the bitterness from her voice.

"Exactly." Nathan sighed, as if he, too, despised everything that Preston Sloane stood for. "They're young and impressionable, and they get caught up in the promises, the draw of what they perceive to be a glamorous life. It's unlike anything they've ever experienced, and he makes it exciting and irresistible to them."

Her lips pursed in anger. "Then comes the alcohol and the drugs, and then they're addicted to more than just Sloane."

"Unfortunately, that's the way men like Sloane operate." His tone was far more reasonable than hers, and she chalked it up to the fact that he was much more seasoned in dealing with the harsh realities of predatory men who took advantage of underage girls.

"You know, tonight I met Holly, who was so willing to do whatever it took to please Sloane. It's just a matter of time before he discards her, if he hasn't already." Her throat felt raw, and her stomach churned with a multitude of emotions—mingling her own personal history with tonight's events. "And while a part of me is infuriated that she allowed herself to get involved in such a degrading situation, another part of me completely understands how it can happen."

He tipped his head curiously. "How so?"

"It's a long story." And one she wasn't certain she wanted to share.

He smiled, the sentiment gentle and caring. "As far as I'm concerned, we have the entire night to talk if you need to."

The compassion in his eyes unraveled her guard, as did the knowledge that he was willing to listen. After everything she'd seen tonight, and recognizing a piece of herself in Holly, the urge to talk about her emotional connection to the girl was strong. Everything was sitting so heavily on her chest, and her own humiliating past clawed with the need to be released and set free.

Except for a college mental health counselor, she'd never confessed to anyone about her relationship with her English professor. She'd been so ashamed that she'd

let someone she trusted take advantage of her, she
hadn't been able to bring herself to even tell her parents
the truth about why she'd fallen into a short bout of
depression after her first term at Columbia University.
Instead, upon returning to college for her sophomore
year, she'd buried all the anguish and grief away and
poured all her time and energy into graduating and then
building a career as a journalist.

She'd believed that particular part of her life was all
behind her, that she'd resolved those issues and moved
on. But tonight's exposure to Holly had unearthed those
agonizing memories and pushed them right up to the
surface, making her feel emotionally stripped bare.

She glanced at Nathan, who was waiting patiently for
her to say something, and she debated on how much to
reveal, if anything at all. In the past few days she'd
learned enough about him to know he was an honorable
man, that he'd be the last person to judge her for the bad
choices she'd made in her past. Sitting next to him in the
dark, she felt safe and secure, and she couldn't remember ever feeling that way with any other man.

She trusted her instincts. And she was about to trust
Nathan with her deepest, darkest secrets.

"When I left my small town in Iowa to attend Columbia University in New York, it was the most exciting
time of my life. I was eighteen and felt so grown-up and
mature being on my own for the first time ever." Looking back, it was easy to see just how young and vulnerable she'd been, ignorant even. A small-town girl with
stars in her eyes and big dreams in her heart.

"I was nervous, a little scared, and at times felt lonely.
But I was determined to study hard, get good grades,
and most especially impress my English professor, since

journalism was my major and I was at CU on a full scholarship based on my writing ability and my solid grade point average in high school."

"Very impressive," Nathan said, sounding sincere.

"Thanks," she said, and smiled for a moment before getting back to her story. "My freshman English professor, Mark Reeves, was a really good-looking guy and had a charming personality to go with it. He was thirty-seven, but he looked exceptionally young, and it was well known that most of the girls in his classes had a huge crush on him."

"Including you?" Nathan guessed quietly.

She nodded. "Yeah, including me. And it was very exciting when he started paying extra attention to me. Out of all the other girls he had as students, he took me under his wing and really made me feel special as a writer, and as a woman. He lavished me with praise, gave me all A's on my essays and tests even when I felt they weren't my absolute best, and he flirted with me in a way that made me feel sexy and attractive. He told me that he saw something special in me and my writing ability, and I honestly believed him."

"You trusted him."

Nathan understood, which was why it was so easy for her to open up and talk to him. "I had no reason not to trust him up to this point. He was perfect, as far as I was concerned," she said, and didn't miss the cynical note in her voice now that she was older and wiser. "I was so infatuated with Mark, and when he invited me over to his apartment to help me with a big writing project, I was not only flattered, but excited to be completely alone with him. He made me dinner and we talked about my current essay and what I could do to make it stronger and better, and then he kissed me and told me how much he wanted me."

She remembered that night all too well. The flurry of butterflies in her stomach as his lips touched hers. The surge of exhilaration that someone like Mark Reeves, an older, sophisticated man, could desire her. His sole attention, along with the seductive, romantic way he treated her, had been like an aphrodisiac, feeding a part of her that felt alone in a new city away from family and friends.

"After that night, the relationship quickly turned intimate, and for me, very emotional, especially after giving him my virginity. The sex was hot, and being with Mark was quite an eye-opener. I was more than eager to learn what pleased him the most because I honestly believed that I was in love with him." She felt the warm rush of old humiliation sweep across her cheeks, but a glance at Nathan told her that she had no reason to be ashamed. That it wasn't her fault Mark Reeves had taken advantage of her youth and innocence.

"A little over a month after we had sex for the first time, Mark started pressuring me to . . . expand our sexual repertoire. At first, I didn't understand what he meant, but I trusted him enough to go along with what he wanted. Some things were . . . interesting, and other things he asked me to do made me uncomfortable."

She dragged her fingers through her hair and exhaled a deep breath before continuing. "I didn't mind when he asked me to dress like a stripper, or we watched porn together, and some of the toys he used were kind of fun," she admitted. "But then those sexual stimulants weren't enough for him, and he started introducing things that made me feel uneasy, like bondage, exhibitionism, and even some S and M."

"Did you tell him you weren't interested?" Nathan asked gruffly.

She nodded. "Yes, and that's when he insisted that I just needed to relax and I'd enjoy it as much as he did. He started giving me these little white pills that calmed my anxiety, and he assured me it was perfectly safe. Whatever it was, the drug definitely lowered my inhibitions, to the point that I let him do things that I normally wouldn't."

Nathan's jaw clenched with a glimpse of fury. "The guy was a real asshole, wasn't he?"

A choppy laugh escaped her. Nathan's question was a rhetorical one that didn't need a verbal reply because the answer was obvious. "About two months later, he started talking about the two of us indulging in a ménage à trois. He told me his greatest desire was to watch me with another man, to share me . . ."

She shook her head, revolted anew at the thought. "I didn't want to do it, but he stepped up the pressure. He told me I was special, that watching me with another man, sharing me, would only heighten what we had together."

Nathan cursed under his breath. "What happened?" he asked gently.

"Because I was afraid of losing him, I gave in and agreed." Her stomach roiled at the memory. "This time, going into the threesome, *I* asked him for one of those little white pills, because I knew I couldn't do it otherwise." Just like Holly had needed drugs and alcohol tonight to get through whatever sexual favors Sloane's men expected of her. Nicole knew exactly what that felt like.

"So, Mark gave me just enough that I was aware of what was going on during the threesome, but I was too lethargic to do anything about it." Her voice grew hoarse. "I thought taking something to relax me would make it easier to let two men take advantage of me, to use me sexually, but it was the worst experience of my life. I felt so helpless, so mortified and degraded—during and afterward."

"I'm sorry," Nathan said softly, compassionately.

She glanced at him, appreciating his comforting presence. "Me, too. About a week after the threesome, the semester ended and a fresh crop of young freshman girls started a new term in his class. It didn't take Mark long to replace me."

Feeling a slight chill, Nicole drew her legs up and wrapped her arms protectively around them. "He ended things with me abruptly and coldly, and as I watched him work his charm on one of the new girls, I literally got sick to my stomach because I realized that I'd essentially traded my virginity, perverse sex, and the use of my body for good grades in his class."

She swallowed hard to push back the knot tightening in her throat. "It all felt so sleazy, and I was devastated emotionally. But while I was in the relationship, it never occurred to me how wrong it all was, not when he was telling me how much he loved me, and how much I meant to him." After the fact, she'd realized that his interest and affection had all been a sham to feed his ego, and she blamed herself for being so stupid and naive and falling for his lies and deceit.

Nathan reached out and gently tucked a strand of

hair behind her ear, as if sensing how tough this conversation was for her. "Reeves never should have gotten involved with a student, let alone tried to push his sexual advances on a young girl, but it sounds as though this was a pattern for him."

"You're right. I wasn't the first, and I know for a fact that I wasn't the last." She dragged her fingers through her still-damp hair, unable to quell the regrets that remained with her to this day. "I should have reported him, but I was eighteen and the sex was consensual. And I was so afraid of my family finding out what I'd done, and how shocked and disappointed they'd be in me, that I decided to bury the whole incident like it never happened."

"That's never a good thing," Nathan said, his tone quiet, but wise.

"I know," she agreed, recalling how all those suppressed feelings had sucked her into a black hole of nothingness and had threatened to consume her. "The weeks after Mark broke things off with me, the shame of what I'd done, and almost did, ate at me, and I fell apart emotionally. I couldn't bring myself to get out of bed in the morning to attend my classes, and my grades started to drop to the point that the university issued a warning that I was going to lose my scholarship if I didn't raise my grades again. That was my wake-up call, and I finally went to a college counselor to help me work through my depression."

She exhaled a deep breath, found Nathan watching her with quiet patience and genuine interest, and finished her tale. "Once I got my head on straight again, I was able to focus on what was most important to me—finishing school and getting my degree. I was determined not to let my experience with Mark ruin my life and future. After that I kept my head down and focused on my grades and graduating."

But she knew that despite the counseling and her outward fortitude, she still harbored unresolved issues and insecurities that affected her relationships with men. After Mark, separating sex and emotion had become crucial for her, because she refused to let herself be that vulnerable ever again.

She still enjoyed sex, but knowing how badly an emotionally based relationship could skew her judgment, it was all about physical pleasure for her. She no longer trusted her instincts when it came to men, and found it much easier to keep things casual, fun, and undemanding. This way she wouldn't risk shifting her focus away from what mattered to her in favor of what a man demanded. Her strategy kept her in control, and her emotions safe and guarded.

Beside her, Nathan shifted and moved as he braced his back more comfortably against the sofa behind him, then he patted his lap. "Come here," he said softly.

The deep rumble of his voice spread through her like a balm, and the offer of comfort was too much for her to resist after the night she'd endured and everything she'd just revealed. She settled on his hard thighs, and his arms immediately slid around her, holding her with a gentle strength that made her relax against his chest and rest her head on his broad shoulder. He smelled good, clean and fresh and all male, and he felt even better. Solid, warm, and reliable.

After a moment of silence, he spoke, his lips moving against the top of her head. "I'm sorry you had to go through that."

The empathy in his voice was real, and while it had been difficult to share her past with him, she was glad she had. "Now maybe you can understand why I feel so passionate about this story and nailing Sloane. No girl or woman should ever be used by any man, emotionally or physically. It's despicable."

She sighed as he rubbed a large hand up and down her back, then kneaded the taut muscles at the nape of her neck. "I survived, and I count myself as very lucky when I think about those girls at Sloane's. They're so young, and the whole situation is reprehensible. Once Sloane is done with them, most of the girls are going to be broken beyond repair." She'd already witnessed the emotional damage with Holly, and she was certain that visions of the young girl were going to haunt her dreams tonight when she finally fell asleep.

"I know," he said, his voice gruff with his own quiet outrage. "I saw this shit all the time during my last undercover assignment when I was a vice cop. It's heartbreaking to watch these girls destroy their innocence and their futures because they get sucked into a life filled with sex and drugs. And as much as I hated seeing so many exploited young girls at Sloane's nightclub tonight, unfortunately we can't save them all."

She lifted her head from his shoulder and stared up at him, catching sight of something dark and haunted in his expression that she couldn't fully grasp. "Why not?" she asked, even knowing how unreasonable she was being.

"Because it just doesn't work that way," he replied, his gaze filled with regret. "We're just two people against a very powerful, well-connected man, and it's up to the feds to bring Sloane down, along with gathering the evidence they need to back up his arrest so the charges stick. You and I have a job to do, and that's to rescue Angela. Even by doing that, we're putting a lot of lives in danger."

She couldn't argue with Nathan's logic, but her head and her heart were torn between her promise to help rescue Angela, and her need to save anyone else she could from such a bleak and lonely existence. Like Holly, who deserved a better future than the grim one she was quickly heading toward.

Nathan caressed the back of his fingers along her cheek, the touch tender and caring and teeming with concern. "This assignment is going to get a lot worse before we're through, and I'm certain you're going to see a lot more of what we witnessed at Bliss tonight. Are you sure you can handle the emotional aspects of this case?"

She knew what he was saying was true and not an attempt to scare her. After her sensitive reaction to the harsh realities of Sloane's world, he was worried about her frame of mind going forward. But no matter how difficult it was to be a part of something so vile, this case had turned personal for Nicole, and she wasn't about to back out now.

"Tonight was tougher than I'd anticipated," she admitted. "But now that I know what to expect, I'll be able to get the job done without falling apart."

"Okay," he said, trusting her to know her own limitations. "But if at any time things get too intense for you and you want out, just say the word and it's done."

She shook her head. "Not a chance. At least we'll be able to give one girl a happy ending."

"That's what keeps me motivated."

A small smile lifted the corner of his mouth, but didn't diminish those shadows still lingering in his gaze. She had her reasons for pursuing this story, and she suspected that Nathan had his that went beyond his obligation to The Reliance Group. But asking for details wasn't her place. If he ever wanted to share, she'd listen, just as he'd done for her tonight. She understood how personal and sacred some things could be for a person.

The night's tension had eased from her body, and she wrapped her arms around Nathan's back and curled up closer to his chest. He tightened his hold, his warm hands stroking along her arms as he enveloped her in the kind of intimacy that was more about respect and affection than the passion and sex she was used to with him.

It marked a slight shift in their relationship for Nicole, one that should have made her panic and retreat. But at the moment she felt protected and secure, and peaceful in a way that had eluded her for years. She couldn't deny that Nathan's embrace calmed her. It was exactly what she needed after digging deep into her soul and telling him about her past.

Knowing the solace was temporary, that soon enough life would intrude and with it the reality of their situation, she decided that for tonight she'd selfishly indulge in any of the tenderness Nathan was willing to offer.

Sunday morning dawned bright and warm with the sun streaming cheerfully through the living room windows. If the newspaper forecast was to believed, it was going to be a scorcher of a day. A normal occurrence for Las Vegas in the summer, and according to Nathan's earlier conversation with his boss, Caleb, a perfect afternoon for the Fourth of July poolside barbecue he planned every year for the TRG crew.

After spending a good half hour discussing last night's events and what Nicole had discovered about Angela, Caleb had asked Nathan if he was coming to the party, and had even extended an invitation for him to bring Nicole if he wanted to. Unsure of how Nicole might be feeling this morning, Nathan hadn't committed to anything and decided to play things by ear.

During breakfast, and even now as he perused the sports section of the Sunday paper in the armchair across from where she was curled up on the couch with her laptop, he glanced her way every once in a while to try and gauge her mood. Ever since waking up, she'd been quiet and subdued. He understood why and tried to respect that personal space she seemed to need this morning.

Last night had been emotionally draining for her—first as a result of her disturbing encounter with Holly, then later, when she'd told him what had happened to her in college. As difficult as it had been for her to open up to him, he appreciated the trust she'd offered. The insight into her past gave him a better understanding of what drove her to write an exposé on Sloane.

But nailing Sloane wasn't their objective. Rescuing Angela was. And he hoped he'd made that clear to her last night.

Hearing her soft sigh, he shifted his gaze from an article on the next big UFC match, scheduled to play out at Mandalay Bay, to Nicole. She looked completely engrossed in whatever she was doing on her computer, but it was the crease lines furrowing her brow that told him there was a lot more going on in that head of hers than she was letting on.

After last night, it was difficult not to see her in a whole different light. He had to admit that he had a newfound admiration for Nicole. Up until this point, he'd only seen her outward strength and confidence, but now he knew that deep inside she was soft and vulnerable. Human. Fallible. A woman with scars and flaws and insecurities.

The two of them weren't that different, especially in the way their tragic pasts now propelled their actions in the present. For different reasons, they both felt the need to make up for old mistakes and set things right, giving them a common objective when it came to Sloane and saving Angela.

Because of all that, he felt connected to Nicole, an emotional bond that went beyond their physical relationship. Holding her in his arms and comforting her had felt good and right—a surprise, but not an unwelcome one.

For the first time in years, he'd allowed himself to feel something for a woman that had nothing to do with sex, and everything to do with tenderness and caring. A scary realization, but it was there nonetheless, and he couldn't ignore the awareness slowly making itself known.

In a very short time, Nicole had gotten under his skin—with her vivacious personality, her sensual nature, and most especially with the way she'd trusted him with her secrets and fears. There was so much more he wanted to learn about Nicole, and he couldn't help but wonder

if maybe, once this ordeal was over with, she'd recon-
sider her friends-with-benefits arrangement and see
if there was something more between them worth pursuing.

But for now, for today, he decided to keep things light,
casual, and fun, and the best way to accomplish that
goal was to get them out of the apartment for the afternoon. He was certain nothing important would happen
today, and being cooped up for hours would only make
them both restless and anxious. He really had no desire
to watch Nicole in her own little world as she con-
versed with men online for her latest article on dating
trends. If she was going to give anyone her attention, he
wanted it to be him.

They needed to clear their heads and regroup, and
he honestly couldn't think of a better way to accomplish that than to be surrounded by the people he'd
come to think of as his second family—Caleb, and the
rest of The Reliance Group team.

He folded the newspaper, set it on the coffee table in
front of his chair, then glanced across the way at Nicole, watching as her fingers moved fast and furious
over her laptop's keyboard. "Hey, can I talk to you for a
minute?" he asked, wanting her complete attention before issuing his invitation.

"Sure. Just a sec." She finished whatever she'd been
typing, then glanced at him curiously. "What's up?"

Leaning forward, he rested his elbows on his thighs
and smiled at her. "Did you happen to bring a swimsuit
with you?"

"Actually, I did." She shut down her laptop, set it on
the coffee table, then lifted her arms above her head

and stretched her limbs. "I figured a place like Turn-berry Towers has an amazing pool and spa that I might want to use."

"It does," he managed to say, even though his mouth had gone dry at the sight of her bare breasts pressing so enticingly against her thin tank top.

They'd slept in the same bed all night long, with her snuggled up to his side, her warm, lush body half draped over his and her hand resting low on his abdomen. It had been a long, excruciatingly platonic night for him, and while he had no regrets about giving her the emotional comfort she so obviously needed, he couldn't deny that even in the light of day his desire for her was as sharp as ever.

And for a brief, crazy moment, he thought about staying indoors and spending the day making love to her in every position imaginable, until they both collapsed from sheer sexual exhaustion. Oh, yeah, his unruly body was totally on board with the lusty idea, but his mind knew that today they both could use some fresh air and a reprieve from the confinement of the apartment.

"Are we going swimming today?" Her eyes lit up, as if the mention of a pool had rejuvenated her, which was exactly what he'd wanted.

"If you want, but not here." She frowned in confusion, and he explained what he had in mind. "Every year on the Fourth of July weekend, my boss has a barbecue at his place in Henderson. I thought it might be a good distraction. And this way you can meet some of the people I work with."

She bit her bottom lip, a quick flash of uncertainty

passing across her expression before it was gone again. "You don't have to feel obligated to invite me. You go and I'll be fine on my own right here in this cushy apartment," she insisted. "Besides, I have some hot online dates to hook up with."

She grinned, and while he knew she was teasing, he couldn't deny the spark of jealousy flaring in the pit of his belly. He knew her online dating was all about research for her article, but damned if he didn't hate the idea of her "hooking up" with another guy, even if it was in an Internet chat room and all business for her.

"I want you to come with me," he said, and meant it. Standing, he walked over to where she was sitting on the couch and splayed his hands on the cushions on either side of her shoulders. He dipped his head close to hers, looked into her eyes, and smiled. "In fact, I'm not taking no for an answer," he said, giving her his best macho-man impersonation.

She blinked at him, all innocent-like—that fun, flirtatious personality that he loved so much finally emerging. "I don't know," she said, her voice slightly breathless with anticipation. "I think it's going to take more than just your say-so to convince me."

Accepting her irresistible dare, he tucked his hands beneath her arms and hauled her up from the sofa and against his chest. Sliding his hands around her back, he fused his mouth against her softer-than-soft lips. When she sighed her pleasure he delved deeper, doing his best to seduce her and melt her so-called resolve. It was all a sexy game, he knew, but it was one he thoroughly enjoyed playing with her.

Before the kiss could get any hotter, before he lost the ability to stop, and forgot all about his good intentions for the day, he forced himself to pull back—even as his aroused body protested.

When he could focus on Nicole's face again, the laughter he saw in her eyes mocked him, as did the mischievous smile curving her kiss-swollen lips. "Oh, come on, Nathan, is that the best you can do to sway me?"

He could think of a dozen other ways to persuade her to say yes, all of them including getting naked and teasing her to the brink of release and not giving in until she agreed. Yeah, the idea definitely had merit, but he'd much rather let the sexual tension build for the day . . . and reap the benefits of all that heat and awareness between them when they got back home tonight.

With that settled, he decided to handle her so-called reluctance with a more barbaric attitude, all feigned, of course. "I'm thinking brute force ought to do the trick."

Before she realized his intent, he bent his knees, wrapped an arm around her thighs, and hefted her over his shoulder like a sack of grain. She gasped in surprise, but quickly caught her breath.

"Ohhh, I just love it when you get all rough and un-civilized with me." Flipped upside down, she was in the perfect position to reach down and pinch his butt, which she did with relish.

Unfazed, he chuckled and playfully smacked her ass in return, causing her to inhale sharply and squirm against his shoulder like a slippery fish. "You'd better behave," he said as he headed toward her bedroom so she could change. "Because there's a whole lot more where that spanking came from."

"Promises, promises," she taunted, but she was laugh-ing, her mood exuberant and the painful memories of last night dissipating as a result of their amusing, sensually charged banter.

And for today, a mental break from the case was exactly what they both needed.

Chapter Twelve

Nicole had no idea what to expect when she and Nathan arrived at Caleb's place in Henderson later that afternoon.

The two-story house was located at the end of a cul-de-sac in a quiet neighborhood. She'd lived for many years in the hub of Las Vegas, a city that lived up to its reputation for never sleeping, and this peaceful suburb felt like a nice slice of normalcy to her.

Other cars were parked in the driveway in front of the house, so Nathan pulled the out-of-place Ferrari up to a vacant curb and killed the engine. He turned toward her, and she drew in a deep breath to help subdue the sudden jumble of nerves swirling to life in her belly.

He smiled, an amused glint in his brown eyes. "Why do you look like you're about to face the firing squad?"

She hated to acknowledge that she was feeling a tad anxious—truly an oddity for her in any kind of social situation. But in this case, meeting the people Nathan referred to as his second family, she wanted to make a good impression. She wanted them to *like* her, and that spoke more to her feelings for Nathan than she was willing to admit to even herself.

"They're your friends and co-workers, and I'm a tag-along in what sounds like an annual ritual," she said, divulging just enough to explain her uncertainty. "I don't want to stick out like a sore thumb today."

His expression held understanding. "Since we're working on this case together, we're partners. I'm sure Caleb told the others about you, which is only fair since I just spent the past half hour giving you a rundown on each of them."

And what a diverse and eclectic mix of people they were, she thought wryly. "I appreciate having that little bit of an advantage."

"Not a problem." He rested his arm across the back of her seat and trailed his fingers over her exposed shoulder, making her tingle as a result of his sensual caress. "Just relax and be yourself and you'll fit right in. I promise."

It was difficult to think straight when he was touching her so intimately, and leaning closer to her in the small confines of the sports car. His lips skimmed along her neck, his breath warm and damp along her sensitized skin, and she closed her eyes and moaned softly as arousal coursed through her veins. The man knew exactly how to melt her resolve, yet at the same time increase her desire and need for him.

"By the way," he said, his voice dropping to a low, husky pitch as he placed his free hand on her bare thigh and nudged her legs slightly apart with his long, strong fingers. "You look really sexy in this little bitty dress you're wearing."

His admission made her smile. It had been like this

between them since that morning. Teasing. Flirting. A slow, heady seduction of body and senses.

When they'd made a quick stop at her apartment so she could grab a few things for the day, she'd changed into a short tube-top dress and a pair of slip-on sandals—a perfect outfit for a hot afternoon in the sun, as well as to tempt Nathan, which seemed to have worked.

"I'm happy you noticed. I wore it just for you." She licked her bottom lip, and he followed the slow glide of her tongue with dark, smoldering eyes. "No bra, skimpy panties, and easy access . . . for later."

"I think I ought to check for myself."

His hand disappeared beneath the hem as his parted lips settled on hers. His kiss was hot and deep from the get-go, and her pulse leapt in anticipation of where those skillful fingers were heading.

A couple of quick, hard taps on the window a few seconds later had Nicole jerking back, abruptly ending the kiss.

"Hey, you two kids. Get a room already," a female voice said in a joking manner.

Nathan wasn't as quick to withdraw the hand that had nearly reached its mark, and the slow, leisurely caress of his fingers along her inner thigh left a trail of heat that wouldn't abate anytime soon. Nicole was grateful that the windows were tinted enough that whoever had interrupted them most likely hadn't been able to see what Nathan had been up to beneath her dress.

Face flushed in chagrin, she glanced out the window to find a cute blonde standing on the sidewalk, hands on her waist and a quirky smile on her lips as she waited for them to emerge from the car.

"Ahhh, that would be Skye Lambert," Nathan said

by way of introduction, even though Nicole had known who the other woman was just by his earlier description. "Come on, let's head up to the house."

They exited the Ferrari and Nathan came around the vehicle to take her hand in his, surprising her with the public display of affection. Then again, they'd just been caught kissing, so hand-holding was fairly tame in comparison.

"What are you, the welcoming committee?" Nathan asked as they stepped up to the sidewalk.

"I saw this Ferrari pull up to the curb and wondered what celebrity Caleb had invited to the barbecue," she said playfully. "I had to see for myself that it was you. Nice ride, Fox." She eyed the sports car with envy and anticipation.

"Don't get all excited," Nathan said. "It's not mine to keep."

"Too bad." Skye sighed in disappointment. "It's definitely a hot ride. I would love to get behind the wheel of a car with such amazing power and stamina."

Nathan chuckled. "Dream on, Skye."

Skye wrinkled her nose at him. "You're no fun," she said, then turned her attention to Nicole and gave her a quick head-to-toe inspection before offering her hand to shake. "Hi, Nicole. I'm Skye. Caleb already told all of us about you being Nathan's girlfriend."

"I'm not really his girlfriend," Nicole said, wanting to clear up that misunderstanding as quickly as possible. "I'm just *pretending* to be while we're working on this case together."

Skye's eyes widened in feigned surprise. "Wow, you two pretend really well. That was some realistic kissing I saw back in the car."

The other woman winked at Nicole in that female knowing way, which did nothing to subdue the warmth suffusing Nicole's face. Nathan stood beside her, his expression bemused. Clearly, he was used to Skye's outspoken personality, and didn't bother to curb her outrageous comments.

As if they were already best of friends, Skye hooked her arm through Nicole's, taking her by surprise.

"Come on, let's go and have some fun." Skye started along a pathway leading to a gate at the side of the garage.

"Behave yourself, Skye," Nathan said from behind them.

"You know I don't have a disciplined bone in my body, so don't count on it, Fox." Skye glanced over her shoulder at Nathan and waved him away with a waggle of her pink-tipped fingernails. "Go and do your guy thing with the boys, while I get Nicole acquainted with everyone and the two of us do the female-bonding thing. I'll take good care of her, I promise."

The last thing Nicole heard from Nathan was a low groan of resignation before they walked into a beautifully landscaped backyard. A large custom-built pool with a free-flowing waterfall dominated the area. There was also a cozy patio with outdoor furniture, and a covered barbecue island with a huge, stainless-steel grill and polished oak bar.

Across the way, on a stretch of green grass, three men were playing a game of lawn darts. Skye steered them in that direction while Nathan veered off toward the bar, probably to get himself something to drink.

As they neared, the men halted their game and Nicole found herself the center of three male stares. Before

Skye could introduce her, a young, good-looking guy with ruffled blond hair and amicable green eyes stepped toward her with his hand extended in greeting.

"You must be Nicole." He grinned, his easygoing manner making her instantly comfortable with him. "I'm Lucas Barnes, the security analysis guy at The Onyx."

She smiled as she shook his hand. "I hear you're pretty amazing with computers." Not only had Nathan told her that Lucas was responsible for creating his new identity as Alex Keller, but he'd also revealed that Lucas had been a kid genius and an expert at all things electronic.

"Yeah, I've been known to crack a code or two in my day," he said, sounding proud of that fact.

The second man stepped forward. A bit older than the rest of the group, he was extremely good-looking with dark brown hair, hazel eyes, and chiseled features. There was a natural air of authority about him, yet his charismatic smile also put her at ease.

"Caleb Roux," he said. "I'm glad you came today."

To Nicole, the name said it all. "Thank you for the invitation."

She hadn't been sure what to expect of Caleb and worried that he might resent her interference in Nathan's case. He was a difficult man to read, but she didn't detect any hostility or annoyance in his reception.

"And the big guy who looks intimidating as hell but is sweet as a pussycat is Kane Briggs," Skye said as she waved a hand toward the man who definitely had the dark and brooding look down pat.

According to Nathan, Kane was a Navy SEAL turned surveillance specialist. He was a big guy, from his broad shoulders to his large feet, and his ink-black hair, intense green eyes, and hard, muscular body only reinforced the notion that he was someone who could pose a very real threat if you crossed him.

"I'd rather not be compared to a dumb beast, if you don't mind," Kane said to Skye before exchanging a warm, courteous handshake with Nicole. "Unless it's something a lot tougher than a damn cat."

Nicole laughed, though the image of a sleek, black panther emerged in her mind, which was more his style. "I'll be sure to remember that."

Nathan joined the group, a bottle of root beer clutched between his fingers just as Skye plucked one of the plastic darts from Caleb's hand. She glanced up at him, a crafty yet vixen-like look sweeping over her features.

"So, Caleb," she said in a soft, sensual drawl. "Want to make a bet that I'll hit the target with this dart in one throw?"

He raised a casual brow at her direct challenge, but there was no mistaking the brief spark of heat in his gaze. "You're not *that* good."

Skye lightly bounced the dart in her palm. "Are you willing to put your money where your mouth is, Roux?"

"Have you not learned your lesson where Skye is concerned?" Lucas piped in, his voice filled with humor. "When she bats those lashes of hers like that, it means proceed with caution, man."

Kane chuckled, the amused sound at odds with his hulk-like appearance.

"Maybe it's time for Caleb to be a little reckless for once," Skye suggested, smiling at the man she was teasing so mercilessly. "Unless, of course, you're afraid you'll have to pay up when I make the shot."

"You're on, Skye," Caleb said without further hesitation.

She smiled her satisfaction. "What are you willing to bet?"

"You name it." Caleb crossed his arms over his chest and waited while she considered her prize.

"A real date," she said without missing a beat. "Drinks. Dinner. Dancing. Maybe something a little more if you're lucky."

"And if you miss the mark?" he asked with mild curiosity.

Skye shrugged. "Then you're off the hook. For *now*."

He rubbed his fingers along his jaw thoughtfully. "Not a whole lot in it for me if you lose, now is there?"

"There is if I *win*." She didn't even try to hide the insinuation in her statement.

Nicole found the lively banter between the two of them fascinating. They seemed to enjoy playing cat and mouse with their attraction, with Skye taking on the role of the feisty feline trifling with an enticing toy she couldn't wait to pounce on and enjoy, while Caleb played the proverbial hard-to-get prey.

"Back up, boys," Skye said as she stood behind a stick that had been laid on the grass to mark the starting line. "I need my space."

Everyone gave her the room she asked for, and with equal parts concentration and determination she eyed her shot, then tossed the brightly colored dart through the air and toward the plastic ring a good fifty feet away. She gasped as the dart landed, less than an inch outside the ring. Then she cursed beneath her breath.

"Bummer," Caleb said. "Better luck next time, sweetheart."

Nicole couldn't tell if he was relieved, disappointed, or a little of both. With laughter erupting from the other guys, the men resumed their game, and Skye once again looped her arm through Nicole's and guided them toward the covered island area.

"Caleb drives me absolutely crazy," Skye grumbled.

"How so?" Nicole was curious to learn more about the history between Skye and Caleb.

"Can I be any more obvious that I want him?" Skye asked, her voice laced with frustration.

Nicole smiled. "From what I can see, the feeling is mutual."

"Oh, I *know* that Caleb is hot for me, except he has this stupid code-of-honor thing when it comes to getting involved with an employee. But one of these days, I'm going to break through all that misguided chivalry of his."

Nicole didn't doubt it. There was obviously more to Skye and Caleb than their surface attraction, but Nicole didn't feel it was her place to pry for details.

They came to a stop at the bar, and the man standing behind the counter greeted them with a devastatingly seductive grin no woman could resist. Coupled with his pitch-black hair and bright blue eyes, along with his gorgeous, masculine features, even Nicole found him extremely attractive.

"Good afternoon, pretty ladies," he said, a lyrical Irish lilt to his voice that was as engaging as his delivery.

Skye rolled her eyes at his attempt to charm. "This is Sean O'Brien, our resident Irish bartender and all-around heartbreaker."

"Hi, Sean," she said, easily believing that this man was a player. "I'm Nicole."

Instead of shaking the hand she offered, he pressed his warm lips to the back of it, lingering longer than was necessary. "What are you doing with a schlep like Nathan?" he teased, the Irish accent no longer present. "Come and run away with me."

Amused by his flirting, Nicole gently pulled her hand back and laughed.

"Better watch yourself, Casanova," Skye cut in wryly. "Nathan is eyeing every move you make and he doesn't look happy that you're already poaching on his territory."

Unfazed by Skye's warning, Sean braced his arms on the surface of the bar and leaned across the counter, a mischievous twinkle in his eyes. "Good. I'll be sure to keep him on his toes this afternoon." He winked at Nicole, confirming his reputation as a rogue.

"I could use a drink," Skye said with a sigh. "What are the specials today?"

"I've got mojitos, blended fuzzy navels, and my special melon martini," he said, showing off by tossing a full bottle of vodka into the air and catching it in his hand as easily as if he were juggling a plastic ball. "Or there's beer."

"Not strong enough," Skye said. "I'll take a melon martini. How about you, Nicole?"

She was more in the mood for something frothy and froufrou, rather than hard-hitting liquor. "A fuzzy navel sounds good."

"Make that two," a female voice said from behind them.

Nicole glanced over her shoulder as a pretty woman approached the bar. Her long brown hair, streaked with gold, fell into soft waves halfway down her back, and her inquisitive brown eyes regarded Nicole with interest.

Skye introduced the woman as Valerie Downing, the casino host at The Onyx. As Valerie grasped Nicole's hand in hers and looked into her eyes, Nicole felt an inexplicable shiver skip down her spine.

"It's very nice to meet you," Nicole finally said, and shook off the strange sensation.

"You, too." Nodding as if she'd satisfied some internal curiosity, Valerie released her hand, and the peculiar awareness between them dissipated.

Sean set two blended fuzzy navels on the counter, and Skye handed one to Nicole and the other to Valerie. "It's about time Nathan got himself a girlfriend, don't you think?"

Nicole shook her head adamantly as she sipped her delicious peach drink. "Really, we're just *friends*." With sexual benefits, yes, but that didn't constitute the kind of relationship Skye kept alluding to.

"Which means I've still got a shot, right?" Sean asked with a grin as he mixed Skye's cocktail and poured it into a martini glass rimmed in sugar.

Skye laughed. "Not unless you want that pretty face of yours rearranged by Nathan's fist."

Sean considered the risk for only a fraction of a second. "Nicole just might be worth it."

"Flattery will get you nowhere with this one," Valerie said, sounding certain of that fact.

Sean's shoulders lifted in an unrepentant shrug. "You can't blame a guy for trying."

"You are trouble with a capital *T*, O'Brien," Valerie said, laughing indulgently.

Skye glanced at Nicole and Valerie as she licked sugar off her bottom lip and raised her glass in a toast. "I say we slip into our swimsuits, enjoy our drinks by the pool, and gossip about the boys."

"Count me in," Nicole agreed, eager to learn more about this intriguing group of people Nathan worked with.

"Me, too," Valerie added as the three of them clinked their glasses together.

They headed inside the house to change, and met back on the patio ten minutes later with Valerie in a modest one-piece with a sarong tied around her waist, Skye in a jaw-dropping two-piece that showcased her amazing curves, and Nicole in a pink-and-white bikini that fell between the two extremes.

From behind the bar, Sean whistled a sexy catcall, drawing the attention of the other guys still playing lawn darts across the yard. The only gaze Nicole noticed was Nathan's, whose stare held a fascinating combination of heat and pure male possession that made her heart beat a little faster beneath her breast.

Sean leaned across the bar. "If any of you ladies need help rubbing suntan lotion on your backs, or anywhere else for that matter, just let me know."

Nicole laughed, and Valerie just lifted her eyes heavenward.

Skye, however, didn't hesitate to put him in his place. "Dream on, O'Brien. Because that's about as close as you're going to get to any of us."

Sean placed a hand over his heart and feigned a wounded look. "You slay me, Skye."

"Someone has to keep you in check," she replied, then turned toward Nicole and Valerie and handed them their drinks again. "Come on, girls. Let's go and enjoy the rest of the afternoon."

The three of them settled on lounge chairs by the pool, and the chatter began in earnest. Skye dominated the conversation with her lively, animated personality. They talked, laughed, and had a great time together, and it didn't take long for Nicole to feel as though she fit right in and had made two new friends.

"So, how did you and Nathan meet?" Valerie finally asked when she was able to get a word in.

Nicole wasn't sure how to answer, considering how unconventional their first encounter had been. "We met at a speed-dating event."

Valerie's brows rose in surprise as she placed her hand on Nicole's arm, as if touching her was necessary at the moment. Then the corner of her mouth lifted in a slow, subtle smile, and those insightful eyes of hers gleamed perceptively.

"Ahhh, so you're *the one,*" she said, and finally pulled her hand away.

There was something about Valerie that made Nicole feel as though the other woman could see much deeper than Nicole was comfortable with. "What do you mean, *the one*?"

"Nathan attended the event as a favor to me," Valerie told her, looking very pleased with herself. "When I asked him how the night went, he told me that he'd met someone, but that it hadn't worked out. *You're* the woman he was talking about."

Nicole's face warmed in embarrassment. "Umm, yeah. That was me. We kind of reconnected." A nice, safe word that didn't give away any details of how they'd *accidentally* run into each other again that night at the art gallery.

"Fate is funny that way, isn't it?" Valerie asked. "Some things are just unavoidable, and I'm glad Nathan found a woman like you. You're exactly what he needs in his life."

Nicole wasn't sure how to respond to that comment, and it appeared that Valerie didn't expect her to. The other woman slipped on a pair of sunglasses and reclined back in her chair. Nicole pondered the odd exchange until Skye launched into a discussion about how some men were able to play hard-to-get better than women . . . referring, of course, to Caleb's ability to resist their very obvious attraction.

The rest of the day passed quickly. What with gabbing with the girls, a game of volleyball in the pool with the guys, and dining on grilled hamburgers, Nicole couldn't remember the last time she'd had such a fun, relaxing day. Friendly ribbing and joking ensued among the boys, with Sean doing his best to deliberately provoke Nathan by playing the part of a philandering ladies' man with Nicole.

There was so much laughter and such positive, cheerful energy flowing, it was a welcome mental and emotional break from all the darkness she'd witnessed at Sloane's club the night before.

And for today, she let herself indulge and revel in the festive environment.

Chapter Thirteen

After such an enjoyable day at Caleb's, Nathan was in no hurry to return to the quiet apartment with Nicole. With only a crescent moon in the clear night sky, he turned the Ferrari onto a deserted back road and steered away from the city toward a long stretch of isolated highway he'd found years ago while driving aimlessly to escape the haunting memory of the case that had gone so horribly wrong.

Tonight, the only thing on his mind was Nicole and how silent she'd become at the end of the evening, while they'd been saying their good-byes to everyone. Up until that point, he knew for certain she'd been having a good time, and he had no idea what had happened to change her mood.

"Hey, are you okay?" he asked, wondering if someone back at the house had said something to make her feel uncomfortable. Hard to imagine after how well she'd connected with the group, but it was a possibility nonetheless.

"I'm good," she said, giving him a smile that didn't

quite reach her eyes. "I had a great time today. Thanks for bringing me along."

"I wanted you there," he said, meaning it.

There was something more going on in that head of hers, and it didn't escape his notice that he was able to read her so well after only a few days together—as though they had an intimate connection that went deeper than physical attraction.

"What are you thinking about that has you so pre-occupied?" he asked.

"How lucky you are to have such wonderful friends."

"They're good people. When we get together, things just click among us."

"I noticed." She rested her head against the back of the seat and sighed softly. "I have to confess that I envy you that close-knit bond you all share. It makes me realize what I don't have."

The wistful note in her voice confused him. "You're close to your family, aren't you?"

"Sure." She stared out the windshield, not questioning where he was taking her, even though they were headed in the opposite direction of the Las Vegas Strip on an isolated road. "I keep in touch with my parents, but I haven't seen them in over a year. With my brother in the military, it's been even longer than that since I've spent time with him."

"But you have friends here in Las Vegas."

"I do, but it's not the same as what you have with your co-workers." She absently smoothed her hands down the skirt of her sundress, then glanced at him, her features softened by the shadows in the car. "There's just something special and unique about your relationship with them. It's hard for me to explain, but it's obvious that you all care for one another very much."

He understood what she was referring to. There was an unconditional acceptance among the members of The Reliance Group, an unspoken trust that went beyond a superficial affiliation or working environment. They all had their own personal issues, some more tragic or scandalous than others, yet there was no judgment because of their imperfect pasts. Within this group, they were equals, and they treated one another as such.

It was difficult to explain.

Instead, he reached across the console and gave her thigh a squeeze. "Well, I know for a fact that they liked you a lot." She'd fit in without effort, as though she'd always been a part of the group.

The smile that appeared this time was genuine. "The feeling is mutual."

"Sean liked you a little too much," he said, still slightly annoyed at the other man's attempts to charm Nicole, even if it was all in fun and meant to bring out Nathan's possessive side.

Which it had.

His comment about Sean made her chuckle. "He's definitely a character."

"Yeah, well, he's damn lucky I trust him so much, or else I would have had to kick his ass for coming on to you throughout the day," he grumbled good-naturedly.

"You're such a tough, macho man," she teased.

He gave her a comical, caveman-type grunt in response, before remembering that there was something he needed to tell her.

"By the way, Caleb found out that Sloane is going

to be at a ribbon-cutting ceremony this week. Sloane donated a substantial amount of money to help build and furnish a new women's shelter," Nathan said, sharing the information Caleb had given him. "I'm going to show up for the ceremony by myself, and make sure he sees me there. We've got to find a legitimate way to get into his estate."

"So, by day the man is an upstanding citizen who comes to the aid of abused women, and by night he's a pedophile. How pleasant," she said, her tone dripping with disgust.

Nathan was equally repulsed by the man's conflicting personalities. But he knew it was Sloane's public image as a humanitarian that served to give the community of Vegas the false perception that he was a charitable man who cared about women's rights.

"You know, I still have that personal invitation from Sloane to see his private art collection," she said, presenting them with another alternative. "It's a guaranteed way of getting me into his estate."

"No." His resolute tone didn't leave any room for an argument. Knowing exactly what Sloane wanted from Nicole, there was no way in hell he was letting her anywhere near the man without him being nearby. "You're not going to Sloane's place alone and unprotected. That's nonnegotiable, remember?"

"Yeah, I remember," she said with a sigh. "Just thought I'd toss it out there for you to consider."

Putting Nicole's life in danger, in any capacity, wasn't an option. "Let's just see what happens at the ribbon-cutting ceremony, and go from there."

Nicole nodded in agreement as she glanced out the side window, then met his gaze in the dim interior of the vehicle, her expression suddenly soft and sultry. The atmosphere in the car shifted, and his body hummed in acute awareness of that provocative look in Nicole's eyes.

All day long there had been an underlying sexual tension simmering between them. In an instant the desire ignited into a full-fledged fire in his belly.

The inside of the Ferrari was small and confined, enabling her to lean across the low console and move intimately closer. She splayed a hand on his upper thigh and skimmed her lips along the side of his neck and up to the shell of his ear.

"Here we are on a pitch-dark, deserted road in a super-fast, hot car," she murmured as her fingers grazed the hard outline of his cock pressing against the front of his jeans. "I'm thinking we ought to take advantage of the moment, don't you?"

He swallowed to ease the dryness in his throat, and dared to ask, "What did you have in mind?" Not that it mattered. When it came to her, he was game for anything.

"How good are you at multitasking?" she asked as she nipped at his lobe, her breath warm and damp in his ear.

Anticipation curled through him as he forced his concentration onto navigating the vast expanse of road in front of them. "Depends on the tasks."

She unbuttoned the top of his jeans, then slowly eased the zipper over the thick bulge of his erection and released his aching shaft, leaving no doubt as to what she intended. "Keep your hands on the steering wheel and your eyes on the road, and I'll do the rest."

He couldn't believe how brazen she was acting, and how badly he wanted what she was about to do.

She unfastened her seat belt, and he curled his fingers tight around the steering wheel as he waited for the pleasure to begin. He inhaled a sharp breath at the first teasing swipe of her tongue across the broad tip, then groaned like a dying man when she took every single hard inch of him deep into her mouth, enveloping him in velvet softness and liquid heat.

His hips instinctively thrust upward, which pressed his cock against the back of her throat. Instead of pulling back, she swallowed around the sensitive head and sucked. The erotic sensation nearly unraveled him, and his foot pressed harder on the accelerator.

Sex and speed mixed together made a heady aphrodisiac, and it was all he could do to hang on for the wild, exhilarating ride.

She continued to take him over and over again, her mouth slick and hot and greedy. Tormenting him with the suctioning swirl of her tongue, she used her hands to stroke his shaft, and his eyes nearly rolled back into his head as she pushed him closer and closer to an explosive climax.

Not certain he could handle such a powerful orgasm while driving, he slowed the Ferrari to a stop in the middle of the dark, abandoned road and killed the engine. She lifted her head, her eyes luminous as she looked up at him, her lips damp and pink, and his cock wet and hard from her talented mouth.

Unable to resist, he tangled his fingers through her hair and brought her mouth to his. The kiss was steamy and passionate. As much as he loved the uninhibited way she'd gone down on him, he wanted to be inside her even more. Judging by the way she was attempting to crawl across the console to get closer, she wanted the same thing.

Taking her inside the Ferrari would have been a wet dream come to life, but it was too cramped, awkward, and impractical to give them both the pleasure they deserved. The seats were narrow, the top of the car low, and her elbows and knees were already jabbing him in uncomfortable places.

He grunted in pain as her hand connected with his rib cage, and he pushed her back to the passenger seat, ignoring the sounds of protest she made.

"Get out of the car," he ordered, and slid out of the driver's side himself. He rounded the front of the vehicle, not bothering to refasten his jeans when he planned to be buried inside her within minutes.

She was standing beside the open door, her hair tousled around her face, watching him approach with a touch of uncertainty. "What are you doing?"

"Improvising." Grabbing her hand, he quickly tugged her toward the back of the car.

Without a soul around for miles, and the only illumination coming from the moon overhead and the interior of the car, the setting was as romantic as he could manage under the circumstances. Not that Nicole ever needed hearts and flowers, but what he was about to deliver was going to be a raw, carnal explosion of unrefined lust.

He couldn't imagine anything hotter than fucking her on the back of a Ferrari. It was every guy's fantasy, and about to become his reality.

Gripping his hands around her waist, he lifted her so that she was sitting on the trunk, her hands propped behind her to keep her upright. He pulled off her sandals so they didn't scratch the paint, then shoved the hem of her dress to her hips and yanked her panties down her legs. Once they were removed, he tucked the scrap of material into the back pocket of his jeans, then braced her heels on the fender and pushed her thighs wide apart, exposing the swollen, weeping folds of her sex to his gaze.

He was so hungry for her, so impatient to feel her clasped tight around his shaft, that spending another second on finesse or foreplay wasn't an option. Wrapping his fingers around his stiff, throbbing cock, he dragged the taut crown though her slick heat, then impaled her with a long, hard thrust that planted him balls-deep inside her.

She tossed her head back with a loud, breathless moan, and he shuddered as her inner muscles pulsed around his shaft. Bending her knees, she locked her legs around his waist and jerked her hips hard against his, seeking a more intense friction and deeper penetration.

His response was instinctive and immediate. He dropped his head to the curve of Nicole's neck and pounded into her, giving her body exactly what it craved, and taking what he needed, too. She trembled with the driving impact of each frenzied stroke, while her hands slid around to the base of his spine and her fingernails dug into his backside in her own show of control and aggression.

He laved her throat with his tongue, then sank his teeth into a tender piece of flesh just below her ear that triggered her orgasm. She bucked wildly against him, her back arching, her hips straining as her mouth fell open on a long, low cry of extreme pleasure.

He watched her face as she came, savoring every moment of her surrender until his own climax slammed into him, forcing the air from his lungs as he ground himself into her, coming so hard it felt as though he'd given her a piece of his soul.

Nicole disconnected the call she'd just received on her cell phone, knowing for a fact that Nathan wasn't going to be happy about her change of plans for the day. While he planned to attend the ribbon-cutting ceremony for the women's shelter in the hope of meeting up with Sloane, she'd agreed to stay at the apartment and wait for him to return. Then they'd discuss their next step in rescuing Angela.

The unexpected call from her editor at *The Las Vegas Commentary* put a major crimp in their agenda.

Releasing a deep breath, she headed toward the master suite and into the adjoining bathroom, where Nathan had just finished taking his shower.

He stood in front of the large mirror above the dual sinks as he shaved, his hair damp and tousled around his head and wearing nothing more than the towel he'd wrapped low on his hips. Water droplets still clung to the smooth slope of his back, and she wondered how he'd react if she licked them off with her tongue.

Despite indulging in lazy morning sex with him only an hour ago, the sight of his half-naked body made her forget the real reason why she'd sought him out. She chewed on her bottom lip, and had to seriously resist the urge to untuck that small knot, let the towel drop to the floor, and have her way with him.

His gaze met hers in the reflection, his smile warm and intimate as he rinsed shaving cream off the razor before lifting it to the left side of his face and ridding himself of the stubble there.

"Don't give me that look," he said, even though his gruff voice was tinged with renewed desire, too. "I don't have time to fool around again."

"I know. I don't have the time, either," she said with a sigh, and leaned against the doorjamb. "It looks like I'm going to be joining you today at the women's shelter."

A frown creased his brows as he swiped the razor beneath the flow of water in the sink. "We agreed that you'd stay here while I go. I want to get Sloane alone so the two of us can talk. He was pretty open about wanting to swap you for one of his girls. I need to work that to our advantage."

She heard the frustration in his tone, but this situation was out of her hands, and his. "I'm really sorry, but I don't have a choice. My editor, Sharon, just called. The person originally scheduled to cover the ceremony came down with food poisoning. It's so last-minute that everyone else has assignments or firm commitments, except me. I need quotes so I can write the article, and a photographer from the magazine will be with me, too, to get some pictures of Sloane while he's cutting the ribbon."

"Shit." Done shaving, he wiped the excess foam from his jaw and neck with a small hand towel, then turned to face her. "Sloane can't see you there as a reporter or our whole cover will be blown."

It was difficult to argue with his logic, but her job was on the line, and she couldn't afford to lose her only source of income. "I've given it some thought, and I think we can make it work."

He looked skeptical as he passed by her into the

bedroom, but she followed and explained. "Sloane has only seen me dressed and made up as a young teenage girl. I can go to the opposite extreme and make myself look completely different and older."

"You look young no matter what you do," he said as he dropped the towel, giving her a glimpse of his tight, muscular butt before he pulled on a pair of boxer briefs. "I don't think it will work."

She believed differently. It was a matter of hairstyle, makeup, and what she chose to wear. "I'll stay at the back of the crowd and I won't make eye contact," she said, still trying to convince him as he finished stepping into a pair of dark brown slacks and shrugged into a long-sleeved shirt. "I know what's at stake here. You're just going to have to trust me on this."

He looped a silk tie around his neck, the grim press of his lips clearly expressing his displeasure over the situation. "Like you said, I don't have a choice. So make damn sure that Sloane won't recognize you."

"I will." By the time she was done with her latest transformation, she was willing to bet Nathan wouldn't be able to easily pick her out of the crowd, either.

Where in the hell was she?

Feeling tense, Nathan scanned the crowd gathered out in front of the beautiful modern building housing the new women's shelter, anxious to find Nicole in the sea of faces so he could keep an eye on her until her job was done. He'd dropped her off at her apartment about an hour ago so she could change and drive her own car, and he hadn't seen her since.

There were many people in attendance, from a multitude of news media, to various politicians who'd helped back the endeavor, to the board of trustees and other supporters of the project. A booklet listed the dignitaries by name and included the mayor, who was currently standing up at the podium commending Preston Sloane for his selfless contribution to the venture, which had made the shelter a possibility.

The mayor's praise was nauseating, considering who and what Sloane really was. But today it was all about Preston and his generous altruism, a perception he worked very hard to cultivate and promote whenever the opportunity arose. And as Sloane sat behind the podium and waited for his turn to speak, on the surface he appeared to be a charitable businessman who cared about today's cause and helping women escape abusive relationships.

A contradiction in every way imaginable, and one that caused Nathan to grind his teeth in revulsion.

Nathan had deliberately declined taking a seat so he could blend in with the overflow of people standing around the stage and move wherever he needed to go. As the guests burst into applause when Sloane took to the microphone to give his speech, Nathan continued his visual search for Nicole, his gaze shifting back to the area in front that had been designated for media.

While Sloane thanked key people for their support and went on to talk about how close this project was to his heart, Nathan scrutinized each female reporter. He overlooked a brunette and a busty redhead, and even a blonde whose face was much too round to be Nicole's. He skimmed past another blonde, his mind automatically discounting the severe upswept hairstyle, dark-rimmed glasses, and navy-blue business suit . . . until she lifted her hand ever so slightly to let him know it was her before returning her attention to the podium.

He did a quick double take, shocked by Nicole's latest metamorphosis that disguised the fresh, youthful appearance he'd grown used to seeing on a daily basis. As his surprise abated and he took in her sophisticated image, recognition set in, enabling him to make out the familiar shape of her face, her expressive eyes, and the confident way she carried herself.

She wasn't in the back as she'd promised, but at least she'd executed a decent job of changing her overall look. She blended in with the rest of the reporters, and that would hopefully be enough to deflect any interest when Sloane passed by.

Sloane went on to enthrall the crowd with his noble pledge to provide a safe haven to homeless and abused women and children, and to promote dignity and self-respect to those who came through the doors of the shelter. Listening to the other man's rehearsed speech with half an ear, Nathan eased over to the media pen. This way he could be close to Nicole and also be in Sloane's path once he exited the stage.

Next up was the ribbon cutting, followed by a closing speech from the mayor to wrap up the ceremony. Nathan waited patiently as Sloane shook hands with important people, then made his way down to where the media were anxious to ask questions and take photos of the businessman who'd made the shelter possible.

That's when Nathan noticed the woman following a few steps behind Sloane, and recognized her from the nightclub. According to Nicole, her name was Gwen and she was Sloane's assistant.

Wearing a pale blue silk blouse tucked into a slim

black skirt and modest heels, she appeared professional, polished, and in control, but it was the subtle longing in her eyes when she glanced at her boss that told Nathan she harbored unrequited feelings toward Sloane. She also seemed very protective of him.

As Sloane neared, the reporters crowded up to the waist-high barrier separating them from the man of the day, shoving Nicole right up front in the process. Nathan caught her startled expression as Sloane looked directly at her, but his gaze didn't linger, nor was there any hint of recognition on his face.

Relief poured through Nathan, and he didn't miss the irony in the older man's reactions, or lack of them. When she was dressed as a real woman and looking more her age, Sloane wasn't interested in Nicole.

She quickly looked away and jotted down notes on her pad as Sloane fielded questions from the media, but it was Gwen who studied Nicole much too intently for Nathan's liking.

Finished with the reporters, Sloane moved on, but Gwen did not. Instead, the assistant stepped up to where Nicole was still standing, prompting Nathan to head in that same direction to distract Gwen if necessary.

Nicole turned away from Gwen to leave, but before she could escape, the other woman grabbed her arm and halted her attempt, forcing her to pivot back around. Nicole remained calm and collected, and even stared at Gwen as though she'd never met the other woman before. A convincing performance, but the whole situation still had Nathan on edge.

He swore beneath his breath and came up behind Gwen just in time to hear her ask Nicole, "Do I know you from somewhere?"

Realizing if he interrupted now he'd likely raise more suspicion, Nathan decided to trust Nicole to handle the confrontation without his help. He knew she'd seen him, but she made no outward reaction that might give his presence away.

Nicole smiled at Gwen, her gaze steady behind the dark frames of her glasses and her facial features convincingly blank. "I don't think so," she said, her voice different than Nathan had ever heard before. Her tone was cool and direct, and a bit raspier, too. "But I'm a reporter, so you might have seen me at other events Mr. Sloane has attended. If you'll excuse me, I need to get to my next appointment."

Nicole's explanation made perfect sense, but as the older woman watched Nicole walk away, her uncertain frown warned Nathan that Gwen was still skeptical.

Disaster averted for now, Nathan lengthened his stride to catch up to Sloane, who was heading toward a black Town Car parked on the curb with a uniformed man holding the back door open for him.

"Preston!" Nathan called out before Sloane could slip inside the vehicle.

The other man turned around, his brows rising in surprise. "Alex. Nice to see you here."

Nathan forced a smile. "I just wanted to stop by and offer my support."

"I appreciate that. I've been meaning to get in touch with you after our chat on Saturday." Sloane checked the gold Rolex watch strapped to his wrist before glancing back at Nathan. "I've got a meeting across town, but if you'd like to join me, we can talk on the way over and then my driver can bring you back for your car."

Nathan wasn't about to pass up the opportunity for more face time with Sloane. "That would be great."

They both settled into the back of the Town Car. Once the driver pulled away from the curb, Sloane pressed a button on the console and a mini wet bar appeared in front of them. He reached for a bottle of Chivas Regal and poured a few inches of the expensive liquor into a short crystal glass.

"Care for a drink?" he asked Nathan.

He shook his head. "No, I'm good. Thanks."

Sloane took a sip of the Scotch, savoring the smooth, rich flavor for a moment before redirecting his attention to Nathan. "Have you thought any more about the discussion we had at Bliss on Saturday night?"

Nathan knew exactly what Sloane was getting at, and he appreciated the man's direct approach since Nathan had no desire to engage in idle chitchat with the man. For Nathan, this was all about business—getting into Sloane's estate and getting Angela out, as quickly and safely as possible.

"Actually, I have given your proposition some thought," Nathan said. He watched as a spark of excitement ignited in Sloane's gaze, and knew it was because of Nicole. With effort, he tamped down the slow burn of anger rising in the back of his throat. "I'm thinking we might be able to come to some kind of agreement, as long as I can find a girl who meets my criteria. I prefer blondes, and none of the girls at the nightclub grabbed my interest."

Sloane finished the rest of the Scotch in one long drink, set the empty glass on the wet bar, then met Nathan's gaze once again. "Tell you what. I'm having a small, intimate get-together at my estate this weekend.

Why don't you come and bring Nikki and we'll see what we can find for you. I'm sure there will be someone there to your liking."

Nathan didn't want to seem overeager and remained quiet long enough to let Sloane believe he was considering the offer. The Town Car slowed, and Nathan had to make a commitment.

"All right," he finally said. "Nikki and I will be there."

"Excellent." Sloane gave him a satisfied smile. "How does Nikki feel about a trade?"

Refusing to think about Sloane touching Nicole, Nathan kept up the pretense of a man who had his woman under his control. "Don't worry about Nikki. She'll do whatever I ask her to."

"That's my kind of girl," Sloane murmured, just as his driver opened the door for him to exit. "I'll have my assistant, Gwen, contact you by cell phone with the address of the estate, and I'll see you and Nikki Friday afternoon."

Sloane stepped from the vehicle, and Nathan waited until the door slammed shut after him before exhaling a deep, tension-filled breath of air.

There were *in* again, and this time they had to make it count.

Chapter Fourteen

Nicole pushed open the glass door leading into the offices of *The Las Vegas Commentary* with her hip, since she held two large vanilla lattes in her hands.

As much as she wasn't looking forward to attending the biweekly, mandatory editorial meeting that morning, she was glad to be out of Nathan's apartment for a few hours. She hated being cooped up so much, and with the two of them heading off to Sloane's estate tomorrow afternoon for what was likely to be a very intense weekend, Nicole welcomed the chance to relax and be herself among co-workers and friends.

She smiled and said a cheerful hello to the receptionist, then made her way through a maze of bland gray partitions until she reached Michelle's small cubicle, which was located right next to Nicole's. While her friend had opted to personalize her little makeshift office with pictures of her fiancé Robert, flowers and knickknacks, Nicole's looked barren in comparison. There was a standard desk and a docking station for her laptop computer, but nothing else to indicate the alcove was anything other than a temporary work space.

For the most part, Nicole preferred to research and write her features outside the main office, and luckily her assignments didn't require she spend a whole lot of time in her cramped cubicle. And in this wonderful day and age of sending in her articles via e-mail attachments, as she'd done with her online dating feature and the commentary on Preston Sloane's involvement with the new women's shelter, she only needed to be present for any required meetings.

Nicole waited for Michelle to finish the call she was on. As soon as she hung up, Nicole stepped forward with her offering. "Hey, girlfriend. I brought you some liquid fortitude for the editorial meeting."

Michelle spun around in her chair, her eyes bright with gratitude. "You are a *goddess*," she said with a grin, and wrapped her fingers around the paper cup before taking a long sip of the sweetened latte.

Closing her eyes, she moaned her pleasure as she savored the coffee drink, and Nicole laughed at her friend's enthusiastic display.

"That's almost as good as sex," Michelle teased, and licked a splotch of foam from her upper lip. "How did you know I desperately needed caffeine this morning?"

Nicole shrugged. "Lucky guess." And she just knew her friend that well. It didn't matter the time of day—Michelle always appreciated a cup of designer coffee.

Michelle set the cup down on her desk, her gaze turning soft and sincere. "I've missed having you around. The apartment is so quiet and lonely without you."

As much as she enjoyed Michelle's friendship, Nicole realized she'd settled into a comfortable routine with Nathan in the short time they'd been living together. *Too* comfortable, if the sudden rapid beating of her heart was any indication.

She'd grown used to having her meals with Nathan, used to sleeping with him throughout the night, and used to their easy conversations, which encompassed a wide variety of topics they sometimes agreed upon, and other times argued about. But even those debates she found stimulating and invigorating because he challenged her intellectually and respected her opinions.

She told herself the familiarity was a result of their proximity, and indulging in the hottest sex of her life on a regular basis was a perk of their agreement. Yet there were times she caught him watching her doing mundane things around the apartment, his gaze so warm and caring she experienced a deep, inexplicable yearning for something more.

At certain times, he made her feel weak—not physically, but emotionally, deep in her heart where it mattered the most. And that realization literally scared the crap out of the strong, independent woman she'd become when she'd sworn she would never allow a man to have that kind of control over her feelings ever again.

Realizing that her mind had traveled down a road better off not traveled, she refocused on Michelle and the discussion they'd been having.

"I thought you and Robert would be taking advantage of the fact that I haven't been at the apartment," Nicole teased, and took a drink of her vanilla latte, which was finally the perfect temperature.

A blush swept over Michelle's cheeks. "Oh, we have, but that doesn't mean I haven't missed you."

"I'll be back before you know it," she said, and immediately dismissed the deep pang in her chest at the thought of leaving Nathan behind. But she would, just as soon as they both finished the job they'd promised to do. "Hopefully after this weekend."

"Really?" Michelle asked, the one word brimming with a wealth of questions she didn't dare voice with so many inquiring ears around.

"We're heading out to the estate tomorrow," Nicole told her, knowing her friend would figure out exactly what that meant.

Michelle stared at her with unmistakable concern in her eyes. "Are you sure you want to do this?"

"Absolutely." Nicole had come this far, and she wasn't going to back out now.

Knowing there was nothing she could say or do to change Nicole's decision, Michelle didn't bother arguing, which Nicole appreciated.

She was ready and willing to do whatever it took to bring Sloane down. She wanted an exposé on Sloane so badly she could taste it, but she also realized that safely retrieving Angela was their main priority. The possibility that Nicole could walk away from all this without a story was a risk she was willing to take if it meant giving even one girl a real future.

Michelle leaned back in her chair and picked up her latte again. "So, how is Tall, Dark, and Handsome?"

Nicole smiled at the nickname her friend had given Nathan. "He's good," she replied nonchalantly, certain she knew where Michelle was heading with her line of questioning.

Michelle regarded Nicole speculatively. Having met Nathan a few times, her good friend insisted there was more than just a sexual spark there.

"Is anything serious going to come of all this between the two of you?" she asked optimistically.

"Of course not," Nicole said, and meant it, but her friend didn't look as convinced. "Look, he's a great guy, and I'm enjoying my time with him. But we have a common goal, and once it's met, we're going our separate ways."

Catching sight of her co-workers heading toward the conference room, Nicole jumped on the excuse to change the subject before Michelle could grill her further. "Looks like the meeting is getting ready to start. We'd better head that way ourselves."

Michelle smirked, seeing right through Nicole's attempt to put an end to the discussion. "You've always been good at avoiding conversations about your love life."

"It's a honed skill," Nicole said, only half kidding. "Besides, love has nothing to do with Nathan and me."

"Too bad." Michelle sounded genuinely disappointed as she stood up and grabbed a file folder from her desk. "He seems like a really good match for you."

Yeah, he was an amazing guy, but Nicole wasn't such a great catch. She was smart enough to face the fact that she carried around a lot of emotional baggage, and she was better off committing to her work than a man.

Together, they walked to the conference room, then took a seat next to each other as the chairs around the large table quickly filled up with co-workers. Finally, Sharon entered and took her place at the head of the table, and the editorial meeting began.

The group gave their input on artwork for a future issue of the magazine, and suggestions for different and unique columns to add to the periodical were tossed out for consideration. Contributing writers were assigned topics to cover for upcoming features, and Nicole was less than thrilled when Sharon enthusiastically informed her that her next two articles would entail a "Date My Friend" party, and a "Dating in the Dark" meet-and-mingle.

Everyone seemed excited to start their next project, except Nicole. As the meeting came to an end and her co-workers filtered out of the conference room, anxious to get a jump-start on all their exciting new features and stories, Nicole found it difficult to drum up even an ounce of enthusiasm for her next two assignments. Instead, she felt an overwhelming sense of dread at the thought of spending the next few weeks researching, and writing about, yet more dating trends.

Everything about the meeting reinforced her decision to start looking for a new job. It was a choice she had to make in order to save her sanity. The fluff pieces were stifling her as a journalist, and didn't give her any kind of mental challenge or creative outlet. She wanted, *needed,* to write stimulating stories and features that inspired people or provided controversy to make them think.

That had always been her goal, and with the *Commentary* focusing more on entertainment, style, and escapism, she was feeling more and more boxed in as a writer. Starting over as low man on the totem pole somewhere new didn't hold a lot of appeal, but life was too short to stay with a job she was coming to hate.

Maybe it was time to really shake up the direction of

her career and move to a bigger city with bigger opportunities. Unfortunately, all she had to her credit was a portfolio of light, frivolous articles and features that most editors at major-league publications would be less than impressed with.

The room was empty except for her and Sharon, and with a tired sigh Nicole gathered her day planner of notes and stood, resigned to writing the next couple of dating articles until she had the chance to put together a strong résumé and a better offer came along.

Sharon stood, too, smiling at Nicole. "I've been meaning to tell you, good job on the feature you wrote on Preston Sloane and the women's shelter. I know it was a last-minute assignment, but I appreciate you stepping in and covering the piece."

"It's my job." Despite loathing the man and everything he stood for, one of the first rules she'd learned when it came to writing for *The Las Vegas Commentary* was to keep her personal feelings out of the stories she wrote. It was all about facts, entertainment, and feel-good features. No one who picked up the *Commentary* wanted to read about a pedophile.

Still, she hated the pretty lies and false perceptions she'd been forced to write about Sloane and his do-good deed with the women's shelter.

Suppressing her resentment and anger, she turned away from Sharon and headed for the door. "Though how we can print such glorified crap about a man who is the epitome of scum is beyond me," she muttered beneath her breath.

"Excuse me?" Sharon asked sharply.

Nicole came to an abrupt stop and squeezed her eyes closed in frustration, knowing she'd overstepped boundaries she never should have crossed at work. The hostile words had just slipped out of her mouth uncensored, and even though she knew she shouldn't have said anything derogatory, she wasn't about to apologize for the truth.

She faced Sharon, who'd crossed her arms over her breasts and looked none too happy about Nicole's disparaging comment.

Well, tough shit, Nicole thought. She wasn't about to sugarcoat her feelings about the situation, or Sloane, even if it meant getting her walking papers for speaking her mind. There were some things she refused to compromise, and one was her integrity.

"I wrote that feature on Sloane and his contribution to the women's shelter because I didn't have a choice," she stated without apology. "As a journalist, I know I have to be unbiased on whatever subject I'm writing about, despite my own personal opinions and feelings, and that's exactly what I did with Sloane. But it literally made me sick to glorify what he wants everyone to believe was an altruistic, compassionate gesture toward abused women when that's exactly what *he* does. The man is a hypocrite when it comes to promoting his public perception, and I hate that I had to support his duplicity."

Sharon's gaze widened in shock at Nicole's outspoken condemnation of Preston Sloane. "You don't know any of that for a fact," she replied carefully.

Oh, but she did. Nicole had up-close, personal, heartbreaking knowledge of Sloane's operations. As much as she wanted to enlighten Sharon, she didn't dare. Not only did she not want her editor to know what she was doing on the side, but Nicole wasn't about to jeopardize Nathan's case in any way.

Still, she wasn't willing to let the subject die just yet. "Can you honestly say you haven't heard rumblings about his preference for underage girls?"

"I won't confirm or deny anything, and it's not your job to go digging in that direction, either," Sharon warned, and ended the discussion by walking out of the conference room.

No, it wasn't Nicole's place to dig into such a controversial story as an entertainment writer for *The Las Vegas Commentary*. But what she did on her own private time was her own business. Someone had to help those girls who'd succumbed to Sloane's promises of affection and material possessions, and Nicole was committed to doing whatever it took to rescue Angela this weekend, and to save any other girl who wanted out.

He'd promised to protect her. He'd promised to make sure she was safe and guarded. And she died. Murdered. Her senseless death was all because he'd failed to shield her from the evil stalking her, waiting for the chance to end her life before she could testify.

With a strangled gasp, Nathan shot upright in bed, his body damp with sweat and his heart pounding hard and fast in his chest. He forced the haunting images from his mind, but the awful sense of grief and failure remained, and he feared it always would.

"Nathan?" Nicole stirred on the bed beside him, her sleepy voice tinged with concern. "What's wrong?"

"Nothing," he lied, his throat raspy and raw. "I'm fine. Go back to sleep."

Knowing any chance of rest would elude him after that rude awakening, Nathan got out of bed, pulled on a pair of sweatpants, and headed into the living room so he didn't disturb Nicole by tossing and turning for the rest of the night.

Standing at the floor-to-ceiling window overlooking the bright lights of the Strip, he splayed his hand on the cool pane of glass and exhaled a soul-deep sigh that did nothing to ease his guilt. The pain of the past still sliced deep, and with the pressure of getting Angela out of Sloane's estate this weekend messing with his psyche, was it any wonder the nightmares had returned?

He curled his hand into a fist and cursed Caleb for giving him this case, for forcing him to relive his past and the mistakes he'd made that had cost a young girl her life. Yet despite Caleb's tough-love approach, Nathan was committed to doing the job, and this time making damn sure no one got hurt in the process. There was no way he'd be able to face Angela's father if anything happened to her. He was determined to reunite Angela with her family, and give her back her life. Give her a future.

"Nathan? What's going on?"

Nicole's soft, caring voice drifted from behind him, and when her fingertips lightly touched his tense back he instinctively flinched away. He immediately regretted the harsh reaction, and when he turned around to face her he hated that he'd been the one to put that hurt look in her eyes.

"I'm sorry," he said gruffly, and noticed that she'd put on one of his gray T-shirts, which looked exceptionally good on her. "I just have a lot on my mind."

"Like what?" she persisted.

He shook his head. "Nothing you need to worry about."

She pursed her lips in annoyance, his dismissive

words seemingly making her more determined to discover what had driven him from their bed in the middle of the night. "I can't just go back to sleep when I know something's wrong," she said, searching his gaze for answers.

He looked away. "Just leave it alone," he said, even though he knew the inquisitive reporter in her wouldn't drop the subject so easily. She sensed a story, and uncovering it was second nature to her.

And he knew she was damn good at her job.

"It's this case, isn't it?" she asked, her voice firm with conviction as she managed to home in on what was weighing so heavily on his mind. "It's personal for you, just as it is for me. I've sensed that from the very beginning. What I'd like to know is how and why?"

"It's ugly," he said, as if that could scare her into backing off.

She crossed her arms over her chest and held her ground. "Everything about this case is ugly and repulsive and horrifying. But right now we're partners, and I'm not some fragile woman who can't handle the truth. There's nothing you could tell me that would shock me, or make me think any differently of the man you are."

He wasn't so sure. Hadn't one woman turned her back on him when he'd needed her support the most? Then again, he knew deep in his gut that Nicole was the complete opposite of Jill, in every way that mattered. Her strength. Her fortitude. Her ability to be vulnerable, yet courageous enough to stand up for what she believed in.

She settled on the cushion next to his. "Why is this case so important to you?" she asked, her tone much softer now.

He could have denied everything, but he couldn't bring

himself to lie to her. She deserved to know the truth about him, and if he was honest with himself, he no longer wanted to carry the burden of his past alone. And trusting Nicole came easily, because he knew she'd never betray his confidence.

He looked at her. The living room was dark, but the glow from the lights of the city gave him just enough illumination to see the caring in her expression, the need to understand what drove him, and a tenderness that affirmed the undeniable connection between them.

"This is my chance to right a wrong," he said, his voice filled with so much pain it hurt to speak. "During my last undercover assignment as a vice cop, I was sent in with a few other guys in my department to infiltrate a prostitution ring. We were to gather enough evidence to bring down the leader, Paulo Rodriguez, and break up the organization. It took months to work my way in, and what I saw during that time turned my stomach. The young girls, the drugs and abuse, the sex trafficking. It was beyond anything I could have imagined."

He dragged a hand down the side of his face and along the taut set of his jaw before continuing. "A lot of the victims were runaways, but others had been either lured in with promises of modeling careers and money, or just abducted right off the streets."

Nicole pressed her fingers to her lips, her eyes wide as she listened to the shocking reality of what he'd witnessed.

He skipped over the more gruesome details of his assignment, because it wasn't something Nicole needed to hear, and it wasn't something he wanted to relive, either, even in his mind. "While I was undercover, I came in contact with a seventeen-year-old girl named

Katie who'd been given to me by Paulo. Katie never could understand why we just talked whenever we were together, but after a while she came to trust me. I learned that she'd once been one of Sloane's girls, until he decided she was too old for him and turned her out on the street. That's when Paulo picked her up. Because Katie didn't think she had anywhere else to go, and she was too ashamed to contact her family for help, she got sucked into a much harsher life of street prostitution."

"Oh, God," Nicole breathed. Tears shimmered in her eyes, and she looked completely devastated by Katie's troubled circumstances, along with the fact that Sloane had been the one to set Katie's tragic future into motion.

"Over time, she supplied me with a lot of information that helped to take down Rodriguez and his organization," he went on. "When vice finally had enough evidence to arrest him, they raided his place just outside Vegas and busted him for prostitution, pandering, sex trafficking, and other drug-related charges. They took the underage girls into custody and released them back to their parents, but the DA needed Katie's testimony to ensure that the charges against Rodriguez held and he was given a maximum sentence."

He dragged in a deep breath, the air burning his lungs like acid. He didn't want to go on, didn't want to revive those awful memories, but now he realized it was a matter of purging himself of years of guilt and grief. He needed the poison out of his system so hopefully he could move on and heal.

He stared at the hands he'd clasped between his wide-spread thighs, remembering the details all too well.

"Katie was so beat up physically, and so scared of Rodriguez, that she initially refused to testify. She kept saying that Paulo would kill her, even though he was behind bars. After promising her that she would be kept safe and secure before the court date, and would go into witness protection afterward, she finally agreed to be a witness for the prosecution."

"What happened?" Nicole asked, and Nathan heard the reluctance in her voice, as if she knew his story didn't have a happy ending, but needed to hear it anyway.

"She was kept at a safe house. The day she was scheduled to testify she was escorted to the courthouse by uniformed policemen," he said, feeling his throat close up with a wealth of emotion he couldn't hold back, no matter how hard he tried. "Just as she reached the doors, Paulo's brother, José, shot her in the head. He killed her so she couldn't testify against Rodriguez. The officers returned fire and killed José, but the bastard died for his brother and sent a pretty strong message to anyone else who might have thought about testifying."

He shoved both hands through his hair, the renewed fury rushing through his veins so strongly he wanted to punch something to relieve his rage.

But then Nicole touched him, her fingers gently curling around his forearm in a show of tenderness and support, calming him. "You couldn't have known what would happen."

"I royally fucked up." He finally looked at Nicole, and was shocked to see the trail of tears down her cheek. She felt his pain, and Katie's, and it made him realize that he'd made the right choice by confiding in her. "I should have protected her better, and instead she was murdered in cold blood. She's dead, and Paulo was acquitted. The bastard walked. The injustice of it was enough to send me into a downhill spiral of self-destruction."

Those dark, depressing days after Katie's death had nearly destroyed him. "I couldn't handle the guilt, and my fiancée at the time, Jill, couldn't deal with my dark moods. I drank to dull the pain."

Or rather, she hadn't even tried to understand. She'd never offered him the comfort and support he'd so badly needed, which had made his downfall even worse. Looking back, he knew her leaving was for the best, that she wasn't the kind of woman he required in his life for the long haul. But at the time, her walking out on him when he'd needed her the most had only added to his pain.

He shifted restlessly beside Nicole, feeling her gaze on him, and sensing her patience and compassion. "I quit the force, because I felt as though the system had let me, and Katie, down. I finally got my shit together and cleaned up my act, and when Caleb hired me on as a surveillance supervisor for The Onyx, I was grateful for a second chance, and a job that didn't put people's lives in danger. Then Caleb recruited me for The Reliance Group because of my skills as a vice cop, and I actually enjoyed the occasional cases that came my way."

"Until now?" she guessed.

"Yeah, until now." He shook his head. "I never wanted to be responsible for another person's life ever again. And now here I am, about to head right back into a similar situation that has the potential of being life-threatening. Caleb knew exactly what he was doing when he assigned me this case. The connection between Katie and Sloane, and the similarities to Angela's situation, are crystal clear."

Nicole smiled, her earlier sadness over Katie's story diminishing. "Caleb's a good man, and he wouldn't give you something he didn't think you couldn't handle."

He hoped to God she was right, because there was no way he could live with another black mark on his conscience. This was his chance at redemption, and he desperately needed something good to come of this case so he could finally put the past behind him and move on.

Coming up on her knees beside him, she framed his face between her cool hands, her eyes locking on his. "Life is rarely perfect, and it's certainly not scripted, which makes things difficult at times. But we're going to get Angela safely out of there," she said, her voice filled with conviction. "She deserves a second chance, and we're going to give it to her."

He believed her. How could he not?

Goddamn. *He loved her*—this woman who wore a tough exterior, but was so soft and vulnerable inside. This woman who gave so much of herself, yet kept her emotions guarded and protected so she, too, wouldn't have her heart trampled all over again. But causing her any kind of pain was the very last thing he ever wanted to do to her.

Love her, yes.

Hurt her, never.

Leaning forward, he settled his lips over hers and kissed her with softness and gratitude for everything she'd given him tonight. Her mouth was warm and sweet and so generous, pulling him in, offering him everything he'd ever wanted. Everything he needed. And in return, he ached to give her a slow, soft seduction that promised to last a lifetime. If she was willing to give them a chance.

He skimmed his hands beneath the loose T-shirt she was wearing and broke their kiss just long enough to draw the top over her head and toss it to the floor before his mouth found hers again. In between lush, soul-deep kisses, he removed her silky panties, along with his sweatpants. Then he gently pressed her back into the plush sofa cushions, his hands reverent as they traced her sweet curves, his fingers devoted to her pleasure as they caressed her sensitive breasts and, farther down, teased and stroked between her smooth, sleek thighs until she was begging him to take her, to ease the slow burning need building inside her.

She sighed blissfully when he finally shifted between her legs, and in a leisurely thrust filled her up. A low, ragged moan escaped her when he pulled her legs high around his waist and sank deeper, losing himself in her heat, the tight clasp of her sex, and the very essence of what made her so sweet and feminine.

In time, he felt her body quicken beneath his, heard the telltale hitch in her breathing, and recognized the arousing signs he'd learned so quickly, and so well. Lifting his head, he stared into her smoky blue eyes and held her gaze, watching as the wild desire softened with genuine emotion just before her lashes fluttered closed and she whispered his name like a litany, over and over, as she lost herself in a shuddering orgasm.

Exhilarated and hopeful, he gave himself over to his own climax—the hot rush of release, and the knowledge that this woman owned his heart and the deepest part of his soul.

Chapter Fifteen

The pressure was on.

As Nathan drove his newly acquired, slate-gray Hummer H2 past the massive iron gates protecting Sloane's estate, he could feel the tension in the car heighten. A quick glance at Nicole sitting in the passenger seat told him she was feeling just as anxious. She'd been quiet on the ride out to Summerlin, and her pensive expression wasn't how he wanted her to greet Preston.

"Take a deep breath and relax, sweetheart," he said just as a long, sprawling mansion came into view. "We're almost there and you need to shake off the nerves."

Right before his eyes, that serious frown on her face disappeared and the rigid set to her shoulders eased. "What nerves?" she asked, flashing him a bright, believable smile.

"Good girl," he murmured, satisfied that she once again looked like the young, carefree girl Sloane expected to see when they arrived.

Outwardly, she'd done an excellent job of hiding any trace of apprehension she might have been feeling. But past experience as an undercover cop had taught him that deep in your gut, there was no way to completely escape the stress that was your constant companion. Knowing you were playing a very risky game with equally dangerous criminals, you were constantly on guard, your level of awareness increased tenfold. All it took was one false move and suspicions were raised, and weeks of building a credible pretense were flushed down the toilet.

They both knew how much was at stake, and like actors getting ready to put on a performance, they'd discussed their roles and spent the day preparing for the weekend and all the possible scenarios that could come up in their attempt to find and rescue Angela. The good, the bad, and the ugly.

Nathan pulled around the circular drive, and as soon as they stopped, a valet opened Nicole's door and offered his hand to help her out of the high vehicle. Then he retrieved their overnight bags from the back and promised to deliver them to whatever room they'd been assigned.

Knowing he needed a sturdy vehicle with more space than the Ferrari in order to get Angela out undetected when the time came, Nathan had traded the sports car for the high-dollar Hummer. It wouldn't come as a surprise to Sloane that the wealthy entrepreneur Alex Keller had more than one vehicle, and the SUV, with its spacious backseats and black-tinted windows, was the perfect distraction.

"Make sure you don't block the Hummer in any way when you park it." Nathan handed the young man a twenty-dollar bill along with the keys. He wanted to make sure he had easy access to the vehicle at all times, and even had a spare key in his wallet just in case the need arose.

The guy pocketed the cash and grinned. "Sure thing."

Tucking Nicole's hand in his, he gave her a reassuring smile and led the way through a courtyard to the front doors of the massive house. They passed a huge, extravagant water fountain with a bronze sculpture of a young girl with two braids, bare from the waist up, pouring water into the first tier of the basin. Throughout the floral gardens surrounding the walkway were smaller statues of naked wood nymphs peeking through the lush foliage.

Nathan exchanged a quick can-you-believe-this-shit look with Nicole before ringing the doorbell. Less than a minute later they were greeted by Sloane himself, dressed casually in a crisp pair of jeans and a polo shirt.

"Alex and Nikki!" he said, sounding pleased to see them. Or at least he was happy to see Nicole, considering that was where the older man's gaze lingered as he took in her soft, loose blond curls, pink minidress, and slender bare legs.

"You look very pretty, as always," Sloane complimented her, his voice low and intimate.

"Thank you," she replied demurely.

Beside Nathan, Nicole remained calm, despite Sloane's blatant visual inspection and approval. She offered the older man a sweet, captivating smile that seemed to mesmerize him even more, and that's when Nathan decided he'd had enough of Sloane's ogling for now.

"Good to see you again, Preston," Nathan said, forcing Sloane's gaze back to him.

As if realizing he wasn't alone with Nicole, the other

man came back to his senses, opened the door wider, and waved his hand inside. "You, too, Keller. Come in, come in."

They entered the huge foyer set with marble flooring. In front of them, a sweeping staircase led to a second-floor landing. A crystal chandelier hung overhead and rare artwork and antiques were displayed throughout the area, adding to the excessive opulence that seemed to be everywhere Nathan looked.

"Amazing place you have here," Nathan said.

"There's so much more for you to see." Sloane stepped up to Nicole, grasped her hand, and tucked it into the crook of his arm. "How about I give the two of you a quick tour of the place?" While his question addressed both of them, Sloane's gaze didn't waver from Nicole's face.

"I'd like that," she said with a nod.

Keeping Nicole's hand secured on his arm, Sloane escorted her into an adjoining room, with Nathan following behind. Under normal circumstances, he would have been more than a little annoyed at feeling like a third wheel, but having Sloane's attention engaged solely on Nicole worked to Nathan's advantage. It gave him the chance to take in the layout of the house and commit as much as he could to memory.

Strolling from room to room, Nathan saw no one but hired staff dressed in black-and-white uniforms, busy preparing for the guests arriving for the weekend. None of the young girls he'd seen at the nightclub were present, but Nathan knew that they were most likely living in one of the three guesthouses that were also on the property.

Sloane pointed out the huge living room where they

would meet later for drinks and a dinner buffet, then the three of them took an elevator down to the lower level of the house to what Sloane fondly referred to as his "playroom." The lighting was dim, but there was no mistaking the provocative vibe of the room, which reminded Nathan of the decor and setting at Sloane's nightclub.

Another flight of stairs led to an indoor/outdoor pool, reminiscent of the Playboy Mansion grotto with caves, waterfalls, hot tubs, and passageways. As they continued to tour more of the house and its amenities, Nathan watched as Sloane poured on the charm with Nicole. The man was suave and debonair, and knew exactly what to say and do to flatter a girl. His touches were light but intimate, leaving no doubt that he was asserting his interest in Nicole and attempting to make her comfortable with his subtle caresses.

Nicole played along, executing a believable wide-eyed innocence and awe that seemed to captivate Sloane.

A good forty minutes later, and none too soon for Nathan, Sloane steered them toward another wing of the house where the guest suites were located and presented them with their room for the weekend.

"The only place I didn't show you was my art gallery," Sloane said to Nicole. "We'll save that surprise for later this evening." He finally released Nicole's hand, but it was obvious to Nathan that the other man was reluctant to part company with her.

Sloane glanced at Nathan. "I'm expecting a few more guests to arrive, but the two of you can relax and freshen up before tonight's get-together. Drinks are at six, followed by dinner, then a night of entertainment. I'll see you then."

There was no question in Nathan's mind what Sloane meant by "entertainment." He'd seen the playroom and the grotto, and most likely that was where the festivities would transition to after dinner. Hopefully, Angela would be there, and Nathan and Nicole could execute the next step in their plan.

Sloane left them alone, and as soon as Nathan closed the door to the suite, he watched Nicole's teenage facade drop away and disgust fill her eyes. She opened her mouth to speak, and Nathan immediately pressed his fingers against her lips and gave his head a hard shake, reminding her what they'd discussed earlier back at his place.

Within the walls of Sloane's estate, they wouldn't talk about anything regarding the case. There was too much of a chance for someone to overhear, and he honestly didn't trust Sloane not to use surveillance devices to keep an eye, and ear, out for what they said or did.

Nicole chose a dark blue lace slip dress with thin spaghetti straps to wear for the evening. She curled her hair, put on a light application of makeup, and swiped shimmering gloss across her lips. Satisfied with her youthful appearance, she headed back into the adjoining bedroom where Nathan was waiting for her.

Wearing black slacks and a white dress shirt, he looked masculine and sexy. For a brief moment she wished they were someplace else entirely, instead of playing dress-up for her to entice Sloane, and for Nathan to express interest in Angela.

They gave each other a quiet look of understanding, then made their way downstairs to the cocktail party. Hand in hand, they walked into the spacious living room where the male guests were already gathered, along with a few young girls who were mingling with the men in the intimate setting.

Curious glances were cast their way, and a few of the girls eyed Nathan with brazen interest, but he didn't so much as give them a second glance—much to their disappointment.

As Nathan led her to a bar set up in the corner of the room, Nicole noticed a couple of the girls from the nightclub, and others she didn't recognize. With the provocative way most of them were dressed, they appeared of legal age, but she knew just how deceiving an outward appearance could be and suspected that most of the girls were minors.

She scanned the room for Holly and anyone resembling the photograph Nathan had of Angela, but didn't see either. The night was still young, though, and Nicole hoped before the evening was over they'd see both girls.

"What can I get the two of you to drink?" the bartender asked.

"I'll take a Johnnie Walker Black on the rocks, and she'll have a piña colada," Nathan said.

The bartender smirked at her frothy choice of beverage, but Nicole was grateful that Nathan had ordered her something light and fruity—definitely a young girl's type of drink with minimal alcohol involved. While hard liquor seemed to be flowing freely, she wasn't about to dull her senses when she needed all her wits about her tonight.

Unfortunately, when she took a sip of her piña colada, she nearly choked on the amount of rum the bartender had added, to the point that she couldn't taste much else. She winced as the liquid burned its way down her throat, and she wouldn't have been surprised to learn that he'd been specifically instructed to kick up the volume of alcohol in the drinks to loosen everyone's inhibitions.

Especially the girls'.

As Nathan led Nicole away from the bar, he glanced at her in concern. "Are you okay?"

She managed a nod and blinked back tears. "This drink started a fire in my belly," she said beneath her breath. "I'll just pretend to sip it until I can discreetly get rid of it somewhere."

"Good idea," he agreed. "By the way, Gwen is in the room, so try to keep your contact with her to a minimum."

Crap. She hadn't expected Gwen to be there.

After their encounter at the ribbon-cutting ceremony, Nicole couldn't risk Sloane's assistant recognizing her, even if Nicole did look completely different from her reporter persona. So, while the other woman made sure everything was running smoothly and the girls kept the male guests happy, Nicole kept her distance and her gaze averted.

Fifteen minutes later, Sloane entered the room, fashionably late, with Holly trailing by his side like an obedient puppy following its master. She was wearing a black halter-style dress that was cut much too low in the front, her expression teeming with desperate adoration as she looked up at Sloane, who appeared completely indifferent to her painfully obvious infatuation.

Sloane greeted a few of the other men nearby, then took Holly by the hand and pulled her forward—not to establish her as his girlfriend, but to introduce her to one of the gentlemen in the group who was staring at her with lust in his eyes. Holly tried to take a reluctant step back, but Sloane's grip on her arm didn't waver.

He bent and said something in her ear that instantly turned her submissive. With one last look of longing at Sloane, Holly allowed the other gentleman to tuck her arm in his and followed him to a couch in a secluded corner of the room so the two of them could be alone.

Without thinking and acting purely on instinct, Nicole started after Holly, and it was Nathan who brought her to an abrupt halt.

"Let it go," he murmured, his tone low but firm. "I know it's difficult to watch, but that's not what we're here for and you don't want to draw Gwen's attention."

Oh, God, she knew he was right and was grateful that he'd snapped some sense back into her. She understood that she couldn't save every girl in this house, but there was something about Holly that made her feel like a protective older sister. It was difficult to watch her self-destruct while Sloane couldn't care less and had no qualms about passing her off to another man.

"Come on, let's mingle," Nathan said, and led her in the opposite direction of where Holly had gone.

They spent the next half hour getting acquainted with the depraved men who'd been invited to Sloane's weekend soiree. From a distance, between playing the part of Nathan's young girlfriend, Nicole continued to watch Holly as she consumed a few martinis, popped some pills, and half smiled at the man who'd pulled her onto his lap and was slipping his hand beneath the short hem of her dress. Holly appeared too wasted to care that she was about to be sexually assaulted.

Unable to stomach the disturbing sight, she turned

away and set her still-full drink on a passing tray holding dozens of other glasses just as dinner was announced. Everyone headed into the dining room and chose their meal from an elaborate buffet spread that Nicole normally would have enjoyed. Tonight, she had no appetite, but forced herself to take some of the fruit and chicken to keep up her energy.

She and Nathan sat down at the far end of the long table, and before the chairs around them could fill up, Sloane came up to them with a petite blonde on his arm. With her hair falling halfway down her back in soft spiral curls, and wearing a pink baby-doll dress, she looked very sweet and much too naive. Her brown eyes were glassy, her body language lethargic, indicating she was either drugged or inebriated, or both.

"Nathan, this is Lisa," Sloane said as he pulled out the vacant chair next to Nathan for the girl to take a seat. "She saw you in the other room and is quite taken with you. I thought the two of you might like to get to know each other better."

"It's a pleasure to meet you, Lisa," Nathan said, and did as Sloane expected and turned his gaze to the young girl.

Clearly, Sloane was anxious to find a girl to Nathan's liking in exchange for Nicole.

Sloane slid into the chair next to Nicole; one of the hired staff set a plate of food in front of him, and delivered one for Lisa, too. He instructed the waiter to pour them each a glass of wine, then he picked his up by the crystal stem and tilted it toward Nicole in a toast. She touched her glass to his and forced a smile.

He looked into her eyes, and she nearly jumped out of her skin when he splayed a hand on her thigh beneath the table and gave it a squeeze. "To an unforgettable weekend."

Her belly lurched at the insinuation in his tone, and unable to find anything witty to say in response, she gave him a nod and sipped her wine. She also very subtly shifted closer to Nathan, and Sloane took the hint and removed his hand from her leg. For now. Unfortunately, her show of modesty seemed to fascinate him, and she had a feeling the man liked a challenge when it came to seducing a girl.

"So, are you having a nice evening so far?" Sloane asked as he cut into his prime rib.

"Yes, I am." With Lisa doing her best to flirt with Nathan and keep his attention on her, Nicole had no choice but to converse with Sloane. She and Nathan had yet to see anyone who resembled Angela, and until they learned where she was, they had no choice but to play Sloane's game his way.

"Good. It's important to me that all my guests are happy, so if there's anything at all you want or need, you only have to ask," he said, his gaze warm and indulgent. "Also, I don't believe I told you and Nathan, but tomorrow night is a masquerade theme, which makes the parties more interesting and fun. I'll have outfits and masks delivered to your room tomorrow afternoon."

She infused a believable amount of excitement into her expression. "I've never been to a real masquerade party before. Will it be like that Mardi Gras parade they have at the Rio?" she said, referring to the Vegas hotel that was well known for its carnival production.

He chuckled at her guileless enthusiasm. "Yes, it's just like that, but so much better here at my place since all of us are a part of the Mardi Gras experience." He winked at her.

Dinner couldn't end quickly enough for Nicole, and as soon as everyone finished eating, Sloane announced that the entertainment would commence in the play-room downstairs. The guests filtered out of the dining room, and Nicole trailed behind with Nathan, not in any big hurry to be in the midst of such vile debauchery.

They were among the last to arrive, and already guests were pairing up with one or two of the girls and heading off to private rooms, the grotto, or hanging out in the main bar area. Out of the corner of her eye, Nicole saw Holly disappear by herself into the restroom she'd seen during the tour Sloane had given them earlier. Since this was most likely her only chance to talk to Holly privately, she decided to take advantage of the opportunity.

"I need to use the restroom," Nicole told Nathan, and deliberately left out the part about her plan to have a little one-on-one time with Holly. "I'll be back in a few minutes."

She headed across the room and slipped into the women's lounge, where a few of the young girls were fussing with their hair and makeup. Because she was a new face in the crowd, they eyed her curiously, but didn't say anything as she walked over to the closed door marked WOMEN and knocked.

There was no answer, but Nicole knew the girl was inside. "Holly?" she said through the door as she knocked again, more insistently this time. "It's Nikki."

"Go away," Holly said, and sniffled.

Nicole closed her eyes for a moment. The despondent note to the young girl's voice nearly broke her heart.

The need to talk to her, to make sure she was okay, made her more persistent. "Let me in, Holly. Please?"

"No."

Nicole sighed but refused to give up. "I'm not going away until you do. If I have to, I'll wait right here until you open the door to leave." The girl had to come out sometime.

Much to Nicole's relief, less than a minute later the locked unlatched and the door opened a few inches. Nicole took it as an invitation to enter and quickly stepped inside, then rebolted the lock behind her so they weren't interrupted.

Her first thought was that Holly looked a wreck, physically and emotionally. Her puffy, red eyes revealed she'd been crying, and her makeup was smudged from wiping away her tears. Her eyes were filled with such hopelessness that Nicole had to resist the urge to reach out and take the young girl into her arms for a comforting hug.

Holly's chin lifted in a show of belligerence. The small, diamond heart pendant glittered from the hollow of her throat, a stark reminder of who she belonged to. "What do you want?"

"Are you okay?" Nicole asked, and leaned back against the closed door.

The other girl crossed her arms over her chest and narrowed her gaze. "Why do you care how I am?"

Holly was back to being the hostile girl Nicole had initially met back at the nightclub. Remembering how she'd been able to reach past those defensive barriers, she attempted to do so again now. "Because I think you could use a friend."

She scoffed at that. "And you think you can be that

friend? You're the one that Preston wants," she added bitterly. "If anything, you're the enemy!"

"I swear I'm not," Nicole said, trying to convince her, and at the same time striving to establish some kind of trust between them. "I don't want Preston."

"Whatever Preston wants, he gets." Holly turned back to the vanity mirror and tried to repair her smeared makeup with her compact.

Not this time, Nicole wanted to say, but couldn't.

Holly dropped the compact back into her purse and met Nicole's gaze in the reflection. "Sloane told me I'm his favorite, and that's why he likes to share me," she said, her unsteady voice not holding as much conviction as it should have, as if Holly had her own doubts but was too terrified to speak them out loud.

God, how Nicole understood how the other girl felt. Hadn't Mark used the same tactics on her to persuade Nicole to engage in a threesome with a virtual stranger? The similarities made her feel nauseous.

"Right now, I'm entertaining one of his friends, and when Preston sees how good I'm being, he'll take me back and not want to share me anymore."

Nicole had to forcibly swallow back her anger at the situation. "Are you sure about that, Holly?"

The young girl's eyes flashed with irritation before she looked away and began digging through her purse. "I *know* he will. I just need a few of my pills to get me through the rest of the night."

Nicole's stomach roiled as she watched Holly shake two white tablets from a small container. "Getting wasted isn't the answer," she said, speaking from her own experience.

Holly clutched the pills in her fist. "I *need* them."

"What are you taking?" Nicole was not only curious, but concerned about what the girl was ingesting.

"I don't know and I don't care." Despair etched Holly's features, and her bottom lip quivered. "Gwen gave them to me to take and they make me feel relaxed and calm. Taking the pills is the only way I can bring myself to let anyone other than Sloane touch me. They make me forget things I don't want to remember."

"It's only a temporary fix, Holly." Nicole took a small step toward the girl, then another. "In the morning, nothing will have changed."

"You don't understand!" Her voice rose in anger, and she popped the pills before Nicole could stop her, then scooped up water with her hands from the sink faucet to wash them down.

Nicole felt so damn helpless, and hated the fact that she couldn't get through to Holly. She watched as the girl closed her eyes, took a deep breath, and tried to recompose herself.

When Holly looked at her again, it was with reluctant determination. "I need to be good," she said, calmer now. "I need to make Preston's friend happy. If I do whatever Preston asks me to do, then he'll know how much I love him."

The anguish Nicole witnessed in Holly's gaze twisted her insides into knots, and she gently touched the girl's arm. "Honey, you're not old enough to know what real love with a man is."

Holly jerked away from her, a renewed fire igniting in her eyes. "So what if I'm only fifteen? I've had more experience than most girls my age."

Nicole didn't hesitate to call Holly on her slip. "Fifteen?"

Panic chased across Holly's face as she realized her mistake, though she did nothing to correct it. Instead, she grabbed her purse and started past Nicole. "I need to get back to Richard before Gwen comes looking for me."

Nicole stepped in front of the girl and blocked her path to the door. "You don't have to do this, Holly. Let me help you. Let me get you out of this place."

"I don't want to leave," Holly said, her voice choked with emotion. "I just want *Preston*."

"What happens when he no longer wants you?" Nicole asked softly, but her words were direct and painfully honest.

Holly shook her head, as if she wouldn't even consider that as an option. "I have to *go*."

Knowing there was nothing else she could do right now, Nicole stepped aside and watched as Holly walked out. Tonight, she didn't have any choice but to let the young girl *entertain* one of Sloane's guests, but somewhere along the way Holly had become Nicole's personal mission.

She wasn't sure how Nathan was going to react to her decision, but Nicole wasn't leaving this hellhole without Holly.

Chapter Sixteen

"See anything you like?"

Nathan wasn't surprised that Sloane had sought him out, especially since he was standing alone in the lounge area of the playroom as he waited for Nicole to return from the restroom. It was the perfect opportunity for Sloane to try to negotiate with him, but Nathan was holding firm until the other man offered him what he'd come here for.

"No, not yet," Nathan replied, smiling amicably at Sloane.

"What did you think of Lisa?" he asked, his gaze both curious and hopeful. "She's quite willing to be your plaything for the night. Just say the word, and she's yours."

The thought of that young, naive girl giving her body so freely to a stranger was enough to turn Nathan's stomach. Thanks to years of undercover work, though, feigning a nonchalant attitude came easily, despite his internal frustration. "Nice girl, but there just wasn't any chemistry with her on my end."

"I've been hearing that a lot lately about Lisa."

Sloane grew thoughtful, a small frown marring his brow. "I'm thinking it's time for Lisa to move on to make room for fresh, new young blood for my friends to enjoy."

Nathan didn't care for the underlying tone in Sloane's comment, and what it implied. "How do you mean?" he asked casually.

"There comes a time when each of the girls has served her purpose, and that seems to be the case with Lisa." He shrugged, as if the two of them were discussing the weather, instead of a human life. "It's time for her to go."

"Go where?" Nathan kept his voice mildly curious, but deep in his gut he knew exactly what Sloane meant. He just needed the man to say the words out loud to confirm Nathan's suspicions.

Sloane leaned closer and let his voice drop in tone, as if he didn't want others to hear what he was about to share with Nathan. "Let's just say I have a very profitable arrangement with a Russian businessman who is more than happy to take the girls off my hands when I'm done with them. Sending them off to Russia keeps things much simpler and cleaner than putting the girls back out on the street here in Vegas."

Jesus. Nathan's mind reeled with the knowledge that not only was Sloane engaging in underage prostitution, he was also involved in human trafficking. The thought of him using these girls, then selling them off to another country to be used for white slavery was enough to make Nathan want to puke.

Somehow, someway, Sloane *had* to be stopped.

"But back to you, Keller, and finding you a girl who'll pique your interest," Sloane went on, forcing Nathan's attention back to the business at hand. "You're a hard man to please."

He shrugged, even as the urgency of getting Angela out of this place heightened. "I'm just very particular, and I want to make this worth my while."

"I completely understand. That's why I've saved the best for last." A crafty smile curved Sloane's lips. "I figured if no one else appealed to you, my Angel definitely would."

Now, *that* grabbed Nathan's attention, and the interest he displayed on his face was genuine. "Angel? Sounds promising."

Nathan followed Sloane's gaze as he glanced across the room and motioned with his fingers. From the shadows, a young girl emerged, escorted by Gwen. From a distance, Nathan could make out flowing blond hair and a petite, slender body draped in a white slip-style dress as she glided toward them on flat slippers.

The illusion of being an *angel* was apparent—from her choice of dress to the fresh innocence of her ethereal appearance. The other men in the room watched in envy while the girl passed by, and as she neared and her vivid blue eyes and face became more visible, Nathan felt a jolt to his system.

Angela Ramsey. *Finally.*

"I haven't shared her with anyone yet, but it's time," Sloane said, keeping his voice low. "I'm offering her up to you first, so you might want to take advantage of the arrangement because she'll be gone in a few weeks."

A chill went through Nathan. "Why's that?"

A twisted smile curved Sloane's lips. "Let's just say that the Russian made me an offer for Angel that I couldn't resist."

Sloane had arranged to sell off Angela. His heart nearly stopped in his chest. "I thought she was your favorite."

"Every girl has her price, Keller," he said like a man who never formed an emotional attachment to any one female, and was only interested in the bottom-line profit. "And every single one of them is replaceable."

Sick, disgusting fuck. Nathan had to forcibly swallow back the inflammatory words, and just in time as Angela came to a stop a few feet away from them.

"Come here, Angel." Sloane held his hand out to her, and she placed her fingers against his palm and let him draw her close to his side. "I'd like you to meet a good friend of mine. This is Alex Keller. Alex, this is Angel."

Nathan smiled at her, noticing the heart pendant necklace she wore, which marked her as a favorite of Sloane's—but not for long.

"You're absolutely beautiful," he said, all too aware of the other man watching him, and his reaction, very carefully.

"Thank you," she said softly.

Her glassy eyes, combined with her docility and too-relaxed demeanor, told Nathan she was on some kind of narcotic. Her dossier had depicted her as a rebellious, troubled teen, yet here in this environment she seemed like a shell of herself, subdued and childlike, and far too innocent to be caught up in such an immoral situation.

And it was up to him to get her out, as quickly and safely as possible before she was lost to them forever—to *the Russian*.

Pushing aside his personal mission for now, he met Sloane's gaze and gave him the impressed response he no doubt expected. "You certainly did save the best for last."

Sloane's chest expanded with conceited male pride. "I only pick the best. Like I said, I've never shared her before, so consider yourself very lucky that you're the first."

It was bad enough that Angela had been subjected to Sloane's sexual advances. Nathan swore it would end there for the young girl.

"Why don't the two of you spend some time alone and enjoy the amenities here in the playroom?" Sloane suggested as he passed Angela off to Nathan. "Or maybe you'd prefer a private room for the evening?"

Nathan knew exactly what Sloane was hinting at. If Nathan opted to spend the night alone with Angela, then the other man would be able to do the same with Nicole, which was what Sloane clearly wanted. Except under Nathan's watch, the all-night exchange wasn't going to happen. Ever.

But he had to get Angela alone to assess the girl's mental state and the situation, and that meant a brief swap was necessary.

"No, not tonight," Nathan said, openly refusing Sloane's offer and making certain the man understood that he hadn't agreed to a trade with Nicole. "I'd like to make sure she's the one I want before I give you Nikki for a night."

"Very well," he conceded, but not happily. "Where is Nikki, anyway?"

"She had to use the restroom." Nathan glanced in that direction and finally saw Nicole heading his way. "Here she comes now."

Nathan immediately noticed that something was wrong. He could see the distress in her eyes, but as soon as she saw Sloane, and then realized the girl standing next to Nathan was Angela, those troubling emotions disappeared. He'd find out later what had upset her, but for now she realized how pivotal this moment was for the two of them—that she needed to leave Nathan alone with Angela in order for him to talk to her.

"Who is this?" Nicole asked as she looked at Angela, her voice infused with a believable amount of teenage jealousy.

"This is Angel," Nathan said, then used a more assertive tone to show Sloane that Nicole was his to command. "She and I are going to visit for a while, and I want you to do the same with Preston."

Nicole stared at him with big, round eyes filled with a plausible mixture of hurt and anxiety. "Okay," she conceded in a soft, obedient voice, which Sloane seemed to appreciate.

Sloane shifted beside Nicole and skimmed his hand down her back. She looked uncomfortable with his caress, and Nathan knew for a fact that her unease was real, not feigned as everything else had been.

"Why don't I take you to see my private art collection?" Sloane suggested. "It's in a nice, quiet wing of the house, where the two of us can relax and talk."

Nicole nodded. "All right."

Sloane reached out and tucked his forefinger beneath Angela's chin, lifting her face so her downcast eyes met his. "Remember what we talked about earlier, Angel," he said, his tone gentle, yet firm. "Be a good girl and do whatever it takes to make Alex happy."

"Okay," she whispered in a small voice.

Sloane transferred his gaze to Nathan. "We'll be back in a while. Enjoy your time together."

Nathan refused to return the sentiment. As he watched Sloane lead Nicole back upstairs, he felt torn between staying with Angela, and following Nicole to make sure the slimy bastard kept his hands to himself. Releasing a deep breath, he focused on what he'd come here to Summerlin to do. He had to trust that Nicole could take care of herself.

Right now, he didn't have a choice.

Taking Angela's small hand in his, he felt her tremble—and sensed her fear as he led her toward one of the draped beds. Angela watched him warily, and in an attempt to put her at ease, he plumped up the pillows so they both could sit up, rather than lie down, as most of the other couples in the room were doing.

He settled on top of the mattress and leaned against the mound of pillows, then patted the vacant spot beside him. "Come and sit down." As soon as he saw the flash of apprehension in her eyes, he sought to relieve her anxiety. "I'm not going to hurt you or do anything you don't want to. I just want to talk."

"Talk?" She eyed him skeptically.

He chuckled, soft and low. "Yeah, just talk. I promise."

She hesitated only a moment before climbing up onto the mattress and sitting beside him—close enough for them to look intimate if anyone should glance their way, yet far enough so that she didn't feel threatened by him. Being with Angela without any sexual contact was the first step to lowering her guard. Next was establishing a friendship and making sure she realized he had no intentions of manhandling her, that he wanted her to feel safe and secure with him.

Angela absently pulled her dress over her knees and glanced at him shyly. "What do you want to talk about?"

He smiled. "You."

A frown creased her light blond brows, as if she wasn't quite sure what to make of his interest in her. "What about me?"

Because he'd given her no reason to fear being with him, she was finally starting to soften, her initial trepidation fading, allowing her to relax more and more with each passing minute. Whatever she was on had a mellowing effect on her, and he took advantage of her docile disposition while he could.

"How long have you been here?" he asked, keeping the exchange between them light and casual. He needed to get a feel for her mental and emotional state and gauge if she was going to cooperate with a rescue attempt, or not.

She shrugged. "A few weeks."

He tipped his head curiously. "Do you like it here?"

"It's okay," she replied softly.

Nathan took her lack of enthusiasm as a good sign. Hopefully, the glamour of being one of Sloane's girls was wearing off and she was starting to realize that running away from home hadn't been the answer to her problems—that it had only created problems of a different kind. Then again, she was young and most likely couldn't see the extreme situation she'd entangled herself in.

"That's a pretty dress you're wearing," he said,

deliberately steering their conversation in a different direction. "Pretty necklace, too."

She blushed at his compliment and fingered the pendant hanging around her neck. "Preston gave it to me. He gives me lots of nice things." A smile wavered on her lips. "He told me that I was special."

"You are special," Nathan said, and smiled to reassure her.

"Then why is he making me do this with you?" Her voice was thick with confusion, and a bit of anger, too.

Because Sloane is done using you, Nathan thought, and wished he was able to give Angela a good dose of tough love to make her realize Preston didn't care about her beyond his own twisted desires. That he'd already agreed to sell her off to another man within the next few weeks.

"We're only talking." Shifting to his side to face her, he propped his head in his hand. He gave her a charming grin. "Am I really so bad?"

"No, you're actually very nice." She met his gaze, her eyes a bit glossy, but sincere. "You don't creep me out like the other guys at these parties."

It was a start—the beginning of gaining her trust. "Tell me more about yourself. What grade are you in?"

Surprise flashed across her delicate features, telling him he'd startled her with his direct, unexpected question—which he'd done intentionally. "I'm . . . I'm not in school," she said nervously. "I'm eighteen."

He studied her just long enough to let her know he doubted her claim. "You look much younger."

"I'm *not*," she insisted.

Knowing if he pushed the issue he'd risk her retreating when he'd already made so much headway with her, he backed off and decided to probe into another aspect of her situation. "So, where do you live, Angel?"

"Here at The Sanctuary." She obviously didn't feel that was a secret she needed to keep. "I'm living in one of the guesthouses on the property."

"Do you live there all the time?"

"Yes," she said with a nod of her head. "I have my own room there."

All good information for him to know, yet there were still so many unknown variables—starting with finding which of the guesthouses she was staying in, and what he'd find once he made his way into the house. Undoubtedly, there was some kind of security involved, whether Sloane employed guards for the girls or used a surveillance system. Either way, he needed time to figure out his options and decide the best way to get her out of the estate.

Going by past experience, rather than skulking around the property in the middle of the night and risking detection, it might be easier to take Angela in the midst of a party—so long as she didn't scream, struggle, or draw attention to the rescue attempt. But he hadn't earned enough of Angela's trust to know how she'd react, and because of that he couldn't even think about an escape tonight.

"Don't you miss your family?" He continued their conversation, asking questions that would make her think of her parents, and hopefully long for the warmth and security of her real home.

"No." The sadness in her eyes contradicted her reply.

"Are you sure about that?" he asked gently. The more he was able to get her to admit to herself that she no longer wanted to live this kind of life, the easier his job would be.

"Maybe I miss them a little," she admitted in a quiet voice. Grabbing one of the red silk pillows strewn on the bed, she drew it to her chest and wrapped her arms around it. "And my cat. I miss Twinkie a lot."

"Twinkie?" He chuckled in amusement, lightening the mood and making her smile, too. "Where did that name come from?"

"Ever since I was a little girl, I've always liked Twinkies." She ducked her head, as if the admission embarrassed her. "I found her at the park when I was ten, and I had to beg my mom to let me keep her. She's this yellow-orange striped color, and her paws and belly are white."

"So she looks a Twinkie?" he guessed.

"Yeah." She laughed, the joyful sound untainted by her current circumstances. "Twinkie slept with me every single night and I loved to listen to her purr."

Angela's whole expression changed as she talked about her cat. She looked so happy, for the moment forgetting that she'd left that childhood behind the day she'd run away from home.

"How about you?" she asked, once she was done regaling him with tales of Twinkie the Cat. "Do you have a dog or a cat?"

"I did growing up." Seeing this as a way to bond with her, he told her about Roxie, the family's golden retriever. He also amused her with stories about his older sisters and made her laugh at his antics as a kid.

While she listened, he glanced at his watch and realized that Nicole and Sloane had been gone for over a half an hour. With each minute that passed, he grew more anxious about where they were, what they were doing, and if Nicole was okay. He decided if they didn't return in the next fifteen minutes, he was going to go and look for Nicole, because if something happened to her on his watch, he'd never forgive himself.

Another long ten minutes passed, and by the time he finished entertaining Angela with his childhood adventures, she was lying on her side facing him, still hugging the pillow to her chest with a sweet smile on her lips. There was a wistful look on her face, the kind that told Nathan he'd stirred up feelings of regret and had also made her reflect about her own family life. That maybe things hadn't been as bad as she'd made them out to be when she'd been living at home. Not compared with her life as Sloane's plaything.

Despite Angela's initial reasons for running away, it was obvious she missed the comforts of home, and the parents who loved her very much. And that, at least, was the first step in changing her thought process around.

For tonight, he'd planted the seeds in her mind. Now he could only hope they grew overnight and helped her realize what a mistake she'd made, and that she wanted to return to her family, where she belonged.

After leaving Nathan with Angela down in the playroom, Nicole followed Sloane as he escorted her upstairs, then to the other end of his huge mansion and into a separate wing of the house where his art collection was on display. She knew it was necessary to give Nathan time alone with Angela, but she didn't like being so far away from him, in a section of the house that was isolated from everyone else—with a man she didn't trust.

To her relief, Sloane started the tour as a consummate

gentleman, his pride and delight in having acquired so
many rare and priceless pieces of art taking precedence
over his attraction to her. For now. Nicole had no doubt
that once the excitement of sharing his treasures with her
was over, his focus would return to what he ultimately
wanted. Her.

The museum-like room was devoted to not only
artwork, but other valuables as well. There were sculp-
tures, vases, tapestries, antiques, and more. But it was
the original paintings by Degas, Monet, and Seurat that
had her in a state of awe. Those creations were truly
magnificent and breathtaking.

As they casually strolled from piece to piece, Nicole
was intensely aware of Sloane constantly touching her
in some way. If he wasn't holding her hand, then his
palm was splayed at the base of her spine, or his fingers
were caressing her bare arm. As he talked, he leaned in
close, his head nearly touching hers as he spoke into
her ear.

In between monologues, he charmed and flirted,
and she had to force herself to laugh at his attempts at
humor, and not cringe when he touched her in a too-
familiar manner. The increasing intimacy of his actions
had Nicole on edge, because she knew where his affection was leading . . . down a path she had no desire to
travel with him.

A glance at an elaborate clock on the wall told Nicole that thirty minutes had passed, and while half an
hour wasn't a long time to be gone, it felt like an eternity
when she had to endure Sloane's advances. Certain that
Nathan had made whatever connection he needed to
with Angela, Nicole was more than ready to return to his
side for the evening.

"Your art collection is amazing," she said, sounding like a young girl who was very impressed with Sloane's wealth. The man would expect nothing less. "But I really should get back to Alex."

He smiled and grasped her hand in his, the look in his eyes darkening with desire. "There's no rush, Nikki. Besides, he's busy with Angel. You and I have plenty of time to spend together."

Nausea swirled in her belly. She'd known this moment was coming; that once they were no longer distracted by his art and other collections, she'd become the focal point of his attention, and obsession. Still, she tried to be as persistent as a teenager would be. "I don't want him to worry about me."

"He knows you're fine," he said in a placating tone, contradicting the firm hold on her hand. "Come sit with me. There's something I'd like to give you."

Instead of resisting him any further and taking the chance of angering him, she let him lead her to a brown leather couch in the room. She settled onto the cushion next to him, her body visibly tense. Not an unrealistic response for a young girl in this kind of situation—but even as a grown woman she was apprehensive of the man.

He tucked a strand of hair behind her ear, his fingers lingering at the side of her neck. "Don't be so nervous," he murmured huskily, his smile inviting. "I don't bite. I promise."

She dampened her dry bottom lip with her tongue and gave him a timid look to divert his seduction. Too late, she realized that her demure reaction only seemed to arouse him more. *Shit.* "I'm . . . I'm not used to being away from Alex."

"We'll go back in a few minutes." He reached for a light blue box wrapped in a white satin ribbon, which was sitting on the table next to the couch, and placed it in the palm of her hand. "This is for you."

She immediately recognized the iconic blue box as Tiffany. Her first instinct was to refuse the expensive gift, but knowing he'd only insist, she went ahead and removed the ribbon and opened the small box. A velvet pouch awaited her, and tucked inside of that was a dainty silver heart link bracelet with a toggle clasp. A classic piece of Tiffany jewelry.

"Do you like it?" he asked.

While most young girls would be thrilled to be the recipient of such a beautiful designer bracelet, knowing what Sloane expected in return for the gift was more than enough to repulse her. "It's very pretty. Thank you."

He smiled charismatically. "Here, let me help you put it on." Taking the box and ribbon from her, he set them back on the table, then turned back to her with the bracelet.

She extended her arm and let him clasp the silver heart around her wrist. Before she could pull away, he gripped her fingers in his and pressed a damp, lingering kiss on the back of her hand. Her stomach twisted in disgust, and she had a bad feeling that this situation was going to get much worse.

"I like to give my girls pretty, expensive things," he said as his thumb continued to caress her hand. "The more they please me, the more I like to spoil them."

Until the sick bastard grew tired of them, she knew.

Leaning in closer, he pressed his body against hers and placed his palm on her thigh. "You know, a kiss would be nice to show your appreciation."

I didn't want the fucking bracelet, asshole.

As a grown, independent woman, that's what she wanted to say to Sloane, but she didn't think he'd appreciate her outspoken rejection. As a nervous young girl, she tried to turn him down gently. "I really shouldn't. Alex—"

He pressed his fingers to her lips, effectively cutting off her words. "Just relax, Nikki. It's just a kiss."

He slid his free hand around to the nape of her neck and pulled her head toward his. The queasiness in her belly returned with a vengeance at the thought of kissing him, and she compressed her lips together, refusing to let his tongue invade her mouth. That didn't stop him from trying, but there was absolutely nothing soft, giving, or inviting about her lips.

When he finally released her, there was a spark of annoyance in his gaze. "You're quite the challenge, aren't you?"

Her heart began a hard, fast beat in her chest. The predatory look on his face told her that she was walking a fine line with him, that if she wasn't careful, the situation could turn ugly. If provoked, Sloane could easily overpower her, assault her, and even if she screamed for help no one would hear her since she was at the opposite end of the house.

"I'm really not feeling very well," she said in a faint voice, and abruptly jumped to her feet. "I want Alex." She deliberately made herself sound like a petulant child—whatever worked to get her back to Nathan.

"Very well, but you and I aren't finished yet." Slowly, he stood up, the corner of his mouth curling with undeniable determination. "Just keep in mind that you can make this as easy, or as difficult, as you want. The decision is yours."

She shivered at the underlying threat to his tone, and decided she'd be better off not responding. He grabbed her hand to escort her from the room, his hold not nearly as gentle as it had been earlier, giving her a taste of the darker personality that lurked beneath Sloane's charming facade.

That glimpse revealed a side to the man she knew she'd be wise not to provoke.

Chapter Seventeen

As soon as Nathan saw Nicole walk back into the play-room with Sloane, his protective instincts went on alert. The tension between the two was palpable, and not in a good way. Nicole's face was pale, the stress in her eyes visible when her gaze met his across the room. Sloane didn't bother to hide his look of irritation—clearly, things hadn't gone well between the two of them.

Concerned for Nicole, Nathan moved off the draped bed and helped Angela off the mattress, too. Taking her hand, he met up with Sloane and Nicole.

Sloane inclined his head at Nathan. "Did the two of you have a nice visit?" he asked of Nathan's time alone with Angela.

"We did." Nathan didn't ask the same of Sloane's visit with Nicole. Something was visibly wrong, and he'd get the details from Nicole later, when they were alone.

"I'm still interested," Sloane said, shocking Nathan with his announcement. Especially since the other man wasn't all warmth and smiles. "How about you?"

"Absolutely," Nathan replied, knowing Sloane was counting on his agreement.

Except there wouldn't be an actual trade, not when leaving Nicole alone with Sloane again would likely put her life in danger. Somehow, he and Nicole had to figure out a way to use tomorrow night's masquerade party as a distraction to smuggle Angela out of the house, *before* the expected swap.

"Excellent," Sloane said, his irritable mood mollified somewhat. "After breakfast in the morning, a few of the girls are going to a spa I own for a day of pampering before the party. Angela and Nicole can go with them. While the girls are out, why don't the two of us talk and make the necessary arrangements?"

"That's perfect." Nathan met Nicole's gaze, and seeing the get-me-the-hell-out-of-here look in her eyes, he took that as his cue to end the conversation with Sloane.

"It's been a long day and Nicole doesn't look as though she's feeling well," he said, taking her hand and tucking it into the crook of his arm. "I think we'll turn in for tonight."

"Good night, then." Finally, Sloane smiled, but the sentiment didn't fully reach his eyes. "I'll see you two in the morning."

Nathan didn't waste any more time getting Nicole away from Sloane, though he wished he could have done the same with Angela. He hated leaving her behind, but consoled himself with the knowledge that by this same time tomorrow night he'd have her out of the estate and on her way back to her parents.

As soon as they arrived in their room, the first thing Nicole did was take off a silver bracelet from around her wrist—a piece of jewelry he knew for a fact she hadn't been wearing earlier. Next, she kicked off her shoes, her movements jerky and angry.

"Nicole?" he asked, knowing she'd hear the concern in his voice.

She shook her head, telling him with that gesture that she didn't want to talk—or couldn't talk about what was really on her mind in a room that might be bugged. "I need a shower."

She also needed time to calm down, and he let her go, giving her a few minutes to herself while he checked in with Caleb. He sent his boss a text message, letting him know he'd made contact with Angela and that he was planning on extracting her tomorrow night, along with the discovery that Sloane was also trafficking the girls. Less than a minute later Caleb responded that he was going to call Angela's parents and give them the update, and they'd deal with the trafficking issue as soon as they were safely off Sloane's estate. Nathan promised to remain in touch as his plans progressed.

By the time Nathan entered the huge, decadent bathroom, Nicole was done shampooing her hair and was rinsing a conditioner from the strands. Knowing this was the best place for them to talk, he closed and locked the door, then took a moment to appreciate the sight of Nicole standing naked beneath the rush of water freefalling from the large, square grid built into the ceiling.

The glass-enclosed shower was luxurious and designed for sensual pleasures, with handholds built into the walls and ledges for sitting. The display of switches on the wall made him curious enough to see what they did. When he pressed a few of the buttons, the main lights went off, but the shower grid glowed with soothing colors of blue and amber, illuminating the falling water and giving the illusion that Nicole was standing beneath a canopy of rain at night.

Nathan grinned, amazed by the spectacular sight and innovative design. "Okay, that's really cool."

"Yeah, it is," she agreed, looking like a sensual water nymph as the luminous water sluiced over her firm breasts and along her lush curves. "Leave it like that. It makes me feel like I'm somewhere other than where I really am."

He understood, and gave her the escape she seemed to need. He quickly stripped off his clothes and joined her under the stream of warm water, already thoroughly, achingly aroused. As much as he wanted to take advantage of the erotic setting and make love to Nicole, there were things they needed to discuss first.

"What happened tonight?" he asked, keeping his voice low as he reached for a large sponge and poured a generous amount of liquid soap on top. Then he motioned for Nicole to turn around so he could scrub her back.

"Where do I start?" she said with a sigh as he began buffing the soapy sponge across her shoulders and the scent of ripe peaches filled the steamy air. "He gave me a bracelet, tried to kiss me, then issued a threat—that it was up to me whether things between the two of us went gently, or roughly, and he didn't seem to mind the latter if that's what it came down to." She shuddered.

Nathan clenched his jaw as he glided the sponge over her bottom, hating that she'd had to endure even a moment of Sloane's vulgar personality. "Did he hurt you?" he asked, kneeling to wash her legs.

"No. But I can't be alone with him again." She turned around again when he urged her to do so, and let him soap and scrub his way back up the front of her body.

"He's not very patient with the hard-to-get routine. Next time, he's not going to take no for an answer."

"I know." Standing again, he dragged the sponge over her belly, then her breasts, trying like hell to keep his mind on business, and not the temptation of her tight, hard nipples and slick, wet skin silhouetted by the erotic rainfall of blue-amber water.

He swallowed hard and placed the soapy sponge in her hands so she could return the favor. But before she touched him, he needed to tell her just how urgent this mission of theirs had become.

"Things here at The Sanctuary are much worse than we originally thought. Sloane is trafficking the girls to Russia once he's done using them," he said, watching as her eyes widened with shock. "He's already made arrangements to sell off Angela and a few of the other girls."

"Oh, my God," she breathed, her face reflecting her own revulsion at the news. "We have to get the girls out of here."

He gently smoothed wet strands of hair off her cheek, knowing how desperately she wanted to save each and every one of the girls here at The Sanctuary. Except the two of them just couldn't do it on their own. It was impossible. Once they were out of this hellhole, it would be up to the authorities to look into the allegations further and gather the evidence they needed to arrest Sloane—and make sure the charges were strong enough to stick.

"We're getting Angela out tomorrow night, before a swap can be made, so you won't be alone with Sloane again," he said, informing her of the more immediate plan he'd formulated. "I'll set things up with Sloane tomorrow when we talk, let him think that after a few hours at the party we'll make the exchange for the night. Except by then, we'll be gone."

"You make it sound so easy." She was washing his back, and while he couldn't see her face, he could hear the frown in her voice. And the doubts.

"No, not easy." He didn't want her to think that anything about getting Angela out of the estate without Sloane's knowledge was going to be simple or uncomplicated. It was a matter of hoping for the best, and planning for the worst. "But it can go relatively smoothly if we have Angela's cooperation. When you go to the spa with her, I need you to establish a friendship with her, let her know she can trust you, and me, and get her in the mind frame to leave. I honestly think she's ready to get out of here, so hopefully it won't be too difficult to sway her."

"Okay. And tomorrow night? How are we pulling that off?"

Her soapy hands slipped between his thighs from behind, and when her fingers brushed across his balls, his cock stiffened even more and he groaned deep in his throat. She continued her way down his calves to his feet, leaving him in sexual agony.

Closing his eyes, he exhaled a deep breath and refocused on their conversation. "We're going to make the masquerade party work to our advantage. Everyone will be masked, which will help conceal our identities and enable us to blend in. Since Sloane will most likely know which masks are yours and Angela's, I need you to find a way to switch your masks with other people's, preferably blondes, to throw Sloane off our trail and buy us some time. Do you think you can do that?"

"I know I can," she said confidently.

"Good." He explained the best way for them to disappear with Angela, and while what he had planned would only give them about half an hour's lead time before Sloane realized they were gone, once they were out the front gates it would be too late for Sloane to do anything at all.

Finished washing his body, she stood in front of him again, both of them beneath the cascade of water. She set the sponge aside, splayed her hands on his chest, and looked up at him, her eyes smoky with desire and a deeper purpose. "I need to ask you a huge favor, especially in light of the fact that Sloane is trafficking the girls to Russia."

He couldn't imagine denying her request, mainly because she'd never asked him for anything. If it was within his power to grant, the favor was hers. "Okay."

"I know I'm not going to get the story I wanted on Sloane," she said, her voice infused with disappointment. "Even though we've both witnessed his sordid lifestyle and just how corrupt he is, and how he's abusing all these girls and that he's also involved in white slave trade, if I wrote an exposé, it would be his word against mine. If I even tried to reveal the truth, he'd literally destroy me, personally and professionally."

Needing to touch her, he placed his hands on her hips and slowly glided them upward over her waist to just beneath her arms. His thumbs absently skimmed the underside of her breasts, and her eyes darkened even more. "Yeah, he would," Nathan said, glad to see that she was thinking sensibly.

"But there is one thing I want out of this and it means more to me than the story," she said in a soft, imploring tone. "I want to take Holly, too."

Shit. Now, there was a complication he hadn't anticipated. Getting one girl out undetected was going to be difficult enough, but two? He shook his head, unsure he could make such a promise.

"Please, Nathan?"

She framed his face in her hands, forcing him to look into her beautiful eyes, past the strong, tenacious woman he'd come to love, to the young, vulnerable girl she'd once been. More than anyone, she understood what these girls were going through and felt she needed to try to save Holly.

"If we don't get her out of this place *now,* she's going to end up in Russia, imprisoned to prostitution for the rest of her life, and I'll never forgive myself for not helping her when I had the chance."

His own devastating past reared its ugly head. He could relate to that feeling of regret all too well, and it was something he never wanted to experience again. Because of that, telling Nicole that he refused to help Holly was impossible.

"We'll get her out," he said gruffly. For Nicole, he'd somehow find a way.

"Thank you." Gratitude filled her voice as she curled a hand around the back of his neck and pulled his mouth down to hers.

She gave him a hungry, emotion-filled kiss of appreciation that spurred his own need for her as all the anxiety and tension of the past few hours flashed over to desire and uncontrollable passion.

Nathan groaned at the feel of her hands moving urgently over his slick, wet body—across his chest and down his belly, until she encircled his erection with her fingers and stroked the rigid length. His own hands squeezed her breasts and lightly pinched her nipples, and she caught her breath and rubbed her thumb over the sensitive head of his cock.

She tore her mouth from his and buried her face against his neck, her soft tongue licking his damp skin all the way up to his ear. "I want you inside me," she murmured. *"Please."*

Aching for the same thing, he walked her backward until they came to one of the built-in seats. He lifted her up a few inches and settled her on the ledge, then pushed her legs wide apart so he could fit in between. She raised her knees, wrapped her legs around his waist, and whispered the erotic words that were his undoing.

"Fuck me," she whispered, her eyes glazed with lust and need.

She didn't want it slow and easy, and neither did he. He dragged the tip of his cock along the slippery folds of her sex, positioned himself, and with a hard flex of his hips he was eight inches deep inside her. He moaned in pure pleasure, and she gasped in surprise, but the hands grabbing his ass and urging him to thrust gave him all the invitation he needed to lose himself completely in the tight clasp of her body.

He pumped into her—fast, rough, and hard—some primitive, male instinct urging him to mark her as his. Her ankles tightened around his lower back as she tilted her hips and pushed herself against him, taking everything he had to give, and more.

As he drove himself home, he felt her shudder and

contract around his shaft, milking him with the strength of her orgasm. Her head fell back, and she cried out as she came, sucking him right into that same vortex of pleasure she was experiencing. His climax ripped through him, and his groan became a deep, guttural growl as he spilled himself inside her.

Once he recovered, he lifted his head and looked at Nicole, the words *I love you* poised on the tip of his tongue, a breath away from being spoken.

But before he could say anything at all, she leaned into him and pressed her lips to his in a reverent kiss. The slow, sweet kind that spoke from the deepest part of her heart and soul. The kind that made him believe that after they were done with this case, they might just have a chance at a future together.

He was counting on it.

After breakfast the following morning, Nicole slid into the back of a waiting white stretch limousine with eight other girls, including Angela and Holly. She deliberately sat next to Angela, who was quiet and subdued compared with all the other loud, talkative teens who were excited to spend a day at the spa.

Being aware of her surroundings, Nicole didn't miss the guy dressed in slacks and a casual shirt who was accompanying the group. While he sat up front with the driver, he was clearly there to watch the girls. For as much as today's outing gave the illusion of a day of fun and freedom, the girls were not allowed to come and go at will. Once outside the estate, their environment was organized and controlled.

It wasn't even noon and champagne was already

flowing from a minibar, and everyone but Nicole and Angela was indulging. Sitting at the opposite end of the limo, Holly had already downed one glass of the bubbly and was working on a second.

While the girls around her were energetic and animated, Holly's expression was sad and bleak, as if last night with Sloane's friend had devastated a part of her—which made Nicole all the more determined to follow through on getting the young girl off Sloane's estate tonight. Then there was the threat of becoming a statistic of human trafficking that added to the urgency of the situation. Not just for Holly and Angela, but for *all* the girls.

Nicole had to find a way to talk to Holly alone today, but right now she needed to take advantage of the fact that she was sitting next to Angela, and no one was paying them any attention. Since the other girl was staring out the tinted windows at the passing scenery, Nicole lightly touched her arm and smiled when Angela looked at her.

"Is going to the spa a regular thing you all do?" Nicole asked conversationally.

Angela shrugged, her demeanor reserved and guarded. "Just usually when there's a big party going on. Like tonight."

Nicole tipped her head, trying her best to engage her. "Do you like the big parties?"

"They're okay," she said quietly.

"Almost everyone seems excited about tonight," Nicole went on. "A masquerade party sounds like fun."

Angela didn't reply. Instead, she stared blankly at the other girls taking advantage of the limo's many luxurious amenities. Nicole didn't believe Angela was being deliberately rude; it truly appeared that she had a lot on her mind, and an afternoon of indulging in a facial or pedicure wasn't on her radar.

Hopefully, longing for her family was.

Still, Nicole persisted. "So, how did you get to The Sanctuary?"

Her inquiry startled Angela out of her thoughts. The other girl met her gaze and was painfully honest with her answer. "Gwen brought me here."

The girl was opening up, just as Nicole had hoped, and she steered the conversation accordingly. "From where?"

Angela wrung her hands anxiously in her lap and glanced back out the window. "I don't know where from. I came here from Arizona, so I'm not real familiar with places. It was by some big hotel with a volcano outside."

The Mirage Hotel and Casino, which was located on the Las Vegas Strip. As Sloane's assistant, Gwen appeared to be in charge of recruiting girls. She'd most likely recognized that scared, out-of-place look on Angela's face and had plucked her off the streets and offered her a safe place to stay. Except Angela couldn't have imagined the strings attached to Gwen's offer until it was too late, or that accepting would change the course of her future, and not in a good way.

"Did you run away from home?" she asked, her voice just high enough for Angela to hear over the other girls' talking and laughter.

Angela glanced back at her, the question triggering a wealth of emotion in her soft blue gaze. "Yes," she whis-

pered, the one word filled with so much loneliness and
pain. "I don't want to be here anymore. I miss my mom
and dad. I miss my cat and friends."

Nicole's heart hurt for the young girl. "Do you want
to go back home?"

She nodded, tears filling her eyes. "I do. But I can't.
Not now. Not after everything I've done." She ducked
her head and wiped away the tears that had spilled over
her lashes, not wanting anyone else to see her crying.
"I'm so ashamed."

Seeing a part of herself in Angela, and recognizing
those feelings of guilt and blame, Nicole took her hand
and gave it a comforting squeeze. "You made a mistake," she said adamantly. "You still have the chance to
make things right and change your life back around."

Angela shook her head. "I don't know how."

"I do."

The young girl stared at her with wide eyes filled
with a mixture of hope and skepticism.

Without a doubt, Nicole knew that Angela was ready
to embrace the opportunity she was about to hand her,
which would make Nathan's job of getting her out of
the estate so much easier. After casting a quick glance
at the other girls to make sure she and Angela weren't
being overheard, she leaned even closer and lowered
her voice just to be on the safe side.

"Remember Alex from last night?"

"Yeah," Angela said with a nod. "He was very nice."

Nicole hesitated a second, then revealed the truth.
"Your parents asked him to find you and bring you
home. They love and miss you very much and want you
back with them."

Shock transformed Angela's features, then panic set in. "But I can't leave," she whispered frantically. "Sloane won't let me."

So he was holding Angela against her will? Sounded like grounds for kidnapping charges to Nicole. "Have you told him you want to go home?"

"He told me that my parents don't want me," she said, her voice choked with emotion. "That they don't love me or else they would have come for me by now."

Goddamn bastard. "Believe me, Angela, they've tried to reach you. They're devastated that you ran away and they do want you back. Badly."

"Why would they?" Angela's bottom lip quivered. "I was so horrible to them. I said such ugly things that hurt them both."

"They love you no matter what. A parent's love is unconditional and isn't based on your actions or what you say or do," she said, not sure that someone of Angela's age could grasp the concept. "They know that being a teenager isn't easy, but it's also their job to be tough on you, to make sure you turn out to be a good person."

"I want to go home." Angela's voice was hoarse, but the look of despair in her eyes said it all. She missed her family terribly.

Nicole couldn't have been more relieved to have Angela's cooperation. "You need to listen to me," she said, making sure she had the girl's full attention before continuing. "As soon as you get to the playroom tonight, go to the women's lounge. I'll meet you there."

"Then what?"

"I'll let you know when the time comes." For Angela's own safety, the less she knew up front, the better.

"Just be there, and we'll get you out. And don't tell anyone what we talked about."

"I won't. I promise," Angela said, just as the limo pulled into a driveway leading to a small, private resort, then parked near a villa that housed the spa facilities.

The girls piled out of the limousine, with Security Guy watching their progress from the vehicle into the spa. Nicole followed behind with Angela, and once inside the exclusive facility, she looked for Holly so she could talk to the other girl next and get into her head a bit.

She caught up to Holly just as she reached the front desk and asked one of the technicians for a private massage and waxing. She was immediately whisked away, leaving Nicole on her own for the next few hours.

Disappointed that she'd lost the chance to bond with Holly, Nicole chose a manicure and pedicure for her spa treatments. She was assigned two young girls— one to polish her fingernails, and the other to tend to her feet.

Settled into a chair that massaged her back, she closed her eyes and relaxed, absently listening to the conversation between the two girls working on her hands and feet. Between envious comments and snide remarks beneath their breaths that they assumed she couldn't hear, Nicole came to the conclusion these girls had once been part of Sloane's harem. She wouldn't have been surprised to learn that he owned the spa and used it to farm out the girls once they got too old for his tastes.

What those girls didn't realize was that they were the lucky ones, if there was such a thing under these circumstances. They were the few who might have been cast aside by Sloane once he'd grown bored of them, but they'd been spared from the hellish life of the white slave trade.

Nearly two hours later, her manicure and pedicure were done, complete with massages, sugar scrub, and paraffin wax dips. With her nails freshly painted, she was told to sit for another fifteen minutes before leaving. So she continued to relax, and when she finally opened her eyes it was to see Gwen strolling casually through the spa, checking on the girls.

For the most part, Nicole had managed to avoid up-close-and-personal contact with Gwen, but there was no escaping the woman now, since she was heading her way and Nicole still had foam separators between her toes. She waited for Gwen to pass by, but the other woman stopped in front of her instead.

Gwen studied her face for a long, uncomfortable moment. Then a slight smile touched her lips. "Are you enjoying yourself?"

"Yes, thank you," Nicole replied, praying that the woman didn't make the connection between her and the reporter at the ribbon-cutting ceremony.

"Good." Her expression gave nothing away. "I'll see you at tonight's party."

Gwen moved on, and Nicole exhaled a deep breath.

Before long, it was time to return to the house, and Security Guy was standing on duty again to make sure that all the girls got back into the limousine. Nicole tried to get a seat next to Holly, but ended up sitting across from her. She wasn't able to talk to the other girl, but she could *see* her, and she didn't look well. After a long full-body massage, she should have been in a great mood. Instead, she seemed sad and depressed.

Nicole knew Holly's situation was only going to get worse, not better, no matter how much Holly claimed to love Sloane. Fortunately for Holly, tonight Nicole was going to give her the chance to change the direction of her life, and her future.

"How was your meeting with Sloane today?"

"Interesting." Nathan glanced in the vanity mirror as Nicole joined him in the bathroom and closed the door, then turned on the shower so they could talk while finishing getting ready for the Mardi Gras party starting in less than an hour.

He still had a towel wrapped around his hips as he shaved his face, but she'd changed into a black push-up bra, lacy bikini panties, and fishnet stockings—all part of her costume courtesy of Sloane, who'd sent the items over earlier that afternoon for her to wear to tonight's party. Too bad the other man wouldn't get the chance to enjoy the provocative ensemble.

"So, is everything set up according to our plan?" She hung her outfit on the back of the door, then stepped into a black-and-purple lace corset and shimmied it up over her hips so it fit against her breasts.

Good God, she looked sexy as sin in her getup, with her hair loose and flowing around her shoulders and the lightest amount of makeup enhancing her delicate features. His lower body stirred, a too-common reaction when it came to Nicole, and he had to force himself to keep his mind on business, where it belonged.

"Yeah, everything is set," he said, and cleared the husky desire from his voice. "But after your encounter with Sloane last night, he claims you're quite defiant."

She laughed in amusement, even as she struggled to

lace up the back of her corset. "That's certainly not going to change anytime soon." Releasing a sound of frustration, she walked over to him, presenting him with the loose ribbons she hadn't been able to reach. "Can you help me out with this contraption?"

"Sure." Finished shaving his five o'clock shadow, he rinsed his razor and wiped the residual lather from his jaw and neck. Before he forgot, he showed her a small plastic bag containing two white tablets. "Sloane feels you might not be as amenable as you should be tonight. So he gave me some pills to guarantee you'll be more accommodating than you were last night."

She yanked the packet from his fingers, her expression both angry and horrified. "What are these? Roofies?"

"Either that, or Special K," he said, having seen too much of the drug as an undercover vice cop. "Though Sloane assured me it's nothing more than a mild relaxant to calm your nerves."

"Jesus." She shook her head in disgust. "I won't be needing them. I don't even want them near me." She dropped the tablets into the toilet and flushed. Once they were gone, she turned so her back was to him once again. "You need to do me."

Despite the seriousness of the situation, her demand made him chuckle. "I'd love to *do you,* sweetheart, but we're a bit short on time right now."

She grinned over her shoulder at him. "Get your mind out of the gutter and lace me up."

"When it comes to you, my mind's always in the gutter," he teased as he gave the silk ties a firm pull, so that the corset fit snugly before finishing the crisscross pattern the rest of the way up to the top. "By the way, as far as you're concerned, there won't be any contact between you and Sloane tonight. I told him that I'd like for us to enjoy the party, and each other, and that we'd swap our girls at ten for the rest of the night. You for Angela."

"Except we won't be here?"

"Exactly." His big fingers fumbled with the thin silk laces as he attempted to make a secure bow. "The party starts at seven. By seven forty-five, we should have our escape plan executed and be on our way out of this place with Angela and Holly. It'll probably take a while for Sloane to realize you switched masks and that all of us are gone. But by then there won't be much he can do about it."

"Sounds like a solid plan." When he was done with the corset, she checked his handiwork in the mirror. "Wow, who would have thought you could make such a pretty, dainty bow?"

"Yeah, it's one of my other many talents, thanks to my older sisters who thought it necessary that I learn the fine art of bow tying," he said wryly. "Trust me, it's not the kind of skill I brag about."

"It'll be our little secret." She walked back to the rest of the costume hanging on the back of the door and retrieved the black, ruffled miniskirt. She stepped into the piece of clothing and zipped it up, then added a pair of black lace elbow-length gloves to complete the too-tempting outfit.

She spun around, placed her hands on her hips, and gave him a sultry pose. "What do you think?"

He found it difficult to *think* at all beyond the small, firm breasts nearly spilling from the front of her corset. "You look like a young courtesan," he said, which most likely had been Sloane's intent when he'd chosen her costume. And she hadn't even donned the exotic, black-and-purple sequined feathered mask yet.

"Hmmm. I guess that's what tonight's party is all about, huh?"

"Yeah, pretty much." He still needed to get dressed, but there were a few more things he wanted to discuss with Nicole before they left the bathroom. "Back to tonight and getting the girls out of here. Holly is the wild card in all this," he said, expressing his one big concern about tonight's extraction. "You do realize that, don't you?"

"Yes, I do." She sighed and dragged her fingers through her loose hair. "I think we'll be okay. Holly started drinking on the drive to the spa this morning. I'm certain she'll be sufficiently wasted by tonight in order to cope with having to entertain one of Sloane's friends, which will work to my advantage in getting her out of the house because she won't be thinking straight."

Nathan still had his doubts about the girl. "We know we have Angela's full cooperation, but you're going to have to make this a game for Holly. Make her think that leaving the house is going to lead to her being with Sloane."

She nodded her agreement. "Good idea. The only way she'll go willingly with me is if she believes she'll be able to have Sloane again."

"Once we're out those front gates, it won't matter what Holly does or how she reacts. She'll be safe." And that's all that mattered to him. "Oh, and I need you to get her real last name as quickly as possible so I can have Caleb run a background check on her and track down her parents."

"Sure, I can do that." She exhaled a deep breath. "It's almost time and you need to get dressed."

He gently caught her arm before she could leave, his gaze scanning her face. "Are you nervous?"

"No. Just determined." The conviction in her voice gave him all the reassurance he needed. "I want this done and over with."

"It will be. Very soon," he promised.

Chapter Eighteen

Wearing her elaborate feathered mask, and with Nathan dressed all in black with a matching black-and-gold mask covering his entire face, the two of them headed downstairs to the playroom at seven o'clock sharp to give them both time to mingle before separating to put their individual plans into action.

First things first. Nicole made sure that Sloane saw her. As he took in the seductive costume he'd specifically chosen for her to wear tonight, his eyes glazed over with lust and a lascivious smile curved his lips. She gave him a demure, *accommodating* nod of acknowledgment that seemed to please him, then turned her attention back to Nathan.

The main lounge area was filled with costumed men and girls in sexy, revealing outfits that ranged from lady pirates to maidens and jesters. Their face masks were decorated elaborately, making it difficult to recognize anyone at first glance. While the guests seemed to find that element of obscurity exciting, Nicole was just grateful that the disguises worked to her and Nathan's favor.

The music in the room was loud and pulsing, and even though the party had barely begun, couples were already grinding against each other and delighting in their brazen behavior. Just like the real Mardi Gras, the mood was bawdy and salacious, with liquor flowing freely and the atmosphere charged with the excitement of immoral temptations. Bright, colorful bead necklaces were tossed to the girls daring enough to flash their breasts, and masked men didn't hesitate to grab and grope the exposed flesh. Squeals of laughter pierced the air, along with cheers and catcalls.

Twenty minutes later, Nathan gave her *the look,* and they gradually separated to execute their plan.

Nicole made her way through the wild, gyrating crowd to the women's lounge, and immediately saw Angela standing at the far end of the long vanity mirror set up for the girls to use. There were at least half a dozen other girls vying for the use of the mirror to check their hair and makeup, but Nicole was only concerned about Angela, who was wearing a provocative blue-and-silver maiden's outfit. Her matching sequined mask was in place, but there was no mistaking how nervous she was about leaving the party without getting caught.

But when she was halfway to reaching Angela, another girl dressed as a court jester in a low-cut blouse and pantaloons stepped in front of Nicole, bringing her to an abrupt stop.

"Oh, my God," the girl exclaimed, her green eyes brimming with envy behind her plain black-and-white feathered mask. "How did you score such an amazing costume?"

Momentarily startled by the interruption when her

mind had been so focused on Angela, it took Nicole a few extra seconds to realize that she'd just been presented with a golden opportunity.

"Amazing?" Nicole injected a believable amount of doubt into her voice. "Personally, I think your outfit is way cuter."

"Are you kidding me?" The other girl shook her head. "I somehow ended up with the most unflattering outfit I've ever worn in my life!" She indicated her loose-fitting top and baggy pants. "I'd love to have that sexy corset and fun skirt instead. The colors are so bright and festive next to my boring black and white."

In this case, boring was good, Nicole decided. Very good. "Would you like to trade?"

The girl's eyes widened with excitement. "Are you serious?"

"Sure." Nicole shrugged nonchalantly. "It might be fun to switch things up and surprise my boyfriend with a different costume."

The girl giggled. "Then let's trade."

They headed into the adjoining bathroom and within five minutes they'd swapped their outfits. The other girl, a brunette with long, flowing straight hair, looked stunning in the tight-fitting black-and-purple corset, skirt, and mesh stockings. In comparison, Nicole looked ordinary and charming as a jester. There was absolutely nothing head-turning about the black-and-white disguise, which gave her the ability to blend in, rather than stand out.

Realizing that they were running about five minutes behind schedule, she quickly donned her feathered mask and exited the bathroom. It took Angela a few extra seconds to register the costume change, but as soon as she had the girl's attention, Nicole slid into the vacant spot next to Angela at the vanity mirror. Reaching into her bra, she withdrew the two hair clips she'd stashed there before leaving her room with Nathan.

She handed one to Angela, then began pulling her own hair back and away from her face to secure the mass at the nape of her neck. "Take off your mask and pin your hair up," she said, wanting to do whatever they could to change Angela's appearance, too.

While Angela did as she asked, Nicole cast a glance at the girls standing to her left, who were talking and laughing while they primped. Three of them had taken off their masks to fix their lip gloss and makeup, and Nicole decided that one of the girl's ugly mustard-yellow and puke-green sequined mask would make a nice disguise for Angela—which she would casually poach when they were ready to leave the lounge.

So far, everything was going smoothly, except for finding the one person who had the ability to put a major crimp in tonight's rescue attempt. Even knowing that Holly was a potential problem, she couldn't leave her behind.

"Have you by chance seen Holly tonight?" she asked Angela.

She nodded. "I saw her getting a drink at the bar on my way here."

And most likely, Holly was still near or around that area. "Okay." Nicole gently grabbed Angela's wrist with one hand, and pilfered the ugly mask with her other as she guided them out of the lounge and away from any listening ears.

Finding an unoccupied alcove, she stopped again and gave Angela her new mask. "Put this on," she said, and

nearly cringed at the grotesque colors now covering
Angela's face. As a disguise, it definitely worked. "I have
to find Holly and I need you to listen to me. While I'm
doing that, you head to the grotto, then make your way
to the outside pool area. There's a darkened pathway to
the left of the cabanas that leads around the side of the
house, and I want you to wait for me there."

She shifted anxiously. "Are you sure this is going to
work?"

God, Nicole hoped so. "As long as you do exactly
what I tell you to, we should be out of here very soon.
Now go, and I'll be there in a few minutes."

They parted ways. Nicole walked the perimeter of
the room, desperately trying to find Holly in a sea of
costumes and masks designed to conceal identities.
She scrutinized shapes of faces, color of hair, and what
would be close to Holly's height. Just as she was starting to panic that she'd never be able to find Holly in
time, she gave the bar area one last look and saw someone dressed in a red, gauzy sorceress outfit who looked
like the young girl.

Wearing a feathered mask and holding a tall drink
that the bartender had just made for her, the girl was
walking away, more than a little unsteady on her feet.
She was definitely inebriated, and Nicole said a little
prayer that she'd finally found who she'd been searching for.

"Holly?" she called out.

The red sorceress spun around, nearly tripping on
the long hem of her gown. She wobbled on her high
heels and just barely managed to regain her balance,
but not before she sloshed half of her drink down the
side of her dress. While she surveyed the damage to

her costume, Nicole lifted her mask to show her face just as the girl glanced back at her.

"Damn it," the girl muttered, then narrowed her gaze at Nicole. "What do *you* want?" she asked, her words slurred.

Even though the other girl was still wearing her mask, Nicole was familiar enough with Holly's angry glare to confirm it was her. Knowing she had to act fast to meet up with Nathan on time, Nicole stepped up to Holly, took the drink from her hand, and set it on a nearby table.

"Hey!" Holly said indignantly. "That's my drink!"

"You don't need it," Nicole said, hooking her arm securely through Holly's to lead her away from the main festivities. But as soon as she started forward, Holly pulled back and stiffened, forcing Nicole to a stop.

"What are you doin'?" Holly asked, clearly not budging unless it was for a good reason.

Nicole planned to give her one. "We have to hurry," she said, the urgency in her voice real. "Preston is waiting for you."

Holly's wide, glassy eyes, framed by flamboyant red feathers, blinked at her. "He . . . he is?"

The soft hope in the girl's voice pierced Nicole's heart, and a part of her hated that she had to lie to make sure that Holly cooperated. But using Sloane as an incentive was the only way to save her, and that's all Nicole cared about.

"He told me he wants to meet with you secretly. Kind of like a Mardi Gras rendezvous." This time when she guided Holly toward the grotto, the young girl stumbled along beside her.

"Where is he?" Holly asked as she pressed a hand to her head.

"I'm going to show you," she said in a soothing voice to make sure she kept Holly calm. "Just keep following me."

There were a few couples in the grotto, already in the process of peeling off their costumes for a dip in the hot tubs. The men were so focused on the eager-to-please girls they were with that they didn't give Nicole and Holly a passing glance.

"He loves me . . . doesn't he?" Holly's words were slowing, as if she was having a hard time stringing her thoughts together. "I knew he did. I told you if I was good . . . and did as he said . . . he'd take me . . . take me back."

"Shhh. You have to be quiet, Holly." They made it through the grotto and up to the pool area outside. There was no one there. Yet. It was only a matter of time before party revelers decided to go skinny-dipping. "He doesn't want anyone else to know that the two of you are meeting."

"You're moving . . . too . . . fast," she complained, sounding like a petulant five-year-old who'd been drugged. "I feel . . . soooo . . . dizzy."

"We have to hurry." It was the truth. Nicole veered toward the left of the cabanas and picked up her pace. She still had Holly's arm looped through hers, but the other girl kept slowing down and falling behind. "I don't want Preston to leave," she said, hoping that would urge the other girl to move faster.

It didn't. If anything, each stumbling step Holly took seemed to be weighted down with concrete. "Me, either," Holly whispered, the sound of tears choking her voice. "Don't leave . . . don't leave . . . don't leave," she chanted.

Holly seemed to become more lethargic, and Nicole was beginning to feel like she was dragging the girl through quicksand. She had to keep her cognizant, and the only way she could think to do that was to keep her talking.

"Holly, what is your last name?" she asked, because she needed the information for Nathan anyway.

"Last . . . name?" Holly sobbed, clearly falling apart emotionally. "I . . . I don't have one."

"Yes, you do. I need to know what it is," Nicole urged as she eased them toward the pathway where Angela was waiting for them. "Preston needs to know what it is. Think real hard, Holly. We can't get to him without your last name."

"Oh, God," she said, crying in earnest now as she honestly struggled to remember her surname. "I . . . It's Holly . . . Holly . . . Davis."

Nicole patted her hand. "Good girl."

"Where's . . . where's Preston?" Holly's breathing was labored, and she was leaning heavily against Nicole for support.

"We're almost there." She guided them down the pathway. Surrounded by lush foliage, they blended into the darkness.

"I'm . . . I'm not going to . . . to make it." Holly tripped and could barely hold herself upright. "I . . . don't . . . feel so good."

Nicole was glad to see Angela just up ahead on the pathway. At least one thing had gone right tonight. "Holly, what have you taken?"

"Just . . . just my . . . pills."

And unknown quantities of alcohol. Shit.

Before Nicole could catch her, Holly unexpectedly

dropped to her knees, clutched her stomach, and threw up on the grass. She moaned as she continued to heave. All the while, Nicole prayed that the sound didn't echo and prompt someone to investigate.

When there didn't seem to be anything left in Holly's stomach, she gave one last groan, then passed out cold.

Nicole stared in disbelief. How in the hell was she going to get Holly's deadweight all the way to the Hummer where Nathan was waiting for them?

Right on time, Nathan left the party and headed upstairs. He stopped for a moment to make sure no one was behind him, then made his way to the front door of the house. With the entryway in his sights, he pulled off his mask and set it on a side table he passed, his mind already on the next phase of the escape plan and hoping everything went smoothly for Nicole.

"Are you leaving, Alex?"

His hand was on the doorknob, but the question stopped him cold. Jesus Christ! Where in the hell had Gwen come from? The only good thing about running into Sloane's assistant was the assurance that she wasn't following Nicole. Remaining calm, he turned back around to face her, an excuse for his abrupt departure already forming.

"I just got a call on my cell," he said, as she stopped a few feet away. She was dressed as a sultry Mardi Gras vixen, her sequined mask in her hand, giving him a clear view of her very direct gaze. "I've got a problem with my Tokyo deal. I have to fix the contract and get it sent back immediately so everything is ready for signatures on Monday morning."

"On a Saturday?" she asked, her tone tinged with skepticism.

He flashed her a smile. "International business never sleeps."

"True," she replied, and seemed to relax. "Is Nikki going with you?"

"No, she's having too much fun at the party," he said easily. "I'll leave her here while I take care of business. I should be back in an hour or so."

Seemingly satisfied, Gwen let him exit the house without further questioning. Even if she immediately reported his absence to Sloane, it would take them both a while to realize that he wasn't coming back . . . and that he had Nicole with him. Longer still until they discovered Angela and Holly missing, too.

He walked toward where the Hummer was parked, which was around the corner from the front of the house, in a darkened area. The vehicle was still parked as he'd requested, with no other cars blocking his escape. Because of his delay with Gwen, he expected Nicole to be there with the girls, but she hadn't arrived yet.

He swore beneath his breath, knowing that their chances of being discovered increased with each minute that passed. He wondered where Nicole was, and prayed she hadn't gotten caught sneaking Angela and Holly out of the house. He worried most about Holly putting up a fight and blowing their escape.

Shit.

Just when he thought he'd have to go searching for Nicole, and possibly abort their escape, he saw three figures come around the side of the house. As they neared, he realized that Nicole, now dressed as a court jester, and Angela were struggling to support Holly between them, straining to keep her upright as they hauled her unconscious form to the Hummer.

Rushing to meet them, he scooped Holly up into his arms and carried her back to the vehicle. Questions would come later, once they were safely out of the estate. As quietly as possible, he got all three girls situated in the Hummer's cargo space and draped a dark blanket over them. For the moment, he was grateful Holly was passed out so there was no chance of her kicking up a fuss and blowing his cover when they reached the guard at the gate. As he rounded the front of the Hummer, his gaze scanned the vicinity to make sure the area was clear and there were no witnesses.

Using the spare key he kept in his wallet, he started the vehicle and headed for the main gate. The security guy waited for him to stop, then came up to the driver's window, which Nathan rolled down.

"Everything okay?" the guy asked.

Judging by the other man's relaxed attitude, Nathan was certain Sloane hadn't yet discovered that the girls were gone. "I just have some business to attend to. I'll be back."

The guard gave him a nod, then returned to his post and opened the gates. Once they were clear, Nathan drove out onto the main road. He immediately called Caleb to give him an estimated time of arrival. His boss let him know that Angela's parents had arrived and that Skye and Valerie were at his place to balance out the male-to-female ratio, and to make sure Angela felt comfortable. Nathan couldn't bring himself to tell Caleb that they'd taken Holly—he'd find out soon enough, and they'd deal with the situation then.

He disconnected the call. Five miles away from Sloane's estate he told Nicole they could come out, but should still lie low.

"What happened with Holly?" he finally asked.

"She passed out on me after throwing up," Nicole told him. "She wasn't very cooperative, either. I'm certain if she was awake she would be fighting to get back to Sloane."

As if on cue, the young girl stirred and moaned. "Where . . . where are you . . . taking me?"

"You're fine, Holly," Nicole said gently, keeping her reply simple and vague. "Just relax and we'll be there soon."

"With Preston?" Holly asked, her voice raspy.

"Yeah, with Preston," Nicole lied, obviously not wanting to upset the girl.

Reassured that Holly didn't need to be rushed to the hospital, Nathan glanced in his rearview mirror at the other blonde they'd rescued. "Are you okay, Angela?"

"Yes." Her voice was soft and low, with the slightest hint of nervousness.

Nathan guessed she was worried about the reconciliation with her parents. But considering the Ramseys had gone to such great lengths to get their daughter back, he knew Angela had nothing to worry about.

He called Caleb again just as he turned down the street, and when he reached his boss's house, the garage door was already open for him. Pulling the Hummer inside, he waited for the steel doors to slide shut before helping the girls out of the back.

Angela was the first to exit, then Nicole. Nathan had to lift a still-groggy Holly from the vehicle, and help her stand. She was unsteady on her feet, and as she looked around the garage, her changing expression reflected her bewilderment.

She looked at Nicole, her gaze dazed and confused. "Where am I?"

Nicole stepped up to Holly and gently grasped her hand. "You're somewhere safe."

Nathan took Angela's arm and led her into the house, with Holly and Nicole following behind. As soon as they walked into the kitchen area, they were greeted by Caleb, Skye, and Valerie. Being in a strange place was all it took to set Holly off.

She glared angrily at Nicole. "Where's Preston? You told me you were taking me to see Preston!"

"He's not here," Nicole said, trying to reason with the girl. "But you're safe and you're going to be okay."

"You lied!" She jerked away from Nicole, stumbling backward and almost tripping on the hem of her sorceress dress. "I want Preston!" Her eyes were wide and wild.

Without asking questions about who the girl was, Valerie and Skye stepped up to Holly, each of them gently taking one of her arms to subdue her. She struggled to break free, but the two women held her without hurting her. They'd been trained for situations like this, and Nathan knew they'd be able to get through to Holly once she calmed down.

"You bitch!" Holly yelled at Nicole as tears ran down her face and smeared her makeup. "I hate you!"

Nicole winced, a pained look on her face. "I know you're upset right now, but in time you'll be glad you're out of there."

"No, I won't," she sobbed. "You had no right to take me away from Preston!"

"Let us take her," Valerie said to Nicole, obviously wanting to defuse the situation. "We'll get her settled in the guest bedroom and calmed down. You go with Nathan and Caleb. Angela's parents are waiting for her in the living room."

"Okay." Nicole sighed as Valerie and Skye led the hostile girl away.

"I want Preston," Holly wailed, the pitiful sound echoing down the hall. "Take me back. Please, take me back."

"We can't, honey." Valerie tried to soothe her. "But you'll be fine here. I promise."

Seeing the worry lines creasing Nicole's forehead, Nathan sought to comfort her. "She's in good hands. Let's reunite Angela with her parents."

Nicole nodded. Putting on a smile, she turned back to Angela. The young girl had been through so much, but she'd survived and had her freedom back, unlike the girls they'd had to leave behind. "Are you ready?"

Angela appeared anxious, but the look in her eyes was cautiously hopeful. "Yes. I think so."

Taking Angela's hands in hers, Nicole gave them an encouraging squeeze. She wanted to make sure there were no doubts in the girl's mind that she'd made the right choice in trusting her and Nathan. "Remember, we did this because your parents *wanted* us to find you. Don't ever doubt that they love you, no matter what has happened."

Tears shimmered in Angela's eyes. "Thank you for

getting me out of there. I was so scared that I'd never see my mom and dad again."

If not for her and Nathan's involvement, she probably wouldn't have. "Then let's go and see them so they can take you home where you belong."

Caleb led the way into the living room, and as soon as the four of them walked in, the man and woman standing by the fireplace stared at the girl still dressed in her Mardi Gras costume. Time seemed to stand still, as if Angela and her parents were uncertain as to who should make the first move.

"Oh, my God," the woman whispered, and pressed shaking fingers to her lips. The heartbreak of missing her daughter shone in her eyes.

"Smidget," the man said in a voice choked with emotion.

The sweet endearment was spoken with such warmth and affection that Nicole had no doubt everything among the three of them was going to be just fine.

"Go on," she gently urged Angela, who seemed to need that extra bit of encouragement. "They're waiting for you."

A sob broke in her throat, and then she was rushing toward her parents, who welcomed her back with open arms, embracing her with unconditional love and compassion. Nicole stood beside Nathan and Caleb, barely holding back her own emotions as the Ramsey family shared hugs, tears of joy, and the kind of reassurances that told Nicole that Angela was going to be just fine.

"I want to go home," Angela said, and her parents were quick to agree.

Tom Ramsey stepped toward Caleb and shook his hand, then Nathan's. "Thank you both for saving my daughter. Considering the police weren't any help, I appreciate your assistance."

"You're welcome," Nathan replied.

"Once I have Nathan's full report written up, I'll be in touch," Caleb told the other man.

"Great. I appreciate it." The relief at having his daughter back was visible on his face. "We have a flight back to Arizona tonight, so we'd better head to the airport."

Nicole knew the Ramseys weren't going to press charges against Sloane. They just wanted their daughter back safely. Since Angela, at sixteen, was at the legal age of consent in Nevada, they couldn't prosecute Sloane.

It made Nicole sick to think that Sloane was getting off scot-free for abducting Angela, and every other girl he'd enticed to The Sanctuary, when he deserved a long sentence in prison.

Everyone said their good-byes, and once the Ramseys were gone, Caleb didn't waste time addressing the other issue still left unfinished.

"Who is Holly and why do we have an extra girl when you were only supposed to extract Angela?" Caleb asked, direct and to the point.

Before Nathan could respond, Nicole stepped forward and accepted the blame. "It's my fault that we took Holly."

She didn't feel she needed to explain her reasons to Caleb, because it wouldn't change anything. Besides, it only mattered that Nathan understood why she'd felt the overwhelming need to save the girl.

"I'm pretty certain that she's underage," Nicole went on, a little intimidated by Caleb's intense, piercing stare and commanding presence. "She slipped up and told me she's fifteen. Her full name is Holly Davis, which should help you locate her family."

"I'll find out who she is," Caleb said.

Before Nicole could ask what would happen to the young girl, Valerie walked into the room.

"How's Holly doing?" Despite knowing the girl hated her, Nicole was still worried about her emotional and mental well-being.

"She's a little calmer and resting, though I'm guessing her obsession with Preston is a result of Stockholm syndrome," Valerie suggested. "It's very common with runaways and girls that are kidnapped to fall in love with their captors, which seems to be the case with Holly."

"How do you know she was kidnapped?" Nicole asked, wondering how Valerie had come to that conclusion.

"I asked Holly how she got involved with Preston, and she told me that she ran away from home nearly a year ago, when she was fourteen." Valerie exchanged a quick glance with Caleb that Nicole couldn't read before continuing. "She was picked up in San Bernardino, California, by someone named Gwen, then brought to Las Vegas and taken to Sloane's estate, where she's been ever since."

Nicole was shocked that the belligerent young girl had shared so much with a virtual stranger. "Wow, you got all that from Holly?"

Valerie shrugged. "I just know how to ask the right questions."

"I have to say, you're good." Nicole still couldn't believe Holly had given up so much personal information so easily. Then again, judging by her own experience with Valerie, there was something very intuitive about the woman. She had a way of reading people that was both unnerving and fascinating.

Nathan glanced at Caleb in pleasant surprise, along with a bit of triumph shining in his eyes. "I'll be damned. Looks like we have enough evidence to bring charges against Sloane in a federal case, outside any influence he has with local law enforcement."

Caleb's look echoed Nathan's satisfaction. "We can bring in the FBI to start an investigation on the charges, as well as look into his connections in human trafficking."

An adrenaline rush of excitement pulsed through Nicole at the thought of Sloane going to prison for what he'd done to Holly, and every other girl he'd violated. No doubt many other girls had been picked up off the street and taken to Sloane's estate to be prostituted out to his buddies. The charges would be myriad, not to mention that Sloane would have a lot of company in prison.

"So, he's going to be arrested?" she asked, needing confirmation that the bastard would soon be behind bars.

"Just as soon as it can be arranged through the proper channels," Caleb replied with a business-like nod. "I'll give the attorney general a call and start the ball rolling, then I'll run a background check on Holly so I can contact her parents."

Nicole breathed a sigh of relief that something good had come of all this. That not only had she rescued Holly from a dire situation, but soon Sloane would no longer be able to prey on young girls' innocence and naïveté.

Caleb left them to make some phone calls, and Valerie headed back to the guest room to check on Holly, leaving Nicole alone with Nathan.

"You did good," Nathan said to her, the admiration and respect in his gaze genuine and warm. "You should be proud of yourself."

"*We* did good." She couldn't have accomplished any of what she had without him by her side, and she'd like to think that she'd been a necessary component to helping him get Angela out of Sloane's estate, too. "You and I make a good team." The words spilled out before she realized the double meaning to them.

"Yeah, we do," Nathan replied huskily as he brushed his thumb along her jaw and his fingers caressed the side of her neck in a tender, romantic touch. "In more ways than one."

He was referring to the two of them—not professionally, but intimately. Beyond the case and working together to rescue the two girls, to the deeper feelings that had developed between them. Feelings she'd desperately tried to keep contained to physical attraction alone, but somehow, someway, they'd evolved into something far more real that scared the hell out of her and threatened everything she'd worked so hard to achieve.

Her heart beat faster in her chest, and an overwhelming sense of vulnerability swamped her. Over the past few weeks with Nathan, from the moment they'd met at the speed-dating event, he'd become her greatest weakness. Sexually, she couldn't get enough of him. But it was the underlying emotions he evoked that struck fear into her heart, because she didn't trust her ability to fall in love and not lose her sense of self all over again.

She took a step back from him, her stiff body language speaking volumes. Knowing it was best that she kept their conversation focused on the case, and off them, she thought about the young girl in the other room. "Thank you for letting me take Holly."

"I don't think you would have given me a choice." His smile was a little sad, as if he realized she was pulling away from him, retreating from everything they'd shared. And that there wasn't a damn thing he could do about it.

"Probably not." She swallowed hard. The hurt she saw in his eyes was much more difficult to bear than she realized. "I'm happy to hear Sloane will get his comeuppance. Knowing that is like icing on the cake."

"Nicole . . . are you okay?" His voice was soft and worried, like no other man's had ever been before.

No, she wasn't okay. She was a wreck, inside and out. She could feel pieces of her heart splintering, and wondered how long the ache in her chest would last. "I'm just tired."

His jaw clenched, and he pushed his hands into his pants pockets, as if that would keep him from reaching out and touching her again, which would undoubtedly be her undoing.

"You and I need to talk," he said.

Not here and not now. She just couldn't handle what was bound to be a painful discussion after the day, and evening, she'd had. She was mentally exhausted, and too emotionally raw.

"I need to be with Holly right now." It was the truth and an excuse, all in one.

To her immense relief, he let her go without a reply, but it was the unspoken emotions lingering in his gaze that told her she'd only been granted a brief reprieve.

Chapter Nineteen

Throughout the night, Nicole sat next to Holly's bed, curled up in the comfortable chair Caleb had brought in for her to use while she watched over the young girl she felt responsible for. Nicole was exhausted and drained, yet a deep, restful sleep eluded her. There was too much going on in her mind—her worry for Holly, thoughts of Sloane's impending arrest, and the disappointment in Nathan's eyes as she'd walked away from him earlier.

The latter still haunted her, in ways she'd never anticipated.

As the hours slowly passed, Holly tossed and turned in her bed, moaning and whimpering as her own dreams, and possibly nightmares, plagued her. The few times she did wake up Nicole made her drink gulps of cool water to help flush the alcohol and drugs out of her system, though Nicole had a strong feeling the young girl was going to feel like crap come morning. By then, the narcotics would have worn off and Holly would be forced to deal in the real world with nothing to dull her anxiety, emotional pain, and the reality of her situation.

She heard Caleb's and Nathan's voices drifting in from the other room, along with an occasional comment from Valerie, and knew they were discussing details of the case, gathering information on Holly, and getting in touch with all the pertinent agencies to take Sloane down.

By dawn, Nicole's heavy eyelids drooped and she snuggled into the blanket wrapped around her and nodded off. When she woke up half an hour later, she found Holly awake, curled up on her side, her vacant gaze staring at the wall behind Nicole. The girl's makeup was smeared, showing her pale complexion, and her hair was a disheveled mess around her face. She looked so empty and alone, and much older than her fifteen years. Her innocence and childhood were gone, stolen by a man who had no regard for the lives he destroyed in his quest for his own sick pleasures.

Nicole sat up in her chair so she was closer to the side of the bed. Holly didn't even acknowledge that she was there, though she knew the girl was well aware of her presence. Most likely, she was still pissed off at Nicole for taking her away from Sloane.

"How are you feeling?" Nicole asked softly.

Holly didn't respond, clearly ignoring her.

Sighing, but by no means defeated, Nicole tried again. "Would you like some breakfast? I can make you some eggs or toast." Eventually the girl would need to put something in her stomach—other than drugs and alcohol.

"I don't want anything from you," Holly finally said, her voice flat and spiritless. "Just go away."

Okay, she was talking. At least that was a start. "Do you remember where you are?" Nicole asked, unsure what the girl recalled from last night. "That I took you away from Preston's estate and brought you somewhere safe?"

Her gaze finally met Nicole's, a spark of renewed animosity flashing in her eyes as last night's events came back to her. "You had no right to take me!"

"We did have the right to take you," Nicole said gently, trying to keep the girl calm. "You're only fifteen, Holly. You're an underage runaway who was kidnapped and taken to Preston's place in Summerlin."

Holly's brows snapped into a frown. "Who told you that?"

So, she didn't remember her conversation with Valerie. "Last night, you talked to one of the other women who is here. You told her you ran away from home a year ago, when you were fourteen, and that Gwen brought you to Vegas from California."

"I wouldn't tell anyone that!" she said, her tone panicked. "I'm eighteen and I want to be with Preston."

Both Sloane and Gwen had done an excellent job in brainwashing the young girl. "What Preston did, what Gwen did, was against the law." Wanting to offer Holly comfort, Nicole reached out to grab the girl's hand.

Holly yanked her arm away, sat up in bed, and glared at Nicole. "I don't care. I'll do anything to be with Preston, to make him happy. He'll find me and he'll come for me. I know he will!"

"He's not coming for you," Nicole said, not wanting Holly to be under any illusions. "As soon as your parents are located, you'll be reunited with them, and they'll take you back home."

Holly shook her head wildly, and tears brimmed in

her eyes. "I don't want to go back. My mother doesn't want me. She's never wanted me."

It didn't escape Nicole's notice that Holly only mentioned the one parent, and it seemed like the relationship hadn't been a good one. It was hard to imagine that a mother would discard a child so easily, and she wondered if Holly's perception of what it had been like at home was somehow skewed after her time with Sloane.

"Why do you think your mother doesn't want you?" Nicole asked. Her own parents would have come for her in a heartbeat, just as Angela's had.

Tears ran down the girl's cheek as memories of her past seemed to overwhelm her. "My mother was always too busy with her boyfriend of the week, and most of them were creeps. She left me alone all the time while she and whatever guy she was dating went out and partied. Sometimes, she didn't even come home until the morning. I wanted to live with my dad, but my mom wouldn't let me."

"Where's your dad?" Nicole asked, curious to know why her father hadn't been a direct part of her life.

"He's in the army," she said, and swiped away the wet tears from her face. "He's stationed in Germany. I miss him so much."

Oh, hell. It sounded as though Holly's home life had been a heart-wrenchingly dysfunctional one. Most likely she'd rebelled in various ways in the hope of getting just a fraction of the attention her mother gave to her boyfriends. When her attempts hadn't worked, she'd decided to run away. And then Sloane had come along and had given her what she craved the most—attention, affection, and gifts to make her feel loved.

"I want Preston." Holly lay back down on the bed, facing away from Nicole this time. "He loves me, I know he does," she said, and Nicole knew Holly believed her own words.

"If Preston loved you, why was he asking you to be with other men?" Nicole asked, hoping the question would break through the girl's stubborn mind-set. It was the same question she'd asked herself over and over, while fighting an internal struggle over Mark's request to sleep with another man.

Holly stiffened. "Go away," she said, choosing not to answer, probably because there was no justification for what Sloane had done to her. "I want to be alone."

There was so much more Nicole could say to Holly to point out all of Sloane's immoral flaws, but in the girl's current mental state, Preston was her hero, the man who'd taken her in and had given her nice things and a false sense of security and love. Never mind that he'd also exploited her and had already started passing her around to other men. Nicole had no doubt that he would have eventually sold her off to his Russian connections for an even worse life, with no chance of ever going home again.

There was no reasoning with Holly in her current frame of mind, and it would be a waste of Nicole's breath to continue trying. The girl required the kind of professional help that Nicole wasn't equipped to provide, and she'd talk to Caleb to make sure she received some kind of counseling to heal her damaged emotions.

But in the meantime, she wanted to be sure the girl had someone to talk to if she needed support. She looked through the nightstand and found a pen and a notepad, then jotted down her name and her cell phone number. She ripped off the piece of paper, came around the bed and tucked it beneath Holly's hand, then gently touched her hair, wishing there was some easy way to make all this go away for Holly. Unfortunately, there was nothing simple or easy about what the girl had been through.

Holly didn't move or acknowledge her touch or the note she'd given her. "If you ever need someone to talk to, that's my cell number. You can call me *anytime*."

Again, Holly didn't respond, but neither did she crumple up her phone number and toss it aside, which Nicole took as a positive sign.

The longer she stared at Holly, the more Nicole saw a part of herself in the young girl. From the very beginning, she'd been drawn to Holly, the need to protect her strong because she knew what the girl was going through.

All too well, Nicole understood the pain of Holly's situation—of once being Sloane's "it" girl, of being asked to do unmentionable things with other men, then being cast off for someone younger and prettier. Mark Reeves had been older and charming—a man who knew all the right words to make a girl's heart beat faster. Yet beneath all that charisma had been a selfish, egotistical player who had no qualms about using his female students for his own sexual gratification.

She'd fallen in love with Mark quickly and completely, and had been willing to do *anything* to make him happy, to make sure he loved her, and only her. To the point that she'd done degrading, humiliating things because she'd been just as obsessed with Mark as Holly was with Preston. Her entire world had revolved around her professor, to the exclusion of everything else.

A shiver rippled down her spine, and the chill of a deep-seated fear touched her heart. After Mark, she'd deliberately spent years in casual relationships, keeping her emotions out of the equation while embracing her independence and working toward building her career as a journalist. She'd learned the difficult lesson that giving any man control over her emotions was the most painful, self-destructive thing she'd ever done.

She'd only known Nathan a few weeks, yet already she couldn't get enough of him. Her strong feelings for him were crossing all those emotional boundaries she'd set for herself, the ones she'd erected to protect her heart and everything else that was important to her.

An onslaught of doubts swept through her, forcing her to question whether her emotions toward Nathan were even real, or if he was nothing more than an obsession, a result of their close proximity over the past few weeks. Was she about to repeat the pattern of her past and risk losing her identity as a journalist and as a woman? And what price would she pay to love Nathan, knowing he could walk away at any given moment?

She feared the answer.

Oh, God. She pressed her fingers to her lips as she looked down at Holly, a clear-cut reminder of what giving her heart and soul to someone could reduce her to. And that's when Nicole knew she just didn't have it in her to take that risk with Nathan, because she'd never be able to survive the heartbreak of losing him.

Nicole had to make a choice, and she knew which one it had to be. She couldn't lose focus as a woman or as a reporter, not when she was on the cusp of something huge with her career. She was about to get the big breakout story on Sloane after all, and she was confident that the exclusive would open up myriad opportunities for her. The kind that would require dedication and commitment to her job. She needed to remain true to herself this time, making the choice to leave before it was made for her. Or before she did something stupid in the name of love.

It was time to end things between them. She knew saying good-bye was going to hurt, that she would miss so many things about Nathan. But she knew it was much easier to shut the door on someone else than have it shut on her. *Their* story was done. It was time for her to move on and heal.

A soft knock on the door startled Nicole out of her troubling thoughts, and she glanced from Holly to Valerie, who stood just inside the bedroom.

"I heard you two talking in here a while ago and thought I'd give you a break," the other woman said, her gaze compassionate. Then, in a lower voice, she said, "Nathan is waiting to talk to you in the other room."

"Thanks," Nicole said, even though she had no intention of having a long, drawn-out conversation with Nathan about them.

Nathan wanted to talk, but for her, there was nothing left to discuss.

Nathan glanced up from the information he and Caleb were reviewing on his laptop as Nicole entered the living room. He was quick to notice she avoided eye contact with him—not that he was surprised. Everything about her body language told him that sometime in the past six hours she'd spent by Holly's bedside, she'd erected emotional barriers and was already closing herself off to him . . . and anything between them beyond this case.

Last night, she'd changed from her jester costume to a large T-shirt and a pair of drawstring shorts Caleb had given her to wear. She'd scrubbed her face clean, and except for the dark circles beneath her eyes, she appeared like a young girl herself. She also looked worn out, and he knew her exhaustion was both emotional and physical.

For now, he'd let business take precedence.

She stood across the room from where Nathan and Caleb were sitting on the sofa. "I found out from Holly that her mother and father aren't together, and she lived with her mother before running away."

"We know," Nathan said. "We have a full background report on her. She's listed as a runaway, and she's only fifteen years old, which helps us finally nail Sloane. We contacted her mother about an hour ago to let her know we have Holly."

A troubled look passed across Nicole's features. "How did her mother react?"

"She was shocked and happy her daughter was alive and okay." A normal response in Nathan's opinion. "Why?"

She ran her fingers through her hair and sighed. "Because the two of them didn't have a great relationship. According to Holly, her mother spent more time with her various boyfriends than with her."

Nathan sensed where Nicole was heading with her comments, and knew he had to get her to start cutting those emotional ties to Holly, despite whatever the girl's family relationships had been. "Her mother is on her way from California to pick her up. She should be here in a few hours." He said softly, "You need to let it go, Nicole."

The concern in her eyes shone bright. "I just don't want to take her out of one bad situation and place her in another. She might be better off with her father, even though he's stationed in Germany."

"It's not our choice to make," Caleb cut in, not bothering to temper the bluntness of his words. For him, this was a cut-and-dried situation, and while Nathan knew that deep inside Caleb was sympathetic, his boss handled all his cases objectively.

"I'll be taking Holly to The Onyx with me. Valerie will stay with her until her mother arrives," Caleb continued, making it clear this was the end of Nicole's involvement with the girl. "We'll probably hold Holly at the hotel for a few days so the FBI can talk to her and everything gets straightened out. Then she'll be released to her mother's custody."

"Okay," Nicole said, though the stunned look on her face told Nathan she wasn't dealing well with the brusque way Caleb was handling the situation. She was having difficulty separating herself from Holly and accepting that her part in the case was done.

Caleb stood and crossed the room to Nicole, extending his hand to shake hers. "I want to thank you for your help," he said, the sentiment genuine. "We appreciate everything you've done to help get Angela back to her parents, and we'll handle everything else from here."

Nathan winced inwardly. Caleb's words sounded like a cool dismissal. But Nathan knew how his boss operated and he was treating Nicole, and the success of the mission, in a professional manner. In Caleb's mind, he'd already moved on to the investigative part of the case and the feds' involvement to take down Sloane.

Caleb headed into the kitchen, leaving Nathan alone with Nicole. He stood up, more than a little tired himself. He'd stayed up all night with Caleb working on the case. They desperately needed a break before the shit really hit the fan with Sloane, and he also needed to get Nicole somewhere safe. After discussing the options with Caleb, they'd both agreed she'd be secure in her apartment until everything was resolved, since Sloane didn't know who she was.

"You've had a long weekend," he said, his voice low and soothing. "I'm going to take you home."

She glanced back at the guest bedroom, her reluctance to leave Holly behind palpable.

"She's in the best hands possible," he said in an attempt to reassure her. Then he held out his hand for Nicole to take, which she did. "Come on, sweetheart. You need a hot shower and lots of sleep, and you'll be more comfortable doing both back at your apartment."

Instead of taking the Hummer, which attracted too much attention, Nathan used Caleb's car to drive Nicole to her place. She sat quietly in the passenger seat, and with each passing mile he could feel her withdrawing and emotionally closing herself off to him. He hated that she could so easily shut him out after everything they'd shared, but he also knew that the stress of what she'd endured was a huge part of the reason she was retreating into herself.

Right now, making sure Nicole was safe and protected was his main priority. Until they arrested Sloane, the man was still a threat. Nathan had already started closing off all the trails for Alex Keller, and Lucas was making sure the identity was completely erased, as if that persona had never existed. As a material witness for the case, he'd be required to give a deposition for the feds, as would Nicole. But until her presence was required, she needed to lie low.

He arrived at her apartment and walked Nicole up to her place. Once the door was unlocked, she stepped inside and turned around, but didn't invite him inside—a telling sign he heeded. For now.

"What happens from here?" she asked, her voice as tired as she looked.

"Until Sloane is in custody, you need to keep out of sight," he said, making sure she was clear on that. "Stay in your apartment and don't go to work. I'll keep in touch so you know what's going on, or you can reach me on my cell at any time."

She nodded. "How long is it going to take?"

"At least three days." He shifted on his feet, trying hard to give her the space she seemed to need, even though the distance between them was killing him. "Less if the feds move quickly."

She rubbed her fingers across her furrowed forehead as she processed his answer. "Then what?"

"We can go back to our regular lives." For him, that meant a future that included her in it. A committed relationship that eventually led to marriage, when she was ready to make that step. "And you can write your exclusive story on Sloane, like you wanted."

He expected an ecstatic response from her, since exposing Sloane had been her goal from the beginning. But she didn't even acknowledge the coup that would be hers, and hers alone.

Instead, she stood there, like an empty shell of herself.

Seeing her so devoid of emotion scared the crap out of him. "All my stuff is still at the Turnberry apartment."

The mundane conversation grated on his nerves, and also set off an uneasy sensation deep inside him. "Caleb has a crew coming in and cleaning everything up. He'll get your things packed, and I'll bring them to you."

She shook her head, her expression suddenly adamant, as was the way she lifted her chin. "No, just have them send everything to me."

The finality of her words hit him in the stomach like a sucker punch. Right here, right now, she was ending things with him, without giving him any choice in the matter. And it royally pissed him off.

His first instinct was to confront her, to lay everything on the line and force her to acknowledge that there was something special between them. To argue that *they* weren't over just because the case was, or because she decided they were done.

Goddamn it, *he loved her.* And he knew she cared for him, too. Their relationship might have started out as strictly sexual, but there was no denying the deep emotional connection that had formed between the two of them.

But she *was* denying her true feelings in the only way she knew how, by reverting to past behavior and walking away before things became even more complicated— just as she'd done the first evening they'd met when she'd slipped out on him in the middle of the night. She was trying to protect her heart the only way she knew how, even if that meant sacrificing her own happiness in the process.

Frustrated by her behavior, he exhaled a deep breath, which calmed his anger and helped him to think straight before he said or did something he'd regret later. He knew the events of the past few days were skewing her judgment. She wasn't trained to deal with the emotional impact of what she'd witnessed at Sloane's. She didn't possess the skills he did to compartmentalize her feelings. His training kept his focus on the mission, and logic ruled his behavior. Everything about this case had affected her emotionally.

She needed time to process everything. She needed space to put everything in perspective, including what was between the two of them. Right now, she was overwhelmed. If he pushed her to examine her feelings for him, she was going to snap. Hell, one of the most valuable lessons he'd learned from his own sisters was that if he made demands of a woman when she was stressed, she was going to make a decision that he'd regret.

And he didn't want any regrets between him and Nicole.

He took a step back, so he was no longer standing in the doorframe. "You and I aren't done yet." His words were short and to the point.

A flicker of sadness passed through her soft blue eyes. Then, without a response, she shut the door on him, closing the door on *them*.

Chapter Twenty

Nicole leaned against the closed door long after she knew that Nathan had gone. Her throat was tight with unshed tears, and she felt so jagged and raw inside. The weekend had stripped her emotions bare and left her defenseless, exposed, and hurting in ways she'd never imagined.

She needed a hot shower. She needed to eat. She needed hours of deep, dreamless sleep. But most of all, she needed to rid her mind of the ugly, unpleasant memories of the weekend. And the only way she knew how to do that was to write the story that was hers alone to tell. The grim facts and details were clawing to get out, and she knew she'd never rest until the experience was purged from her soul.

Since her laptop was still at the Turnberry apartment, she turned on the desktop computer in her bedroom. Michelle had spent the weekend with her fiancé, and Nicole was grateful to be alone. She sat down at the desk, opened a new Word document, and put her fingers to the keyboard.

The story of Sloane, his exploitation of young girls,

and his involvement in human trafficking spilled out of Nicole faster than she could type. But then her past collided with the present, and she realized that she wasn't just writing the story for her career; it had also become a huge cathartic release for the shame and humiliation she'd carried with her for so many years, along with the fears that kept her from risking her heart again. It all poured out of her, a wealth of fear and heartache, and all the anger she'd kept buried for much too long.

It wasn't until hours later, when she was nearly done with the piece, that she became aware of the wet trail of tears on her face. She was supposed to be a dispassionate journalist, yet she was an emotional mess. But despite the pain of reliving the past, and the anxiety of rehashing what she'd witnessed at Sloane's estate, she felt as though she'd set a part of herself free in writing what had become a very personal story for her. In her mind, she'd finally righted a wrong, and bringing down Sloane would save many other girls from falling victim to a man's manipulations.

The knowledge gave her a heady, uplifting feeling of triumph.

Beyond spent, her mind and body completely tapped out, she saved the document, pushed her keyboard aside, and laid her head on the cool surface of her desk. She really did need food, a shower, and sleep, and she told herself she'd get up in just a minute . . .

The ringing of her cell phone jolted Nicole upright. Her head felt heavy, her mind unfocused. It took her a moment to realize that more than a minute had passed. As she blinked to clear the slumberous haze from her vision, a squinty-eyed glance at the clock on her desk told her she'd been asleep for nearly three hours.

Her phone rang again. She cleared her throat before flipping it open and answering the call. "Hello?"

"It's . . . it's Holly."

Getting an unexpected call from Holly was enough to snap Nicole to immediate attention. "Are you okay?"

"No. I need you."

Nicole's heart leapt into her throat. Holly sounded scared, and an uneasy sensation filled Nicole. "Where are you? Where is your mother?"

"I left the casino and I came back to The Sanctuary to be with Preston."

Nicole heard a gruff, angry voice in the background, then what sounded like a slap.

Holly started to cry. "He's going to kill me if you don't come. He wants you."

The line disconnected.

Oh, God. Nicole had no idea what Sloane knew about her and Nathan, but the man was obviously obsessed with her and wanted her back. And she had no doubts that if she didn't arrive quickly, Holly would pay the price. And if that happened, Nicole would never, ever forgive herself.

With adrenaline rushing through her veins, and her stomach in knots, she slipped into her flip-flops. She grabbed her purse and keys as she passed through the living room and out the door. In less than a minute she was in her car, heading toward Summerlin.

Panic made her heart race as she sped to the outskirts of the city. Knowing she couldn't save Holly by herself, she called Nathan's cell phone number, and cursed when she was sent directly to voice mail.

She knew he was most likely meeting with the feds, and prayed he'd get her message quickly. "It's Nicole.

Holly just called me and she's back at Sloane's. He threatened to kill her if I don't come. I'm on my way there now."

Minutes later, she arrived at the closed iron gates. The guard was obviously expecting her because he opened the gate and let her through. Her car came to a screeching halt in front of the house, and she jumped out and ran toward the entrance, her only thought to get to Holly before something horrible happened to the girl.

As soon as she stepped into the entryway, Gwen was there to greet her, a gun pointed directly at Nicole's chest. As always, she looked the polished, professional assistant, and more beautiful than such an evil woman should.

A bitter smile curved the other woman's red lips and hatred gleamed in her eyes. "So nice of you to join us."

The gun scared Nicole. Especially when it was in the hands of someone so obviously unstable. "Where is she?" Nicole demanded.

Gwen ignored her question. "I don't know why Preston thinks you're so special," she sneered, her voice dripping with jealousy. "But he'll get tired of you soon enough. You're just a passing fancy, as are all the other girls he's fucked. And then he'll either kill you, or send you off to Russia like all those others, where you'll spend the rest of your life lying flat on your back for other men to screw."

A deranged light flickered in Gwen's eyes. "I'm the only one who truly loves Preston, and you bitches have always gotten in the way of what I've wanted!" She waved the gun wildly between them. "He'll come back to me because I'm the only one who stayed and protected him. I've watched him go through all those girls while I've been the perfect executive assistant, handling his business affairs and cleaning up all the messes you girls have made. He can't live without me. One day, Preston will get too old for all this shit. The girls will no longer want him, and he'll turn to me and finally be *all* mine."

Nicole realized that at one time, in her youth, Gwen had been one of Sloane's "it" girls. But unlike so many of the girls who were cast aside, Gwen had found a way to make herself indispensible to Sloane, with the hope that he'd one day want her, and only her.

The woman was delusional and dangerous. It was a frightening sight to behold.

Gwen circled her and pressed the barrel of the gun against her spine, urging her up the spiral staircase. Nicole slowly started climbing.

"Preston is going to get what he wants, and then we'll just dispose of you both," Gwen continued matter-of-factly. "And then there's the little matter of Alex, your protector. He stole from Preston. We have plans for him, too. He reneged on a deal, and no one breaks a deal with Preston. Alex is going to pay for betraying his trust. He's going to die, just as you and Holly are."

Nicole swallowed hard as Gwen directed her down a hallway. Despite her outward courage, Nicole was terrified inside. If Nathan didn't get her message soon, she feared that she and Holly would end up dead.

Reaching the end of the corridor, Gwen shoved Nicole into a large, spacious master bedroom. The first thing Nicole saw was Holly sitting on the huge bed, the dress she was wearing ripped and torn. She was sobbing, her cheek red where she'd been slapped, probably more than once.

"I'm so sorry," Holly whispered in a quivering voice, and Nicole believed that the girl regretted her decision to return.

"Come on in and join the party," Sloane said, drawing Nicole's attention to where he stood off to the side by a large dresser. He was casually holding a gun, seemingly relaxed and in complete control of the situation.

With Gwen's prompting, Nicole moved farther into the room, watching Sloane warily as he strolled closer, his eyes raking over her. She was still wearing the T-shirt and drawstring shorts that Caleb had given her, her hair a tangled mess, but he didn't appear put off by her unkempt appearance.

He had revenge on his mind, and she was it.

"You can leave now," Sloane said, dismissing Gwen as if she were nothing more than a servant.

The woman hesitated, but a sharp look from Sloane had her walking out of the bedroom and closing the heavy double doors behind her. Sloane pressed a button on the wall, and Nicole heard the unnerving sound of metal bolts securing the doors.

She swallowed hard. She and Holly were well and truly locked inside, with no escape.

Nicole kept an eye on Sloane, and knew the only way to save herself and the young girl was to keep the man talking, to distract him until help arrived.

"You want *me*," Nicole said, trying to bargain with Sloane, anything to keep Holly out of harm's way. "Let the girl go and you can have me."

"I don't think so." Sloane stroked the cold steel barrel of his gun along Nicole's cheek. "Holly can send me to prison, and that's not going to happen."

He was going to prison anyway, but Nicole wasn't

about to enlighten him. She casually stepped back to create space between them. "She won't say anything," Nicole said, keeping her voice calm, while inside she was trembling with terror. "I swear."

He laughed, the sound maniacal and evil. "Neither of you will have the chance to say anything to anyone."

A spark of rage burned inside Nicole, making her lash out. "You're pathetic."

He shrugged, her words having no impact on him. Instead, he kept the gun on her and decided to get down to business. "Take off your clothes," he ordered.

She lifted her chin defiantly. No way was she making any of this easy on him, even as she knew that defying him could result in horrible consequences. It was a chance she was willing to take. "No."

"We can do this the easy way, with you cooperating, or the fun way, with me forcing you." A malicious smile curved his mouth. "I do like it rough."

The man was depraved. If Nicole had had anything in her stomach she would have puked all over him. "You're nothing but a pathetic pervert who doesn't know what to do with a real woman," she spat at him. "You're a pedophile that preys on girls who are vulnerable, and you make me sick!"

"Bitch!" He backhanded her so hard she staggered on her feet and saw stars.

Behind her, she heard Holly scream.

"Shut the fuck up!" he yelled at the girl, his face flushed red with fury. He grabbed a handful of Nicole's hair, twisting it around his fingers until she gasped from the pain ripping at her scalp.

She had no choice but to follow him as he pulled her toward the bed.

He turned the gun on Holly. "Get off the bed!"

Crying hysterically, the girl scrambled off the mattress. The next thing Nicole knew, she was being pressed down onto the bed, crushed by the heavy weight of Sloane's body. He was bigger and stronger than her, yet she refused to let him rape her. She was a fighter, a survivor, and she wouldn't, couldn't, let him win.

Because once he was done with her, he was going to kill her.

Nathan needed to check on Nicole. After leaving her apartment, he'd given her time to recover from everything that had happened, and he just needed to hear her voice and know that she was okay—despite her belief they were finished as a couple.

He'd finished up the initial meeting with the feds, and while there was more to come, he desperately needed a few minutes to himself before being grilled for another few hours.

"I'm going to take a break and give Nicole a call," he told Caleb, who gave him a nod of understanding. He pulled his cell phone from his pant pocket, which he'd kept on silent during the intense interrogation, only to discover that he had one missed call from Nicole and a voice mail that had been left over thirty minutes ago.

He listened to the message, his blood turning to ice in his veins as Nicole explained that Holly was back at Sloane's, and she was on her way to the estate to get the girl out.

"Shit," he said, his gut ripping to shreds as he met Caleb's concerned gaze. Rick, an agent with the FBI, stared at him in curiosity. "Holly and Nicole are at Sloane's estate."

"That's impossible," Caleb replied with a shake of his head. "Holly, her mother, and her boyfriend are in a suite here at The Onyx."

"Are you sure about that?" Until he had evidence proving otherwise, he believed Nicole's story. And that meant he didn't have time to waste on Caleb's say-so.

Nathan's skeptical tone had Caleb reaching for the nearest phone to call the suite he'd put the Davis family in. When there was no answer, he called hotel security, ordering them to immediately locate Holly's mother, Wendy Davis, and bring her and her daughter to his office.

"I can't wait that long," Nathan said, shifting his gaze to Rick. Chances were, Holly wasn't here. "I need a warrant and I need backup."

"We can't get a warrant in less than two hours," Rick said. Frustrated, Nathan wanted to say the hell with protocol. Lives were at risk. Nicole was in danger.

Caleb reached down to his ankle and removed the snub-nosed .38 strapped there, then handed the weapon to Nathan. "Take this with you. I know a friendly federal judge. We can have a warrant in less than an hour."

Thank God for Caleb and his connections. He gave Rick a pointed look. "Don't be far behind me."

The agent's lips pressed into a grim line of disapproval. "You shouldn't go in alone."

"Just try and stop me." The woman he adored was in mortal danger. She'd called him, needed him. He wasn't about to let her down.

Rick unclipped the handcuffs from the case secured to his belt and tossed them to Nathan. "Take these, too, just in case. You might need them."

Nathan pocketed the cuffs and tucked Caleb's gun

in the back waistband of his jeans beneath his jacket. He was on the road in minutes, driving as fast as he could go. But not fast enough for his peace of mind. With every second that passed, his chest tightened with anxiety. His past flashed before his eyes—images of young Katie. The crime scene photos of her lifeless body on the courthouse steps. He blamed himself. He'd failed to protect her, and she'd paid with her life.

Nausea rose up into his throat as he relived his worst nightmare. If he didn't make it in time, Nicole's fate would be the same.

He thought of Nicole's quiet courage, her laughter, and the vulnerable side she'd shared with him. He recalled how steady she'd been during the mission, despite her own fears. She was the kind of woman he admired the hell out of and respected. And loved with a strength and depth he'd never believed possible.

And he knew if he lost Nicole, he'd never recover.

The guard at the gate recognized him from the night of the party, and after Nathan told him he had business with Sloane, which he did, the young man opened the gates. Nathan assumed the guard had no idea what was going on up at the house.

Just as Nathan parked behind Nicole's car, his cell phone rang. Seeing that it was Caleb, he answered.

"I have Holly's mother in my office," Caleb told him. "Holly is gone. Wendy said she left Holly in the suite two hours ago so she could go downstairs and gamble with her boyfriend."

Nathan swore. What kind of mother left her traumatized daughter alone after a year apart? "Then she's here," Nathan said, grateful for the verification. "Get that backup here ASAP!"

He hung up, jumped out of the vehicle, and ran through the courtyard. He slowed when he reached the front doors. Entering the house quietly, he listened for sounds of Holly or Nicole. He moved into the nearby living room, startling Gwen with his sudden appearance. The woman spun around and trained a gun on him.

"Where the fuck is she?" he asked, not mincing words as he strode toward the woman despite the gun.

"She's upstairs in Preston's room with Holly," she said, taking a step back and finding herself blocked by the sofa. "But you can't get to her."

The weapon in Gwen's trembling hand wavered, telling Nathan that she was all talk and no action or she would have shot him by now. She'd given him all the information he needed, and he didn't have time to waste. Opting for the element of surprise, he grabbed the hand with the gun and twisted hard. She let out an agonized cry and released the weapon. Before she could recover, he spun her around and jammed her arm halfway up her back so she couldn't move.

She whimpered in pain. "You're hurting me!"

"Too fucking bad." None too gently, he guided her into the entryway. Retrieving the handcuffs from his pocket, he snapped one silver bracelet around her wrist, looped the cuffs through a few of the iron-rod stair rails, and shackled her other hand so she couldn't go anywhere.

She jerked against her restraints, her expression furious. "You can't do this!" she wailed.

"I just did." He took the stairs two at a time to the second landing. Remembering where Preston's room was located from the tour he'd given them, he headed silently in that directly.

As he neared the closed double doors, he pulled out his gun. His heart beat fast and furious in his chest. Hearing muffled sounds coming from inside the bedroom, he pressed his ear to the door. He could make out screams and Sloane cursing—none of it good. Alarmed, he tried to turn the knob, but the doors were locked as tight as Fort Knox.

A sinking sense of despair nearly brought Nathan to his knees.

There was no busting down the steel doors.

And no saving Nicole.

Nicole refused to die. And she refused to let Sloane violate her. Despite Sloane's brute force, she fought him off with every ounce of strength she had in her—and it was a surprising amount considering how exhausted she was. She kicked and screamed and bit whatever exposed flesh she could find. She caught his cheek between her teeth, and he howled in pain as she bit down so hard she drew blood.

He smacked her, subduing her for only a few seconds before she was clawing at him with her fingernails and using her knees to kick him where it counted. He swore, his voice a low, threatening growl that sent chills down her spine—and still she didn't stop fighting for her life, because she had a whole lot to live for.

Somewhere in the room Holly was bawling and pleading for Sloane to please, please, stop.

Nicole felt the gun pressing against her side, and made a grab for it, but Sloane was faster. They struggled for the weapon, but he overpowered her and shoved the barrel of the gun into her stomach.

She kneed him in the groin, and he pulled the trigger.

She gasped as a blinding, searing pain ripped through her side, stealing her breath from her lungs. Someone pounded on the door. She could have sworn she heard Nathan yelling her name. Then again, it could have been her mind playing tricks on her.

"Stupid bitch," Sloane sneered. Still on top of her, he pressed the muzzle of the gun against her throat, and Nicole knew he was going to kill her with the next shot. "You're just not worth the trouble."

She closed her eyes, wishing she'd had the chance to tell Nathan she loved him. Because she did. With all her heart. And he'd never, ever know. The pain in her side was nothing compared with the ache in her heart.

She heard a loud, sickening *thud*. Then she felt Sloane's body go slack, his weight crushing her. She thought she was going to suffocate.

Holly knelt on the bed and shoved Sloane's unconscious body off her. Her face was drenched with tears, her gaze devastated and contrite. "I'm sorry. I'm so sorry, Nicole. He was going to kill you and I couldn't let him."

"What . . ." She sucked in a breath as a sharp burn began spreading through her, and her vision blurred. ". . . did you . . . do to him?"

"I hit him over the head with one of his bronze statues," she said, and in that moment Nicole was so proud of the girl. "Oh, God, Nicole, you're bleeding so much."

Nicole touched her hand to her side and winced as she saw the slick red substance coating her fingers. The pain was nearly unbearable. She couldn't move, and she wondered if she was going to die after all.

"Nicole!"

This time, there was no mistaking Nathan's frantic voice, and she tried to stay focused. Just for a few more precious minutes. "Holly . . . unlock the door . . . and let him in."

The sound of a gunshot going off behind the locked doors stopped Nathan's heart. That distinct feeling of helplessness swamped him, and he continued his futile pounding on the door, hoping, praying, that she was okay.

Down below in the entryway he heard a loud commotion, and knew his backup had finally arrived—maybe too late.

Just as law enforcement came barreling down the hallway, the doors to the bedroom opened. The men charged inside, guns drawn, but as soon as they realized that Sloane was out cold and the threat had been defused, they reholstered their weapons, took Sloane into custody, and started securing the crime scene.

Holly stood off to the side, obviously in shock as one of the men made sure she was okay, while Nathan quickly made his way to Nicole where she was lying on the bed, a crimson pool of moisture staining the bedspread beneath her. There was so much blood, and while she was still alive, he had no idea the extent of her injuries.

"Get an ambulance here," he yelled out. *"Now."*

"They're already on their way," someone called back.

He sat down beside Nicole and took her hand, careful not to jostle her body or cause her more pain. Her eyes were glassy, her breathing slow and shallow. His throat closed up on him, making it difficult for him to talk.

She smiled up at him, her lips as pale as her face. "Did they get him?" she asked, her voice hoarse.

"Yeah, we got him," he said. "*You* got him."

"Good." She moaned, and gasped for breath. "That's all that matters."

She closed her eyes, and then she passed out.

Chapter Twenty-one

Nicole woke up slowly, her head foggy and her midsection feeling as though she'd been in a boxing match. Her lashes fluttered open, and she stared at unfamiliar white walls and an IV hooked up to her arm. It took her a moment to remember that she'd been shot, and now she was obviously in the hospital after surgery.

She turned her head, and her heart softened in her chest when she saw Nathan sitting on a chair beside her bed, his dark head resting on the mattress by her hip as he slept. He was holding her hand, as if he was afraid of letting go of her. Afraid she'd leave him.

She wasn't going anywhere, not without him. And she planned to let this amazing man know just how much he meant to her. Seeing her life flash before her eyes while a crazed man held a gun to her throat had a way of putting things into perspective. There was no denying that Nathan was the best thing to ever happen to her. She was just a little slow on the uptake when it came to facing her feelings, and believing in them.

Not anymore. She'd spent years avoiding a commitment, her fears crippling her ability to give any man her whole heart and fall in love. Or maybe it was just a matter of the *right* man coming along and sweeping her off her feet and shaking the very foundation of who and what she thought she was. A man who'd always treated her as an equal and admired her strength and determination to succeed. A man she could count on, no matter what.

That man was Nathan. She was so ready to take a chance on him, on *them,* because what she felt for him was real and solid and pure. Not a young girl's infatuation, but a grown woman's love.

Releasing a soft, content sigh, she slid her hand from beneath his and touched his silky hair, then trailed her fingers along his chiseled jaw, rough with a day's growth of stubble. He stirred, and gradually opened his gorgeous brown eyes, then lifted his head to look at her. He seemed surprised to see her staring back.

She smiled, embracing the overwhelming emotions filling her full with lots and lots of love. "Rough night?"

Humor tugged at the corner of his mouth. "Yeah, you could say that, though yours was a helluva lot rougher."

She shifted closer and groaned when she felt a sharp pinch in her side. The one now stitched and bandaged. "Damn. Bullets hurt."

"At least you're going to make it," he said gruffly, and grabbed her hand again, as if he needed to touch her to make sure she was really okay. "The bullet missed vital organs and went clean through. You should be out of here in a few days."

It could have been much worse, she knew, and shivered at the thought.

A deep frown furrowed his brows. "You scared the

hell out of me, and I don't *ever* want to see you like that again."

She had no doubts he'd faced a few of his own demons when Sloane had shot her. God, what a pair the two of them made. "Hey, I'm tough," she teased.

"Yeah, you are," he said, his thumb caressing the back of her hand as he held her gaze. "More than you realize."

"Holly, she did it," Nicole said, wanting to give credit where it was due. "She saved me."

"Holly." Nathan chuckled and shook his head, his expression incredulous. "Who would have thought, huh?"

"I'm so proud of her." The girl had come a long way in a short amount of time, though Nicole knew Holly would probably need plenty of therapy to help get her life back on track. But at least she did have her life, and future, back. "It couldn't have been easy for her to hit Sloane over the head with that bronze statue, considering how in love she was with him."

Nathan nodded somberly. "I think she saw a side to him that scared her straight."

"I hope so," she said, and tugged at the thin blanket covering her lap. "What else did I miss?"

"Gwen is in jail for attempted murder, and Sloane is being held without bond. They're still gathering a list of charges against him, including prostitution, kidnapping, and human trafficking. Also, the feds discovered that Sloane has quite the movie collection."

She tipped her head curiously. "Movies?"

"Sex videos," he explained. "Blackmail against the rich and powerful. There's going to be a whole lot of indictments coming from this bust."

"Thank God," she breathed, pleased to hear that everyone who'd taken part in Sloane's prostitution ring would be prosecuted. "And the girls at the estate?"

"The ones who were found at Sloane's are now with child protective services," he told her. "We're looking into locating their families and they'll be reunited as soon as possible."

"They'll need counseling," she said, knowing that would be imperative to the healing process.

He smiled. "Trust me, they'll be able to afford it once they sue Sloane's estate."

"And Holly?" More than anything, she wanted the girl to be okay. Starting with knocking some sense into her mother.

"She's a ward of the state of California." His fingers absently stroked the center of her palm, making her skin tingle all the way up her arm. "Caleb managed to locate her father in Germany, and he's going to come to the States and get her. He's always wanted Holly to live with him, but Wendy Davis wouldn't give him custody. Now she has no choice."

That was the best news yet. Holly deserved to be happy, safe, and secure. The case was truly over, except for one last outstanding thing. "Now I can finish my story."

He laughed, the sound warm and genuine. "Sweetheart, you have one hell of an exclusive. Your career is about to skyrocket."

At one time, making a big name for herself as a journalist would have thrilled her. But now, there was something else she wanted just as badly, and she was confident she could balance the two—if Nathan gave her the chance.

She took a deep breath and put it all out there, along

with her heart and soul. "What about you and me?" she asked, surprised by just how nervous she felt. "Can we be exclusive, too?"

He mulled over her request, and for a moment she felt a sense of panic, until she caught the playful glimmer in his eyes. "What, you're willing to give up your friends-with-benefits motto?"

He wasn't going to make this easy on her, but honestly, why should he when she'd put him through an emotional wringer? If she had to beg and grovel, it would be worth it in the end. *He* was worth it.

"I have to say, that friends-with-benefits arrangement worked pretty damn well for us," she said with a seductive sigh. "But isn't it a woman's prerogative to change her mind?"

He stood up, and for a brief moment she thought he was going to turn around and walk out. But then he braced his hands on either side of her head and leaned in close, his gaze so rich and deep she wanted to drown in their depths.

"That all depends on what you want," he drawled, his words and tone daring her to be open and honest with him, to trust what was between them.

She did. Utterly and completely. Nothing had ever felt as perfect as being with Nathan.

She pressed her hands to his unshaven face, amazed how one man could bring out the best in her. In every way. "I want a commitment," she told him. "I want a lover. I want forever. And I want all that with you."

"Hmmm." He considered her heartfelt request. "That's a lot to take in all at once."

She gave him even more, having saved the best for last. "I love you, Nathan Fox."

"Ahh, those were the magic words I was waiting to hear." He grinned, a sexy, charming rogue. "I love you, too. I have for a while now."

Oh, wow. Unable to top that, she pulled his mouth down to hers and kissed him, pouring every ounce of emotion into the fusing of their lips, the tangling of their tongues. Until she moved the wrong way and a stitch in her side reminded her that she needed to take it easy.

He touched his forehead to hers. "Marry me, Nicole."

"Yes." She smiled as he kissed her softly, reverently, and wondered if she'd ever felt so happy. So whole. So complete.

She didn't think so.

Not until this very moment.

Not until Nathan.

Read on for an excerpt from
Janelle Denison's
next book

NIGHT AFTER NIGHT

Coming soon from
St. Martin's Paperbacks

Sean followed Zoe into the foyer of her apartment at the Panorama Towers, a luxury high-rise known for its exclusive amenities and outstanding views of the Las Vegas skyline. She led the way into a spacious living room with a wide wrap-around couch, a glass-topped coffee table, and a mahogany entertainment center with a flat-screen TV. The contemporary décor was uncluttered and precise, yet warm and inviting.

Just like the woman who lived there.

"Nice place," he said, catching sight of the adjoining kitchen with stainless-steel appliances and beige granite countertops.

"Thanks. It's small, but functional. Only a thousand square feet and two bedrooms, but it's really all I need."

After setting her purse on a side table, she strolled through the living room in front of him, drawing his gaze to the provocative sway of her hips and a pair of long, slender legs that had his fingers itching to touch all that silky, bare skin.

"But it was the outside balcony and amazing view of the strip at night that ultimately sold me on this place."

She pushed open the sheer curtains covering a glass sliding door and floor-to-ceiling windows, revealing a spectacular sight of bright neon lights that stretched for miles.

She unlocked the sliding door and stepped outside, and he did the same, standing beside her at the concrete-and-rod iron railing securing the area. Even at twenty-one stories up, a balmy evening breeze reached them, lifting and playing with the few loose strands of her hair that had escaped the wide gold clip she'd used at the nape of her neck. Her smooth shoulders, completely exposed by the low, sexy neckline of her dress, gleamed like alabaster in the moonlight.

Pulling his gaze from her profile, he looked out over the city, so deceptively beautiful at night. "I bet this sight never gets old, does it?"

"Nope." She curled her fingers around the rod iron and slanted him a sidelong glance filled with a beguiling amount of heat. "Especially on a night like this. Clear. Warm. *Sultry.*"

The soft, throaty way she spoke the last word evoked images of steamy, erotic kisses and hot, lazy caresses in intimate places. Ever since she'd asked him back to her place, the attraction between them had become a slow tease of sexual awareness. The onslaught of arousal thrummed through his system, and she wasn't helping matters by looking at him like *he* was dessert.

God, she was messing with his head, and making him want her more than was wise considering how he felt about her cheating, lying father and Grant Russo's part in making sure that Sean's father spent years in prison for a crime *both* men had committed. And judging by the information Caleb had collected for their client on this case, it was clear that Russo was still in the business of scamming people.

Sean had agreed to accompany Zoe to her place to discover anything else he could about her father. Based on their exchange at dinner, it seemed like she had a somewhat close relationship with her dad, but after listening in on her conversation with her mother and watching her reactions, Sean was pretty much convinced that she wasn't aware of her father's shady dealings and genuinely believed he was on a business trip—in *Chicago*, she'd told her mother.

Sean planned to pass that bit of information on to Caleb as soon as he left Zoe's tonight so they could get a jump on that lead and see if that found Russo, or if it was nothing more than a diversion.

Ultimately, Sean's main objective was to remain as close to her as possible in the hopes that she heard from her father. Zoe was his daughter, and contact with him had to happen *sometime*. And when it did, Sean wanted to be around to learn where the cowardly bastard was hiding out so the Reliance Group could take him down.

Obviously, he couldn't be with Zoe 24/7 to monitor her actions and calls, but one of the Reliance Group's team members, an ex–computer hacker, had already put a tap on her cellphone, enabling them to track her incoming and outgoing calls, as well as text messages. They couldn't actually listen in on her conversations, but they were able to monitor her contacts and approximate where they originated. So far, there had been plenty of business calls, but no interaction with her father.

"Let's head back inside," she said after a few quiet minutes, and he followed her into the living room.

"Make yourself at home." She waved a hand in the general direction of the entertainment center. "There's a CD player in the wall unit. Why don't you put some music on and I'll be back in a few minutes."

As she started to walk away, he couldn't help but ask, "Where are you going?"

She stopped, tipped her head, and gave him one of those slow, sweet smiles that made him feel sucker-punched. "To get out of this restrictive dress and change into something more comfortable," she said, as if that should have been obvious.

She disappeared into a nearby bedroom and shut the door behind her, leaving Sean alone to contemplate what, exactly, she'd meant by *comfortable*. All his fertile male imagination could conjure was something flimsy, with silk and lace and lots of bare flesh. He groaned and tried like hell to shove those images from his mind before they got him into trouble.

He was a man who was used to fast women and mindless sex when the opportunity arose—no names necessary. Admittedly, he was a player, and he never made excuses or apologized for his preferences for casual, one-night stands. Because of his less-than-favorable past as a con man, cultivating any kind of lasting relationship had never been on his agenda, and most likely never would be.

Because, at the end of the day, what woman wanted a long-term commitment with a man who'd spent most of his adult years scamming people, only to spend time in prison for his stupidity? With such a huge black mark on his resume as potential husband and father material, he'd found it much easier to keep things with women simple and uncomplicated.

Fulfilling his physical needs had never been a problem for him before . . . until now. Because the woman he wanted was someone he shouldn't touch. Not only did they reside in completely different worlds socially, but even more damning was the fact that he was dating her under false pretenses. He was using her for information, and if she ever discovered his deception, she'd undoubtedly, and rightfully, hate his guts.

Knowing all that, however, didn't stop him from wanting her. Far more than was wise.

Feeling warm and knowing it had more to do with his internal temperature than the outdoor weather, he removed his jacket and tossed it over the back of a chair, then discarded his tie as well. He unbuttoned the too-tight collar of his shirt as he made his way to the compact disc player, where he selected one of John Mayer's earlier CDs, then adjusted the volume so the music wasn't too loud.

Waiting for Zoe to return, he stood by the sliding glass door, hands in his trouser pockets, and gazed out at the brightly lit horizon, until he finally heard her bedroom door open again.

Not certain what to expect, he turned around, initially relieved to find that there wasn't a bit of silk or lace on her anywhere that he could see. She wore a pair of pink drawstring sweatpants and a white camisole–type top with thin straps, and while there was nothing overtly revealing about what she'd changed into, the casual outfit showcased everything her dress had concealed—the tantalizing curve of her waist and hips and the full, rounded shape of her breasts. She had a stunning figure, the kind that had the ability to bring a man to his knees—for all the right reasons.

"Dessert is in the kitchen." Giving him a coy look, she crooked her finger at him to follow as she walked by.

The playful overture in her voice was unmistakable. *Dessert* took on a very suggestive meaning, and as he turned to follow her, he nearly groaned when he caught sight of the word JUICY stamped across her perfect ass, which accurately described the way she smelled. Like a ripe, succulent peach he wanted to suck and savor before taking a big bite out of.

He shook his head. Hard. God, she was going to kill him with all her innuendo before the night was over. He was sure of it.